RISING SUN, FALLING SHADOW

BY DANIEL KALLA
FROM TOM DOHERTY ASSOCIATES

RISING SUN, FALLING SHADOW

DANIEL KALLA

A TOM DOHERTY ASSOCIATES BOOK
NEW YORK

RISING SUN, FALLING SHADOW

Simultaneously published in Canada by HarperCollins Publishers Ltd

Copyright © 2013 by Daniel Kalla

A Forge Book
Published by Tom Doherty Associates, LLC
175 Fifth Avenue
New York, NY 10010

www.tor-forge.com

Forge® is a registered trademark of Tom Doherty Associates, LLC.

The Library of Congress Cataloging-in-Publication data is available upon request

ISBN 978-0-7653-3764-1 (hardcover)
ISBN 978-1-4668-3501-6 (e-book)

Forge books may be purchased for educational, business,
or promotional use. For information on bulk purchases, please contact
Macmillan Corporate and Premium Sales Department at 1-800-221-7945,
extension 5442, or write specialmarkets@macmillan.com.

First U.S. Edition: September 2013

Printed in the United States of America

0 9 8 7 6 5 4 3 2 1

03184 7864

To the memory of my grandparents—Celia and Leo Hornung and Elizabeth and Vilmos Kalla—good people who lived through a terrible time.

I

Chapter 1

January 20, 1943, Shanghai

Soon Yi Adler—"Sunny" to almost everyone—craved a few moments of fresh air. She still had hours to go in her shift and would be alone with the patients once Irma had changed out of uniform. The older nurse was reluctant to leave the refugee hospital, but Sunny insisted. Irma's husband had developed a fever and, like most refugees, she was terrified of malaria. The mosquitoes that carried the parasite were dormant in wintertime, but the paranoia of it lingered year-round like the stench from Soochow Creek.

Still, Sunny had to escape the ward, if only for a minute or two. The demands of running a hospital through wartime occupation—the constant shortages of food and medicine, the frequent disruption of the power and heat and the unexpected seizures of what little supplies they had—weighed on her more heavily than ever. Especially today, when the embodiment of all her frustration and futility lay on a stretcher in the hallway draped by a fraying cotton sheet.

Magda Fleischmann had died less than fifteen minutes earlier. She was twenty-eight years old, six months younger than Sunny. The *shomer*, a male volunteer, had already arrived to sit with the body to accompany her soul while awaiting the burial, which, by Jewish law, had to be conducted within two days. Had Frau Fleischmann come to the hospital only a week earlier, when the dispensary still possessed a few sulpha pills, her fate might have been so different. Without antibiotics, Sunny could do nothing but administer fluids, morphine and hollow words of encouragement while the typhoid fever ravaged the young mother of two in front of her eyes.

The tragically familiar pea-soup odour—the hallmark of typhoid deaths—still hung in the air as a ghostly reminder of the woman's departure. Desperate to escape the smell, Sunny bolted down the hallway, yanked open the door and stepped out into the afternoon chill. It was not yet five o'clock, but the sun—hiding behind the layer of cloud that seemed to permanently enshroud Shanghai this winter—had already begun to set.

Sunny heard men shouting in Japanese and froze halfway down the short pathway between the hospital and the street. She blanched when she spotted the source of the commotion. Four soldiers, their white armbands marking them as members of the dreaded Kempeitai, were shoving two boys, maybe fifteen or sixteen years old, toward the abandoned building across the street. Sunny recognized the taller boy as the son of one of the Jewish women on the ward. His face was ashen with terror but, unlike his companion, he silently complied with the Kempeitai men.

The other boy's arms flailed as he desperately tried to resist the manhandling. "*Es war nur ein Scherz!*" he cried before switching to English. "It was only a prank! We were not going to take it."

One of the Kempeitai men wheeled around and rammed the butt of his rifle into the boy's midsection. The boy clasped his belly as he crumpled to his knees. Another soldier grabbed the scruff of his jacket and dragged him through the street.

"Just . . . a misunderstanding," the boy gasped as he was hauled along.

As soon as they reached the wall, the soldiers spun the boys around to face the road. The taller teenager's eyes locked onto Sunny's, imploring her to help. But her feet felt as though cast in clay, her tongue as if glued to the roof of her mouth. She had a flashback to a violent night four years earlier, when she had been attacked in the street by a drunken Japanese sailor—and the much greater tragedy that had followed.

Sunny hid her terror behind what she hoped was a comforting

expression, the same one she had offered Magda Fleischmann in her last conscious moments. Her chest ached from the shame of her passivity, but she managed to sustain eye contact with the petrified boy.

"Stand straight!" one of the Kempeitai men barked in English.

Two of the soldiers stood shoulder to shoulder in the street, ten feet in front of the boys, and simultaneously raised their rifles. Dread overcame Sunny, and her throat tightened.

The taller boy began to tremble. His companion raised his arms to shield his chest and face. "Please, please!" he whimpered. "Our families were hungry. We have to eat. We are not thieves!"

The door whooshed open behind Sunny. She glanced over her shoulder to see Irma filling the doorway. The plump woman instantly appreciated what was happening and rushed toward the soldiers without hesitation.

Sunny shot a hand out to stop her, but Irma swept past. "*Stop!*" she shouted. "They are only boys! This is madness!"

One of the soldiers spun around. The muzzle of his rifle flared twice. Sunny flinched at the crack of gunshots, a cry lost in her throat.

Irma dropped to the pavement in midstride, as though someone had cut her legs out from beneath her.

"*Gott hilf uns!*" the shorter boy screamed.

The rifleman turned back toward the boys. Sunny covered her face, unable to watch. She could hear one of the men calling out in Japanese and, from his cadence, could tell that he was counting.

"No, no, no," she muttered.

Two more shots rang in her ears and echoed along the street. A sulphuric smell drifted toward her. In the silence that followed, she kept her eyes squeezed shut, unwilling to face the inevitable.

Moments later, Sunny heard footsteps pounding the pavement as the soldiers marched off. Finally, once the worst of her shaking had subsided, Sunny opened her eyes.

Irma lay face down in the street. The two boys were slumped at the foot of the wall like a pair of discarded rag dolls.

Chapter 2

February 18, 1943

Franz Adler's black oxfords—twice resoled and polished until the leather had thinned—sank even deeper in the field's muck. The wet breeze seemed to penetrate his coat's lining, and he fought off another shiver. Franz didn't mind the cold, but the dampness was dismal. He would have gladly traded Shanghai's dreary rain for the snow that often blanketed Vienna at this time of year.

Franz's gaze drifted to the oval fence surrounding him. It outlined the track where the horses had once run, but he barely recognized the Shanghai race course. How different the place had looked on his previous visit, before the war. That sunny afternoon, Franz rubbed elbows with American and British Shanghailanders, along with the wealthiest of local Chinese. The city's upper crust snacked on eclairs, strawberries with cream and chilled champagne, many betting more on a single horse race than most of the sampan families—who often spent their entire lives aboard their houseboats on the Whangpoo River—would see in a lifetime. With its vibrantly painted stands and ultra-fashionable guests, especially the women in bright silk cheongsams, the track had been an explosion of colour. But now, everything around him—the sky, the grounds and even the people—looked grey. In his mind's eye, he framed a photograph. The scene epitomized the kind of faded glory that he loved to capture through the lens, although these days a roll of film was a rare and precious commodity that was usually beyond his means.

Several Shanghailanders stood near Franz, but little about the ragtag crowd hinted at its members' former standing or prosperity. Most stooped under the weight of overstuffed knapsacks. Pots and pans dangled from their packs, clanging noisily. They might have resembled a gathering of one-man bands if not for the sense of gloom that engulfed them. The men wore red armbands imprinted with a single letter; almost all read "A" for American. A few women hovered near their husbands, their worry palpable. The Japanese were trucking the men off to the internment camp, which they insisted on referring to as the "Chapei Civic Assembly Center." No one knew when, or if, the wives would join their husbands.

Infantrymen in khaki uniforms and brimmed caps formed a loose ring around the captives. Some soldiers stood at ease, rifles slung over their shoulders, while others held their guns across their chests, at the ready. The soldier nearest to Franz tapped his finger on the weapon's trigger casing as he viewed the prisoners with unconcealed loathing.

Simon Lehrer nodded at the scowling guard. "What do you figure, Franz?" he asked in a low voice, winking. "Is that the guy to turn to for special treatment?"

Franz covered his mouth with his hand and muttered, "Take care with him, Simon. With all of them."

"You know me, Franz. I'm only about self-preservation."

Franz hoped that Simon's show of bravado was intended to calm his wife, Esther, who clung to his arm. Franz's own wife, Sunny, stood on the other side of them, silently surveying the tense scene.

Simon stood out among the American prisoners. Not only was he taller than most, but his was the only smiling face. He had drifted to Shanghai five years earlier to avoid managing his family's furniture business in the Bronx but, ironically, ended up shouldering a far greater responsibility as the director of the CFA, the Committee for Assistance of European Refugees in Shanghai. Since the attack on Pearl Harbor, the American and British citizens who ran the CFA, including Simon, had all been deemed hostile aliens. They were, arguably, even worse off than Shanghai's twenty thousand German refugees, many of whom they had once helped to house and feed.

Another gust of wind swept over the track. Franz flipped up the collar on his tattered coat and dug his gloveless hands deeper into his pockets. Unlike the Americans, he had come to the racetrack voluntarily, and only to say goodbye to his friend. Franz was not a prisoner of war. Not yet, at least. As an Austrian Jew, he held no official nationality. The Nazis had stripped him of his citizenship—along with his academic standing, his career and his savings—years before, back in Europe. In the eyes of the Japanese, Franz was a stateless refugee—"a nothing, a no one, a non-person," as one of his refugee colleagues often put it.

Why now? The question had been on the lips of Shanghailanders for weeks. The Japanese had originally conquered Shanghai in pieces, over-running the Chinese-controlled neighbourhoods five years earlier and then seizing the International Settlement—the European enclave—on the same day that their bombs decimated Pearl Harbor. They had frozen bank accounts, appropriated assets and rationed everything from rice to heating oil, but had allowed most Allied citizens to live relatively freely for the past year. Some speculated that the sudden roundup was in retaliation for the wartime internment of Japanese citizens abroad, while others saw it as a sign that the Japanese were running scared after a series of military setbacks at Guadalcanal and in New Guinea. The rumour mill ran rampant among Shanghailanders still awaiting internment. Stories of food shortages, lice and beatings inside the prison camps electrified the ever-shrinking Shanghailander community.

Esther wrapped Simon's arm in both of hers. The bulge of her seven-and-a-half-month pregnant belly was visible through her wool coat, though her face appeared thinner than ever. With her deep-set eyes and stoic gaze, she was usually the epitome of poise, so it was unsettling to see her now on the verge of panic.

Franz understood her anxiety only too well. Esther had once been married to his younger brother, Karl. Four years earlier, on the night of Kristallnacht, Franz had found her crouched in the alley behind her husband's Vienna office building, bleeding from her lacerated arm. Out front, Karl's body dangled from the lamppost from which a Nazi mob had hanged him. Now, seven months into a precious unexpected pregnancy, Esther was facing the prospect of losing a second husband.

She tugged at Simon's arm. "*Ich will mit dir kommen,*" she implored in a thick voice. "Let me come with you. Please, Simon."

"To have our baby born in a prison camp?" He patted her belly. "Never, Essie. It's better this way."

Esther clasped his hand against her abdomen. "She needs her father."

"Soon, Essie." Simon stroked her cheek. "Meantime, his aunt and uncle will have to look out for the little fella."

"Of course we will," Sunny spoke up. "After all, Essie and the baby will stay with us until your release."

"I'm still not convinced that is necessary," Esther murmured.

Sunny laid her hand on Esther's shoulder. "Necessary or not, you are family."

"There is more than enough room for you and the baby," Franz said. "We want you with us, Essie."

"It will give me a whole lot of peace of mind, too." Simon grinned. "After all, what Jewish parent alive wouldn't want his kid living with a couple of doctors?"

"Besides," Sunny added with a small laugh, "Hannah has already decided for you. You do realize that she intends to be the baby's amah?"

Franz bit back a smile. His daughter would be a teenager in a few months. Despite her mild left-sided weakness—a consequence of her difficult birth, which had also claimed her mother's life—Hannah had adapted to life in Shanghai better than anyone else in her family. She spoke Mandarin and Shanghainese fluently. And ever since Hannah had learned of her aunt's pregnancy, she had been preparing for the new arrival as though the baby would be her own.

Esther nodded in gratitude, but her expression showed little relief. She continued to speak softly in German so as not to be overheard by the guards and other prisoners. "Simon, these camps . . . the rumours . . . How will you manage?"

"I'll be fine." Simon winked. "You'll see. I will be the one on the inside with all the cigarettes and chocolates. Silk stockings, too, if you need those."

Esther was unappeased. "The last time the Japanese took you away . . ."

Simon winced. Franz shared his friend's revulsion. The previous summer, the feared Kempeitai had arrested both of them on suspicion of spreading a rumour among the refugee community that the local Japanese government was complicit in an SS plan to exterminate Shanghai's Jews—a plan that, thankfully, had never come to fruition. Those six days of interrogation and torture at Bridge House still haunted Franz. Some nights he would wake in a cold sweat, still able to taste the mouldy towel that had been stuffed in his mouth and the foul water that had trickled down his throat, choking him.

Simon shook his head. "This time is different, Essie. We're being interned, not arrested."

"How does anyone really know?"

Simon cupped her face in his hands. "We'll be one happy family—all three of us—in no time. Trust me, Essie."

"I do, darling." Esther switched to English. "I am being selfish. I will miss you so much. I so want you to be here when . . ." She looked down at her belly.

Simon tapped his chest. "They can't keep us apart."

"No. Never." Esther showed her first smile of the day. "Besides, this is not so bad as the catastrophe that befell your precious Yankees."

"You got a point there." Simon laughed. He had sulked for days when the radio broke the news that his beloved Bronx Bombers had lost the 1942 World Series to the St. Louis Cardinals.

One of the Japanese officers lifted a bullhorn to his mouth and shrieked, "All American men line here for transport you to Civic Assembly Center. All now! All others to go immediately."

The soldiers advanced toward the prisoners with their rifles levelled.

Sunny hugged Simon and kissed him on the cheek. "We will bring you supplies as soon as we can."

Simon grinned. "I would never say no to more of Yang's treats, that's for sure. Kosher or not, I love your housekeeper's rice balls."

Franz stepped forward. Lost for words, he simply clapped Simon's shoulder and shook his hand.

"I give the Nazis and the Japs six months tops," Simon said, though Franz doubted his friend believed that fantasy any more than he did.

Sunny reached for Franz's hand and guided him back a few steps, allowing Simon and Esther a moment of privacy.

Even after the other prisoners had fallen into line, Esther and Simon stood with their foreheads touching, exchanging whispered words. A Japanese soldier hurried over and jabbed Simon in the back with the butt of his rifle. After regaining his balance, Simon kissed Esther on the lips, then turned and headed for the end of the line without a look back.

*   *   *

Sunny, Esther and Franz trudged down Bubbling Well Road in sombre silence. Tall neoclassical and art deco buildings loomed overhead, including the city's tallest skyscraper, the Park Hotel. Rickshaws and pedicabs rushed down the four-lane road. Until recently, roaring American automobiles and coughing trucks had lined the thoroughfare, but the Japanese, in their need to stockpile fuel, had since prohibited the use of non-military vehicles in the city.

They reached the main road, named Avenue Edward VII on the north side and Avenue Foche on the south. Until Pearl Harbor, it had served as an informal border between two separately administered entities within the city: the International Settlement and the French Concession, known by most as simply Frenchtown. The sovereign distinction was long gone. Still, it was hard to ignore the sudden shift in architectural style from the prim and proper British rigour that dominated the International Settlement to the more laissez-faire approach of Frenchtown.

"Why don't you come home with us, Essie?" Sunny asked. "We can collect your belongings later."

"No, thank you," Esther murmured. "I need a little time to organize my home first."

Franz suspected that she also needed private time to grieve. His heart ached for Essie. After more than a decade as a widower, he could not stomach the idea of being forcibly separated from Sunny again. Their eight-month marriage had been the bright spot in an otherwise dark and difficult few years. During the week that he had been held captive in Bridge House, the idea that he might never see her again was harder to endure than the physical torture.

Franz had met Sunny on his first visit to the refugee hospital more than four years earlier. She was the only volunteer nurse there who was neither German nor Jewish. After years of unofficial apprenticeship at the side of her father, a prominent local physician, Sunny was as knowledge-able as any doctor. Franz offered to mentor her in surgical technique and, within a few years, she was performing at the level of a junior surgeon or better. He had been struck from their first encounter by her delicate Eurasian features: her teardrop-shaped eyes, sloping cheekbones and glowing alabaster skin. But it was her poise, compassion and empathy—the way she could read his mood in a glance and know exactly when to offer him a reassuring smile—that had stolen his heart.

Franz and Sunny walked Esther home through the damp, lit-tered streets of Frenchtown, passing luckless merchants and skeletal beggars, but like most others in the street, they had nothing to offer them. Eventually, they reached Avenue Joffre in the heart of Little Russia: a neighbourhood populated with White Russians who had fled to Shanghai after the Russian Civil War. Since Japan and the Soviet Union had signed a neutrality pact, the Russians—including a large Jewish contingent—were faring better than most, but even Little Russia had suffered in the face of constant rationing, inflation and shortages. The broken windows, backed-up gutters and stench of stale garbage reaffirmed for Franz that Shanghai was a shell of her former self, little more than a ruin in the making.

A girl rushed down the street toward them. Even before Franz could make out her features, he recognized his daughter by her slightly lopsided gait. He opened his arms to greet her, but Hannah stopped short and thrust a sheet of paper out to him.

"Papa, have you seen this?" she panted.

Franz took the page from her. "No, *Liebchen*."

"What is it, Hannah?" Sunny asked.

"A proclamation! The Japanese have posted them all over."

Sunny and Esther crowded in while Franz read the English words aloud: "Proclamation concerning restriction of residence and business of stateless refugees." The hairs on his neck stood up. "Due to military necessity, places of residence and business of stateless refugees in the Shanghai area shall hereafter be restricted to the under-mentioned area."

"They mean the German and Austrian Jews, Papa," Hannah murmured. "Us."

Franz locked eyes with his daughter. He considered telling her that everything was going to be fine, but he realized she would see right through the lie. All he could muster was a meek "Yes, Hannah-*chen*."

The proclamation went on to declare that all stateless refugees had until the eighteenth of May to sell their homes and businesses and relocate to a narrow area within Hongkew, one of the most crowded boroughs in the city. It concluded with an ominous threat—"Persons who violate the proclamation or obstruct its reinforcement shall be liable to severe punishment"—and was signed by the military governor.

Sunny squeezed Franz's hand until her nails dug into his skin. Franz knew that she must be thinking about her parents' house—the only home she had ever known—but all she said was "Three months, Franz."

Before he could reply, Esther's gaze darted frantically from Sunny to Franz. "A *ghetto!* Just like the Nazis created in Poland. Like Warsaw and Łódź."

All the local Jews had heard horror stories of the ghettos in Eastern Europe. "Essie, you cannot jump to—"

Esther's anguished expression silenced him. "My baby . . . born in a ghetto. His father gone. *Mein Gott,* what next?"

Chapter 3

The winter sun finally nudged through the canopy of clouds that had hovered over the city for weeks. But the brightness did little for Sunny's mood as she tromped along Ward Road beside Franz.

Reminders of Simon's absence were everywhere. At the end of the block stood the bomb-damaged schoolhouse that he had helped to transform into a functional hospital. Across the street loomed the largest of the *heime*, the hostels, that the CFA ran to shelter and feed the thousands of Jewish refugees who had no means of supporting themselves. Without Simon, and his magical ability to pull supplies out of thin air, what would become of all those hapless refugees? *Would they starve?* But Sunny was too worried for her close friend to dwell on the fate of the rest of the community.

Franz reached for Sunny's hand. "You know Simon. He always manages to land on his feet, as he likes to say."

Not since her father, who had died four years earlier, had Sunny known anyone who could read her mind as readily as her husband. At times, she found it uncanny. "But with the baby so close."

Franz shook his head. "To have to miss the birth of his own child."

Sunny studied Franz, trying to discern his thoughts. She longed for a baby of her own and, while Franz seemed to share in that desire, he already had a twelve-year-old daughter. Did he really need a newborn? Besides, with their existence growing more precarious by the day, was it fair to anyone to consider it now? She had yet to feel certain enough to leave the issue to chance in the bedroom.

Franz scanned the street. "Can you imagine, Sunny? Another ten thousand of us forced to live here in Little Vienna."

Half the city's Jewish refugees already lived in the square mile that replicated the Austrian capital right down to cafés and bakeries; according to most, it even smelled like home. The Jews shared the cramped space with a hundred thousand Chinese, who had proven remarkably tolerant of their new neighbours. "It will be tight," Sunny said. "At least the refugee hospital is already inside the borders."

Franz shrugged. "Perhaps that will just be one more luxury we have to forego."

She pulled her hand free of his. "We can't give up now, of all times! The hospital is going to be needed more than ever."

"Yes, I suppose it will." His expression fell somewhere between apologetic and resigned.

As they approached the footpath that led to the hospital, Sunny experienced a familiar sinking feeling. Involuntarily, her eyes shifted toward the abandoned building across the street. The weeks of rain had helped cleanse the walls, but she could still make out reddish-brown streaks. The slaughter of the two boys and Irma flashed to her mind so vividly that it felt as though the execution were unfolding in front of her all over again.

She had never learned what the teenagers had allegedly stolen. Summary executions were so commonplace in Shanghai that she had come to expect such violence from the Japanese. Still, her cheeks burned with shame. Never had she felt more helpless or cowardly than in the aftermath of that impromptu firing squad.

Franz gently tugged at her sleeve. "Poor Irma. So brave, but so rash. And for what? Thank God you kept your head, Sunny."

Sunny understood that his reassurance was meant kindly, but it only exacerbated her self-disgust. She broke free of him and headed down the pathway to the hospital.

From the outside, the single-level structure looked as uninspiring as ever. Inside was a different story. Since opening in 1938, the hospital had weathered a world war and a hostile occupation without ever turning away a patient. The single open ward, with its twenty-one beds, housed anywhere from a handful of patients to a hundred at a time, as during the cholera outbreak of the previous spring. The staff consisted of nine nurses—all, aside from Sunny, middle-aged or older refugees—and seven doctors, whose specialties ranged from dermatology to psychiatry. Sometimes the staff tripped over one another in the small ward, while other times a single nurse managed the entire hospital on her own. Many lives had been saved inside the hospital, not a few of them in the operating room, where Franz and the others had performed surgeries that should have been impossible to successfully conduct in such a rudimentary facility.

In recent months, the Japanese had actually helped to supply the hospital. A year earlier, four critically injured Japanese sailors had been rushed there after the Chinese Underground had allegedly detonated a bomb at the wharf nearby. Three of the four victims survived. Ever since, the Japanese had used the refugee hospital as a backup facility for their injured and ill. Sporadically, and always unannounced, canvas-covered trucks would rumble up to the sidewalk, and soldiers would dump crates, often marked only in Japanese, outside the doors. The supplies, a hodgepodge of bandages, non-perishable food and medications (some long past their expiry dates), rarely corresponded with the hospital's needs, but Simon and his second-in-command, Joey, managed to trade them on the black market for what was most urgently required.

As Franz and Sunny made their way down the main corridor, they slowed at an open door. Inside the office, Maxwell Feinstein ran a makeshift pathology lab. As expected, they found the sixty-year-old internist hunched over a desktop microscope, wearing his usual spotless lab coat and polka-dot bowtie. Max and his wife, Sarah, had been among the first German refugees to arrive in Shanghai as war loomed in Europe, but their daughter and her husband had refused to leave Hamburg with them. Their son-in-law had been convinced that someone he knew at the American consulate would secure them a visa to the United States. By the time he realized his mistake, the war in Europe had cut off the escape route to Shanghai. Max had not heard a word from his daughter or two grandsons in more than two years. He never spoke of them, but his grief was a persistent underlying presence.

Max wasn't alone in the office. Li Jun—"Joey" to everyone at the hospital—paced what little space he could find on the other side of Max's desk. The wiry twenty-one-year-old was dressed in his usual attire: a navy three-piece suit left to him by a patient's widow.

Though Joey rarely spoke of his past, he had once drunkenly told Sunny how he had ended up in Shanghai, at the age of twelve, after a typhoon and subsequent flood killed his family and wiped out his village. Joey had made the hundred-and-twenty-five-mile trek to Shanghai on foot. In the city, he barely escaped the life of street prostitution that so many rural girls and boys drifted into. Instead, he worked as a coolie—the lowest echelon of Shanghai labourers, who regularly worked themselves to death or died on the street from exposure in the winter and dehydration in the summer. Joey might have fallen victim to the same fate had Sir Victor Sassoon, an Iraqi Jew and the city's most influential businessman, not taken a shine to him. Impressed by the way the young rickshaw runner bartered over a fare, Sir Victor brought Joey onto his household staff, where he acquired languages as easily as he learned his other tasks. Sir Victor had hand-picked Simon to run the CFA, and the New Yorker had come to rely on Joey—who spoke Mandarin, Shanghainese, English, German, French and even a smattering of Russian. Joey, for his part, idolized Simon, treating him as a cross between a big brother and a mentor.

Joey wheeled toward Sunny. "What have they done with Mr. Simon, the *Rìběn guǐzi?*" he demanded, using the common Shanghainese pejorative, meaning "Japanese devils."

"Simon will be all right, Joey," Sunny soothed. "He has gone to an internment camp with many other Americans."

"You can't trust those Japanese dogs," Joey spat in Chinese before switching to German. "What about the hospital and the heime? Who will help them now?"

Franz motioned to Joey. "We are counting on you to fill in."

"I am no good at that stuff." Joey flexed one of his scrawny arms. "I am only the muscle around here."

Franz and Sunny shared a chuckle. Joey was a very able negotiator, especially with the local black marketeers.

Max viewed the others impatiently. "How is any of this funny? The hospital cannot survive without Simon."

"It has to, Max," Franz said with a glance toward Sunny. "We will make sure of it."

Max grunted skeptically. "What difference does it make, anyway? You saw the proclamation. The Japanese are herding us together in a ghetto. Probably at Hitler's request. It will make it that much easier to get rid of us."

Franz shook his head. "The Japanese had no appetite for it last year when the SS showed up with their poison gas and plans for us."

"Only because your friend, the colonel, intervened."

Max had a point. The High Command in Tokyo might have never interceded to stop the Nazis' plans had Franz not solicited the help of Colonel Tsutomo Kubota, a British-schooled Japanese officer who had always been sympathetic to the refugees' plight.

"And where is Colonel Kubota now to protect us?" Max continued.

Neither Franz nor Sunny had an answer. No one seemed to know where Kubota had ended up after being dispatched from Shanghai in disgrace for overstepping his professional bounds by helping the Jews.

"Besides, the war is not going so well for the Japanese," Max said. "Perhaps this time no one will object to Hitler's plans for us. Never forget how they handled Irma and those boys."

Sunny fought off a shudder. Franz shook his head repeatedly. "We are already at their whim," he pointed out. "If the Japanese want to hand us over to the Nazis, they don't need to go to the trouble of relocating all of us into another section of the city."

"It's true," Sunny agreed. "If they planned to hand the Jews over to the Germans, it would make far more sense to round us up in camps, like they have done with the British and Americans."

Max arched an eyebrow. "So why move us at all?"

Franz shrugged. "More living space for their own people?"

Joey waved a hand toward the window. "The harbour is so close. And the radio towers are nearby. Even the rail lines crisscross here."

Franz snorted in laughter. "*Ja,* of course. Joey is right. There is no more strategic location in all of Shanghai than Hongkew."

"So why in God's name cluster us here then?" Max asked.

"As a deterrent," Franz said.

Max raised an eyebrow. "They are concerned about Jewish saboteurs?"

Joey gestured to the ceiling. "Allied airplanes. The bombers."

"Are you suggesting that the Japanese plan to use us as human shields for their military installations?" Max chuckled grimly. "The fools!"

"What is so foolish about it?" Sunny asked.

Max gave her a compassionate look that he usually reserved for patients. "You dear, naive girl. When in the history of mankind has the potential loss of Jewish lives ever deterred anyone from doing anything?"

Franz sighed. "You are as cynical as they come, my friend, but you might have a point."

Joey began pacing again. "Where have they taken Mr. Simon?"

"To Chapei," Sunny said. "They have converted the Great China University into a prison camp for Americans."

Joey nodded to himself. "Good. I won't have to cross the river."

Franz put his hands on hips. "Joey, you are not thinking . . ."

Joey gaped at him as though Franz were simple-minded. "We can't leave just leave him to rot at the hands of the *Rìběn guǐzi*."

The image of the two teens crumpled at the foot of the wall flashed again into Sunny's mind. She reached out and squeezed Joey's shoulder.

He reddened at her touch. She had always found his schoolboy crush endearing, but now she chose to use it strategically. "Joey, promise me you will not do anything rash," she said softly in Shanghainese. "If something were to happen to you, I would be lost. You know that."

Joey turned crimson, and he dropped his gaze to his feet. "I only want to go see how he is doing."

"It's too dangerous," Sunny said.

But Joey persisted. "Last week, I crossed the Whangpoo to the Pootung Camp to bring food to the Kaplans. That kind old British couple from the CFA executive." He shrugged slightly. "There were only a few soldiers outside. No one stopped me from going in."

Sunny gave his shoulder another squeeze before letting go. "Just so long as you do not try anything reckless."

"I won't," he mumbled.

"You must promise me—" Sunny began to insist, but a panicky voice cut her off.

"*Franz!*" Esther croaked from the doorway.

Sunny looked over to see Esther swaying at the threshold. Her face was ghostly pale against the collar of her black coat, and she propped herself up in the doorframe with a trembling hand.

Franz rushed over and slid his arm behind Esther's back. "What is it, Essie?"

Esther fumbled for her belly and her coat flopped open. She clutched her bulging abdomen. "The baby," she whispered.

"Is it coming? Now?"

Esther only grimaced. Sunny's eyes were drawn to the woman's legs, where dark red blood trickled down the inside of her knee.

"When did the bleeding begin?" Sunny demanded.

"Fifteen minutes, maybe," Esther whimpered uncharacteristically. Her expression exuded sheer panic. "It keeps coming. Clots, too. What is happening to my baby?"

Before Sunny could reply, Esther's eyes rolled back in their sockets. Her legs buckled and she collapsed in Franz's arms.

Chapter 4

Esther didn't regain consciousness until Franz lowered her limp body onto the nearest stretcher. She stared up at him through glazed eyes. "*Ach,* Franz, will I lose the baby?"

Franz knew it was not the time for false promises. Besides, he was even more concerned for her survival. "It's too early to say, Essie."

"But it is likely?" Esther asked calmly.

Sunny looked up from where she crouched at the bedside, preparing to insert an intravenous needle into Esther's arm. She squeezed Esther's hand supportively but said nothing.

Franz ran his fingers along the firm mound of Esther's abdomen, pausing every few inches to press deeper and to study her face for a response. "Does this hurt?" he asked.

"There is no pain. Only bleeding. So much blood," she said, panting heavily.

Franz pulled his hand from her belly and glanced over at Sunny. "At least it's not an abruptio," he said as much to himself as to the others.

Sunny continued to focus on Esther's arm. She poked the needle through the skin and eased it deeper until a drop of blood formed, confirming the tip had entered a vein.

"*Abruptio?*" Esther grimaced. "What is this, Franz?"

"In the final months of a pregnancy, there are only two likely causes for such heavy bleeding: placenta previa or placenta abruptio." He deliberately kept his tone clinical. "Both are related to complications with the placenta, or the afterbirth, which nourishes the fetus. In abruptio, the placenta separates from the wall of the womb and causes bleeding. The mother experiences pain and tenderness in her belly. In previa, the placenta lies low—too low—below the fetus, at the level of the cervical opening. It is painless, but the bleeding can be heavy. I suspect that must be your diagnosis."

Esther nodded bravely. "What is the treatment?"

"We must deliver the baby by Caesarean section. Immediately."

Esther's thin lips tightened until their colour almost vanished. "But Franz," she murmured, "the baby is only seven and half months. It is too soon."

"There's no choice, Essie. You have already lost too much blood."

"I have plenty more." Esther mustered a small laugh. "Too much blood is a family curse. The doctors in Vienna used to have to bleed my Onkel Klaus regularly. Please, Franz. Can we not wait a day or two more and see if the bleeding stops?"

Franz placed a gentle hand on her shoulder. "Essie, you will only continue to hemorrhage."

"I am willing to take that chance," she said in a small voice.

The intravenous connected to the bottle, Sunny rose to her feet. She tenderly pushed the hair away from Esther's brow, but when she spoke her tone was firm. "Without you and your beating heart, there is no baby, Essie. We need to deliver right away. It is not a matter of choice."

Esther's eyes defiantly held Sunny's for a moment, and then her face crumpled. She raised her hands to cover her tears. "Yes, of course, you would know best," she said, her voice breaking. "Do what has to be done."

"It's for the best, really," Franz murmured, embarrassed by the hollowness of his words.

Esther lowered her hands, then looked from Franz to Sunny and back to Franz again. "Please, you must promise me, Franz. Whatever happens during the surgery, you will save the baby first."

Franz and Sunny exchanged charged looks before Franz turned back to Esther. "You know we will do everything possible for you and—"

Esther reached up and clutched his wrist with surprising force. "But if it anything goes wrong, you will save the baby! Please, Franz."

Franz clasped her hand in his and held it tightly for a moment. A silent promise.

Another nurse, Berta Abeldt, arrived pushing a portable stretcher ahead of her. "The operating room has been prepared, Dr. Adler," she announced.

Together, they lifted Esther onto the stretcher and then Berta wheeled her away.

As Franz scrubbed for surgery, his thoughts drifted back to the night of Hannah's birth. His wife, Hilde, had been so excited when her water finally broke a week after her due date that she cried from joy rather than discomfort, at the first contraction. Between labour pains, Franz and Hilde playfully argued over names. They both favoured "Albert" for a boy, but they could not agree on a girl's name; Franz preferred "Elise," while Hilde had her heart set on "Hannah."

By Hilde's sixth hour of labour, Franz sensed trouble. The baby's head had hardly progressed down the birth canal. After twelve hours, Hilde was too exhausted to push any more. Franz's mentor, Dr. Ignaz Malkin, had rushed into the hospital at four in the morning to perform an emergency Caesarian section. Franz had to beg the older surgeon to allow him into the delivery room; husbands were always kept outside. Franz had never felt as terrified or helpless. Hannah came out navy blue and not breathing. Dr. Malkin's vigorous rubbing finally coaxed a breath or two from the tiny girl. But the damage had been done. The newborn's brain had been deprived of oxygen for too long. Franz soon noticed how little his daughter's left arm and leg moved compared with the limbs on her right side. He was devastated, but Hilde remained unfazed. She persuaded him to be grateful for the miracle of their daughter's survival. And he was, too, until Hannah's fourth day of life, when Hilde developed a fever. Less than twenty-four hours later, his wife was dead from an overwhelming post-operative infection.

"Esther is on the operating table," Sunny announced from over his shoulder, snapping him out of the memory. "We are ready, Franz."

His heart pounded in his throat. Esther and he were closer than most siblings. They had been the only adults in either of their families to escape Nazi-occupied Vienna, four and a half years earlier. During their first three years in Shanghai, Esther had lived with Hannah and Franz in a one-bedroom apartment. Esther was more a mother than an aunt to Hannah. Franz could not imagine life without her.

Sunny reached a hand out to him. "I have performed several Caesarian sections, Franz. If you would prefer . . ."

He smiled grimly. "I have to do this, Sunny. I promised her."

"Yes. Of course."

As Franz stepped into the operating room, he reminded himself that there were no true medical parallels between Hilde and Esther's conditions. Still, he had to force himself to slow his breathing and focus on the procedure, not on Esther, who was already on the table, covered from the neck down. Her pregnant belly rose from a gap left between two sheets. Her abdomen was painted with brown iodine in preparation for surgery, but her complexion better matched the white sheets draping her. She managed a quivering smile for him. "If it's a girl, she must be "Ruth." But if we have a boy, Simon and I both like the name "Jakob." After your father, Franz."

"A good name, Essie." The lump in his throat almost choked away his words.

Jakob Adler had outlived his younger son, Esther's first husband, Karl, by only a few weeks. Emphysema, not the Nazis, had taken his life, but it still troubled Franz that Jakob had survived long enough to witness his younger son's lynching.

Sunny stepped up to the operating table, across from Franz. Another nurse, Liese, stood at the head of the table, assuming the role of anaesthetist. She held a breathing mask and a bottle of ether that Simon had managed to secure through the black market just the day before he was interned.

Franz leaned closer to his sister-in-law. "Are you ready, Essie?"

"Not for any of it—not surgery, not motherhood or . . ." She uttered a small laugh. "But please do not let that stop you."

Franz looked over to Liese and nodded.

"I am going to put you to sleep now, Frau Lehrer," Liese said as she lowered the mask over Esther's face and tilted the bottle, slowly dripping the ether.

The sweet, acrid smell of the anaesthetic filled the room. After seven or eight drops had saturated the mask, Esther's eyelids began to flutter, and soon her eyes closed altogether.

Franz's stomach flip-flopped as he realized again that, despite the routine nature of the procedure, so much would be beyond his control. He lifted a scalpel from the surgical tray, surprised by the steadiness of his hand as he lowered the blade to the skin below Esther's navel. He poked the tip through, drawing blood, and waited for Esther's reaction. She remained still and silent, so he dug the blade in deeper and sliced vertically downward until he reached the level of her pelvic bones.

Sunny followed the blade with a sponge, dabbing away the blood. As soon as Franz pulled the scalpel back, she eased two retractors inside the long incision and spread the skin apart. Franz reached his gloved hand into the wound until he touched the firm bulge of Esther's uterus, which tightened against his fingers in a sudden contraction. Once the spasm passed, he placed the scalpel against the womb and cut through the brownish-red muscle, being careful not to let the blade penetrate too deeply and nick the baby tucked inside. Once the scalpel pierced the uterus, dark blood gushed out through the incision, obscuring Franz's view

Sunny sponged up as much of the blood as she could, and Franz glimpsed a tiny hand and arm poking through the incision. He dropped his scalpel on the tray and slid his hands inside Esther's uterus until they wrapped around the infant's warm, slippery body. Franz resisted the urge to yank the baby free. Instead, he gingerly eased it out, while Sunny clamped off and then cut the umbilical cord.

The tiny boy weighed no more than four pounds, but those details hardly registered with Franz. Covered in mucus and blood, the baby flopped limply in his hands. His skin was as blue as the Danube, and he neither moved nor breathed.

Franz went cold. For the first time since Hannah's birth, he froze inside the operating room.

Berta plucked the child from his hands, then swaddled him in a towel and laid him on the pillow on top of the table that had been set up as a makeshift cradle.

Franz held his own breath as he studied the baby's chest, desperate to see a sign of respiration. But the boy remained absolutely still.

"Is he?" Sunny asked slowly.

Unwilling to meet her eyes, Franz just stared at the table.

Berta applied her knuckles to the baby's small chest, her fist covering its entire surface as she rubbed. "Take a breath, *Kleiner*."

Nothing.

"Please, *Schatzi*," Berta cooed. "Breathe for your auntie."

Drops of perspiration ran down Berta's brow as she continued to rub, murmuring gentle words of encouragement.

"Franz!" Sunny called. "We have an arterial bleed!"

Franz spun and saw that Sunny had plunged her hand wrist-deep through Esther's incision. Bright red blood was welling up around Sunny's arm and running down the sides of Esther's abdomen.

"Damn it to hell," Franz muttered, realizing that one of the arteries that fed the placenta must have ruptured spontaneously once the pressure of the fetus's head against it had been released. He grabbed for the biggest clamp on the tray and swung back toward Esther. "Let go, Sunny."

She hesitated. "You won't be able to see anything through all the blood."

"Then I will do it blindly."

Sunny pulled her hand free. Almost immediately, the blood began cascading over the edges of the surgical wound like the overflow from a backed-up sink.

"Dr. Adler." Liese spoke in a hush from where she stood at the head of the operating table, her fingers against Esther's neck. "The pulse is very weak."

Franz thrust his hand back inside the wound, blood engulfing his glove and warming his hand. He felt around until his fingers found the left uterine ligament, and the artery and vein below it. He firmly clamped them off. He shot his hand over to the other side of the womb and explored until his fingers gripped the structures on the right side. Sunny handed him a second clamp, which he fastened onto the blood vessels. He hesitated before slowly withdrawing his hand.

Sunny wadded sponges into the wound. The blood soaked through them on contact. She prepared to stuff more inside, but Franz waved her off. "Wait, Sunny."

They both stared at the incision. No fresh blood appeared.

"The pulse, Liese?" Franz addressed the anaesthetist.

"There is little change, Dr. Adler." Liese paused. "Perhaps a smidgeon stronger."

Franz pointed to the clamps protruding from Esther's abdomen. "Even if she survives, I have to remove her uterus now. *Ach,* there will be no more children."

"What choice was there?"

He dropped his chin to his chest, defeated. "I promised her."

Sunny's gaze shifted to Berta. Her eyes lit up. "Franz, look!"

He turned to see Berta cradling the baby in her arms and singing softly. For a moment, Franz wondered if the song was a prayer of mourning that he didn't recognize, but her words were in Yiddish and the tune was that of a lullaby. Then Franz heard what sounded like mewing. And then he saw something move. It was the baby's hand.

Chapter 5

February 23, 1943

Sunny peeked through the curtains that separated Esther's bed from the others on the ward. She watched with affection tinged with envy as Esther eased little Jakob's head up to her breast. The infant rooted around for a moment or two before his mouth latched on to the nipple.

Sunny had not expected either mother or child to survive the traumatic birth. And yet, less than a week later, both were thriving. Esther's skin was still pale, almost translucent, but she had recovered as quickly and resiliently as her son had.

Esther smiled bashfully. "He seems to be finally grasping the concept."

"I would say so," Sunny said as she watched the baby suckle with gusto. "How are you, Essie?"

"Tired. Lost. Useless." She sighed contentedly. "And still so very grateful for the *nes*—the miracle—of this little one's survival." She shook her head. "Sunny, if not for you and Franz . . ."

Sunny raised her hands in mock denial. "It had far more to do with your stubbornness. Both of you. Your insistence on surviving, despite the odds." She stepped forward, letting the curtains fall shut behind her. "Do you have any pain?"

"Nothing worth complaining about."

"Have you been eating?"

"Here and there," Esther said as she gently rocked Jakob. "He doesn't give me much time for such luxuries."

"But you must, Essie. Otherwise there will be no milk for Jakob."

"Of course." Esther wrapped her other arm protectively around her son.

Sunny studied the baby's face. His rosy cheeks stood out against Esther's pale flesh. "He's beautiful."

Esther laughed. "You really think so? To my eye, he looks a little too much like his father."

"He could do worse."

The smile slid from Esther's lips. "I wonder if Simon even knows."

"Joey went out to the camp to tell him."

Esther looked away. "Knowing might only make it that much harder for him."

Sunny could not disagree and lapsed into silence as she continued to watch Esther feed her baby. After a few minutes, Jakob's eyes closed and his lips stopped smacking. Esther gently pried him free of her breast. She looked up at Sunny. "Would you burp him for me?"

Sunny eagerly tucked Jakob against her chest. As his warm body undulated with his gentle breathing, the longing for a child of her own stirred inside her.

Esther's eyes brimmed. "He likes you."

Sunny patted Jakob's back and rocked him back and forth. She pressed her cheek to his smooth head. The scents of talc and baby only intensified her heightened emotions. "Let's hope he does. The poor little fellow has to live with us for the foreseeable future."

Esther frowned. "Sunny, I have been thinking about our living arrangements. I wonder if it would not be best—" She stopped in mid-sentence as the curtains swooshed apart.

"*Simon?*" Sunny gasped, shocked to see his tall frame filling the gap.

Simon's hair stuck up in messy spikes. His pinstriped suit was stained across the sleeves and torn below one pocket. He looked thin, frail and exhausted. But he sported a huge smile as he rushed to his wife's side. "Gorgeous! Oh, I can't even trust my eyes! I must be dreaming!"

"Simon, I . . . I don't . . ." Esther sputtered as he swallowed her up in an embrace.

Simon smothered her face with kisses before straightening and turning to Sunny with a wild grin. "Hiya, Sunny!" He kissed her on the cheek and then held out his hands for Jakob. "May I?" His voice was thick.

Sunny passed Jakob to his father, who cradled him gingerly, as though holding loosely packed crystal. Without taking his eyes off his son, he muttered, "Can you believe it, Essie? Our beautiful boy!"

Esther reached up and clutched her husband's arm. Her eyes misted over. "How, Simon?" She cleared her throat. "How is this *nes* possible?"

Simon shrugged. "A stroll in the park after what you and little Jakob have been through."

Esther tugged at his sleeve. "Simon, tell me."

Before he could answer, the curtains parted again and Franz stepped through. "So it is true! How did you get out, Simon?"

Simon laughed. "I'm not feeling particularly welcome back home. All anyone cares about is my escape."

"Escape?" Esther blanched. "Oh, Simon, you didn't!"

Simon swaddled Jakob more tightly in the blanket and held him closely against his body. He leaned forward awkwardly and kissed Esther on the lips again. "After I heard what you went through, Essie, there was no way they were going to keep us apart."

"And the Japanese let you just waltz out of prison?" Franz asked.

"Not sure that the Japs are big on waltzing." Simon chuckled again. "But Chapei camp is no Bridge House. The guards are enlisted men, not those Kempeitai sadists."

Franz frowned. "It's still a prison, is it not?"

"The Japs only ever call it the 'Civic Assembly Center.' Then again, it's not like they treat us that well. My old springer spaniel would have turned his nose up at the slop they feed us." Simon sighed. "But it doesn't feel much like prison. There are even some kids inside. Security is pretty loose. Joey smuggled me in some cash. For ten bucks, the night guard in my barracks looked the other way. I snuck out just after curfew."

Esther struggled to sit up, using her husband's arm for support. "They will be looking for you."

Simon waved away the suggestion. "They've got tens of thousands of Allied prisoners to worry about. What is one less to them?"

"You are not just any prisoner," Sunny pointed out. "Everyone around here knows who you are, including the Japanese."

"So I guess I will just have to become another nameless refugee," Simon replied in almost accent-free German as he snuggled Jakob closer. "Who's going to know any better?"

"Colonel Tanaka will," Franz said, wiping the cheerfulness from Simon's expression.

Tanaka, the leader of the Kempeitai in Shanghai, had enthusiastically overseen the two men's torture at Bridge House. There was little doubt that Tanaka would take a personal, and possibly lethal, interest in Simon's recapture.

Esther's hand fell to the bed. "It is not safe for you to be here, Simon. Not for you." She looked away, and when she spoke again, her tone was firm, almost expressionless. "And especially not for Jakob."

Crestfallen, Simon stared down at his sleeping baby and nodded. "I just had to see you both. I didn't think it through. Essie, you know I would never endanger either of you." His voice dropped to a whisper. "I will go."

Chapter 6

"It's a little easier to get a table these days, isn't it?" Ko Jia-Li chuckled through a veil of exhaled smoke.

Sunny saw her point. The Peking Room of the Cathay Hotel was nearly deserted. The sight was surreal. Not long before, only celebrities and the ultra-wealthy stood a chance of securing a table for the hotel's high tea, which people still referred to by the old British term of "tiffin." The art deco gem, situated at the intersection of Nanking Road and the riverside Bund, had been the city's crowning glory. Sunny had recently heard an elderly Shanghailander widow reminisce reverently about the hotel's opening-night gala, thrown thirteen years earlier. According to the old woman, the guest list read like that of a royal wedding. Apparently, Noël Coward missed the party because of the flu, completing his play *Private Lives* while lying in bed five floors above the ballroom.

"Are you really so surprised?" Sunny asked. "Who is left to even come for tiffin?"

Jia-Li waved her cigarette toward the gilded ceiling. "Still, the occupation hasn't dampened the city's nightlife much."

"I wouldn't really know. I never got out much, even before." Between work, school and her apprenticeship with her father, Sunny had never had much opportunity to take in Shanghai's bustling social scene.

Besides, even before the Japanese occupation, she had never been interested in the city's myriad nightclubs, cabarets and discreetly welcoming opium dens. The one evening Jia-Li had dragged her out to a nightclub on Broadway, Sunny had not lasted long. She managed to swallow only two sips of her throat-burning martini and eventually found the sight of the gorgeous but aging Russian taxi dancer—who drifted from one table to another, haplessly soliciting men to purchase dances—too sad to bear.

"Trust me, *xiǎo hè*." Although they were speaking English, Jia-Li still referred to Sunny by her Chinese nickname, which meant "little lotus." "*I would know.*"

The nightlife had been Jia-Li's profession for almost half her life. At twenty-eight, she was still one of the city's most sought-after singsong girls. She had worked in Frenchtown's leading brothel since the age of fifteen, when her first boyfriend dragged her into a life of opium addiction and prostitution and then abandoned her to fend for herself. She had battled addiction ever since. Sunny ruefully thought of the many episodes of opium withdrawal through which she had nursed her friend. But Jia-Li had impressed her of late with her longest run of sobriety yet, having not touched an opium pipe in nearly a year.

Eager to change the subject, Sunny asked, "How is Dmitri, *bǎo bèi?*" Jia-Li's childhood nickname meant "precious."

Jia-Li took another drag from her cigarette. She wore no makeup, but it made no difference. With her magnetic eyes and ivory complexion, she was the most beautiful person Sunny had ever seen.

"Depressing." Jia-Li sighed. "Aside from the Japanese, no one has it better in Shanghai than the Russians. But I think that bothers Dimi. He finds purpose only in suffering and pessimism."

Sunny had nothing against the scrawny poet whom Jia-Li was dating, but Dmitri had always struck her as gloomy to the point of morbid. She could not see his appeal, but that was almost to be expected with Jia-Li's lovers. Ever since that first boyfriend, there had been a consistently self-destructive pattern to Jia-Li's choices in men.

Jia-Li flicked away her romantic concerns along with the ash of her cigarette. "What about your dashing doctor? How is Franz?"

Sunny smiled sadly. "He works himself beyond exhaustion."

"And you?" Jia-Li blew out her cheeks. "You worked two full-time nursing jobs while your father put you through his own private medical school. You have not slowed down since."

"It's non-stop with Franz. He works at the refugee hospital seven days a week. When he's not tending to patients, he's trying to find enough supplies to keep the doors open."

"That must be a struggle, with Simon in the camps." Jia-Li nodded in sympathy. "How will all those refugees cope without their American messiah?"

Sunny glanced over her shoulder and then leaned in closer. "Simon is not in the camps," she whispered.

Jia-Li's eyes narrowed ever so slightly. She lowered her voice, too. "What happened to him?"

"He escaped."

"Escaped?" Jia-Li breathed out another curling tendril of smoke. "Simon? A fugitive? I can't see it."

"He was so worried for Essie and the baby." Sunny told her of Esther's unexpected collapse and Jakob's urgent delivery.

"So he had no choice then," Jia-Li said with finality.

"No, I suppose not."

"Still, I don't know how much better off he is outside the camp." Jia-Li shook her head. "Shanghai is a mess. That is why I choose to keep my head firmly buried in the sand."

Sunny knew better, but she didn't comment. Instead, she reached for Jia-Li's free hand. "The hospital is the first place the Japanese will look for him."

"And your home will be the second."

"True."

Jia-Li squeezed Sunny's hand. "So what are we going to do with him?"

"I was hoping you might have an idea."

Jia-Li bit her lip, deep in thought. Her pensive expression only heightened her beauty. After a few seconds, she broke into an amused grin.

"What is so funny?"

"Do you remember that night a few years ago?" Jia-Li asked. "When Simon took us to that fabulous party at Sir Victor's mansion on Great Western Road?"

"Of course."

"Simon played piano and sang us all those Cole Porter and Irving Berlin songs? Drunk as he was, he wasn't half bad."

"I don't see how—"

"The Comfort Home could always use another piano player."

Sunny's jaw dropped. "You are not suggesting that we hide Simon in your brothel?"

"Why not?"

"Aren't the Japanese your best customers?"

"Hardly our best," Jia-Li snorted. "But perhaps our most dedicated."

"So why would we ever take such a chance with Simon?"

Jia-Li smiled patiently. "They might be the most tenacious and paranoid race in the world, but you must understand: the Japanese never mix work and pleasure."

"Still . . ."

Jia-Li patted Sunny's hand. "Not to worry, *xiǎo hè*. I'm only joking about the piano. The *Rìběn guǐzi* will never catch sight of Simon. It will be just like with the others."

Chapter 7

March 2, 1943

The path meandered through the sprawling gardens, which were sprinkled with magnolias, gingkos and wildflowers, before leading to the mustard-coloured Spanish villa that was perched on a slope overlooking the grounds. A steady breeze rustled the leaves as Franz and Esther made their way toward the grand house. There were no signs on the premises, but anyone familiar with Frenchtown would have recognized it as the Comfort Home.

Franz had visited the brothel before. On the previous occasion, he had come in search of Jia-Li after his release from Bridge House when he had been unable to find Sunny or Hannah and was frantic. He was returning now against his better judgment, for he couldn't resist Esther's appeals any longer.

"What if I never see him again?" Esther had wondered aloud the previous evening.

"It does no good to think like that, Essie," Franz said.

Her gaze fell to her lap. "Not only did I ask him to leave, I accused him of endangering our child."

"And you were right to. It was a rash thing Simon did." He shook his head. "Just as taking you there to see him would be."

"Why? No one has even come to search for him."

She had a point. The Japanese had yet to come to their home or the hospital in search of Simon. Franz found their absence almost as disconcerting as one of their raids. "Trust me, Essie. They will search for him."

"His own son, Franz. Simon only wanted to see us. To ensure we were safe. And I sent him away."

The memory of Esther's shattered expression bolstered Franz's resolve as he neared the Chinese guard who blocked the final few steps of the pathway. Over six foot five and at least three hundred pounds, the black-suited goliath would have been an intimidating sight were it not for his gap-toothed grin. "A pleasure to see you again, Dr. Adler," he said in impeccable English. His gaze drifted to Esther and the baby in her arms, but his smile held fast.

"Good to see you, too, Ushi." Franz motioned to the others. "This is Esther, my sister-in-law. And little Jakob."

"Nice to meet you, ma'am." Ushi turned back to Franz. "How is Sunny?"

"She is well, Ushi. And you?"

"I'm still here," he said wistfully. "Have you come to see Jia-Li?"

Before Franz could even nod, Ushi turned toward the house, saying, "You will have to wait in the drawing room."

According to Sunny, Ushi had been a punter, or bodyguard, at the Comfort Home his entire adult life. Jia-Li and he had been close ever since her first day, when he had sat up the whole night beside the bed where she eventually sobbed herself to sleep. Jia-Li viewed Ushi as the big brother she never had. For his part, he had been in love with her for years but had long since accepted that his feelings would go unrequited. Still, Ushi watched over her as ferociously as a mother bear protecting her cubs, something several overly aggressive clients had learned to their dismay.

Franz and Esther followed Ushi as he veered off the main pathway and headed around the building to the rear entrance. They walked up an elaborately carved mahogany staircase and entered through a massive doorway. The drawing room was furnished with elegant French Baroque pieces and decorated with inlaid wainscoting and a coved ceiling. It smelled of pipe tobacco, wood polish and old money. Franz had never been inside any other bordello, but he knew the Comfort Home was far from typical. The mansion had been originally built for the family of a French aristocrat—a major in the army—who had returned home from the Great War a broken man and promptly drank and gambled away his entire fortune. The city's foremost crime syndicate, the Green Gang, had claimed the home as a gambling debt and turned it, under the watchful eye of Madam Chih-Nii, into the most distinguished brothel in Frenchtown.

Franz was studying a large oil portrait of a pretty but stern-faced French woman—and wondering if her husband was the one who had trifled away the family fortune—when Jia-Li swept into the room in a red cheongsam and matching four-inch heels. Her cheeks were flushed, and a few strands of hair had escaped from her otherwise perfect coiffure, but she didn't appear the least surprised to see two old friends, one of whom held an infant, standing inside her place of work.

"We are sorry to surprise you like this," Franz said.

Jia-Li only shrugged. "Simon will be ecstatic to see you."

Esther rushed over and placed her free hand on Jia-Li's wrist. "You are truly a godsend."

Jia-Li laughed. "I've been called many things, but never that before."

"But you are," Esther said as she freed the other woman's arm.

Jia-Li straightened her hair and smoothed her dress before leaning forward to peer at Jakob.

"Would you like to hold him?" Esther asked.

Jia-Li's eyes lit up as she took Jakob in her arms. She gently swung him to and fro and nuzzled his nose. After a few minutes of cooing, she reluctantly transferred him back into his mother's arms and glanced over at the grandfather clock against the far wall. "We had better get moving."

They followed Jia-Li down a corridor. As they turned a corner, Jia-Li almost bumped into two Japanese soldiers who were heading toward them. Esther's finger surreptitiously crept around Franz's elbow, while Franz struggled to keep his face calm as he glimpsed the white armbands that marked the men as Kempeitai. Their faces were flushed from alcohol, and one's shirt was untucked. The other warbled an unidentifiable tune.

Jia-Li breezed past the soldiers as though they were street beggars. Franz hurried after her, pulling Esther and the baby along with him.

Suddenly, a fleshy Chinese woman appeared in the middle of the hallway, blocking it with her wide frame. Franz could almost taste her heavy cinnamon perfume. Chih-Nii's hair was pulled back tightly around an ivory comb, and her face was caked with powder and rouge. She wore a voluminous jade-coloured cheongsam that was embroidered with gold. Her appearance verged on caricature, but Franz knew that the getup was nothing more than a costume. Chih-Nii was among the shrewdest business people in Shanghai. According to Sunny, she had created her persona from the pulp-fiction ideal of the Oriental madam and exaggerated it even further after the Japanese invasion.

Chih-Nii looked from Esther to Jakob and touched a bright pink fingernail to her red lips. "Certainly, not my usual clientele," she said in a singsong voice. "But all are welcome at the Comfort Home."

Jia-Li introduced Franz and Esther by their first names only. Chih-Nii tilted her head, squeezing one of her jowls against her shoulder. "So the friends have come to visit my *bǎo bèi?* The most prized flower in my lovely garden."

Franz and Esther shared a nervous glance. Jia-Li shook her head. "I am taking them to the basement."

Chih-Nii stiffened. She spat some words in guttural Chinese, a marked contrast to her earlier musical tone.

Unperturbed, Jia-Li nodded to Esther. "Simon, the American. His wife and baby."

Chih-Nii folded her arms over her chest. She muttered further in Chinese before finishing in English. "No one," she growled. "Could I have been any clearer?"

Esther stepped forward. "This is my fault. I have come here uninvited and unannounced." She touched Chih-Nii's golden sleeve. "I am so grateful for your help. I have no business being here, but our baby—he came so close to dying. My husband risked everything to see him, but as soon as he arrived, I sent him away. I want to make it right. I must."

"A sad story, indeed." Chih-Nii glanced coolly at Esther's hand on her arm. "But Shanghai is bursting at the seams with sad stories. No one can make any of them right."

"Only this once." Esther said. "I will never return. I swear."

"And what about the others?" Chih-Nii snorted. "They will want their wives and babies to visit, too. Mark my words: this can only end badly for everyone."

Franz wondered how many fugitives were hiding in the Comfort Home. He opened his mouth to intervene, but Jia-Li spoke up first. The two women conversed in Chinese. Franz had the distinct impression that he was witnessing a negotiation.

Finally, Chih-Nii stepped to one side and swept her arm behind her with a flourish. "Go. Go see your man," she said to Esther, her tone as welcoming as before. "After all, wives are rarely so pleased to find their husbands inside the Comfort Home."

They followed Jia-Li to the end of the hallway. "What did you promise her?" Franz asked in a low voice.

Jia-Li rolled her eyes. "Nothing. She cannot afford to lose me."

Ushi met them at the top of a staircase. "He will take you from here," Jia-Li said as she turned away. "I have . . . appointments."

Ushi led Franz and Esther down the steps. In the basement, the guard had to stoop his head and neck to clear the low ceiling. He stopped at a door and glanced to both sides before entering.

Franz and Esther followed Ushi into a long, narrow wine cellar that smelled vaguely of must. The guard latched the door behind them and then led them past row after row of bottles: wines, spirits and others that were too dusty for Franz to identify. He stopped at one rack and pounded his fist four times against the wooden frame, barely rattling the bottles in its shelves. Ushi rapped four more times rapidly. A moment later, four muffled knocks came in reply.

Ushi placed his palms against the top shelf of the rack and pressed upward. The entire rack popped off the wall with a click, but not a single bottle shifted as he laid the frame on an angle against the other wall. He grabbed one of the screws that stuck out from the exposed wall and pulled. A short section of the wall slid toward them: a false front.

Ushi pressed a finger to his lips and nodded toward the opening. Franz turned sideways and sidled through the gap, with Esther following. After they had taken a few steps, he heard Ushi slide the wall back into place behind them.

Franz expected to step into the kind of torch-lit dungeons familiar to his imagination from the radio dramas and B movies of his youth, but instead he emerged from the short passageway into a spacious room furnished with a table, chairs and even a basic kitchenette. Two floor lamps lit the room. The staticky sound of a BBC broadcast floated softly from an upright wireless that stood in a corner. Another Chinese guard, imposing though not quite matching Ushi's stature, stood facing the passageway. His arms were folded across his chest, his face expressionless. "You wait," he grunted.

Jakob whimpered in Esther's arms. She rocked him, trying to hush her son. "Papa is coming," she soothed.

After a moment, a door swung open and Simon rushed out. He crossed the floor in a few eager strides and flung his arms around his wife and baby, kissing them both repeatedly.

"I am so, so sorry, darling," Esther murmured when he finally released her.

"Not a reason in the world to be sorry, gorgeous." Simon stroked her cheek. "I am so happy you came."

Franz took a step back, feeling like an intruder, but Simon turned to him with a grateful smile and an extended hand. "Thanks, Franz."

"Your gratitude is misplaced." Franz shook his friend's hand self-consciously. "If I had any say in the matter, none of us would be here."

Still beaming, Simon slipped Jakob out of Esther's arms and held him overhead. "How about you, little fella? You wanted to come visit your *tate*, didn't you?" He studied the baby thoughtfully. "He has your eyes, Essie. Lucky little guy."

Esther ran her hand through Simon's hair, which had been shorn into a crewcut. She frowned as she assessed his outfit. The blue button-down shirt he wore billowed around him, and his black slacks were at least three inches too short. "I must bring you clothes."

"Not necessary, Essie." Simon chuckled and plucked at his loose shirt. "We don't get out much around here."

"And food?"

"They treat us well. A lot better than we deserve. They're risking a lot to protect us."

"Who is 'us'?"

The guard glared at Simon and shook his head once.

"Best if I don't say too much," Simon said.

Esther nestled her head into the crook of Simon's neck. "If only there was a way that we could all be together."

"Soon, Essie. Soon."

Franz took Jakob from Simon's arms. The infant cried as Franz repositioned him against his shoulder, prompting a flood of memories of pacing miles with baby Hannah as she fussed away night after night with colic.

Simon glanced at his son with concern. "Is he hungry?"

Esther wrapped her arms around her husband and pulled him into a tight hug. "He can wait a few minutes."

Esther and Simon swayed silently in each other's embrace, while Franz bounced Jakob and tried to distract him. The baby suckled on his finger for a moment and then cried even louder. Jakob's howls were just then joined by an urgent pounding that came from down the passageway: two rapid knocks, followed by a brief pause and then two more rapid knocks.

The guard snapped to attention. He shot up a hand to silence the others. "A raid! *The Kempeitai!*" he spat in a hushed tone as he launched into motion.

Franz glanced helplessly at Simon. His friend's face was calm but his eyes held an unfamiliar tinge of terror.

The guard reached for the radio and flicked it off before dousing one of the lamps. When he turned back to the others, he held a hunting knife. He waved the blade at the baby. "Shut him up," he growled in a low voice.

Esther grabbed Jakob from Franz. She turned away, pulled at the top of her dress and fumbled with her slip. She jerked Jakob to her chest just as the guard extinguished the other lamp, throwing the room into darkness.

Jakob's howls died away. All Franz could hear was the sound of the baby nursing and the clipped breathing of the others in the room. He had a terrible thought that the Japanese might have secretly followed them to the Comfort Home: that would explain why they had not raided the Adlers' home or the hospital. *Did we just lead the Kempeitai to Simon's hiding place?* The fear weighed on his chest like piled bricks.

The ceiling shook from the stomping of boots overhead. Then a muffled voice barked orders from somewhere on the side of the wine cellar. Even through the walls, there was no mistaking the Japanese inflection.

The sound grew louder as the voice rose in pitch, exasperated. Franz expected to hear the false front scraping open at any moment. Bracing himself for another arrest, he thought with dread about his days at Bridge House. He considered storming into the passageway to confront the soldiers. *Could bullets be any worse than another visit to the torture chamber?*

The seconds crawled past.

Esther panted in fear, and Simon stroked her hair to try to calm her. The shouting on the other side of the wall only escalated.

A single gunshot cracked through the silence. Esther gasped. Franz stiffened.

Two or three more agonizing minutes passed. In the electrified quiet, Jakob's suckling seemed to rise to the intensity of a jackhammer in Franz's ears.

More stomping came from the other side of the false front. Barely breathing, Franz listened intensely. But hard as he tried, he could not tell whether the footsteps were moving toward or away from the hiding place.

II

Chapter 8

May 28, 1943, Hongkew, Shanghai

As he surveyed the oppressive little room, Franz suppressed a sigh. The walls were blistered and the smoke-stained ceiling peeled at the corners. Even at midday, little natural light penetrated the single window. The oily stench of the neighbours' cooking saturated the room all day long.

Still, it was home now.

To comply with the Japanese Proclamation concerning refugee Jews, the Adlers, including Esther and her baby, had been forced to trade homes—temporarily, they faintly hoped—with a Japanese family who lived in the heart of Hongkew. Like most of the refugee families, they fared poorly in the exchange: trading Sunny's charming colonial-style house in Frenchtown for this dingy apartment that lay within the borders of what the authorities referred to as the "Designated Area for Stateless Refugees," though most Jews who lived inside spoke of it—albeit in whispers or *sotto voce*—as "the ghetto."

Franz knew his family was luckier than most. Their flat had indoor plumbing. Most of the other alleyway apartments—the unique Shanghai phenomenon known as *longtangs*—possessed only commodes or waste buckets, which were emptied every morning by "night soil men," who carried away loads of human waste on bamboo poles across their shoulders.

Until now, Sunny had never lived anywhere but her family's home.

Franz had to admire her: rather than mope or complain, she focused her energy on converting the one-bedroom flat into home. She had scavenged an old bamboo table and chairs from somewhere and patched up an abandoned couch whose springs had torn through its upholstery. She decorated the walls with Franz's black-and-white photographs of some of Shanghai's most iconic buildings and transformed the last of her mother's old dresses into curtains. But she was fighting a losing battle. The flat was too small and too dismal to be much more than a functional shelter.

Esther and Jakob slept on a mattress laid every night in the main room, while Franz and Sunny slept in the bedroom and Hannah bedded down in the shallow loft. Esther did the cooking and helped where she could, but her baby and her worry over her husband drained much of her energy.

Esther had not seen Simon in three months—not since the evening they had huddled tensely in the Comfort Home's basement hideaway, fearing the worst while the walls shook with the stomps and shouts of Kempeitai men. Almost an hour had passed before Ushi freed them from the hiding place. No one knew whether the Japanese had followed them to the brothel or raided it coincidentally, but Chih-Nii was apoplectic—even Sunny didn't know the terms of the deal Jia-Li had struck with the madam so that Chih-Nii would not toss Simon out on the street. Esther and Franz had to swear on their lives to never return to the Comfort Home.

In the months since, Jia-Li had functioned as a go-between, delivering weekly letters between Simon and Esther. Despite Simon's upbeat tone—his letters were peppered with humorous anecdotes about living one floor below the busiest brothel in Shanghai—Esther remained convinced that the Kempeitai would soon track him down.

Franz felt for his Esther but, of late, his daughter was monopolizing his thoughts. No one had coped better with the family's arrival in Shanghai, four years earlier, than Hannah. She had embraced the experience of living in the exotic city and its many cultures as one great adventure. However, now her beloved Shanghai Jewish School had been forced to close, and in the past two months, her mood had plummeted. It had only worsened after their move, to the point where even Jakob's presence no longer cheered her up.

With those thoughts weighing on him, Franz climbed the rickety ladder to the cramped loft space. "It's time for breakfast, Hannah-*chen*. The others have already left."

Hannah lay on her mattress with a book propped up on her chest. "I'm not hungry, Papa," she said without even looking up. "Besides, I can't face another bowl of that watery rice pudding."

"Breakfast is not a luxury, Hannah. You must eat. Do you realize how fortunate we are not to have to go hungry?"

"Yes," she muttered into her book. "We Jews are the most fortunate people in the world."

Franz exhaled slowly as he fought the temptation to react to her sarcasm with some of his own. "Among German Jews, we probably are, yes," he said evenly instead.

Hannah only nodded.

"Of course, knowing it does not make our situation much easier, does it?" Franz allowed.

"Not really, no."

Franz climbed over the ladder's last rung and into the loft. He hunched forward, pressing his back against the slanted ceiling as he sidled along to the end of Hannah's mattress. He sat down and placed a hand on his daughter's arm. "Is it the move, *Liebchen?*"

She shrugged.

"You miss your old school, don't you? Your British and American friends? The ones in the internment camps."

"I do, yes," she said noncommittally.

"Is there something else?" Franz squeezed her arm. "Perhaps a boy?"

"My school, my teachers, my friends—I miss them all," she said irritably. "But most of all I miss the way things were before."

"Before the Japanese came?"

"That, too, I suppose."

"I don't understand."

"It's not important, Papa."

Franz frowned. "Hannah, do you mean before Sunny and I were married? Before we all moved in together?"

Hannah shrugged again. "It's not Sunny, really." Her eyes fell to her book. "When we were in our old home on Avenue Joffre . . . everything was simpler."

Franz had never before sensed the slightest tension between Hannah and Sunny. The evidence suggested they shared a closeness that transcended a typical stepdaughter–stepmother relationship.

Before Franz could probe further, Hannah rolled away to face the wall. "Papa, I'll come down and eat breakfast soon. Do you mind if I rest another few minutes? I did not sleep well last night."

Franz stared at her back for a moment before he nodded to himself. "All right. I have to leave for the hospital now. But, please, Hannah, you must eat. Do you understand?"

*　　*　　*

As Franz stepped onto the ward, he was greeted by the sight of Berta draping a sheet over the man in the nearest bed. "*Barukh atah Adonai Eloheinu melekh ha'olam, dayan ha-emet,*" the nursed murmured the Jewish prayer of mourning.

Franz surprised himself by echoing the refrain. He had arrived in Shanghai a committed atheist and, like his father before him, distrusted all religions. However, over the past four years, Judaism had crept back into his life. He was still not convinced that he believed in a higher power, but he had even begun to attend Saturday Shabbat services, something he never would have dreamed of doing in Vienna.

"So Herr Liffmann is finally gone," Franz said as much to himself as to Berta.

"Amazing the poor man hung on as long as he did," Berta said.

The typhus had ravaged the fifty-year-old cobbler's body, and he had been no more than skin and bones in recent days. "*Ja,* he was a fighter," Franz agreed with a pang of unexpectedly profound sorrow.

Before the Japanese Proclamation, the Liffmanns had lived relatively well in the International Settlement. As the May relocation deadline drew near, Liffmann lost his job and couldn't secure accommodation for his family inside the ghetto. Rather than move into one of the under-supplied hostels, the heime, alongside the crowds of impoverished refugees, Liffmann chose to ignore the deadline. Two days after the proclamation went into effect, the Kempeitai rounded up the Liffmanns and the others who had refused to move. The soldiers dumped the women and children at the Ward Road heim and dragged the men to Bridge House for interrogation. Those who survived the week of torture emerged from prison overwhelmed by typhus, acquired in the lice-infected prison cells. The staff at the refugee hospital tried everything, but without antibiotics or adequate intravenous fluids, it was futile. Liffmann had been the last one to survive. He never once showed a flicker of regret for his defiance. Even as he lay on his deathbed, he joked, "I fled the Nazis in Munich to Shanghai. Since I have no way of getting to the North or South Pole, I think my only other possible refuge will be a hole in the ground."

Franz felt a hand on his elbow and turned to see Sunny. Suddenly angry, he motioned around the ward with a frustrated wave. "What is the point of all this?"

"At least Herr Liffmann's suffering has ended."

"But what do we do here anymore?" he demanded. "Who do we help?"

"Have you forgotten that we saved Hannah's life in that very bed?" Sunny released his elbow and pointed to the stretcher where they had brought Franz's daughter back from a near fatal brush with cholera the previous year. She turned her finger toward herself. "And don't forget, you saved my life in our operating room." Sunny had required emergency surgery, four years earlier, after being stabbed in the street by a Japanese sailor. "And what of Esther and Jakob? Where would *they* be without this hospital?"

Franz waved away her arguments. "That was before, Sunny. When we still had surgical supplies. We ran out of anaesthetic weeks ago. Every day we watch people suffer and have nothing to offer aside from empty words." He shook his head. "I am as good as useless."

"You're still a doctor, Franz."

"No, Sunny, I'm a surgeon. That is the only kind of medicine I know."

"You run this hospital." Sunny folded her arms. "Besides, look at Wen-Cheng. He cannot perform surgery either, but he still works as hard as any other doctor here."

Dr. Wen-Cheng Huang and Sunny had worked together at Shanghai's Country Hospital since before the Adlers arrived in the city. Franz knew that Sunny and Wen-Cheng had once shared an attraction that could have evolved into much more, had the married surgeon been willing to leave his wife. Wen-Cheng's wife had since died in a traffic accident, and Franz was convinced that the only reason the Chinese surgeon volunteered at the Jewish hospital was to be near Sunny. He tried to quiet his suspicions, but they had resurfaced the previous week when he stumbled upon Sunny and Wen-Cheng huddled in a corner of the ward, locked in a hushed conversation in Chinese. There was nothing uncommon about a doctor conferring with a nurse, but their reaction to his presence struck him as unusual: Sunny turning red with embarrassment, and Wen-Cheng slinking away after a few hasty words of excuse.

Franz eyed Sunny for a long, cool moment. "Dr. Huang is a man of many talents."

Sunny held Franz's gaze. "You are just as capable, Franz. We all have to adapt. There is no choice."

Franz opened his mouth, but a sudden commotion stopped him before he could speak. Two men were approaching them, both wearing drab grey suits. One man was dragging the other along, propping him up with an arm around his companion's waist. The man on the verge of collapse was Chinese; the other, who had long, unruly hair and an uneven beard, looked European.

Franz gawked at the bearded man as though seeing an apparition.

"My God, Franz, are you a sight for sore eyes!" Ernst Muhler cried.

"Ernst! How is this possible?" Franz said in surprise.

He had not seen or heard from his friend in over a year—not since the painter and his lover, a Chinese man named Shan, had escaped Shanghai, with the Kempeitai in full pursuit. The authorities had discovered a series of oils Ernst had painted based on reports of the massacre in Nanking. One painting in particular still haunted Franz: a woman impaled on a Japanese standard, naked from the waist down, staring plaintively out from the canvas as the life seemingly drained from her. The paintings had so enraged and embarrassed the Japanese that execution would have been a mercy had Ernst been captured. He and Shan had fled west, to Free China, in search of the mountain villages where the Communist Resistance congregated, but Franz had no reason to believe that they had reached their destination or survived the journey.

A hundred questions ran through Franz's head, but the condition of Ernst's companion was his immediate concern. Franz slid a hand behind the man's back. Together with Ernst, he shuffled him to a nearby vacant stretcher. The man was too weak to climb onto the bed, so Franz and Ernst had to hoist him. As his fingers brushed over the man's sweaty brow, Franz instantly recognized a high fever.

"Thank you," the man gasped in English as his head flopped back on the mattress.

Sunny hurried over to join them at the bedside.

"Look at you, Soon Yi!" Ernst exclaimed. "What a delicious vision you are."

Sunny gave him a quick smile but kept focused on the ill man. "Where is the infection?" she demanded.

Ernst pointed to the man's right leg, and Franz saw that the material covering it was stained black from blood. Sunny gently rolled up the pant leg to reveal an angry, glistening wound. The man winced but said nothing as she continued to expose more of his leg.

Ernst flicked a finger in the direction of his companion's shoulder. "If that's not damage enough, my unfortunate friend here took a bullet to his arm, too."

"That is nothing," the man murmured, his eyes still closed.

Franz hunched forward to inspect the injured leg. Ignoring the putrid stench, he saw that the thigh just above the knee bulged from a large abscess. He almost missed the bullet's entry point because it had nearly swollen shut. As he prodded the skin lightly, his fingers met with resistance. "The bullet is still lodged in your thigh, correct?" Franz asked, and the man nodded. "We will have to remove it and drain the pus."

"Of course, doctor," he breathed.

Ernst sighed. "We didn't travel over a hundred miles and cross enemy lines simply for hospital food. Although, at this point, I wouldn't pass up a meal of any kind."

"We will feed you both soon, Ernst." Franz turned back to the other man. "What is your name?"

"Chun." The man finally opened his eyes. An arresting almond brown, they showed a glimmer of amusement. "Or Charlie, as Ernst insists on calling me."

"Ernst has not yet managed to rename me. I am Dr. Adler. Franz."

"While here, I actually prefer Charlie."

Franz didn't understand the distinction, nor did he dwell on it. "May I examine your shoulder, Charlie?"

Sunny helped Charlie remove his jacket and shirt. The exit wound near his shoulder was even larger than the entry wound through the deltoid muscle, but the large-calibre bullet had clearly missed any vital structures. The wound looked clean and uninfected.

"Your shoulder will not require surgery," Franz said. "But we must operate on your leg immediately. It cannot wait."

"I understand," Charlie said.

"Unfortunately, our hospital has all but run out of ether." Franz looked away. "We do not have enough anaesthetic, do you understand?"

Charlie mustered a brave smile. "It will not be pleasant, I realize, doctor. Nor will it be my first operation without anaesthetic."

Franz glanced at the swollen leg again, wondering if gangrene had already set in. "I cannot promise that we will be able to save the leg."

Charlie closed his eyes again. He nodded once. "What has to be done has to be done."

Two nurses arrived at the bedside. As they prepared Charlie for the operating room, Franz and Sunny led Ernst to the small staff room. Once inside, Sunny threw her arms around their friend and hugged him fiercely. Franz clapped the artist's shoulder, feeling only bone. Above the tawny beard, grey in patches, his cheeks had hollowed but, despite his scrawniness, Ernst somehow still looked robust. His once-pale complexion had become ruddier, and his eyes burned as brightly as ever.

"Not a word in over a year," Franz said. "I had assumed the worst, my friend."

"And who says you weren't right to?" Ernst said. "Have you ever spent a year of your life in a backwater Chinese village? Trust me. It doesn't get much worse."

"You are home now," Sunny pointed out.

"Home? I have no idea where that is." Ernst smiled. "But, by God, of all my deprivations from civilization, what I miss most is a little gossip." He looked pointedly at Franz and Sunny. "So tell me. What of you two?"

Sunny raised her left hand to show Ernst the wedding band that had once belonged to Esther's grandmother. Ernst clutched his chest theatrically. "I knew it! You see—love can still prevail, even in this *godforsaken* place."

"Speaking of love," Sunny said. "Where is Shan?"

"Still in the village," Ernst said. "He had a bad fall—sometimes we're forced to travel in the darkness. He broke his ankle."

"Is it serious?"

"He will recover." Ernst looked away. "I left without telling him. Shan would have insisted on trying to come with us, but his injury was too serious."

Sunny touched Ernst's cheek. "You were only protecting him."

"To be truthful, I was protecting myself. It was hard enough getting Charlie here on that game leg of his. I have come to appreciate that, behind enemy lines, two legs are a decided advantage." He breathed out with a sigh. "Sadly for me, my Shan is not always the forgiving kind."

Franz eyed the artist. "Who is Charlie?"

"A trusted friend," Ernst said flatly, suddenly serious.

"He looks familiar," Sunny said. "His English is so good, but he's not from Shanghai, is he? His accent . . ."

Ernst ran a hand through his dirty-blond hair. "Trust me. The less you both know about Charlie, the better."

"But you brought him here," Franz said. "To our hospital."

"I didn't want to. Believe me, I had no choice." Ernst shook his head helplessly. "I would make the world's absolute worst doctor, but even I could see that Charlie would die if we left him in that village. I could think of nowhere else to turn."

"You were right to bring him here," Sunny said.

Franz nodded. "We might be able to save his leg yet."

"It's always the same with us, isn't it?" A pained smile crossed Ernst's face. "You help me, and I repay the kindness by endangering you even further."

"And in spite of that, we still missed you."

"Of course you did," Ernst said with exaggerated panache. "Parasite or not, my appeal is irresistible."

"Will you stay?" Sunny asked.

"Only until Charlie is well enough to travel again."

"That will be a long while," Franz said. "Meantime, isn't it terribly dangerous for you to be in Shanghai?"

Ernst waved the suggestion away. "Sexual peccadilloes aside, I am a German gentile. A purebred Aryan. I could not be more welcome here. The Japanese adore us."

"They certainly do not adore you."

"They will never recognize me."

"And if they do?"

The levity drained from Ernst's face. "I will tell you this, my friends. We will have far bigger problems if they recognize Charlie."

Chapter 9

There were no soldiers, guard dogs or barbed wire, not even a fence. Aside from a simple checkpoint posted at the intersection with Muirhead Road, Wayside Road appeared no different than it had before the proclamation had established the Jewish ghetto. It would have been easy to step off the curb and amble across the road, but Hannah wasn't that reckless. The Japanese had set a brutal precedent the week before when it came to dealing with those who ventured out of the ghetto without passes, as three hapless young men who had simply been following their boss's order to go to Frenchtown to buy flour for his bakery had discovered.

Hannah had not seen the public flogging, but two neighbourhood boys had snuck out to the busy intersection to watch it. The next day, Hannah had joined a cluster of kids outside the Kadoorie School to hear the boys' account. Revelling in their moment of celebrity, they spoke over each other as they competed to share lurid details. Apparently, two of the three bakers had sobbed openly by the third lash. One of the men fainted with the seventh stroke but, as the boys exclaimed, "not before pissing himself!" Each prisoner received fifteen lashes in all before being dumped in a twitching heap in the middle of the road. The boys agreed on one point: the snap of the whip as it struck the men's backs sounded louder than gunfire.

Hannah assumed that the boys had been exaggerating, but her chest still drummed as she neared the checkpoint. An elderly balding refugee manned the post, his official status signalled by the yellow rag tied around the sleeve of his suit. Lean and stooped, he resembled a schoolteacher far more than a policeman. But Hannah found little reassurance in his paternal smile. She had heard that the refugee guards were often spied upon. They had no choice but to report irregularities to the Japanese soldiers they answered to.

Since she was under eighteen, Hannah did not require a pass to leave the ghetto. However, she had not told her father that she was planning to leave, let alone that she was smuggling contraband. The brooch jabbed into the skin below her waistband, as though deliberately reminding her of the risk that she was taking. She imagined that she must look as obvious as one of those Hollywood gangsters with a gun bulging beneath his jacket.

Fighting back her anxiety, Hannah approached the checkpoint. She had given her word to Freddy and was determined not to break it. She could still picture his lopsided grin as he playfully punched her shoulder. "I just knew you were a brave soul," Fritsch Herzberg, known by everyone at school as Freddy, had announced earlier that morning.

"Not so brave." Hannah caught herself chewing her lower lip. "They will not search me, will they?"

"No one will touch you." Freddy's deep voice cracked, as sometimes it still did. Freddy was German, but he preferred to speak English and, at times, his deportment struck Hannah as pure American, right down to his self-chosen moniker. "I wish I could carry it myself, but the guards are on the lookout for my family." Freddy shrugged helplessly. "Last week they caught Papa trying to sell one of my mother's necklaces. He spent three days in lock-up. None of us is allowed to set foot outside the ghetto now."

Hannah swallowed, feeling her mettle slip a notch. "They caught your father?"

"Only when he got to Frenchtown. They didn't search him at the checkpoint or anything. They never do, Hannah. You will be fine."

"How did they catch him?"

"He was trying to pawn the necklace off to a jeweller in the International Settlement." Freddy tapped his temple with a forefinger. "We think the owner ratted him out. Probably had a deal with the Japs to split the profits after confiscating it."

Hannah's expression must have betrayed her nervousness, because Freddy reached out and placed a reassuring hand on her shoulder. "Hannah, you only need to get the brooch to Papa's contact in Frenchtown. He will take care of it from there." He smiled broadly and winked. "You will do well. Guarantee you."

Hannah nodded, distracted by the pressure of his hand on her arm.

Freddy was the only the boy in her class who ever touched her. He did so often—clapping her arm, mussing her hair and even draping an arm affectionately over her shoulder—and without a trace of self-consciousness. At first, Hannah had shrunk from the contact, afraid he would detect the extent to which cerebral palsy had withered her left arm, the one she always hid beneath a long sleeve. But he seemed oblivious to the asymmetry of her limbs, and after a while she came to look forward to his touch.

Hannah had known Freddy for years and, like most of the girls at the Shanghai Jewish School, had long idolized him from afar. Although he was more than a year older and a class ahead of her, after the proclamation they had wound up being seated side by side in the classroom at the Kadoorie School, where they had been transferred. Despite her shyness, Freddy had been friendly toward her from the first day. They soon discovered a shared fascination for the local culture. Unlike Hannah, Freddy couldn't speak Shanghainese or Mandarin, but they amused one another by chatting in pidgin English, the city's unofficial language of commerce. Sometimes they would hold entire conversations with local merchants in pidgin, fighting back giggles. "My no savvy. This price b'long true?" Freddy would cry in mock outrage. And, if the laughter had not already given him away, he would always decline the peddler's persistent sales pitch with a curt, "No puttee book. No can do."

Hannah had convinced herself that Freddy saw beyond her handicap. She dreamed of sharing a kiss with him like the one she had once secretly witnessed between two older students behind the school. But that fantasy collapsed the day she spotted Freddy strolling along Ward Road hand in hand with Leah Wasselmann. Hannah maintained their friendship as though nothing had changed, but a gloom descended over her that even she recognized as being out of proportion to the pain of an unrequited crush. She had faced far worse in her short life—hunger, homelessness and cholera—and had always made it through with her spirits intact. But in the weeks since she spied Freddy and Leah together, her curiosity and enthusiasm for life seemed to seep away, and she felt helpless to stop it. Nor could she shake her fear that she would always be an outcast: a freak who would never find love.

She was grouchy all the time, too. Hannah felt guilty for her constant irritability, which more often than not ended up directed toward her father. When he confronted her about her mood, Hannah had allowed him to assume Sunny was to blame only because she could think of no other excuse. She was too embarrassed to set the record straight, and felt even more ashamed for it.

Hannah had never before hidden anything from her father but, as she approached the checkpoint with Freddy's brooch poking into her hip, she realized that lying to him was becoming habitual.

"*Guten Tag, Fräulein,*" the guard said, bowing his shiny head. In the long tradition of the Chinese neighbourhood watch, or *pao-chia*, the men guarding the checkpoint had been selected from local volunteers. Hannah had heard that positions in the *pao-chia* were coveted among the refugee men because they came with a small food ration and preferential access to exit passes.

Uncertain how to respond, Hannah returned the bow.

The man clasped his hands together. "Of course, a lady of your tender years needs no pass to leave the Designated Area. I am, however, obligated to ask the purpose of your excursion."

"I have a friend, Natasha—Natasha is Russian—she lives in

Frenchtown," Hannah sputtered. Her tongue felt thick and her words unnatural.

The guard's eyes narrowed. "And you think this is a wise trip to undertake?"

For a panicked moment, Hannah assumed that he suspected her real motive. She just gaped at him, unable to find her voice.

"To be going alone to the French Concession?" The guard glanced to either side before lowering his voice. "Shanghai is no longer the same. Soldiers and other . . . types . . . roaming the streets." He shook his head grimly. "For a girl of your age . . ."

Hannah steeled herself with a deep breath. "Thank you, sir, for your concern. I lived in that neighbourhood before the proclamation. I know it well. I will be fine."

The guard sighed and then nodded reluctantly. "You do understand that you must return to the ghet—" he coughed—"the Designated Area before eight o'clock. Believe me, Fräulein, you must not miss the curfew."

Before Hannah could reply, someone yelled in German behind them. "Stop! Stop this very instant!" It was a man's voice, high-pitched and bearing a Japanese accent.

Hannah glanced over her shoulder to see a Japanese man in a trench coat, flanked by two soldiers, trotting toward them. The man was at least a head shorter than either of his escorts, and he wore a brown fedora that looked as out of place on him as a cowboy hat.

Ignoring Hannah altogether, the little man strode up to the refugee guard, stopping only inches from him. "What is the meaning of this?"

The guard lowered his head deferentially. "I do not understand, sir."

"This." He jabbed his thumb behind him to indicate Hannah. "I did not see you check any papers from the girl."

"No, Mr. Ghoya. I was told that minors do not require papers."

"Bah! And how do you know she is a minor? Did you see her identification?"

"No, sir. It is clear—"

Without warning, the little man reached up and slapped the guard's cheek hard enough to swivel his head to the side. "It is never clear without proof! You always need to check! I told all of you this myself!"

The guard rubbed his reddened cheek. "I am so very sorry, sir," he said shakily. "In the future, I will always—"

"No future! No future!" The man unleashed a second, louder slap across the stunned refugee's face. "You are finished. I do not tolerate such incompetence. You will go beg for your food with the others. Yes, yes, go begging!" He snapped his fingers at the soldiers, who stepped forward in unison and clamped a hand on each of the guard's arms. The little man spun around to face Hannah, and she was hit by a heavy whiff of sweet citrusy aftershave. He snapped his fingers impatiently again. "Identification!"

Hannah dug a trembling hand into the front pocket of her skirt, terrified that she might dislodge the brooch and drop it on the curb. As soon as her refugee card emerged from her pocket, the man snatched it out of her hands.

He studied it. "Adler? Like the doctor?"

"Yes," Hannah whispered. "My father."

"Hmm," the man grunted. "What business has a thirteen-year-old girl leaving the Designated Area all alone?"

"To . . . to visit a friend," she stammered.

"To visit a friend?" he echoed in a low suspicious voice.

"Yes, sir."

"Visit a friend?" He screamed it this time.

Hannah instinctively leaned back, expecting to be slapped.

"There is a war, girlie! A war!" He raised his hand and let it hover near her cheek. "We did not create the Designated Area for you to wander off to a friend's home for tea and playtime."

"I . . . I . . ."

"Do you have any idea who I am, girlie?"

She looked down her feet. "No, sir."

"I am Ghoya, assistant director of the Bureau of Stateless Refugee Affairs. But everyone in Shanghai knows me by a different name."

Silence descended between them. Finally, Hannah felt compelled to ask. "Which name, sir?"

He dropped his arm to his side. His eyes lit up, and his face broke into a Cheshire cat–like grin. "Here in Shanghai, I am King of the Jews!"

Chapter 10

Charlie's eyelids flickered a few times before opening. The rice wine combined with three drops of anaesthetic that Sunny scavenged from the bottom of a discarded bottle of ether had turned out to be more than enough to sedate the gaunt young man, who had been unconscious for almost four hours since his surgery. Sunny suspected that the raging infection contributed to his post-operative stupor.

Charlie's face remained remarkably placid as his eyes focused and then shifted from Ernst to Sunny. Sunny knew that he must have been suffering intense pain from his wound, but he didn't show it. Instead, he summoned a rubbery smile. "My leg," he croaked in English. "I can still feel it."

"Largely because it is still attached to the rest of you," Ernst said through a cloud of cigarette smoke.

Sunny shot her friend a sharp look before turning back to Charlie. "We removed the bullet and drained a lot of pus from the site of the infection. We had to excise—to cut out—a fair bit of flesh around your thigh."

"You did not have to amputate," Charlie said in an almost detached tone.

"No." Sunny hesitated. "But we do not yet know how the wound will heal or, Charlie, *if* it will."

"I understand." Charlie shifted slightly.

Sunny lifted the glass syringe she had been clutching in her palm and held it up to the light. She tapped it with her fingernail, knocking the air bubbles to the top and expelling them. "A dose of painkiller," she explained as she pinched the skin over his shoulder and injected the morphine.

Charlie was stoic. "Today I still have two legs, which is more than I expected."

Ernst sucked heavily on his cigarette. "And really quite advantageous from the point of view of balance."

"Ernst, please," Sunny said.

Charlie waved off her concern with a chuckle. "Without Ernst, we would have little opportunity for laughter in our village."

"Marxists." Ernst rolled his eyes. "Never will you meet a more sanctimonious or humourless bunch. They will stamp out every last trace of irony and sarcasm long before they get around to addressing the class system."

Charlie viewed his friend straight-faced. "That's entirely possible."

Sunny wondered again where Charlie had learned his flawless English. She could tell from the few words he had uttered in Mandarin, together with his features and darker complexion, that he was not Shanghainese. She suspected that he came from somewhere much further north. Although his heritage remained a mystery, she could not shake the sense of familiarity she felt looking at him.

The curtains parted and Franz approached the bed wearing a lab coat that had begun to fray at the sleeve from repeated washings. "Ah, Charlie, good afternoon. No doubt Sunny already informed you. The operation went as well as it could, all things considered."

"Thank you. Both of you." Charlie struggled to raise his head and shoulders but, exhausted by the effort, flopped back down to the bed. He looked over to Ernst. "An hour or two, and I should be ready."

"Ready for what, Charlie?" Sunny asked.

"To go home."

Franz squinted at him. "Home? That is out of the question. You will not be leaving the hospital for weeks."

"I am afraid I must," Charlie said.

Franz folded his arms across his chest. "If you leave now, you will surely lose your leg. Provided you survive long enough for even that to happen."

"Dr. Adler, I have the highest regard for your medical opinion, but I can assure you that my life will be in even more danger if I remain here."

Ernst sighed. "Sadly, Franz, he might be correct."

"Besides . . ." Charlie yawned as the morphine took effect. "The sooner we leave, the better for your hospital."

"Our staff is capable of extreme discretion," Sunny said. "No one else need ever know that you are here."

"Trust me . . ." Charlie yawned again. "They will find out."

"Find out what?" Sunny grimaced. "None of us even know who you are."

Charlie's eyes drifted shut. "They will," he murmured.

They watched him doze for a few moments before Franz motioned toward the door. "Maybe a good sleep will bring him to his senses."

Ernst and Sunny followed Franz through the ward and into the deserted staff room. An empty cup, dried tea leaves stuck to the bottom, stood on the table as testament to the last time a nurse or doctor had had an opportunity for a rest. As soon as Franz had closed the door behind them, he wheeled around to face Ernst. "Who is he?"

Ernst shrugged. "I told you—"

Franz stabbed a finger at him. "Nonsense. We need to know who we are dealing with here."

Sunny touched his elbow. "Please, Ernst."

Ernst looked at each of them in turn before pulling out another of his hand-rolled cigarettes and igniting it with the lighter that never seemed to leave his hand. "His name is Bao Chun. More precisely: General Bao Chun."

"The Boy General, of course!" Sunny almost slapped her forehead.

"That's why he looks so familiar." She could picture old newspaper articles and their grainy photographs of the young officer.

"He can't even be thirty years old," Franz pointed out. "How is it possible that he's already a general in the Chinese army?"

"There is no Chinese army per se," Ernst said. "There are the Kuomintang and the Communists. And despite the so-called Unified Front, the two sides expend far more energy, bullets and lives fighting each other than they do the Japanese."

"So Charlie and you are both Communists, then?" Franz asked.

"Me a Communist? Bite your tongue, Franz! I'm just a queer painter. A lapsed bohemian. Nothing more." His cheeks flushed. "Most nights I fall asleep on a dirt floor praying that I will wake up on my lumpy old bed in my studio in Vienna. Before the Japanese, the Nazis and the Communists conspired to banish me to a village—not even—a camp, really—a thousand miles from the nearest whiff of civilization—" He stopped mid-tirade. The storm left his eyes and a more familiar devil-may-care expression settled on his face. "As for Charlie, he fights for the Communist army. Whether he is truly a Marxist at heart, I cannot say. But he is the exception to the infighting rule among the Chinese. He never wastes a bullet on the Kuomintang. He focuses all of his effort on the Japanese."

"Charlie is from the north, isn't he?" Sunny asked.

"Manchuria. He was just a boy when the Japanese first invaded in '31. But according to his men—at least the ones who speak anything other than that rural mumbo-jumbo—he was born for the fight. Fearless. A natural leader and a brilliant tactician." He took another long drag on his cigarette. "The men worship him. Most Chinese divisions—entire armies, even—survive months at best on the front. Staggering losses. Not Charlie. He has kept his battalion together for five years. Even the Japanese fear him."

"Fear him?" Sunny said in disbelief. "The Japanese?"

Ernst pointed his cigarette at the windowless wall. "It's so different out there. Once you get beyond the city, the countryside goes on forever.

The Japanese cannot control Charlie or the other partisans. At most, they can contain them. Even in the regions that the Japanese have conquered, they only truly control the points and lines."

Franz grimaced. "What are those?"

"Just markings on a map—the cities and the railroads. The Japanese cannot police the whole countryside. It's far too vast. All they will ever capture are their precious points and lines." He snorted. "And for those, they have killed millions. *Millions!*"

"Where is Charlie's army based?" Sunny asked.

"We often hunker down in the little village where Shan is now. But Charlie's army has no real base per se. It's the reason for their success. Most of the time, they live behind enemy lines," Ernst explained. "They ambush Japanese patrols and sabotage the railway, disrupting transport and lines of communication, before retreating back into the forests and mountains. It's a game of cat and mouse—lethal sometimes—but Charlie plays it very well. He is a legend among the partisans."

Franz turned to Sunny, his face suddenly pale with concern. "If the Japanese learned Charlie is here . . ."

"What's that silly term Simon used to use?" Ernst snapped his fingers. "Public enemy number one."

"And we are sheltering him in our hospital," Franz said quietly. "Our *Jewish* hospital. Can you imagine what the Nazis would do if they were to ever find out?"

"The Nazis?" Ernst groaned. "When it comes to Charlie, those louts should be the least of your concern."

"On the contrary, Ernst," Franz said. "Last year, after you were already gone, the SS tried to persuade the Japanese to annihilate us Jews. The Nazis argued that we were a security risk. They almost had the Japanese convinced. Certainly the local Kempeitai. If we are caught harbouring a hero of the Chinese army in our hospital, imagine how that would bolster the Nazis' argument." He turned back to Sunny. "At the very least, the hospital would be finished."

Sunny's heart ached for Franz. The weight of the responsibility of running the hospital since Simon's departure had worn her husband down as much as the war itself. Grey hair and crow's feet had appeared almost overnight. He was a changed man, and Sunny longed to see more of the old Franz, the one whose passion extended beyond the walls of the hospital.

"This is precisely why refugees cannot participate in any form of resistance," Franz continued. "We cannot afford to give the Japanese a reason or excuse to follow through on the Nazis' plans for us."

"So you agree then, Franz," Ernst said. "Charlie must leave the hospital. Premature discharge or not."

Sunny saw the conflict in her husband's troubled eyes. She wanted to reassure him somehow, but she shared his torn feelings: it would be best for everyone—except the patient himself—if Charlie left.

Franz ran a hand through his hair. "Charlie will never reach home alive. Not in his current condition." He squared his shoulders. "No. He has to stay. And, Ernst, you must find a way to persuade him."

*   *   *

Sunny left the hospital an hour later, telling Franz that she was off to the market to gather food and supplies. But this was only part of the truth.

Joey insisted on accompanying her, intending to track down one of his black market contacts who had "a line" (another phrase he had picked up from Simon) on a fresh supply of ether. Invariably, that meant his contact had stolen the anaesthetic from another woefully undersupplied civilian hospital. The refugee hospital had been victimized by similar thefts, and it sickened Sunny to think that she might be indirectly complicit in such activity. But she couldn't stomach the thought of performing another emergency surgery while a patient stared up at her in ashen-faced agony, or the idea of her husband marginalized to the point of uselessness by a lack of basic medication. So she swallowed her misgivings and reluctantly endorsed Joey's illicit trading.

Outside, the afternoon sun seemed confused about the date. Although it was still only spring, the sunshine beat down upon them as though trying to melt the pavement the way it would at the height of summer. Sweat beaded on Joey's brow, and Sunny could feel her cotton dress becoming damp under her arms and around her neck. The heat intensified the stench of the rotting garbage that had been dumped on the sidewalks and the buckets that passed for toilets in the decrepit lane houses.

Once they reached Chusan Road, the smells of espresso and baking came as a welcome relief. As they headed along the ghetto's main street, they passed cafés, a newspaper office and a dance hall. The theatre in the middle of the block still performed revues three nights a week in both German and Yiddish.

Sunny felt a surge of pride at the refugees' remarkable resilience. They faced constant, often deadly, threats: overcrowding, disease, starvation and hostility from two world powers. Yet, somehow, the refugees not only persevered but also managed to foster culture, the arts and a sense of community. Sunny, who had never met a German Jew until her first day volunteering at the refugee hospital, found it all quite beautiful. She had grown up largely in the Chinese world, where family meant everything but community mattered little. And while she had never before experienced anything close to the bickering and complaining that seemed normal among the refugees, neither had she ever witnessed such generosity and compassion between strangers connected only by their religion and language. When Sunny married into this eccentric society, they had accepted her as one of their own, as though she had been born to a kosher butcher in Munich or a cantor in Leipzig. As a Eurasian, Sunny had grown up feeling like a perpetual outsider, never fully accepted by either Shanghailanders or Shanghainese. The sense of belonging she had found among the refugees was unexpected and precious, and it heightened the protectiveness she felt toward them.

Sunny and Joey approached the guard posted at the ghetto's exit, a beanstalk of a man with a yellow rag tied around his rolled-up sleeve. As Chinese citizens, they were exempt from the restrictions imposed on the refugees. The guard gave them only a cursory glance as they bypassed the queue of Jews waiting to leave the Designated Area.

As they walked away from the ghetto, Joey remarked, "The hospital doesn't see many Chinese patients."

"We do from time to time," Sunny said.

"Not really."

"You know what the Shanghainese are like, Joey. Most would never go to a hospital in the first place, and those who do choose the Shanghai General or the Country Hospital. Most of the locals are not even aware that we run a hospital."

Joey stopped. "Charlie is not a local."

Sunny slowed, then came to a halt. "No, I suppose not."

"He's from Manchuria."

Sunny turned to face him. "How do you know that?"

"I recognize him from the newspapers and magazines. He is a hero."

Sunny lunged toward Joey, then looked around anxiously, confirming that no one was within earshot. "You cannot tell anyone who he is," she hissed in a low voice, laying a cautionary hand on his shoulder. "Do you understand?"

Joey shrank from her touch. "I would never say anything except to you!" He squinted in indignation. "I haven't even told Charlie that I recognize him."

"Of course. I'm sorry, Joey." But her chest pounded all the same. "We must prevent word from getting out. His life . . . the hospital . . . everything depends upon us protecting his identity."

"None of the Jewish people will recognize him. And there are only a few Chinese who work at the hospital."

"What about the cleaning men? Or the coolies who do the carrying and lifting?"

Joey nodded, deep in thought. "We could cover Charlie's face with a mask like we do during the flu outbreaks."

"That would only attract more attention," Sunny said. "But we should draw the curtains around his bed at all times, and keep the locals away from the ward."

Joey nodded briskly. "I will see to it as soon as I return."

Despite Joey's cooperation, Sunny was shaken by his revelation. If he had recognized Charlie so easily, then others were bound to as well. She was so preoccupied that she almost forgot the primary reason she had left the ghetto with him. "Joey, why don't I meet you at the market in an hour?" she said, remembering.

His face creased with suspicion. "Are you going somewhere else now?"

"To Frenchtown. I have to sell something."

"What?"

Sunny withdrew the brass watch from her pocket and held it up by its gold chain. "It was my father's."

A few months earlier, the idea of pawning Kingsley's treasured pocket watch would have been unthinkable. Her father had been murdered by a Japanese sailor while trying to defend her from an attack on the street, and Sunny had resisted parting with any of his possessions. Until Franz and Hannah moved in with her, she had not touched his bedroom. Yang, the family's long-time housekeeper, treated the room with equal reverence, entering only to clean and dust. They still kept everything in her father's office as it had always been—from expired vials of insulin to stacks of old journals and the Audubon Society magazines he had prized. But the Adlers were broke. They had already poured their scant savings into maintaining the hospital and received no wages from it. Franz was unaware of the extent of their poverty: Sunny had been hocking her father's possessions for the past two months without telling him. From time to time, she had even accepted money from Jia-Li, who constantly offered it. Sunny hoped the watch would bring a good price; she was ashamed to rely on her friend's charity.

"I'll come with you," Joey declared.

"Thank you, but I can do this alone."

"Whatever they offer, I will get you a better deal. Trust me."

"I do, Joey." If she wasn't so agitated, Sunny might have hugged the wiry boy. She had no doubt he would be able to get her more for the time-piece, but even more than the money, she needed privacy. "This is very special to me. I don't remember a day when I didn't see my father wearing it. To have to sell it now . . ."

Joey's face flushed, and he dropped his gaze to the ground. "I have people to meet, too. I'll see you in the market in an hour."

Sunny watched Joey walk away. She took a moment to gather her composure before heading off for the International Settlement. She crossed the Garden Bridge and walked into the Public Garden, the colonial-style park that jutted out into the Whangpoo River. Bamboo, weeds and dirt had replaced the manicured lawns and vibrant flowerbeds that had once made the Public Garden one of Shanghai's jewels. Sunny was heartsick to see that the red-roofed gazebo where her father used to bring her in the summertime to watch brass bands play had been vandalized, too.

Pushing aside thoughts of the neglected grounds, Sunny spotted Wen-Cheng Huang seated on a bench across from the twisted hull of the gazebo. Clearly, he saw her too, but, as they had agreed, he pretended not to recognize her. Instead, he raised an open newspaper until it hid his face.

Sunny glanced from side to side and, satisfied that no one was watching, hurried over to him.

Chapter 11

Franz tasted coal dust as he almost choked on the dark smoke that billowed from the stove. But he didn't dare stop fanning the charcoal briquettes inside, trying to coax them to life with as much oxygen as possible. Their traditional Shanghainese oven, which always reminded Franz of an overturned flowerpot, was loaded with briquettes recycled by the locals and compacted with river mud. They took forever to ignite and would extinguish on a whim.

"Will Sunny be home for supper?" Esther asked from the couch behind him, where she sat rocking Jakob to sleep in her arms.

"I hope so," Franz said. "As we were leaving the hospital, an elderly woman arrived with a rapid heartbeat. Sunny gave her our last tablets of digitalis."

"Did her condition improve?"

"It helped, but you know Sunny. She won't leave until the woman's heart has settled down to the rate of a sleeping athlete's."

Esther nodded approvingly. "She's a wonderful nurse."

"And a good surgeon, too, Essie," he said with a tinge of pride. "Her judgment is as good as her dexterity, and far beyond her experience."

Franz noticed that the glowing embers had begun to dim. He waved the fan even more vigorously, like a toreador provoking a bull with his cape.

"I remember the ovens in Vienna being more responsive," Esther said.

"I have seen corpses more responsive than this cursed contraption."

Esther chuckled. "And even when it does burn well, we still have to buy our hot water from the water man."

It was true. The traditional stoves didn't produce enough heat to boil water. Before meals—which for many refugees now came once a day at most—people could be seen lining up all over Hongkew at the water stores and carts to buy a ladle or two of boiling water. They would rush their steaming pots home, being careful not to spill them, and hoping the water would still be hot when they arrived.

"What shall I prepare for supper?" Esther asked in jest.

"Perhaps a spicy sauerbraten with spaetzle and red cabbage, followed by your strudel, Essie. With whipped cream."

Esther smiled. "Or we could stick to rice with bland greens."

They had not eaten meat in months. Rice was now the mainstay of their diet. Depending on their cash reserves, on a given day, they would garnish it with soybeans, bamboo shoots or flavourless greens for which no one seemed to know the German name.

Still, Franz was pleased to see Esther in good spirits. She rarely complained, but her faraway eyes often betrayed the loneliness and worry she felt in Simon's absence.

Esther carefully positioned Jakob on a pillow in the bamboo basket at her feet. The infant was the only one eating well in their home. Esther's breast milk had become plentiful and reliable since Sunny had insisted on increasing his mother's daily rice ration, and Jakob had doubled in size by the end of his third month of life. He was always a contented baby, and in the last few days he had begun to smile. His angelic grin had even recaptured Hannah's attention.

Once the baby was asleep, Esther reached for Simon's latest letter. As usual, his words brought a smile to her face. This time it evolved into a chuckle that soon turned into tears of laughter. "Listen, listen Franz," she choked out. "Simon writes: 'After months down here, I can recognize the ladies of the house by the sound of their footsteps above us. Jia-Li glides over the floor. You have to concentrate to hear her: she is like a cat padding lightly overhead. Nelly—that's not her real name—but whoa, Nelly! She stomps above me like a deranged hippopotamus. That's exactly how I picture her: a hippopotamus wearing lipstick and black stockings and leaning seductively against the mantle, smoking from a long-stemmed holder.'" Esther dissolved into giggles. "'As I write this, I hear Bambi overhead. She skitters and trips in her high heels like a fawn flailing across a frozen pond.'"

Franz marvelled at Simon's sensitivity. Imprisoned beneath a brothel, not knowing if he would ever see his wife or son again, he found only amusing anecdotes to share with his wife. Lately, his perpetually upbeat tone had begun to have an effect. For the first time since their forced separation, the practical and level-headed Esther of old re-emerged.

With the briquettes finally ignited fully, Franz felt safe turning his back on the stove. He stood up and stretched. "Essie, have I mentioned that Wen-Cheng Huang is volunteering at the hospital?" he asked, trying to sound as casual as possible.

Lowering the letter, Esther tilted her head up. "Did anyone ask for his help?"

"No. He just showed up a few months ago, offering his services."

"That was very decent of him."

"Very. Yes." Franz cleared his throat. "It is somewhat of a coincidence."

"That he should volunteer at the same hospital as Sunny?"

Franz nodded. "Of course, there are only four hospitals still open in the city. And most of them, like us, barely get by. Before the Japanese, there were ten hospitals and—"

"Obviously, he has come because of Sunny."

Franz straightened up involuntarily. "Do you think so?"

"A Chinese doctor coming to volunteer in a *Jewish* refugee hospital? His sole connection being the woman who used to be . . ." She paused to search for diplomatic words. "The object of his affection. What other reason could there be?"

"None, of course."

"But surely Dr. Huang is not so stupid," she said. "Sunny and he shared a working friendship for years. There is no reason to assume his intentions are anything but honourable."

"No, I suppose not."

"Besides, Franz, what matters is how Sunny feels, not Dr. Huang." Her face creased with an understanding smile. "And you have nothing to worry about on that account."

"It's almost too trivial to mention but . . ." Franz felt his face beginning to burn. He loved Esther dearly but, even with Sunny, he sometimes struggled to voice certain emotions.

"What is it Franz?"

"Last week, on the ward, I came upon the two of them talking—of course, that is nothing out of the ordinary. It's just that . . ."

"Tell me."

Growing more embarrassed by the second, he looked away. "They were speaking in Chinese. I have no idea what it was about, but they were standing close and talking in hushed tones. There was something . . . secretive about it."

"Sunny? Never." Esther shook her head adamantly. "It's not even worth considering."

*　　　*　　　*

Franz was relieved to step outside into the blazing sunshine. He had been mortified to confess his marital insecurities to Esther, and he left feeling only vaguely reassured.

As he trudged to the hospital, he was reminded everywhere of the war. Buildings bore battle wounds like veterans returning from the front: bullet holes and mortar damage disfigured their facades, and most of the windows were boarded up. Many shops were closed or simply abandoned. Soldiers and military police roamed the streets with unconcealed menace. Skeletal rickshaw pullers stood by their empty carriages, no paying fares in sight.

When Franz had first arrived in Shanghai, he had been struck by the city's obsessive attention to fashion, particularly among the impeccably dressed Chinese women who roamed the city's shopping districts, often in giggling packs. Their glittering cheongsams epitomized the fusion of East and West, with hem lengths, collar styles and the closeness of their fit varying from season to season and influenced as much by the styles of Hollywood as those of Asia. But the gorgeous patterns and eye-popping colours were long gone. Now, Jews and Chinese alike scurried about in drab clothes too loose for their shrunken bodies.

In happier moments, Franz took pride in the triumph of the refugees' will over circumstance: the sense of culture and community that somehow blossomed under a constant shadow of persecution and deprivation. But in his current dark mood, it seemed to him that survival had become the only object of their existence.

Franz reached the hospital and hurried up the pathway, eager to find shelter from the sun and his miserable ruminations. The instant he entered, he spotted two Japanese soldiers at the end of the corridor, their peaked hats and epaulets marking them as officers.

Franz froze. *Have they come for Charlie? Please, no, not so soon.*

One of the young officers wheeled around to face him. "You are Dr. Adler?" he demanded in English.

"Yes."

Both men rushed toward him. Neither laid a hand on him, but their sombre faces and urgent manner sent a chill down his spine. He looked from one soldier to the other. "May I ask the meaning of this?"

The first officer indicated the doorway with a rigidly outstretched arm. "Mr. Ghoya requests you."

Ghoya? The man who gives out exit passes? Franz felt his stomach unknot. *They have not come for Charlie after all.*

Still, his apprehension rose as he headed for the door. Stories abounded among the refugees about the strange little official. He had already earned the Yiddish nickname of "Meshugana Ghoya," or Crazy Ghoya, and was said to be as unpredictable as he was flamboyant, parading around his office like a pint-sized tyrant. He would routinely deny refugees passes based on arbitrary criteria such as appearance, particularly with the taller men, whose height he presumably resented. It was said that he had forced Moshe Kaplan, a concert musician who had played with the Berlin Philharmonic, to play a violin duet with him. When Ghoya could not keep time, he accused the musician of sabotaging the piece and attacked Kaplan, slapping him and snapping the fingerboard off his Stradivarius.

Franz followed the officers outside, expecting to see a military vehicle parked at the curb, but the street was clear. "We walk," one of them announced.

Franz was sweating by the time they reached a nondescript building at the corner of Muirhead and Ward Roads. Above the front door, a hand-painted placard announced the Bureau of Stateless Refugee Affairs.

Although it was already mid-afternoon, fifty or more people were queued outside the office, waiting to apply for exit passes. The soldiers marched him past the withered-looking men and women. Franz realized with a pang of sympathy that they had probably been standing in line in the hot sun since early morning.

Inside, the stuffiness was oppressive. Franz and the officers had to walk single file along a narrow hallway to reach the office at the far end. Through the open door, Franz saw a diminutive man sitting behind a desk. Noticing the new arrivals, the man hopped to his feet and waved frantically, as if trying to flag down a speeding car. "Come in. Yes. Come, come!"

The man kept beckoning Franz forward, until he stood inches from the desk. The two officers snapped salutes and left the room, leaving the door open behind them. The man stared at Franz with a grin. Not much taller than Hannah, he wore an out-of-fashion navy suit with thick pinstripes. His face was pockmarked and either his head was too large for his frame, Franz thought, or his neck and shoulders too small. Mr. Ghoya appeared exactly as Max Feinstein had described him: "A man who looks as though he has stepped into the wrong country in the wrong decade while wearing the wrong suit." But Franz was not amused then or now. He had heard too many stories of refugees who had underestimated Ghoya, based on first impressions, and had come to deeply regret it.

"Dr. Franz Adler from Vienna," Ghoya trumpeted. "You are a surgeon. You run the Jewish hospital."

Franz waited for a question, but none came. Ghoya interlaced his fingers behind his back and began to pace back and forth behind his desk. After a few seconds, he stopped and said, "Your daughter, did she have fun playing with the Russian girl in Frenchtown?" Then he muttered to himself, "I don't know why I let her go. Too soft. Always, too soft."

Bewildered, Franz wondered if maybe the nickname of "Crazy Ghoya" was less exaggerated than he had assumed. "Excuse me, sir?"

"Your daughter," Ghoya snapped. "Did she have a good romp in Frenchtown after she left the Designated Area?"

"Hannah has never left the Designated Area," Franz said.

"Yes, yes! Of course she has!" Ghoya cried. "I let her go myself, just yesterday. I remember everything, and you would be wise not to forget that." His lips twisted into a smug grin. "So she left without informing her own father?"

Franz wondered what could have possessed his daughter to leave the ghetto, but all he said was, "Hannah is very grown-up for her age, sir. I do not always check on her whereabouts."

"Yes, yes." Ghoya sighed, seeming to have lost interest in the subject. "You know who I am, correct?"

"I believe you are Mr. Ghoya, sir."

Ghoya darted around the desk and stopped only inches from Franz, the smell of his aftershave overpowering. Hands still clasped behind his back, Ghoya tilted his chin up to glare at Franz. "I am not 'Ghoya' to you. You will know me as the other stateless refugees do, as the Christians know their saviour. To you, I will be 'King of the Jews'!"

For a moment, Franz wondered if Ghoya might be joking, but his expression said otherwise. "Yes, sir. The King of the Jews."

"So I am the king of your hospital, too. Do you understand?"

"Yes," Franz said warily. "I understand, sir."

Ghoya nodded. His tone suddenly turned conversational. "Tell me more of this hospital of yours."

"What would you like to know, sir?"

"What does it do?" Ghoya threw a hand up, nearly striking Franz. "Can you make operations? Do you deliver babies?"

"Yes and no, sir. We can only run our operating room when we have the supplies to do so."

Ghoya brought a finger and thumb to his chin. "And where do these supplies come from?"

Franz shifted on his feet. He was leery of what Ghoya might do with the answer, but he also understood that withholding it could be a grave mistake. Ghoya might already know the truth. "Various individuals donate supplies or money. The Russian Jews in Frenchtown have been particularly helpful. As has the Imperial Japanese Army, which has been the most generous of all."

"Tell me, doctor, what about the local Chinese? Do they have a hospital of their own?"

"I do not believe so, sir."

"Aaahhh." Ghoya drew out the word. "And the citizens of the Imperial Japanese Empire who live in Hongkew, do they have their own hospital?"

Franz hesitated. "The Shanghai General, sir, is managed by the Japanese navy—"

"*The Shanghai General!*" Ghoya screamed. "Does that sound Japanese to you?"

"No, sir."

Without warning, Ghoya vaulted on top of his desk. He perched at the edge of the tabletop while gesturing wildly down at Franz. "So why do you Jews get your very own hospital? Tell me. *Tell me!*"

"I . . . I . . . am not certain that we—"

"What is so special about you Jews?" Ghoya cried.

"Excuse me, Mr. Ghoya, may I have a word?" A familiar voice came from over Franz's shoulder.

Chapter 12

Sunny and Wen-Cheng sat at opposite ends of the bench, leaving enough space for two people between them. They did not exchange a glance, let alone a word, for five long minutes.

An old Chinese man in a tattered grey Zhongshan suit stood a few yards away, staring at the wrecked gazebo. Slightly round-backed, he kept his arms glued to his sides and his head hung low. Sunny sensed great sadness in him. For some reason, she imagined him to be one of Shanghai's many bird fanciers who used to bring their caged pets to parks and other public places for "airings." Sunny had heard that, since the invasion, many of those enthusiasts had been forced to eat their beloved pets.

Finally, with a slight nod to Sunny and Wen-Cheng, the old man turned and shuffled off toward the street. As soon as he was out of sight, Wen-Cheng looked up from his newspaper and glanced around. Satisfied that they were alone, he smiled, and his distinctive pale eyes lit up. Not so long ago, before Franz entered her life, that expression had melted Sunny's heart. It had almost led her into an affair with Wen-Cheng, who had been married at the time.

Neither the war nor the death of his wife in a car accident had diminished Wen-Cheng's attractiveness. Unlike those of most in Shanghai, his face was as full and smooth as ever, and his teeth still ivory white. He was handsome enough to be a double for one Shanghai's local film stars. He had lost most of his wealth when the Japanese appropriated his family's ceramics factory and converted it to an armaments plant, but Sunny knew that Wen-Cheng had invested much of what he had left in buying supplies for the refugee hospital. She was flattered, and a little frightened, to think that he might be doing it primarily for her sake.

Wen-Cheng arched his back and stretched. He exuded a kind of tranquility that belied the troubled times. "Thank you for coming, Soon Yi," he said in Shanghainese.

She broke off eye contact, letting her gaze fall on the gazebo's decrepit, but still brightly coloured, roof. "I am still not certain, Wen-Cheng."

"You do not have to decide this very moment."

Another wave of guilt washed over her.

"It's so beautiful today." He motioned to the bright blue sky, ignoring the blistering heat. "Shall we walk?"

They rose and headed deeper into the park, toward the river. Weeds had made the once glass-smooth pathway uneven. At one point, Sunny stumbled over a bamboo root. Wen-Cheng caught her by the upper arm, holding her for an extra moment after she had steadied herself. Stomach flip-flopping, she nodded her thanks while still avoiding his eyes.

They came to a halt as the path curved along the western bank of the Whangpoo River. The yellow-brown water churned, and the day's heat intensified the smell of the sewage that continuously drained into the river. Suddenly, a long skinny rat, its tail no more than a stump, appeared from under the rocks at their feet. It scurried along the path for a few feet before diving under another set of stones. Sunny had never been superstitious, but she still found a sliver of comfort in the traditional Chinese belief that suggested the appearance of a rat, even one so mangled and scrawny, was a good omen.

"Did you see his tail? Even our vermin suffer under the *Rìběn guǐzi*." Wen-Cheng gestured out toward the harbour, which teemed with ships flying the Rising Sun. Most were freighters or troop transports. One battleship, the *Idzumo,* dwarfed the other vessels. Its massive gun turrets pointed inland as though warning Sunny to reconsider what she was doing.

Sunny turned to Wen-Cheng. "Will someone else meet us?"

He shook his head.

"Then why have we come?"

His lips parted in another easygoing smile. "I enjoy your company, no matter what the circumstances."

"Wen-Cheng, you promised me a meeting."

He only shrugged. "They are exceedingly cautious, Soon Yi. Out of necessity. I am sure they are watching."

"When will I meet them?"

"Later. Perhaps never." He lowered his voice. "I have only met with them a handful of times. We usually communicate through signals or notes that are left in secret locations. We rarely meet in person, and we never use the telephone or even the radio."

"You have a radio?" She had heard that anyone caught possessing a transmitter would face interrogation, torture, even a firing squad.

"I have access to one, yes." Wen-Cheng dug a hand into his pocket and extended a pack of cigarettes to her. Sunny waved him away, so he lit one for himself and looked out at the Japanese armada.

The butterflies in her stomach fluttered harder. Although Sunny knew that Wen-Cheng was somehow involved with the Resistance, the idea of connecting directly with the shadowy movement felt surreal. Two months before, on Nanking Road, she had walked past the twisted hull of a transport truck that had been sabotaged with an explosive. Aside from a few such tangible examples, it was impossible to know how far and wide the Underground's reach extended. The city was abuzz with rumours of brazen acts of sabotage. Some, such as the truck bombing, were easy to attribute to the Resistance, while others, like the sinking of a Japanese cruiser in the harbour in broad daylight, taxed belief. The rumour mill whirled in a self-perpetuating frenzy, building the Underground into a mythical secret force that had the mighty Japanese army running scared. The more she heard of the Underground, the more indistinct and legendary its status grew in her mind. Sunny had no idea how effective the Resistance was in undermining the enemy but, like most Shanghai natives, she desperately wanted to believe in it.

Wen-Cheng's eyes narrowed in disgust as he continued to stare at the harbour filled with Japanese vessels. "They have no right to be here," he grumbled.

"They have the ships, the planes and the guns." Sunny looked at the *Idzumo's* huge turrets. "Might makes right, does it not?"

Wen-Cheng puffed on his cigarette silently. "Once in a while, right must fight back." He inclined his head. "Isn't that why you have come today, Soon Yi?"

"I suppose." In truth, her motives were far more complex, but Sunny felt too unsettled and uncertain to delve into them with Wen-Cheng. Besides, she was the one who had demanded the meeting.

Originally, Wen-Cheng had hidden his subversive activity. Sunny's suspicion had been piqued two months earlier when Berta at the hospital told her that she'd run into Wen-Cheng in the Yuyuan Garden on a day when he had announced he would be visiting an ill aunt in Wuxi. According to Berta, Wen-Cheng had barely acknowledged her, offering only a curt nod as he hurried away. Days later, Sunny confronted him. He claimed to have been running late for a date and then uncharacteristically lashed out at the dependable Berta for being a wild gossip. But Sunny had not believed him. A few weeks later, she pulled Wen-Cheng aside again and said, "*Wo yào bāngzhù.*"

He shook his head. "You want to help whom?"

"The Underground," she whispered.

"Why would you tell me? I have no access to them."

"I think you do."

"You are mistaken."

"I think not," she said. "But if am wrong, I will keep making enquiries until I find someone who can put me in touch with them."

Hesitating, he glanced over at Franz, the pen in the doctor's hand held still against the patient's chart as he watched them carefully. "This is not the place, Soon Yi," Wen-Cheng whispered.

Two more secret conversations at the hospital eventually led to this rendezvous in the Public Garden. Sunny glanced around her again, but the park still appeared deserted. "Can any one of us really make a difference?"

"Probably not, no." Wen-Cheng shrugged. "But if none of us tries, what hope is there?"

"The Japanese will never defeat America."

"They do not have to." He gestured with his palms up. "The Americans are already fighting in Europe and Africa. Eventually, they will lose their appetite for another war in Asia. Any peace between the Japanese and the Allies would mean the end of China. Shanghai would be lost forever."

Sunny saw his point, and it saddened her. Before the Japanese invasion, she would never have considered herself a patriot. Her country had been consumed by civil unrest and regional strife since before she was born. China was more of a loose affiliation of regional cultures, languages and ethnicities than a single nation. And nowhere was that more evident than in Shanghai. Politically and culturally, the city had always seemed to her as British or French as it ever did Chinese—more its own entity, a city state, than part of China. But Sunny loved her hometown with all her heart, and she embodied the paradox of East meeting West that was Shanghai. The idea of living the rest of her life under the Japanese was too horrible to consider. She thought of Simon forced into permanent hiding while his wife raised their baby alone. And what about her own family's legacy? Although she would not be perpetuating the family name, she owed it to her father to continue his lineage. But how could she introduce a child of her own into this mess?

Wen-Cheng studied her intently. "Does Franz know?"

"That I was coming here to meet you? No."

He nodded knowingly but said nothing.

Sunny remembered the last time she had raised the subject of the Resistance with her husband. Franz had responded angrily, one of the few times he had ever raised his voice with her. "Anyone from the ghetto who assists the Underground is no more than a selfish fool!" he cried. When she wondered how someone could be considered selfish for risking their own life, he snapped back, "To aid the Resistance is to risk the lives of *everyone* in the ghetto."

Guilt bubbled inside her. "Franz is dead set against refugees participating in subversion of any sort."

Wen-Cheng snorted. "It's not their fight, is it?"

"It's not that at all. Franz hates how the Japanese treat the locals. To him, it's no different from how the Nazis bully the Jews." She exhaled slowly. "He worries that if any refugee were to be caught aiding the Underground, it would have devastating repercussions for the whole community."

"And for his hospital."

"That, too, of course."

Wen-Cheng considered it for a moment. "You are not a refugee, Soon Yi."

I am not really anything, she thought. "My husband is. And so is my stepdaughter. If I was ever implicated, it could be just as damaging."

"My wife is dead. I have no children." Wen-Cheng paused. "Franz is right. You cannot afford to be involved. Forget all of this, and go home to him now."

But Sunny could not. The Japanese had raped her homeland. They had murdered her beloved father. And she would never forget Irma or those two teenagers, or the imploring look the taller boy had given her. Sunny folded her arms across her chest. "I am ready to contribute."

Wen-Cheng's expression had hardened, and his eyes darkened. "Once you commit, there is no turning back."

"I realize this."

Wen-Cheng dropped his cigarette to the dirt and stubbed it out with the toe of his shoe. He had always been a fastidious dresser, but his once-gleaming black shoes were now so scuffed they appeared grey. "How far are you prepared to go, Sunny?"

Sunny had no idea, but she answered anyway. "As far as is necessary."

"Even if your actions lead to death?" His stare was unsettling. "And not only for Japanese soldiers."

Sunny could feel doubt creeping over her like a blush, but she refused to waver. "As far as is necessary."

Chapter 13

Franz looked at Colonel Tsutomo Kubota with equal parts awe and relief. Ten months had passed since their last conversation, and Franz had never expected to see him again.

Ghoya hopped off the desk and immediately bent forward at the waist in a deep bow. "Taisa Kubota," he said, then mumbled a few more deferential words in Japanese.

Kubota limped toward them from the doorway with the aid of a cane. Franz was struck by how much the colonel had aged in a year. His face was pale and lined, and his once proud posture had given way to a hunched stance. Franz noticed that his left hand trembled coarsely.

Kubota nodded once to Franz, then turned to Ghoya. "I hope you do not object to my presence at this meeting?" he asked in English.

"But of course." Even though Kubota had just witnessed Ghoya lambasting Franz from atop his desk, the little man now gestured affectionately toward Franz. "The good doctor here was just apprising me of the situation at the refugee hospital."

"So it appears," Kubota said dryly.

"Yes, yes, most honourable *taisa*," Ghoya said, seemingly oblivious to the colonel's sarcasm. "It is impressive that the Jewish people have been able to keep open such a busy hospital."

"They do have a reputation for industriousness," Kubota said.

Ghoya nodded wildly. "I have noticed it myself. It's true. Most true!"

"Mr. Ghoya, would you mind if I borrowed Dr. Adler for a few moments?"

"Certainly not, Taisa Kubota." Ghoya arched his back. "I still have many refugees to see concerning passes. I have time for almost nothing else these days."

Kubota led Franz out of the office and to a staircase around the corner. Franz noticed that the colonel mounted the steps with only his right foot, dragging his left foot behind as he held the railing with one hand. At the landing, he tucked his cane under his arm, straightened his shoulders and limped down the hallway. At the end of the corridor, he opened a door and stepped into an office that was no bigger than Ghoya's and furnished just as plainly.

Kubota motioned to the chair in front of his desk as he walked around it. "Ah, Dr. Adler, you appear just as I remember you. These days, that is high praise indeed."

Franz was markedly thinner than when they were last face to face, but he merely nodded. He couldn't return the compliment with any sincerity. Franz wondered if Kubota's one-sided tremor and stiffness were the result of a stroke. He waited to see if the colonel would volunteer a medical explanation, but none came. "I did not think I would see you again so soon, Colonel," Franz finally said.

"To be frank, Dr. Adler, I did not imagine that we would ever meet again. However, in my experience, fate rarely takes our expectations into consideration."

Franz was so accustomed to hearing rudimentary English from Japanese soldiers that he had almost forgotten that Kubota—who was Cambridge schooled and had lived among the Shanghailanders for years—was so eloquent. "If I may say so, I am most pleased to see that you have returned, Colonel."

Kubota looked away. "In the past year, I have been posted to Burma and Malaysia. And yet this does not seem like a homecoming at all."

"Shanghai is not the same as it used to be, is it?"

"Very true, Doctor," Kubota said. "Of course, I have also returned to a vastly different posting. I now oversee the Bureau of Stateless Refugee Affairs."

Kubota's tone and expression remained neutral, but Franz sensed shame behind his words. The colonel had once ranked second in command only to the city's military governor, General Nogomi. He had returned to Shanghai as an administrator of a half-mile-square ghetto and its unwanted residents. Franz felt responsible for the colonel's fall from grace. Had he not pleaded for Kubota's help the year before when the SS had lobbied the Japanese for permission to annihilate the refugees, the colonel would surely never have been demoted. However, had Kubota not intervened and appealed to the High Command in Tokyo to spare the Jews, Franz might well not have lived to feel his current guilt.

Franz coughed into his hand. "Colonel, I cannot tell you how indebted we are to you. And I am so deeply sorry—"

Kubota shook his left wrist clumsily. "We have a saying in Japan: *Kako wo mizu ni nagashimashou.* Let the past drift away with the water." He nodded. "I trust Mrs. Adler is well?"

"Yes, thank you. Sunny is fine. She will be delighted to hear that you have returned."

"I am most pleased to hear it." Kubota's smile was fleeting. "And your friend, Mr. Lehrer? I understand that he disappeared from the Chapei Civic Assembly Center."

"We have not seen Simon in months." Franz misled with the truth. "We are very concerned for him."

"Most understandable." Kubota sounded distracted. "Have you heard news of Dr. Reuben and his wife?"

The Reubens were third-generation Jewish Shanghailanders. Samuel, a surgeon of many years' standing, had given Franz his first job in the city, but there was no love lost between the two. "I have not heard a word about Samuel and Clara since they were interned last winter."

"They are getting by. I visited them myself in the Lunghua Camp last week." Kubota emitted a small sigh. "Even though they are British citizens, I was able to convince the camp commander that the Reubens have a long-standing affiliation with the refugees." He paused to wait for a reaction, but Franz said nothing. "I have made arrangements to transfer the Reubens here. To the Designated Area."

"I see."

"I was hoping that you might help them adjust to life in the Designated Area. Perhaps even find work for Dr. Reuben in the refugee hospital?"

"Of course, Colonel. We could always use another surgeon." While Samuel and he had rarely seen eye to eye, Franz owed his life to the colonel. For his sake alone, he would do anything he could for the Reubens.

"Thank you." Kubota nodded. "Incidentally, I agree with Mr. Ghoya. It is most impressive that you have managed to keep the hospital functioning."

"In no small part thanks to you, Colonel. Even after you departed, the supplies from the Imperial Army have continued to arrive regularly."

Kubota only frowned. "My colleague, Mr. Ghoya, his methods are somewhat . . . unconventional. Nonetheless, I believe he is committed to his role." He paused. "It is not my place to intervene on matters under his jurisdiction."

"I understand."

"That is good," Kubota muttered. "Very good."

"Is there something wrong, Colonel?" Franz asked.

Kubota gazed up at the ceiling while his left hand trembled silently on the desk. "I find myself more directly involved in the affairs of the Jewish refugees than ever before, Dr. Adler." His eyes then locked onto Franz's. "And yet, ironic as it may sound, I have never been in less of a position to advocate on behalf of your people."

*   *   *

Franz was still mulling over the conversation as he approached the ghetto checkpoint at Wayside Road. Out of the corner of his eye, he saw a woman hurrying across the street, holding a bamboo sack at her side. Turning his head, he was surprised to recognize Sunny. As a refugee, Franz was unable to go beyond the sidewalk that represented the boundary of the ghetto without one of Ghoya's passes, so he stood and waited for his wife at the curb.

Face flushed, Sunny greeted him with a kiss to his cheek.

"Where have you been?" Franz asked.

Sunny raised her bag but avoided his eyes. "Joey and I went to the market for supplies."

"So where is Joey?"

"He stayed behind after we left the market." She lowered her voice. "He is confident he will return with more ether."

Franz forced a chuckle. "He is our Chinese Simon."

"We could use the real Simon. More than ever. Those black marketers . . . I worry for Joey."

"Joey is shrewd. When it comes to the black market, he's more worldly than either of us." Franz laid a hand on her elbow. "Sunny, Colonel Kubota has returned."

Her mouth fell open. "You saw him?"

Franz described his summons by Ghoya and the subsequent meeting with Kubota. "It's more than just how aged he looks. His spirit is broken, too. He was very clear that he would not—that he could not—offer us any assistance. Even when it comes to Ghoya."

"The colonel has done enough already, Franz."

Franz closed his eyes and nodded. "When Ghoya's men came for me, I was certain they knew about Charlie."

Sunny laid her hand over his and squeezed. "Oh, Franz, I must tell you—Joey already recognized Charlie as the Boy General."

The warmth of Sunny's touch evaporated. "So easily?"

"From photographs in newspapers and magazines."

"So it's only a matter of time until others recognize him, too," he grunted. "The wrong people."

"What else can we do, Franz?"

"We can let him go home." He prickled with shame even as the words left his lips. "After all, that is what he wants."

"But Franz, you said . . ."

"What I said was correct. To send him out now . . ." He rubbed his temples and avoided her eyes. "But there is an entire community to consider."

Chapter 14

A throng of students, ranging in age from seven to eighteen, lined up at the door of the Kadoorie School, anxious to escape the airless old building. Hannah didn't mind the jostling. She barely even noticed how overheated she felt in her wool tunic. She'd hung on to it from her days at the Shanghai Jewish School, though her new school had no uniforms.

Freddy Herzberg had that effect on her. Hannah had not felt as excited in months. He had invited her to his home. She still couldn't believe that a whole Hershey's chocolate bar was waiting there for them. Hannah had not seen, let alone tasted, chocolate in over a year. Her mouth watered every time she thought of it, but just as importantly, it also meant that Freddy didn't mind her meeting his parents. The small offer had revived her crush. *Perhaps Leah Wasselmann won't be Freddy's girlfriend forever?*

"Herzberg gratitude," Freddy had labelled the promised chocolate during lunch break, as it was still called, though few students had the luxury of a regular noontime meal. "For the hero who put food back on our table."

"It was nothing. Just a short walk."

"Yeah, but smack through the heart of enemy territory!"

"You make it sound a lot more impressive than it was." She brushed off his praise, through her chest fluttered with pride.

Hannah had told Freddy about her run-in with Ghoya but downplayed her panicked reaction. She could hardly believe that the hysterical little man had let her leave the ghetto after the grilling he gave her. Once she cleared the checkpoint, she had to walk over a mile to reach the address on Avenue Joffre that Freddy had made her memorize. He need not have bothered to give her directions, though; the building was a block away from the flat where she used to live with her aunt and father.

Along the way, she had passed numerous Japanese soldiers on the streets. The sight of them terrified her, but aside from a few curious glances and one vicious scowl, Hannah went otherwise unnoticed. A Russian man with a few days' worth of stubble on his cheeks met her at the door to the apartment. He swayed at the threshold, reeking of alcohol, while trying to persuade her to join him inside for lunch. Resting a hand on her shoulder, he offered her something he called "*plain shchi,*" which as best she could tell was some kind of meaty soup. Hannah wriggled free of his grip, handed him the brooch and, explaining that she was late to meet a friend, hurried away.

Hannah returned home feeling exhilarated. She was not a helpless cripple after all. She wouldn't mind doing it again, she told Freddy. He assured her that more missions awaited her. "There's a lot more than just food money involved, too," he added in a conspiratorial whisper that thrilled her. With her new-found sense of purpose, and Freddy's attention, her months-long melancholy dissipated like a rising fog.

Hannah was so eager to head home with Freddy now that she didn't notice her father among the crowd of students and parents—a few of whom wore the traditional black coats and hats of the Hasidim, despite the heat—until he called to her from the sidewalk.

"Papa, why have you come?" she asked as soon she reached him. "Is something the matter?"

"Who is your friend, Hannah-*chen?*"

Hannah flushed. Before she could say anything, Freddy thrust out his hand. "I am Freddy Herzberg. It's a pleasure to meet you, Dr. Adler."

Franz returned the boy's handshake. "Will you excuse us, Freddy? I must take Hannah home."

"Can it not wait an hour or two, Papa?" Hannah pleaded. "Freddy and I were going to his apartment to open the—" She caught herself. "We have homework to complete."

"No, Hannah. This cannot wait."

Though her father spoke quietly, Hannah could tell from his tone that something had upset him. Still, she persisted. "Please, Papa. I will be home very soon."

Freddy held up his hand. "It's all right, Hannah. We can do the homework tomorrow. I will not touch it until you are free."

"But, but . . ." Hannah was dying to sink her teeth into a chocolate bar, but she was equally upset about missing the chance to accompany Freddy home. She doubted that either opportunity would wait for her.

"You will come home now, Hannah," Franz said with cool finality.

Burning with embarrassment and disappointment, she did not even make eye contact with Freddy as she mumbled her goodbye.

Franz did not speak for several blocks as they headed along East Yuhang Road. Once they turned off onto quieter Ward Road, he stopped abruptly and placed his hand firmly on her shoulder. "Hannah, did you leave the ghetto without telling me?"

She felt ambushed. "I . . . well . . . I . . . I did, Papa."

The pressure on her shoulder intensified as his fingers dug into her tunic. "Why?"

"I went to visit Natasha."

Natasha Lazarev, who had lived with her family near the Adlers' apartment, was the first friend Hannah had made upon landing in Shanghai. But in recent years, as their lives and interests diverged, they had seen less of each other.

Her father's eyes simmered, but his tone remained calm. "And you didn't think to ask me before leaving?"

"You . . . you were at the hospital."

"Which is not so far from home."

She looked away. "I didn't think it was necessary."

"Not necessary?" His voice rose in volume and pitch. He glanced over either shoulder before gritting his teeth and continuing in a hushed, angry tone. "Not necessary to tell me that you planned to stroll out of this . . . this prison as though you were just off to the park? How could you be so foolish?"

She shifted from foot to foot. "I should have told you, Papa."

He stared at her for a long painful moment. "There was a time, *Liebchen,* not so long ago, when we shared everything."

His disappointment pierced her deeper than his harsh words. She was overcome by remorse along with a sudden urge to confess everything: her feelings for Freddy, the smuggled brooch, Ghoya's outburst and the priceless chocolate bar. But for reasons that she didn't fully understand, she lowered her head and said only, "Next time I will ask, Papa."

Chapter 15

As always, Sunny felt strangely at home inside the brothel. She had visited Jia-Li intermittently at the Comfort Home since they were both teenagers. Most of the prostitutes welcomed Sunny like an old friend. The proprietor, Chih-Nii, had been playfully trying to recruit her for years. "Half Eastern, half Western, you would be a delicacy to both worlds," the madam would say. "We could make a fortune together, my Eurasian buttercup."

Ushi had escorted Sunny into the drawing room, then went in search of Jia-Li, leaving her alone on the chaise longue. Sunny studied the paintings that had belonged to the house's original French owners, wondering again why the portraits still hung on the walls. Perhaps Chih-Nii thought they imbued the room with a sense of history or European flair? Sunny found them depressing. She was relieved not to have left any pictures of her family behind when she and Franz had been forced out her parents' home. She cringed at the idea of someone using photographs of her parents to add character to her old home.

Jia-Li entered the room in a form-fitting, embroidered maroon cheongsam, slit up one side to the top of her thigh. Her bright lipstick was perfectly applied, and not a strand of hair was out of place, but to Sunny, Jia-Li was never quite as composed as she pretended to be at the Comfort Home. While Sunny was well aware of the circumstances that had forced her friend into this world, she never understood how someone as beautiful and intelligent could continue to sell her body. Or why, now that she had been free of the opium pipe for over a year, she still needed to. She thought about Jia-Li's recent financial generosity toward the Adlers with another flush of guilt.

"I thought I was meeting you Thursday," Jia-Li said as she kissed the air on either side of Sunny's face.

Sunny took in the smells of cinnamon and jasmine. "I am sorry, *bǎo bèi,* this could not wait."

Jia-Li lowered herself into the chair beside Sunny, lighting a cigarette as she did. She brought her lips to the holder and inhaled languidly, then broke into a luminous smile. "I welcome any visit from you, regardless of the reason, *xiǎo hè.*"

"You might not say that after you hear me out."

"Let me guess," Jia-Li said through a stream of smoke. "You want to speak to Simon."

"Very much so. But that's not why I have come."

Jia-Li arched a painted eyebrow. Sunny glanced around suspiciously. "We are alone," Jia-Li assured her. "You can speak freely."

Sunny was tempted to tell Jia-Li about her meeting with Wen-Cheng. Sharing her secret would have been a huge relief, but somehow the subject felt too raw to broach inside the confines of a brothel. Instead, she said, "There is a patient at our hospital. A Chinese man with a nasty leg infection." She paused. "From a gunshot."

Jia-Li released an elegant ring of smoke. "I take it this man is wanted by the *Rìbĕn guĭzi?*"

"He would be if the Japanese knew he was in the city. Very much so." Sunny nodded. "We cannot keep him at the refugee hospital. He stands out like a sore thumb, as Simon would say. Besides, there is nowhere to hide him."

"Shanghai used to be the easiest place in the world to lose yourself," Jia-Li said wistfully. "But such hiding places have become another precious commodity, haven't they?"

"*Bǎo bèi*, I hoped that maybe . . ."

"How sick is he, Sunny?"

"He could lose his leg at any time. He might not even survive long enough to be moved anywhere."

Jia-Li shook her head. "He would only fare worse here. It's so musty downstairs."

"At least he would be safe."

"Safe?" Jia-Li gasped. "The Kempeitai have raided us twice more since the day Franz and Esther came with the baby. Chih-Nii is beside herself. She is refusing to take in anyone else. And she is desperately trying to get rid of the ones who are still here. There is talk of trying to sneak them out to the country."

Sunny had not held out much hope that the Comfort Home could help Charlie, but she still felt a sting of disappointment.

"Look at you, *xiǎo hè*." Jia-Li leaned forward and stroked Sunny's cheek with the back of her hand. "It breaks my heart to see you so sad."

"There is nothing more to be done for this man. We cannot keep him. He will die, and we might die because of him."

"There is always something." Jia-Li laughed quietly. "Besides, there are no rules left in Shanghai. Only guidelines. I will speak with Chih-Nii. We will figure out a way."

Sunny kissed the back of her friend's hand. "Thank you."

Jia-Li leaned back in her seat pensively. "This man? Is he part of the Underground?"

"No. He is a soldier."

Jia-Li nodded. "Ah, a member of the Kuomintang? That will be tricky."

"Not exactly the Kuomintang."

Jia-Li sat up straighter. "If he's not Kuomintang—"

"He fights for the Communist army, though he is not politically inclined himself."

"*The Communists!*" Jia-Li sprang out of her chair. She looked around urgently, then murmured, "Your soldier would be in greater danger here than with the *Rìběn guǐzi.*"

"You can't be serious!"

"I've never been more so. Chih-Nii works for the Green Gang. You know this, Sunny. For Du Yen Sheng." She whispered the name of the overlord of Shanghai's criminal world. "Du is a sworn enemy of the Communists. He gets along better with the Japanese. His men would skin this man alive." She paused and squinted. "Unless . . ."

"What is it, Jia-Li?"

"No one were ever to find out that he is a Communist."

Sunny remembered how Joey treated Charlie like a matinee idol. "I am afraid that's not possible. Someone is bound to recognize him."

"Why? Who is he?"

"Bao Chun."

Jia-Li's eyes grew wide. "The Boy General? *That* Bao Chun?"

"Yes."

"He's a national hero."

"But he's also a Communist."

"Yes, yes. We could never keep him here."

Despondent, Sunny rose from the couch. "I will have to look elsewhere."

"If it's of any help to you, I might be able to arrange to get the general out of Shanghai."

"Perhaps. I will see." Sunny smiled gratefully. "As if I haven't already burdened you enough, could I visit Simon now, *bǎo bèi?*"

*   *   *

Ushi insisted on taking Sunny down to the cellar himself. He led her into the wine cellar, then slid down the tight passageway like a crab and into the concealed room.

Simon threw his arms around Sunny, almost knocking her to the ground. "Oh, Sunny!" he cried as he righted her. "Next to a visit from Esther and my boy, it doesn't get better than this. You ready to see a grown man bawl?"

Simon was clean-shaven and smelled fresh, but he had lost so much weight that his eyes were sunken and his Semitic nose more prominent than ever. "You look well, Simon. Thin but well."

He shook his head. "And you look more gorgeous than ever. I'm not only saying that because I've been trapped down here forever with only men. Though God knows you do make a nice change of scenery."

Sunny glanced around, but Ushi had already vacated the room, and no one else was in sight.

Simon motioned to another door. "The others are behind there. We're not supposed to have visitors, but if we do, the rest stay out of sight." He wiggled his fingers in a give-me gesture. "Please, Sunny, tell me about Esther and my boy."

"They are well. Every morning Jakob seems to have grown more. And he smiles now. He's so adorable, Simon."

Beaming, Simon dug his fingers into his shirt pocket and extracted a weathered photograph. He studied it for a moment before reluctantly handing it over to her. Franz had taken the photo. In the black-and-white shot, a smiling Esther held a wide-eyed Jakob up to the camera with both hands. Sunny remembered that Franz, who usually preferred to photograph buildings, had used his last roll of film on the shoot. At the time, she had wondered why her husband had insisted on snapping so many photographs. Now she understood.

Sunny returned the photo to Simon. "Picture Jakob with your big smile and you'll know what he looks like today."

Simon's grin faded. "I am sick of picturing it, Sunny. I want to be with them. To hold my baby. To just smell him. And I want to kiss my wife again." He screwed up his face. "Is that so much to ask?"

It really wasn't, but Sunny couldn't muster the right words in reply. Instead, she only shook her head.

Simon studied the cement floor. "I have to get out of here."

"Soon, perhaps."

"Not soon. Today."

"You're not thinking with your head."

"I don't care, Sunny. I'm going to leave."

"The police will be looking for you."

"Then I will change the way I look. I'll grow a beard or shave my head or put on some old glasses. Hell, I'll even throw on a bamboo hat and pull a rickshaw if I have to. Whatever it takes."

"What about Esther and the baby?"

"Don't worry. I won't come near your home or the hospital. I wouldn't endanger Essie or my son like that. Not ever again." He swallowed loudly. "But even if it means only seeing them from across the road. Even if they don't know I'm there." He tapped the pocket that held his photograph. "It would still be a thousand times better than just looking at this."

"Where will you go?"

He shrugged. "I know people."

Sunny paused, then squinted at him. "You might have to stay here for a few more days."

"Why?" Simon grabbed her arm excitedly. "What is it?"

"There *is* someone who can help us."

Chapter 16

Franz had hardly slept and, according to the night nurse, neither had Charlie. Around midnight, the injured man had begun to tremble violently, as though he were having a seizure. His temperature spiked, and the fever didn't break until sunrise. All the while, Charlie refused more painkillers.

Franz slipped between the curtains surrounding Charlie's bed to find the young general locked in an urgent conversation with Ernst. His complexion was tinged grey and his face drenched in perspiration. Still, Charlie greeted Franz with a stoic smile.

Ernst looked up, an unlit cigarette dangling from his lips. His beard was still scraggly, but his hair had been combed back and his suit was less rumpled. "Ah, Franz. Good morning. Everyone survived the night. Isn't that a delicious little miracle?"

"Every morning." Franz turned to the patient. "How does the leg feel, Charlie?"

"Less painful. Perhaps I will be able to stand on it soon?"

"Good, yes. Hopefully." Franz found it difficult to hold the man's gaze. "May I have a look under the dressing?"

Charlie nodded. Franz pulled up the sheet and gently removed the bandages from the wound. The redness around Charlie's knee had lessened and the skin was less painfully taut, but the fresh surgical wounds puckered. Their black edges troubled Franz. They did not look promising, especially without further surgery. He loosely rolled the bandages back into place, feeling like more of a fraud than a doctor.

"What is your opinion?" Charlie asked.

"The wound has a long way to go," Franz said in a circumspect tone.

"Don't we all?" Ernst studied the cigarette he now held between his fingers. "My last smoke until God knows when I find some more. I hear they last longer when you don't light them."

Franz cleared his throat. "Charlie, are you still keen to leave Shanghai?"

Ernst shook his head in dismay. "What nonsense is this? He is in no shape to leave the hospital. You were clear about that yesterday."

"That was yesterday," Franz mumbled weakly.

Charlie studied the ceiling for a pained moment, then nodded. "I think it would be for the best, yes."

"Look at you!" Ernst cried. "You're the colour of a storm cloud. We will never get you home."

"We can try," Charlie said.

Ernst turned angrily to Franz, shaking a finger at him. "*Was ist passiert?* Why the change of heart?"

"People recognize Charlie."

Ernst's eyebrows rose in surprise. "Which people?"

"Joey."

"Can you not trust the boy?"

"Of course we can trust *him*. But he recognized Charlie straight away. Others will too. He is too well known to keep hidden here."

"Ah." Ernst nodded bitterly. "So you are no longer willing to risk the exposure."

"This is not only about me," Franz said evenly.

Ernst was about to respond when Charlie propped himself up. He gasped from the effort and swayed from side to side but held himself upright. As soon as he caught his breath, he turned to Ernst. "The doctor would be a fool not to send me away," he snapped with sudden authority.

"And I would be an even bigger fool to stay. I would never risk a whole company for the sake of one fallen man. It is no different for Dr. Adler and this hospital."

"You are not just any man," Ernst pointed out.

"They have removed the bullet," Charlie said firmly. "It was the only reason you persuaded me to come, Ernst. It is time to go."

Franz reached into the pocket of his lab coat, dug out a bottle of anti-biotic pills and passed it over to Charlie. "Sulpha medicine. To help keep the infection in check. You will need to take one tablet three times a day until they are gone."

Charlie accepted the bottle with a shaky hand. It contained the last of the hospital's antibiotic supply, but to Franz this was little more than a token gesture. "Thank you, Doctor," Charlie said.

"This is bloody lunacy," Ernst muttered. "Can you not see it?"

"I am leaving, Ernst," Charlie said. "It is decided."

"What is decided?" Sunny asked from behind the curtains. She pushed them apart and stepped inside. Jia-Li followed her in before the drapes fell closed behind them both.

Exasperated, Ernst looked from Franz to Charlie and back. "These two agree that Charlie is far too hale and hearty to waste any more time in hospital."

"No one said that," Franz said quietly.

"There are risks either way," Sunny said, giving Franz a supportive look that did little to alleviate his conscience.

"A pleasure to see you again, Ernst," Jia-Li said.

Ernst extended his hand to her. "Ah, well, if it isn't my saviour herself."

Charlie viewed him quizzically. "Your saviour?"

Ernst nodded. "Last year, when the Kempeitai were scouring Shanghai for Shan and me, this . . . this vision arranged for two rather shady—or perhaps 'colourful' is the word—characters to whisk us out of the city in the dead of night."

"Lum and Vu colourful? Never." Jia-Li laughed. "Shady, yes, but not colourful."

"Oh, Jia-Li, how I wish I had my brushes." Ernst sighed. "I've painted you in my head a thousand times since I last laid eyes on you."

"I am not sure whether or not to take that as a compliment."

"Why not?"

"The only subjects of yours that I am aware of are the wild pheasants," Jia-Li said, referring to the lowest class of dockside prostitutes. Ernst's portraits of the wretched young women had made his reputation in the pre-war Shanghai art scene. "And the victims of the Nanking massacre, of course."

Ernst brushed her comment away with a flip of his wrist. "I'm done with all that. I've seen more than enough ugliness for a lifetime. Next time I paint—if there is a next time—I will capture only beauty and light on the canvas."

Jia-Li glanced over at Charlie. "Ernst, will you not introduce me to your friend?"

"How rude!" Ernst gasped. "A year away from civilization and I've lost all my manners. As though raised by wolves. Jia-Li, allow me to introduce Charlie."

Jia-Li approached the bed. Her huge brown eyes lit up. "Ko Jia-Li." She added several words in Chinese.

Charlie wiped his brow with his sleeve and chuckled. "So you are responsible for sending Ernst to our village," he replied in English.

Jia-Li nodded to Franz and Sunny. "I only arranged the truck. The rest is their doing."

"Then I hold you all equally responsible," Charlie said as he lowered himself back onto the mattress, exhausted.

Sunny laid a hand on his elbow. "Charlie, we thought Jia-Li might help arrange your transport out of Shanghai."

"That would be most helpful," Charlie said. "My men can meet me outside the city, but for them to travel inside is somewhat of a challenge."

"A *challenge?*" Ernst groaned. "Suicide, more like it. Only blind luck got us through the Japanese soldiers on the way in."

As he studied Charlie's wan complexion, Franz doubted that anything could be more of a threat to the man's well-being than his near-gangrenous leg. He felt small for keeping the thought to himself.

"I would be honoured to assist you." Jia-Li bit her lip, appearing uncharacteristically bashful. "You do so much for China."

Charlie looked away, embarrassed. "I am one of millions."

"One *in* millions." Ernst turned to Jia-Li. "How would you get us out of the city alive?"

"Not us, only me," Charlie said.

"I would come too, of course."

"No, Ernst. You must stay."

Ernst's face fell. "I have to escort you home. I gave my word."

"We need you here in Shanghai," Charlie said definitively.

"I never even told Shan that I was leaving."

Sunny wrapped an arm around Ernst's shoulder and drew him nearer. "He will understand."

"You clearly do not know Shan as I do," Ernst muttered.

Jia-Li coughed into her hand. "My boss's boss, Du Yen Sheng, is an influential man. He supplies the Japanese with certain commodities."

"Opium?" Franz asked.

"Among other things, yes," Jia-Li said. "They truck it in from the countryside. His men are among the few Chinese who receive gasoline rations and permits to drive."

Sunny frowned. "In the back of an opium truck? That is how you intend to send Charlie home?"

Jia-Li rolled her shoulders in a can't-be-helped gesture. "There is a truck arriving today. After unloading its cargo, it will head straight back out of the city."

Charlie wiped his brow again, but sweat continued to drip off his face and down his neck. "And they will take me?"

Jia-Li nodded. "I have to warn you, Charlie. It will not be comfortable." She glanced down at the sheet covering his infected leg. "Under all the boxes and crates there is a false compartment that they use for such . . . emergencies."

Charlie held Jia-Li's gaze for a moment. "Trust me. It will not be the worst ride of my life. What time does the truck leave?"

"At one o'clock precisely," Jia-Li said. "You would have to meet them at a warehouse near the wharf."

"How do we get Charlie to the wharf in broad daylight?" Ernst consulted his watch. "In less than three hours?"

Jia-Li held up a hand helplessly.

"Utter lunacy," Ernst said again.

Franz had a sudden revelation. "The Japanese allow us to bury our dead."

Ernst rolled his eyes. "Well, that will come as some consolation to Charlie and his men."

"I was thinking that we could send Charlie to the warehouse inside a casket."

"But Franz, you know how paranoid the Japanese are," Sunny said. "They often look inside the caskets when they are being transported through the streets."

"Yes, you are correct," Franz muttered.

Sunny squinted. "Unless . . ."

"Unless what, Sunny?"

"The night soil men come through the ghetto all the time."

Jia-Li grimaced in disgust. "Surely, *xiǎo hè*, you are not suggesting . . ."

Reddening, Sunny turned to Charlie with an apologetic frown. "Charlie, we could wrap you in bamboo and other coverings. If we stood you up inside the barrel, with all that . . . waste . . . above you, no one would dare look inside."

Charlie only shrugged. "War is war."

Chapter 17

For the first time in days, clouds crowded the sky. The temperature had dipped to one more typical, and tolerable, for late spring, and yet today Sunny was sweating more heavily under her dress than on the previous scorching afternoon. She wondered how she could possibly be of any help to the Resistance when a simple reconnaissance mission was making her so nervous.

Franz seemed calm as he walked beside her down Ward Road, but Sunny sensed that something other than Charlie's predicament was troubling him.

She had noticed a similar coolness the night before when they had lain in bed together, discussing Simon's intent to leave the Comfort Home. "I convinced him to stay for another few days while I arrange things with Yang," she said as she stroked his arm.

"You think your housekeeper will take him in?" Franz asked.

After the Adlers had been forced to move into the ghetto, Yang had followed them into the same neighbourhood, claiming she had nowhere else to live but in her youngest sister's apartment. Sunny knew, though, that Yang had other siblings who resided in better areas and would have also welcomed their big sister into their homes. "Yang has an extra room in her flat since her sister moved in with her son," she said.

"But you know how terrified Yang is of the Japanese," Franz pointed out. "And she refuses to speak anything other than Chinese."

"She will speak English if she's forced to. Besides, she's lonely. She may be crusty, but she is desperate to help. Why do you think she moved into the ghetto?"

"To be close to you."

Sunny nestled in tighter, her chest pressing into her husband's side. "I like being close to you," she said in an inviting tone.

He turned his head and gave her a listless kiss on the cheek. "I'm exhausted, darling. Good night," he said as he rolled away from her.

Sunny had little time now to dwell on her husband's uncharacteristic coolness as they walked past two more Japanese soldiers, these ones standing on the corner and laughing uproariously at some private joke.

Her heart fluttered even faster. "Franz, there are so many soldiers," she said quietly in German. "It's a long trip to the wharf in broad daylight. Especially for a night soil man."

"True."

"Who knows how many times he might be stopped? What if the soldiers hear Charlie inside? What if something else goes wrong?"

"We have no choice," Franz muttered, focusing his gaze on the men approaching them from the other end of the block.

"There must be another way to get Charlie there," she said. "If only I could—"

Franz clamped a hand on her elbow. He spun away from the street to stare at the boarded-up window of the empty storefront.

Sunny mimicked his pose, wondering what the sudden threat could be. "What is it, Franz?" she whispered.

He lowered his head and turned to retrace their steps, pulling her along with him. "Those men behind us—don't look back!" he said in a hush. "The short one is Ghoya."

"The one who calls himself the King of—"

"Yes. And the other man. I recognize him from the newspaper."

"Who is he?"

"Baron von Puttkamer," Franz said.

"Is he a refugee?"

"A Nazi. People call him the 'Goebbels of Asia.'"

A shrill voice called out to them. "Dr. Adler, Dr. Adler!"

They froze in place. Franz squeezed Sunny's elbow before releasing her. She understood. He would do the talking.

They slowly turned to face the approaching men. Ghoya wore a fedora and a flamboyant pinstriped suit. The man beside him, in contrast, was tall, athletic and fashionably dressed in a navy blazer and tie. He strolled down the street like someone who expected to have an entourage trailing him. Two younger men kept a deferential distance behind him. One resembled a youthful Ernst, while the other was Asian but looked neither Chinese nor Japanese. Korean, Sunny decided.

Ghoya reached them first. "Ah, Dr. Adler. Allow me to introduce you to one of your countrymen." He held his small hand out to the man beside him. "Baron Jesco von Puttkamer."

No handshakes were offered, but von Puttkamer nodded crisply in what Sunny understood to be the Prussian manner. "Dr. Adler." He did not introduce his two subordinates and ignored Sunny altogether.

"I was just taking the baron and his men on a tour of the Designated Area," Ghoya announced.

Franz's expression remained neutral, but Sunny sensed his soaring apprehension. "Of course, Mr. Ghoya," he said, keeping his tone steady. "However, the baron and I are no longer countrymen. The German government rescinded my citizenship years ago."

"Technically, that is correct, Dr. Adler," von Puttkamer said in a low, silky voice. "Still, I understand that most of the Jewish residents in the Designated Area are German-born. Citizens or not, my government maintains an active interest in all such peoples."

His tone was conversational, polite even, but the words "active interest" sent a chill through Sunny. Franz fidgeted uncomfortably but said nothing.

"Yes, yes," Ghoya said. "The baron is most interested in seeing how the Jews get by here. Most interested. I was just taking him to the school now."

Hannah! Sunny immediately thought. *Leave those children be!* she wanted to scream. *What does the school matter to you thugs?*

Franz stiffened. "The school? Really? There is not much to see inside that ramshackle building."

"No doubt." Von Puttkamer nodded. "Still, I am most interested to see it for myself. Do Jews not prize education above all else? How else can all your little ones grow up to be lawyers and bankers?"

"And doctors," Ghoya added with a giggle.

"So many Jewish doctors," von Puttkamer grunted. "Which reminds me. Mr. Ghoya was telling me that you have built your very own hospital here in Shanghai."

Sunny's eyes darted over to Franz. His jaw was clenched even tighter now. "It's not much more than an abandoned building with a few beds inside," he said.

"It is much more than that!" Ghoya exclaimed. "You told me so yourself."

"We have hardly any medicines or supplies left in our cupboards, Mr. Ghoya," Franz said. "The hospital is basically a convalescence home. A place where we can sometimes keep people a little more comfortable before they improve or they die."

"I think you are being most modest," von Puttkamer said. "I would very much like to tour this hospital of yours."

Franz shrugged his shoulders and held out his palms. "You would be wasting your time, Baron."

The younger German man lunged forward, looking for a moment as if he might tackle Franz. "The baron does not take advice from a rotten Jew!"

Von Puttkamer smiled in a paternal manner. "Please excuse Gerhard's exuberance, but my young colleague does have a point, Dr. Adler. I would like to see the hospital for myself."

"Yes, yes," Ghoya said. "We will go there right after the school and the temple."

*   *   *

Sunny resisted the urge to run as she and Franz returned to the hospital. "How long do you think we have, Franz?"

"Half an hour? An hour at the most. How long can it possibly take them to tour the synagogue and school?"

"So there is no time for the night soil barrel," she said.

"Absolutely not. We must get Charlie out of the hospital immediately."

"I'll find a straw hat." Sunny thought aloud. "We have to just bundle Charlie up in a rickshaw and send him to the warehouse. I will go with him."

Franz stopped and caught her arm again. "No, Sunny! If you were to be caught . . . I should go."

"You are not allowed out of the ghetto without a pass. It's too risky for you, Franz."

"Then Ernst will have to take him."

"That would draw even more attention. No one will take notice of two Chinese riding together."

"Joey, then."

"It's not fair to ask him." She marshalled her courage. "I will do it. There is no other choice."

Before Franz could argue further, they reached the door to the hospital. Panicky voices could be heard inside. Ernst's was the loudest.

Franz took off down the corridor, and Sunny followed. They reached the ward to see Charlie staggering across the room in a shirt but no pants. Ernst supported him on one side, while Max Feinstein supported him on the other. The dressing around his leg had unfurled, and blackish blood trailed behind him. Panting heavily, Charlie was reaching his hands out in front of him as though trying to catch imaginary butterflies that were fluttering past his head.

"You have to go back to bed, Charlie," Ernst commanded, but Charlie continued to grasp at air.

"He is delirious from the infection." Max shook his head. "His fever is through the roof. Gangrene must have set in."

Sunny rushed over. Wordlessly, she pushed Ernst aside and slid an arm behind Charlie's back. Even through his damp shirt, she could tell that his skin was on fire.

"The railway station," Charlie mumbled to her in Mandarin. "Don't you see? It is the key. We must get to the station."

"We will, yes," Sunny reassured him as she forcefully guided him back toward the bed. Charlie didn't resist, but he could barely hold himself upright. Max and Sunny had to drag him onto a stretcher, manoeuvering him past a line of patients, who watched with expressions ranging from bewildered to petrified.

With Franz's help, they hoisted Charlie back onto the bed. He kept trying to lift his head up off the mattress, despite being too weak to hold it up. "The explosives," he mumbled. "How will we get the explosives in?"

Max squinted at Franz. "You must take him to the operating room and remove more tissue. Surely it is his only hope."

"There is no time, Max," Franz blurted. "Ghoya is on his way over. Von Puttkamer too."

Max's face blanched. "That vicious Nazi is coming here? *Mein Gott! Why?*"

"I have no idea," Franz said. "We must get Charlie out of here before they arrive."

"Why would they care about Charlie?"

Sunny waved her hand. "We will explain later, Max," she said in a tone that left no room for argument. "Go get Joey. Straight away."

Max hesitated as if to argue but then turned and went in search of Joey.

Franz gazed at her. "What do we do now, Sunny?"

He looked as lost as she had ever seen him. "Joey and I will take Charlie home," she said.

"*Home?*" Franz asked incredulously. "To Hannah, Esther and the baby?"

"Just until we can find somewhere more suitable."

"And what will we possibly do for him there?"

She looked down at the blackened wound on Charlie's thigh. It had begun to blister around the edges. "We have to take care of that," she said softly. "You must bring home the necessary equipment."

Franz watched Charlie thrash at the air above him. "Ernst was so right. This *is* lunacy."

Joey popped his head through the curtains and seemed to immediately understand what was happening. "What do you need?"

"Go get a coolie with a rickshaw—someone you trust, Joey—and have him wait out front," Sunny instructed. "And find a straw hat if you can."

As soon as Joey left, Sunny retrieved Charlie's trousers from their heap under the bed. With Max pinning his shoulders down and Franz holding his thighs, Sunny managed to slip the stained garment over his legs. Charlie screamed as the fabric rubbed against his raw wound. Berta arrived at the bedside holding a syringe of morphine and two Aspirin tablets. Together, they managed to sit Charlie up. He choked on the water but swallowed the pills. Sunny exposed a patch of skin on his shoulder and injected the painkiller, then wrapped a blanket around his torso while Berta dabbed at his brow with a compress. Throughout it all, Charlie kept muttering about railways and explosives.

"The coolie is waiting," Joey said from the end of the bed, where he stood holding a ratty bamboo hat.

Franz turned to Sunny. "Let me come with you."

"No. You have to be here when Ghoya arrives."

Joey and Sunny hoisted Charlie to his feet. Joey secured the hat firmly on Charlie's head. He was like dead weight now and mumbling incoherently. Together they dragged him across the ward and down the corridor.

"I will check the street." Franz darted out the door without waiting for a response.

Charlie's eyes were closed, even as he continued to mutter. Joey stared silently at the door. Sunny's pulse pounded in her ears. Moments later, Franz burst back inside. "There is a soldier at the end of the street. Just standing there. I'm not sure which way he will go."

"And the coolie?" Sunny asked.

"He's at the curb out front."

"We have no time to wait for the soldier to go." Sunny shuffled Charlie toward the door and Joey followed her out.

They practically carried Charlie down the pathway to where the coolie stood beside his rickshaw, viewing them with only mild interest as he held tight the handles of his carriage.

Joey hopped inside the rickshaw and helped Sunny manoeuvre Charlie into the seat beside him. Just as she squeezed in herself, the soldier marched up to the rickshaw. He waved his rifle at Charlie and barked at them in Japanese. Joey and Sunny shrugged to indicate that they couldn't understand him.

The soldier took a step closer to the rickshaw. He studied Charlie, then motioned for them to remove his hat. Fighting to steady her hand, Sunny feigned indifference as she pulled the hat off Charlie's head. The soldier leaned forward and examined his face.

Sunny's breath caught in her throat.

Suddenly, Joey let out a loud cackle, and the soldier turned to him in surprise. Joey formed a bottle with his thumb and his fist and pantomimed drinking from it. He nodded toward Charlie. "This one starts very early in the morning," he said, laughing.

The soldier's lip curled into a disgusted scowl. "No-good drunk Chinaman."

Chapter 18

Franz stepped inside his bedroom to find the others crowded around the bed where Charlie lay glassy-eyed. His calmness suggested that he had emerged from his delirium. Still, despite the breeze from the open window, the faint smell of decayed flesh hung over him.

Sunny stood at the head of the bed speaking to Charlie in a low voice while pressing a compress to his brow. Wen-Cheng, dressed in a surgical gown and gloves, had wedged himself between the bed and the wall and was assembling an impromptu surgical tray from tools he had smuggled over from the hospital. A hacksaw perched ominously on the far end of the tray.

Sunny looked over her shoulder at Franz. "What happened with Ghoya and the Nazis?"

"We can discuss it later." Franz could still picture the crazed little man leading the Nazi contingent around the silent ward as though showing them an apartment whose tenants he was about to evict.

Charlie winced. "This is too much."

"What is?" Sunny asked. "The pain?"

Charlie shook his head slightly. "Just let me go," he croaked.

"We cannot allow that," Wen-Cheng said. "We are your doctors. We know how to fix you."

Charlie's eyes drifted over to the saw. "Fix me?"

"Dr. Huang is correct," Franz said. "You should improve once we—"

"And if I don't?" Charlie asked.

Sunny dabbed his brow again. "Do you not owe it to your men to try?"

"A soldier has to . . . to know when to abandon his losses," Charlie said.

"You are not lost yet, Charlie." Franz held a hand out to him. "So let us to do what has to be done."

Charlie's eyes drifted shut. Sunny spoke to him in Chinese, her tone soft and soothing. After a few moments, he nodded.

Franz looked from Wen-Cheng to Sunny. "The ether?" he asked.

Sunny lifted up a small smoked-glass bottle. "Joey's contact cheated him. He mixed it with water. I am not sure there is enough ether to be effective."

"What choice is there?" Franz asked, though inwardly he was horrified at the prospect of amputating the leg of someone who might still be awake.

Wen-Cheng held up his gloved hands. "I am already scrubbed. May I perform the surgery?"

Franz had no idea why Wen-Cheng would want to take the lead but was relieved that he wouldn't have to use the saw himself. "I'll assist you," he said.

Franz donned a gown and mask, then scrubbed his hands with the last sliver of soap in the basin of lukewarm water. He dried his hands on the pillowcase that was serving as a towel and then slipped them into the rubber gloves.

Wen-Cheng draped Charlie's right leg with thin sheets, exposing the edges of the blistering wound. He cleaned the area with a soapy sponge. Sunny covered Charlie's face with the ether mask and dripped anaesthetic onto it. Franz could tell by the faintness of its odour that the drug didn't possess its usual potency.

Sunny shook the bottle to extract a final drop or two, but Charlie remained alert. She looked from Wen-Cheng to Franz. "He is not anaesthetized."

Franz squeezed into a spot across the bed from Wen-Cheng. "The quicker we do this, the better." He took a scalpel off the tray and handed it to his colleague, feeling irrationally complicit in something terrible.

Wen lowered the blade to a spot two-thirds of the way down Charlie's thigh, at a point where the skin still looked like human flesh. He glanced over at Franz, who nodded his agreement. Wen-Cheng sliced through the tissue in one fluid movement.

Charlie groaned and kicked his leg. Wen-Cheng's hand froze. His eyes darted over to Sunny. She grimaced as though the knife was cutting into her own leg. "I have nothing more to offer him for pain."

Franz fixed Wen-Cheng with the commanding stare that he had once summoned to motivate hesitant surgical interns. "Do not stop now!" he barked.

Wen-Cheng sliced the blade across the man's thigh. Charlie moaned again, but his leg held still. Franz followed the incision with his sponge, dabbing away blood. The unwholesome odour intensified the deeper Wen-Cheng cut, as did Charlie's stuporous groans. Wen-Cheng deftly dissected out layers of diseased flesh and muscle, then used two sutures to tie off Charlie's femoral artery and vein, the large blood vessels responsible for supplying the leg with blood.

Franz lifted the saw from the tray and, heavy-hearted, passed it to Wen-Cheng.

Chapter 19

Most of the class had been elated about the sudden cancellation of the school day. Not Hannah. The instant she had spotted Ghoya in the hallway, she assumed he had come for her and had almost bolted in the opposite direction. Only her fear of drawing his attention stopped her.

Hannah recognized from the newspapers the tall man who accompanied Ghoya. She couldn't remember his name—did he have some kind of aristocratic title?—but she was certain he was a leader among local Nazis. Despite his distinguished appearance, Hannah sensed malice behind his smile. An Asian man and a young German followed behind, the latter screwing his face into a permanent scowl, as though he were being led through a pigsty.

When Hannah informed Freddy Herzberg of the visitors, he did not seem the least bit concerned. Even when she explained who the men were, he shrugged it off with his usual bluster. "Did you see any soldiers with them?"

"No."

"Are they armed?"

"They're wearing suits."

"So what is there to worry about?"

"A Japanese commander of the ghetto brings Nazis to our school! Doesn't that seem bad?"

For a moment his face darkened, but he brushed her off with another shrug. "We have the day off. We ought to enjoy it."

Hannah did not know how Freddy could be so cavalier, but there seemed to be no point in arguing. She turned down his offer to visit the market and instead headed straight home to share the news with her family.

Hannah found Esther sitting still and silent on the chair in the corner of the living room. She was staring dead ahead at the closed bedroom door, while Jakob slept at her feet in his basket. It took Esther a moment to register Hannah's arrival, then her head snapped toward her niece as though she were emerging from a trance. "Hannah! What are you doing here?"

"They cancelled school today, Tante Essie. We had visitors come to the—"

"You must go now," Esther snapped before Hannah even had a chance to finish. "Frau Eckstein has a skirt that needs hemming. Go fetch it for me. Straight away!"

"Tante," Hannah pleaded. "Ghoya came to the school today. He brought Nazis with him!"

But Esther would not listen. "We will discuss this later. You must go now."

"Why, Tante?"

A loud moaning sound reached her from under the bedroom door, then Hannah heard voices on the other side. She recognized her father and Sunny but could not make out their words. More groans came from inside the room.

Hannah started for the bedroom door.

"No!" As Esther jumped up from her chair, her foot knocked the basket holding Jakob. She dropped to her knees to steady it as Jakob began to howl.

Hannah froze. "What is it, Tante?"

Esther reached into the basket and lifted up Jakob. She cradled him under one arm. "Shush, my darling," she cooed as she gently bounced him up and down.

Jakob settled quickly in her arms. Esther looked over to Hannah. "Your father and Sunny are in the bedroom. They are not alone."

"Who is with them?"

"Dr. Huang." Esther hesitated. "And a patient from the hospital."

Hannah felt her fists clench. "Why would Papa bring a patient into our home?"

"This man is special."

"Special how?"

"He is a friend of Ernst's."

Hannah's heart skipped a beat. "Is Onkel Ernst here, too?" She had not seen him in a year. *Was he really back?*

"Yes. Well, no. He had to . . . to step outside."

Hannah opened her mouth to inquire further when another noise from the bedroom stopped her. She hesitated, then placed it: it sounded like wood being sawed.

Chapter 20

The surgery lasted less than twenty minutes. Although Charlie had remained semi-conscious the whole time, his moans eventually subsided. After Wen-Cheng tied the final suture, he wrapped thick cotton bandages over the freshly created stump.

Charlie swivelled his head drunkenly from side to side while Sunny discreetly tucked the sack holding his amputated limb under the bed.

As Franz was slipping his gloves off, Wen-Cheng said, "Surely you cannot keep the general here."

Franz jerked his head up, one glove still hanging from his hand. "How long have you known?"

"Since the moment I laid eyes on him," Wen-Cheng said as he bent over to finish wrapping the wound.

"Another one," Franz muttered, struck again by how fortunate they were to have not already been arrested. He doubted that their good fortune could hold up for much longer. "I never dreamed Charlie would end up here in our own home."

"He cannot stay." Wen-Cheng pointed to the door. "Not with children out there."

"Absolutely not," Sunny agreed.

Wen-Cheng frowned, deep in thought. "Perhaps we could keep him at my apartment."

Sunny shook her head. "No, Wen-Cheng. That would be too great a risk for you."

Wen-Cheng stared at her for a moment before he turned his attention back to the bandages around Charlie's stump. "Bao Chun has sacrificed far more than I ever have." He paused. "Or ever will."

"Frenchtown is full of spies and informants, Wen-Cheng," Sunny murmured. "What if the Japanese found him in *your* home?"

Franz tried not to read too much into the intimacy of his wife's tone. "Besides, how would we get Charlie to Frenchtown?" he asked. "He's in no shape to travel."

"This is true," Wen-Cheng said.

Franz massaged his temples. "It would be best to take Charlie somewhere nearby."

Sunny nodded. "In the ghetto. Somewhere any of us could tend to him."

"What more can any of us do for him now?" Wen-Cheng asked.

Franz saw the doctor's point, but his pessimistic tone still irked him. "The kind of care—dressing changes, painkillers and so on—that we would offer any post-operative patient," he said pointedly.

"Franz? *Sunny?*" Ernst's frantic voice penetrated the bedroom door. "Is it over?"

Wen-Cheng motioned toward the door. "Go talk to him. I will stay and watch Charlie."

Franz followed Sunny into the apartment's main room, closing the bedroom door firmly behind him.

Esther sat holding Jakob to her chest under a blanket. Ernst stood near the door with an arm draped protectively over Hannah's shoulder. He had found another cigarette and he waved it at them with his free hand. "Well?"

"Hannah-*chen!*" Franz cried. "What are you doing home?"

"They cancelled school today, Papa."

"Yes, lucky for me they did." Ernst pulled Hannah tighter against him. "Now, please. How is Charlie?"

Sunny gave Hannah a little grin before turning to Ernst. "There were no surprises," she said, electing not to mention the ineffective anaesthetic.

"Can I see him?" Ernst asked.

"Give him a few minutes," Sunny said. "He has not fully woken up."

"Papa, Mr. Ghoya came to our school," Hannah said. "He brought Nazis with him. They went through the classrooms. They even spoke to the principal and some of the teachers."

Ernst made a face. "What could those cretins possibly want with your school?"

Franz didn't want to alarm Hannah any further with the news that the same men had trooped through the hospital as though they owned it. "You know the Nazis, *Liebchen*. They have to know what we are up to at all times."

Hannah's face quivered. "Why can't they just leave us be?"

As she clung to Ernst's side, Franz saw Hannah's teenage defiance melt away. She was still just his child. "Doesn't matter what they are up to, Hannah." Franz forced a smile for her. "Colonel Kubota is now ultimately responsible for the refugees. And he will not let them harm us."

"Do you really think so, Papa?"

"Absolutely." He hoped he sounded more certain than he felt.

"So what happens now?" Esther asked from her chair.

Sunny looked blankly to Franz. Before he could answer, they heard a sharp knock at the apartment door.

Silence swallowed the room. No one moved. The knocks only grew louder.

Sunny started for the door, but Franz shot out a hand to hold her back. He considered trying to hide the women and children but realized that it would be pointless. There was nowhere to conceal them.

Go away! Leave us be! Franz thought as he moved toward the door, his heart in his throat. His hand trembled as he slowly pulled the door open. Recognizing Joey and Yang at the threshold, Franz almost laughed in relief.

Joey burst into the room, anxious for details. Yang entered warily, reminding Franz of a stray cat that sensed danger but was too hungry to pass up the prospect of milk. The tiny woman looked even more frail than the last time Franz had seen her. Most of the locals were justifiably frightened of the Japanese, but Yang's terror ran deeper. Soldiers had gunned down her little brother and sister-in-law in the first days of the invasion. Her brother, whom Yang had practically raised, had still been alive when she found him on the sidewalk, clutching at his wife's cold wrist and whimpering for help that was never to come.

Sunny rushed over to Yang and enfolded her in a hug. They chatted in Chinese for a moment, then Yang glanced over Sunny's shoulder at Franz and muttered in Shanghainese.

"What did she say, Sunny?" he asked.

Still embracing Yang, Sunny turned to Franz with a smile. "She will take Charlie in, too."

"Into her home?" Franz asked. "Here in the ghetto?"

"Yes," Sunny said.

Franz pointed to the bedroom door. "Yang, do you understand who that man is in there?"

She nodded without meeting his eyes.

"And you are still willing to take him in?"

"I am." They were the first English words Franz had ever heard Yang speak.

Chapter 21

September 23, 1943

Sunny could see Yang's entire apartment from the doorway. She couldn't imagine how Charlie, Simon and Yang had shared these cramped quarters for the past four months, especially considering that neither man could leave the apartment's confines without risking all of their lives.

Still, Sunny had not seen her old amah so energized since before her father's murder, almost five years earlier. Yang had flourished in her new role as protector of the two fugitives. She guarded them with the same fierce care with which she had once swaddled Sunny. Simon had commented that Yang was like a mother, a cop and a grade-school teacher all rolled up into one tiny terrifying package.

The smell of rice and fish wafted over to Sunny. Yang glanced over from the single burner where she tended to a small pot. "No one saw you enter, Soon Yi?" she demanded.

This was typical. Yang had never been particularly trusting, but of late she was suspicious of everyone, and for good reason. The Kempeitai had ramped up their raids and roundups of locals, often responding to allegations that were imagined or exaggerated. Neighbours were directing suspicion to one another to deflect it from themselves, and Shanghai was infested with informants, some motivated by better rice rations for their hungry families, others driven by opportunism or even spite. Sunny had heard of a woman who, after having felt slighted at a family gathering, had falsely charged her younger brothers with spying. If the rumour were to be believed, all four had been executed. Becoming an informant was as easy as finding an English-speaking Japanese soldier. Sunny knew the risk of exposure was greater than ever.

"I was careful, Yang." Sunny smiled. "No one saw me."

Simon hurried over and crushed her in a hug. His face was still gaunt, but somehow Yang had not allowed either him or Charlie to lose any more weight under her watch. "Essie? Where is she?" were the first words out of Simon's mouth.

"Jakob is napping," Sunny said. "They will visit as soon as he wakes."

Yang had stipulated that Simon's wife and son could visit only on Thursday afternoons, when her elderly neighbours headed out to a friend's home for their weekly game of mah-jong. She worried that the sounds of the mother and baby would seep through the flimsy walls and draw the attention of the old couple, despite their being relatively deaf. Simon and Esther had accepted her condition, since the situation was still preferable to the open-ended separation they had endured during his time at the Comfort Home.

Sunny held up the two English-language books that she had managed to find in the past week. She knew the men would lap up the dog-eared works, especially Charlie, who loved the hard-boiled style of American crime novels.

Simon eagerly accepted the books and studied their covers. "Dashiell Hammett, Charlie!" he called over his shoulder. "We hit the mother lode this week."

Charlie made his way toward her on the old wooden crutches he had borrowed from the hospital, his pant leg pinned up to his thigh. His agility had improved remarkably. Now he was almost graceful. "I hope Sam Spade returns in this one," he said.

Charlie had accepted the loss of his leg without a word of complaint or self-pity. Still, for him, as for everyone else living in the ghetto, the last four months had been anything but easy. A week after the amputation surgery, he developed a pulmonary embolus from a blood clot that had formed in the veins in his other leg and eventually lodged in his lungs. No one expected him to survive. One evening, as Jia-Li and Sunny sat at his bedside listening to him struggle for breath, out of nowhere the previously taciturn general had suddenly announced, "My father killed her."

"Killed who?" Jia-Li asked.

"My mother," he whispered.

Sunny wondered if Charlie had slipped back into a delirium. "Your parents aren't here, Charlie," she said softly.

"No, no," he said. "In Harbin. My home in Manchuria. I was only six."

Jia-Li leaned closer. "Your father murdered her?"

"He beat Mother all the time. She would tell my sister and me that she was clumsy and fell." He paused to try to catch his breath. "But we used to hear the shouts and the beatings from our bed. My sister, Dao-Ming, she is older than me, but I still remember her crying into my shoulder."

"How wretched," Jia-Li murmured.

"One day we woke up and Mother was gone. 'Died in a fall,' Father told us. But we knew better," Charlie grunted. "The next day he left us at the orphanage run by the Methodists."

"Ah," Sunny said. "Is that where you learned to speak English so well?"

Charlie nodded. "They were kind, those missionaries. Every night, the old English reverend, Dr. Woodard, used to read to us. Milton, Shakespeare and always from his old leather-covered Bible." He chuckled weakly. "Dr. Woodard told us we had to learn to speak properly, since God only understood the King's English."

Jia-Li smiled. "Sounds like a better home than your father's."

Charlie stared off into space. He gulped for air, never seeming to swallow enough. "Once I was thirteen, I left the orphanage to track him down. It was how I learned to fight. How I ended up in the army. Even after the Japanese invaded . . . I only wanted to find him . . . to restore Mother's honour." He shut his eyes. "I will never get that opportunity now."

Jia-Li pressed her forehead to his. "Stay with us, Charlie. Please. Do not waste any more time hunting the ghost of your father."

Within hours, Charlie had slipped into a coma that Sunny assumed would prove fatal, but later that day he somehow fought back to consciousness. Within another week, he was breathing more easily, though he had never regained his previous lung capacity. A few turns around the flat could wind him now.

Charlie had never since mentioned his childhood or his desire for revenge on his father. Lately, he had begun to focus his energy on returning to the countryside. Now, he leaned on one crutch and scraped the floor with the other. "The time has come for me to return to my men," he declared quietly.

Yang glanced over her shoulder at him from the stove but said nothing.

"And how do you plan to get there?" Sunny asked.

"Perhaps with the assistance of Jia-Li's . . . employers."

Sunny knew that Jia-Li would do anything for Charlie but also that it would break her friend's heart to see him go. She had never admitted to her feelings, but she was transformed in Charlie's presence. Jia-Li never flirted with him, which was unusual in itself, but it was her awkward self-consciousness around Charlie that told Sunny how hard her friend had fallen. She had even broken off her relationship with the Russian poet.

"No offence, Charlie," Simon said. "But how much help can you be in the field on one leg and half a working lung?"

Charlie shrugged. "Only time will tell, my friend."

Simon rolled his eyes. "No, I am pretty sure the first pothole you overlook will tell."

Charlie only laughed. "Until then, I might be of some use."

"Listen, pal, there are people fighting this war from the inside, too."

Charlie nodded. "The Underground? Here in Shanghai?"

"Underground . . . Resistance . . . whatever they call themselves," Simon said. "We've all heard the stories of the ships they've sunk and convoys they've sabotaged. Not to mention the assassinations. Word is they've got the Japs checking over their shoulders these days."

"I am a soldier, not a spy," Charlie said. "Besides, can you imagine anyone more conspicuous than me?"

Sunny had to agree. She suddenly felt irrationally conspicuous herself. She hated having to conceal her connection to the Underground from her loved ones, but she knew how vehemently they would object, especially Franz.

"I belong with my men," Charlie continued. "Not lying around here, nothing more than a burden and a liability."

"Enough foolishness!" Yang piped up in Chinese, having followed the conversation despite their speaking in English.

"Yang is right," Sunny said. "You are both wanted men. And, Charlie, you are in no shape to go anywhere. The only place for both of you is right here."

The doorknob rattled, and everyone's eyes turned toward it. Yang inched back from the stove as though edging away from a rearing cobra.

Sunny didn't share her amah's alarm. She knew that the Japanese didn't arrive so quietly. The door opened a sliver and Ernst slid through. Carrying a sack of rice under his arm, he flashed Yang a grin. But she turned back to her pot with a scowl, muttering a stream of Chinese curses at him for this unannounced visit.

"I really think that one is warming to me." Ernst motioned to Yang with his lit cigarette. "I do hope she will not be too devastated to learn that my romantic tendencies lie elsewhere."

Simon laughed. "I think you're pretty safe on that front."

Ernst deposited the rice at Yang's feet. She grunted her gratitude in Chinese without looking up.

Ernst was the only person Sunny knew who had gained weight in the past four months. His cheeks had fleshed out and were covered by a full beard. During his time back in Shanghai, he had grown increasingly confident in the anonymity his long hair and scruffy beard afforded him. His attitude verged on cavalier. "Admit it, Sunny," he had recently remarked. "We white devils all look exactly the same to you. Imagine the Japanese trying to recognize me behind this glorious mane."

Daniel Kalla

Ernst had rented an apartment outside the ghetto, in Germantown—a predominantly European-populated neighbourhood within the International Settlement. Adopting the alias Gustav Klimper—a play on the famous Austrian artist Gustav Klimt—he had begun to paint again. Rather than continuing with the raw portraits that had made such a splash on the art scenes of Vienna and Shanghai before the war, he had taken to painting mountainous landscapes featuring fields of wild edelweiss and cityscapes filled with classical architecture. Or, as he described it, "The kind of trite bunk that the Nazis simply cannot get their fill of."

Ernst greeted Sunny with a kiss to either cheek. "Can you believe it?" he said with an amused grin. "They are insisting that I attend one of their meetings."

"Who is 'they'?" she asked.

"My neighbours," Ernst said. "The couple who have bought not one but *two* of my renderings of the Brandenburg Gate. They tell me that Baron von Puttkamer—that megalomaniac from the wireless—will be speaking."

Sunny cringed at the mention of von Puttkamer's name. A month earlier, she had inadvertently tuned in to one of his speeches on Jia-Li's radio. Von Puttkamer spoke softly and with more restraint than many of the other Nazis, but he expressed a similar hateful philosophy, cloaked as always in the grand rhetoric of German nationalism. She understood how he had earned the moniker "Goebbels of Asia."

Simon frowned. "Come on, Ernst, you don't actually plan to go see von Puttkamer in person?"

"A free comedy? Why not?" Ernst looked from Simon to Sunny and the flippancy drained from his expression. "Besides, the Germans here, they mention the Jewish refugees often—too often."

Simon shook his head. "I guess they don't have enough worries, what with the Italians surrendering and the Ruskies advancing westward every day?"

Ernst ran a hand through his thick hair. "The Nazis are nothing if not singularly German in their fixation with Jews."

Sunny remembered that late spring day when she and Franz had run into the Nazi contingent touring the ghetto. Von Puttkamer had been seen in the ghetto on two occasions since. Franz had told her that his visits were just meant to intimidate the refugees, but Sunny could see in her husband's eyes that he too worried that the Nazis might have something more sinister in mind.

"What do you expect to find out from the baron?" Simon grunted. "You think Hitler has had a change of heart? Maybe he wants to rebuild all those synagogues he levelled on Kristallnacht?"

Ernst frowned, as though he were seriously considering Simon's suggestion. "Seems rather unlikely. Still, my neighbours are under the impression that I belong to the Party. After all, I have earned a reputation as a painter whose works glorify the Reich. You never know. Perhaps they might allow me into their inner circle."

"To spy on them?" Simon squinted at him. "Is that what you've got in mind?"

Ernst shrugged. "They trust me so far."

"And if someone recognizes you as Ernst Muhler?" Sunny asked.

"*Ach*, not to worry," Ernst said confidently. "Those fools think they have wiped out the entire avant-garde. Besides, they don't believe in fairies any longer."

*   *   *

Sunny left Yang's flat with a growing sense of unease, and not only because of the inherent risk of Ernst's plan. Her worry deepened as she headed toward the Public Garden. Wen-Cheng had requested another meeting with her there.

Wen-Cheng had thus far been Sunny's only connection to the Underground. He had only ever approached her with an assignment once, three months earlier: a simple task that she had completed by the end of July. Wen-Cheng had asked her to track the movements of a certain Kempeitai officer, Captain Kanamoto. The captain had lost most of his foot to a landmine in Burma. Whether out of convenience or because of his lack of faith in the Shanghai General, Kanamoto had taken to visiting the refugee hospital to have the bandages changed on what was left of his foot. The chronic wound required frequent cleaning, and though any nurse could have tended to it, Kanamoto had started insisting that Sunny perform the procedure.

The captain was fluent in English and coolly polite. He hardly spoke more than a few words to her, and his face never hinted at the agony that he must have endured as she teased away the dressings that invariably stuck to the raw flesh. And yet, behind Kanamoto's impassive eyes, Sunny sensed a hardness and violence. Her stomach turned each time she saw him; more and more, Kanamoto came to remind her of the sailor who had assaulted her and ended up murdering her father.

Sunny surprised herself with the conspiratorial thrill she took in recording the details of Kanamoto's visits: the time of day he arrived, the length of his stay, the number of soldiers accompanying him and the type of vehicle they drove. She kept logs in code, recording series of numbers on the inside flaps of envelopes. To further disguise the communications, she stuffed the envelopes with letters written in Shanghainese to a fictional uncle. Wen-Cheng had sent her to a series of destinations to drop off the envelopes. Once she had deposited them in a hole in a wall created by a mortar shell; another time she slid them under the door of an abandoned shop.

Near the end of July, Kanamoto stopped showing up at the hospital. Sunny realized that the Underground had to be responsible for the captain's disappearance but, when she questioned Wen-Cheng, his only response was a shrug. To her surprise, and slight horror, Sunny experienced no remorse or regret. In fact, she felt a certain satisfaction that verged on thrill—as if her role in Kanamoto's undoing had somehow avenged her father's murder and restored her family's honour.

Sunny suspected that first mission had been as much a test of her resolve as anything else. After all, Wen-Cheng could easily have gathered the same information on Kanamoto himself. As months passed without Wen-Cheng even mentioning the Underground, she had begun to wonder if she had failed her audition. In truth, she hoped that there would be no further missions.

But then, two days earlier, Wen-Cheng had asked her to meet him in the park again. Sunny's heart sank. Despite her initial enthusiasm, the Resistance seemed more mysterious, nebulous and frightening than ever to her. Who were they? The question troubled her. She would catch herself staring at shopkeepers, waitresses and even coolies, wondering whether one of them was carrying a secret message or even concealing a bomb. Although she still felt guilty about Irma and the two teenagers, Sunny rationalized that she was contributing to the war effort enough by helping to hide and care for Charlie. It was about more than just the risks, too. The dark, vengeful side of herself that she had glimpsed after Kanamoto's disappearance scared her almost as much as the danger of being caught.

She entered the Public Garden warily to find the park almost deserted. The scorching summer and subsequent monsoon season's floods had battered the grounds beyond recognition. Sunny spotted Wen-Cheng at the bench where they had met before. To her surprise, across the pathway stood the old man in the grey Zhongshan suit, the one she had pictured a bird fancier. Hoping he would leave soon, she strolled around the perimeter of the park, tripping once over the wild bamboo roots that wove across the pavement like exposed telephone cable.

Finally, when it was clear that the old man was not about to go anywhere, Sunny meandered over to the bench and joined Wen-Cheng. He didn't acknowledge her arrival. They sat together in taut silence, staring out at the withered park.

After a while, the old man finally began to move down the pathway. Sunny assumed he was on his way out of the gardens, but instead he stopped in front of their bench and slowly pivoted toward her. The sun had made his face leathery, and the bags under his eyes resembled rawhide pouches.

"Your husband," the man said in a genteel Shanghainese accent. "In the hospital, he has tended to members of the local Japanese leadership. Is this so?"

Sunny's head swam. Wen-Cheng offered her an encouraging nod, but it took her a few moments to accept that the wistful-looking old man was, in fact, Wen-Cheng's Underground contact. "Yes, yes, it ... er ... is," Sunny stuttered. "Last year, he operated on General Nogomi."

"He saved the governor's life. It was a perforated stomach ulcer," Wen-Cheng offered.

The old man nodded. "And the other leaders—Colonel Tanaka, Vice-Admiral Iwanaka and Colonel Kubota—Dr. Adler is familiar with these men as well?"

"Yes," Sunny said, deciding to not mention that Tanaka had overseen Franz's torture in Bridge House, while Kubota had saved his life and possibly the entire refugee community.

The old man's craggy face was an expressionless mask. If anything, he looked saddened by her answers. "Has your husband been inside the homes of these men?"

Sunny glanced over at Wen-Cheng, unsettled. "No, of course not."

"Their offices inside the Astor House building, then," the old man said. "Has your husband been there?"

Sunny nodded. "I believe Franz has visited all their offices but, as I understand it, Colonel Tanaka's office is not at Astor House," she said. Tanaka was the head of Shanghai's Kempeitai and headquartered elsewhere. "At least, it was not there when the colonel interrogated Franz."

"This is correct," the old man said, his face unreadable. "Tanaka keeps his office at Bridge House, where he can hear the screams from the prisoners below."

Sunny felt embarrassed but said nothing.

"Have you yourself been to their offices?" the old man demanded.

"Only Colonel Kubota's," she blurted and immediately regretted it. She felt as if she had betrayed a friend.

The old man grunted. "We need you to speak to your husband. To learn as much as you can about each of these offices."

She shifted in her seat. "What sort of information?"

"The precise locations. Which floor. Which side of the building.

Where their desks are situated. How many guards are posted inside and out." His tired gaze fell to the ground. "Anything you can possibly find out will be of use."

"My husband—" Sunny began to say but caught herself.

Wen-Cheng laid a hand on her wrist. "Her husband is not involved."

The old man nodded, looking as though he had lost his capacity for surprise. "Surely a clever wife can learn anything that her husband knows."

Chapter 22

"*Warum bin ich lila, Herr Doktor Adler?*" Frau Engelmann demanded from her back. Lying on the stretcher, she held her arms outstretched above her and rolled her wrists left and right to show him that her skin had acquired a violet hue.

Franz stifled a laugh. "You have Dr. Feinstein to thank for that, Frau Engelmann. Of course, you also have him to thank for saving your life."

At the mention of his name, Max Feinstein crossed over from the other side of the ward. "You had two choices, Frau Engelmann," he said without a trace of sympathy. "Be purple or be dead."

"What is the cause of this?" she said, studying her arms with wonder.

"This has been a terrible summer for malaria," Franz said. "The humidity, the flooding, the crowding and all those mosquitoes . . ."

The woman nodded sombrely. Her expression, never naturally cheerful, turned grave. "I lost my niece only last week to malaria. *Aleha hasholem.* God rest the dear soul."

"God?" Max shook his head and sighed. "He seems to be on sabbatical these days."

"Dr. Feinstein!" Frau Engelmann scolded.

Franz held out a hand. "We used to get quinine, our anti-malaria remedy, through the Dutch East Indies but—"

{142}

"*Ach*, that was before the Japanese decided to pillage the Far East—before the Nazis could get there," Max grunted. "I tried violet bismuth because it bears a chemical resemblance to quinine. It's a poor stand-in. Nowhere near as effective. And anyone who takes it will turn one shade or other of purple from head to toe."

The woman laughed humourlessly. "On balance, Dr. Feinstein, I would rather be purple than be dead."

Max let out a snort, as if doubting the wisdom of her choice. Without another word, he turned away.

Frau Engelmann stared up at Franz. "Will the doctor be all right?"

Franz considered it. "I wish I could answer that."

"I heard about Dr. Feinstein's daughter and her poor children . . ." Her voice dropped to a hush. "They never made it out, did they?"

"No."

Max had not heard a word from his daughter in three years. Although Max had never said as much, the internist had clearly resigned himself to the fact that his only daughter and her family was already lost. Max and his devoted wife, Sarah, never spoke of their daughter in front of him, but Franz found it difficult to spend time with the couple, especially at their home. Photographs of the family papered their walls, and their daughter's absence was a spectre in the room.

Frau Engelmann's face creased with concern again. "Dr. Adler, do you believe the . . . the rumours?"

"Who knows what to believe anymore?" Franz still tried to convince himself that the persistent whispers among the refugees about mass murders in Eastern Europe were nothing more than hysteria and fear mongering. But it was no use. Last year he had spoken with a man named Aaron Grodenzki, a Polish Jew who had escaped from the concentration camp at Chełmno. Franz had met the man only once, and the Pole did all the talking. He could still picture Grodenzki struggling to grasp his coffee cup with his damaged hands; frostbite had spared only one finger. He could hear Grodenzki's mechanical description of SS men cramming trucks full of men, women and children—including Grodenzki's own parents and sister—then redirecting the exhaust back inside and running the vehicles until the screams died away. Grodenzki's empty eyes, more than his words, had convinced Franz that he was telling the truth. His last doubts vanished two weeks later when Grodenzki leapt to his death from the twentieth floor of the Park Hotel.

Franz turned from the bedside. "I will check in on you later, Frau Engelmann."

His thoughts wandered to his own family. Few days passed when the loss of his father and brother did not cross his mind. But it was almost a relief not to have left any relatives behind to suffer as Max's presumably had.

*   *   *

As Franz headed down Ward Road, the bright sunshine lifted his mood. The late August heat wave had abated and the monsoon season had come and gone. Three weeks before, a typhoon had pounded Shanghai, flooding the streets and causing mayhem for those with ground-floor apartments, like the Adlers. Water had pooled ankle deep inside, but they had managed to dry out their home over a few days. Still, Sunny's antique rugs, a cherished inheritance from her father, had been ruined and, despite the windows being kept open, the sewage-stained water all around gave off a smell strong enough to quell Franz's appetite.

The Adlers had weathered other storms, too. The Japanese still had not connected Charlie to the refugee hospital but, in the early summer, the donations of medical supplies had ceased as abruptly as they had begun. Only an impassioned plea from Franz to the leaders of the Russian Jewish community—with Joey translating almost in pantomime—had persuaded the Russians to continue funding the refugee hospital, albeit at a bare-bones level. The availability of medication was more sporadic than ever, and sometimes the hospital ran only by candlelight. But it had remained open for the summer, and with the help of Max's violet bismuth concoction, they had already saved numerous lives during the malaria outbreak.

Franz's concerns over his daughter's mood had lessened, too. He was pleased to see glimmers of her old joie de vivre. Esther's spirits had also improved. Now that she had weekly contact with Simon, she had truly become a fawning Jewish mother—fussing over Hannah and the adults almost as much as she did Jakob. Esther had reason to take joy in her son. At seven months old, Jakob had a smile for everyone and possessed an infectious tinkling laugh.

Franz was pulled from his thoughts by the sight of two men approaching from across the street. They wore red, white and green armbands and were locked in a lively conversation, their hands as busy as their lips. Franz knew that, up until a few weeks earlier, the Italian government had been allied with the Japanese. However, after the Italian defeat in Europe, overnight her citizens had gone from welcome guests to hostile aliens in Shanghai. The Italians were facing the same threat of internment that had befallen the local British, Dutch, American and Canadian nationals.

Italy's sudden switch of allegiance typified the confusing and contradictory nature of recent war developments. Franz had no access to a wireless at home. He had turned down the offer of a free radio from a grateful engineer from Potsdam whose appendix he had removed. The penalty for possessing unauthorized radios was steep, and Franz wasn't willing to gamble on Hannah's or Jakob's safety. Despite the danger, many refugees, including some of the nurses and doctors at the hospital, did conceal wirelesses, and Franz sometimes dropped in on their homes to catch up on war news. The reports were inconsistent and changed by the hour. Depending on the weather, the signal from Allied stations such as the BBC or CBS was often too weak to pick up, so they were often forced to listen to the Japanese-censored or even local German broadcasts, which invariably told a very different story. Regardless of the source, though, the facts were inescapable: the Allies were steadily gaining ground in Europe and the Pacific. With each success—the Soviet recapture of Kharkiv, the sinking of the German battleship *Tirpitz* or the fall of the Solomon Islands—the optimism among the refugees grew. But Franz's own hope was tempered by the steadily worsening conditions in the ghetto. Franz feared that the refugee community might not be able to sustain itself until an Allied victory, if it ever came.

The two Italians waved to him, and Franz reciprocated. As he rounded the corner, he ran into Hannah and Ernst walking arm in arm. He was surprised by the sight: of late, she steadfastly avoided physical contact with her father in public.

"Papa!" Hannah's face beamed. "Onkel Ernst just bought me a strudel at Kaplan's. The absolute best in the world."

"*Wunderbar.*" Franz tried, unsuccessfully, to remember when he'd last tasted strudel. Still, he fed off Hannah's contentment. "It's good you have such a rich uncle."

Ernst stuck out his lower lip. "The worse I paint, the better the Nazis pay me. If I produce much more of this schlock, they just might make me Führer like they did with that crazy little third-rate painter."

Hannah giggled. "Stop it, Onkel Ernst. Someone might hear."

Ernst rolled his eyes. "Let them."

Hannah slid her arm free of Ernst. "I must go meet my friend."

"Would this friend be Freddy, by chance?" Ernst asked.

"We have homework," Hannah mumbled. She spun away just as the colour crept into her cheeks. "Thank you again, Onkel Ernst. Bye-bye, Papa," she called over her shoulder.

Ernst watched her hurry off. "You do realize that your daughter is in love."

"Ernst, you exaggerate," Franz said. "Only a teenage crush, surely. She is just a schoolgirl, after all."

"Love is love."

"What has she told you?"

"Nothing, really." Ernst tapped his temple. "You might not know it from my recent work, but I still have the eye. I am attuned to emotion. Besides, the girl positively glows at the mere mention of his name."

Franz bristled at the thought of his daughter having romantic feelings. He knew precious little of Freddy or his family. Besides, she was his little girl. Franz was not ready to accept any of it. "Precisely, you are an artist. Prone to romanticism, fantasy and excess."

"Guilty on all counts." Ernst held up both hands in a *mea culpa*. "Still, I am not wrong about Hannah."

Eager to change the subject, Franz looked up and down the street to convince himself that no one was within earshot. "Have you visited Simon and Charlie recently?"

Ernst nodded. "This morning. I spent most of the time trying to talk Charlie out of sneaking out of the city."

Franz sighed. "Never mind his leg, with those weakened lungs of his ..."

"Charlie wouldn't stand a chance on two legs, let alone one. But at heart, he is a soldier. It's all he knows, really."

"Will he stay, then?"

"This week, perhaps." Ernst inclined his head. "He will not stay indefinitely. Of that, I am certain."

"We must delay him as long as we can."

"Agreed." Ernst leaned in close enough for Franz to catch a whiff of his hair grease. He lowered his voice. "I went to that rally last night."

Franz frowned. "Ernst, you are still a fugitive."

Ernst flicked at his long hair and then stroked his beard. "The Japanese don't recognize me. And those philistines I sell art to as Gustav Klimper have never heard of Ernst Muhler or any real artist of my generation."

Franz was not convinced, but he was too intrigued to argue. "The rally?" he prompted.

"Von Puttkamer spoke. He is something, that baron."

"What did he say?"

"Oh, the usual Nazi doublespeak and claptrap. More nonsense about how all the recent retreats and withdrawals are part of some brilliant strategy. As best as I can tell, Hitler and Göring plan to win the war by fighting backwards."

Franz laughed nervously but didn't comment.

"Still, von Puttkamer is very persuasive." Ernst lowered his voice to a hush. "He spent much of the time talking about you."

Franz felt his gut tightening. "The refugees?"

"All of the city's Jews. The Russians and Shanghailanders too."

"What did he say about us?"

"That you have no business being here."

"Some surprise," Franz snorted.

"Like a scratched recording, I realize. However, there was something different about it this time."

"Different in what way?"

Ernst dug a cigarette out of his shirt pocket and lit it. "He sounded almost . . . smug. As though . . ." He frowned, searching for the right words. "He kept talking about what he called the 'Jewish question.' It was as if he had some kind of plan."

More than fearful, Franz suddenly felt drained, as though he had not slept in days. Almost five years and ten thousand miles separated him from Vienna—and Kristallnacht—and yet here he was being dragged back into the snake pit of anti-Semitism. It would never end. "Did the baron mention any specifics?" he mumbled.

"None." Ernst shook his head. "Maybe it's nothing. I could be wrong. I hope I am. But on my way out, I overheard a group of young men talking about their visit to the ghetto and how it could not come soon enough."

Fighting off a shudder, Franz considered von Puttkamer's recent visits to their neighbourhood. He had long suspected that they represented some form of reconnaissance, but what could the Nazis possibly have in mind? An old-fashioned pogrom? Like the way the Cossacks used to raid Jewish villages?

Ernst kept talking, but Franz was lost in his own thoughts. Before long, the artist stopped and stared at him expectantly. "Should I go, Franz?"

"Go where?"

"To meet von Puttkamer," Ernst said impatiently. "In person. He and my neighbour were school chums in Berlin. He says he will take me to dinner with the baron and his inner circle."

"You really think you can infiltrate that group?"

"Why not?"

Before Franz could list the many reasons that came to mind, the growl of an engine drew his attention. Moments later, a Japanese military vehicle pulled up to the curb beside them. As soon as it crunched to a stop, the driver climbed out and hurried over to open the rear passenger door. A young officer emerged, followed by Ghoya in his usual pinstriped suit. After Ghoya, Colonel Kubota emerged and struggled to pull himself upright in the street. He waved off the young officer's extended hand and eventually reached his feet without assistance.

Ghoya motioned to Franz and exclaimed, "Dr. Adler!"

Franz's stomach plummeted. His eyes involuntarily shifted to Ernst, who, despite a slight pallor, looked as calm as ever. Ernst had once practically ripped a painting off Kubota's wall to protest the atrocities the Japanese were visiting upon the Chinese, particular the family of his lover. Franz knew that Ernst's new hairdo and beard would never deceive the colonel.

Ghoya led Kubota over to them. The little man waved a hand at Ernst as though he were not even present. "This man. I do not recognize him, Dr. Adler. He is not a refugee?"

"No." Franz said, meeting Ghoya's gaze. "We are old friends from Vienna."

"Is he a Jew?"

Franz's heart beat in his throat. "No, as I said—"

"I have been called worse." Ernst chuckled as he extended a hand to Ghoya. "My name is Klimper. Gustav Klimper."

Looking surprised, Ghoya met the handshake. Ernst turned and offered a hand to Kubota. The colonel viewed him carefully, but his lined face gave away nothing. Finally, he transferred his cane to his unsteady left hand and reached out with his right. "I am Colonel Kubota." A small smile appeared on his face. "Your name, it sounds very similar to that famous Austrian artist."

"Gustav Klimt."

Kubota nodded. "Yes. I greatly admire Klimt's work. In fact, I have become somewhat partial to Austrian art in general." He paused. "Except, of course, those paintings that possess more political overtones. They do not interest me in the least."

Chapter 23

Hannah pressed her lips to the soft folds of Jakob's belly and blew noisily. The infant squealed with delight and broke into a giggle that spread through the room. Even Franz chuckled as he knelt in front of the Chinese stove. Moments earlier, he had been mired in frustration as he struggled to ignite the damp charcoal briquettes.

"He adores you, Hannah," Sunny said from where she stood beside Esther at the countertop, picking maggots out of uncooked rice.

Hannah shrugged. "He would love anyone who blew on his tummy."

"He might laugh for anyone," Esther said. "But love? No, Sunny is correct. You are one of his favourites."

Jakob stared up at Hannah with liquid brown eyes and a wide grin. She warmed at the thought of being her little cousin's favourite. "Rabbi Hiltmann says that it's a *bracha*—a true blessing—to have a baby in our home."

"I agree with the rabbi." Sunny's eyes darted over to Franz, whose back was turned to the room as he wrestled with the uncooperative briquettes.

Hannah had seen that look on her stepmother's face before. She often gazed at Jakob with more than just affection; there was longing in her eyes, too. For months, Hannah had been expecting her father to announce that a baby sibling was on its way.

One day the week before, as she helped Sunny change Jakob's diaper, Hannah had asked her, "Do you and Papa not want a baby?"

Sunny smiled as she slid off the wet rag. "Who wouldn't want to have little Jakob?"

"No. A baby of your own."

Sunny's hand froze, the soaked diaper dangling from her hand. "It's not so simple, Hannah," she said quietly.

Hannah remembered one of her teachers at the old Jewish school telling her that, as much as she loved children, she and her husband were not capable of having their own. Hannah flushed with embarrassment, assuming that Sunny meant something similar. "I'm sorry. I did not . . . er . . . know that you could not . . ."

"No, Hannah, it's not that." Sunny smiled. "I believe your father and I could have babies. I—we—would love nothing more than to have a little playmate for Jakob. But it would mean another mouth to feed." She looked away. "I am not convinced that would be fair to anyone, especially the child."

"Fair? What does that have to do with anything? If you want a baby, we would all help. We would find a way. He could have some of my rice. I'm so sick of it anyway."

"Oh, Hannah." Sunny leaned forward and kissed her on the cheek. "You are so special, you know that? I hope you don't object, but I think of you as my child—well, hardly a child—but you understand."

"I would never object." Hannah wrapped her arms around Sunny in a tight hug. Her stomach fluttered guiltily when she remembered having led her father to believe that Sunny was somehow responsible for her low mood months back.

Hannah let go of Sunny. "Can I ask your advice?" She felt her face begin to warm again and looked down at Jakob, who shook his rattle contentedly.

Sunny bit her lip, stifling a grin. "Does it concern Freddy?"

Hannah nodded without looking up.

"He's a charmer, that one."

"Exactly. He is so charming to everyone. I cannot tell if . . . if Freddy views me any differently from the others."

"But surely you already know, Hannah. He spends so much time with you. He is always looking for you."

"That is only because I help his family."

Sunny's eyes narrowed. "You help his family? How so?"

"No. No!" Hannah waved her hand, desperate not to raise suspicion. She had not yet told anyone about her illicit courier activities. "I . . . I help Freddy with his homework. He is hopeless at mathematics. And sometimes I help Frau Herzberg around the home while I am there."

Sunny nodded impassively. "Listen, Hannah, no boy would spend so much time with a girl simply for help with mathematics. Or for any reason like that. Unless he felt something more for her."

"Do you think so?"

"I know so." Sunny grinned. "Look at you. You're so beautiful. What boy wouldn't want to be with you?"

"I am not like other girls. I'm only half-Jewish. And . . ." she held up her left hand.

"Oh, Hannah, I know what it means to be different, too. Look at me. I am neither white nor Chinese." Sunny winked. "But being a little different only makes you that much more special."

Jakob pulled Hannah out of the memory by pawing at her arm for attention. Hunching forward, she blew into his belly again and was rewarded with another eruption of giggles.

Sunny looked over to her husband. "Franz, I had to pass Astor House yesterday. I had not seen it in ages."

"Oh?" Franz said, still struggling to light the stove. "Why were you in that part of town?"

"I met Jia-Li for tea. She insists on going to the Bund, even though most of the restaurants and stores are closed." Sunny dug another maggot out from the rice. "The Japanese still govern the city from that lovely old hotel, do they not?"

"As far as I know, yes," Franz said.

"You have been inside the governor's office."

Franz craned his neck to look at her. "Only the once."

"There were still so many guards posted out front of Astor House." Sunny shook her head. "If I know the Japanese, General Nogomi must have a grand office. Is he in one of the penthouse suites?"

Franz shrugged. "He was last year. On the sixth floor."

"What was his office like?"

Franz flung his free hand up in the air. "I hardly noticed. We were only there to plead our case. You remember we had to beg Nogomi to stop the Nazis—" Making eye contact with Hannah, he stopped short of finishing the sentence. He would have preferred to shield her from the truth, but at school she had already heard all the rumours about the Nazis' plot to exterminate Shanghai's refugees.

"Still, I can only imagine that Nogomi's office must be quite something," Sunny persisted.

"The meeting didn't go as planned, remember? The general threw us out. And then I ended up in Bridge House."

Hannah remembered her father returning from Bridge House with his face bruised almost beyond recognition and a plaster cast covering one arm from fingers to elbow. She had pestered him for details, but all he would offer was a forced chuckle and jokes that the food was inedible and the mattress uncomfortable. Hannah knew from his eyes that he had endured hell during his week of captivity, but she never heard him discuss it.

"With any luck, none of us will see the inside of the general's office again." Franz looked up at Sunny. "Why are you so interested in what it looks like?"

She exhaled softly. "As you say, Nogomi almost sealed our fate. Everything that happens in Shanghai, for all of us . . . it all rests with him and *that* office. I am curious to picture it in my head."

"Me too, Papa," Hannah said. Even Esther nodded her agreement.

The perplexity left Franz's face and he broke into a small grin. "It's grander than you might imagine. Nogomi has a fancy Chinese desk and antique Victorian furniture everywhere. He's in the centre of the top floor of the hotel and has a stunning view of the ships and sampans floating on the Whangpoo. But his desk faces away from the window." He nodded to himself. "I will never forget how it smelled. So strongly of jasmine. But I never spotted a single flower in the whole room."

Hannah lowered Jakob into his makeshift playpen on the floor. He looked up at her, seemingly more disappointed than upset. She excused herself, explaining to the others that she had to meet a friend to finish their homework. Sunny flashed her a knowing look but said nothing.

*   *   *

Freddy Herzberg was already waiting out front for her. He wore the much-admired bomber jacket that his parents had given him at the beginning of the school year, though the weather was still warm enough to go comfortably in shirtsleeves.

"Hiya, Banana." The nickname still made her blush. "What took you so long?"

Freddy threw an arm around her neck and pulled her toward him in a friendly headlock. She picked up the alcoholic scent of his aftershave and realized that he must shave every morning like her father did. For some inexplicable reason, this excited her. As their faces neared, she thought—hopefully, nervously—that he might kiss her. But it wasn't to be—at least, not now.

"I was helping my family with supper," she said.

He laughed. "How hard is it to make rice and water?"

"You shouldn't joke, Freddy. At least we have food."

He flashed a broad grin. "If you want to call it that, Banana."

As always, Freddy spoke English. Hannah had a hard time imagining him in Vienna; lately, she was even having trouble seeing him as Jewish. He sounded and acted far more like Mickey Rooney than someone who was born "Fritsch Herzberg." Then again, she had heard that many of the matinee idols in Hollywood were Jews who anglicized their names. *Surely not Mickey Rooney?*

"You ready to go across again tomorrow?" he asked.

In the past month, Hannah had smuggled more than just jewellery out of the ghetto for the Herzbergs. Two weeks earlier, she had practically waddled past the checkpoint after concealing perfume bottles in her skirt. She was terrified that they would clank together and draw the attention of the refugee guard. Rumour was that Ghoya had been demanding better "results" from his *pao-chia* guards—meaning more arrests and confiscations. The day before, two more refugees had been flogged on the ghetto's main street after being caught sneaking back into the ghetto twenty minutes after curfew.

"Pop has an idea that will fill our plates with a lot more than rice," Freddy continued.

Her face tensed. Every time Freddy's father had a new idea, it seemed to involve something risky. "Oh, what is it now?"

Freddy folded his arms across his chest. "Nah. Doesn't sound like you want to hear it. Just forget it."

She reached out and touched his elbow. "Tell me, Freddy."

A big smile spread across his face. His eyes swept the street and he lowered his voice. "Okay, up until now, all we do is carry stuff out. Basically, we're fencing the last of our own belongings for a few miserable bucks."

Hannah could feel the muscles in her neck and chest tightening. "And so?"

"Some people inside the ghetto still have money." He chuckled. "We are, after all, Jews, aren't we?"

Hannah didn't like his tone, but still holding on to his elbow, she merely nodded.

"What do the people stuck inside the ghetto need most, Hannah?"

"Food, medicine, clean water . . ."

"Yeah, yeah, yeah. The essentials." He dismissed them with a wave of his hand. "But what one thing do they really want?"

It took a moment, but she had the answer even before Freddy raised two fingers to his lips. "Cigarettes."

"Cigarettes," he echoed, beaming.

She dropped her hand from his elbow. "You want me to smuggle cigarettes *into* the ghetto?"

Freddy nodded eagerly. "Think about it. Outside the ghetto, you can buy cigarettes from the Chinese merchants on Nanking Road at ten or twenty cents on the dollar. A single run, and we could make twenty or thirty dollars. Maybe more." He stared at her hard. "Imagine how much more than just rice that would put on our dinner tables."

She could feel the hairs on the back of her neck standing up. "How would I carry cartons of cigarettes past the guards?"

Freddy patted the front of his bomber jacket and chuckled. "First step is to get you a roomier coat."

Chapter 24

"Do you think anyone still calls it the 'Jewel of the Bund'?" Jia-Li asked Sunny as they strolled past the columned entrance of the Hong Kong and Shanghai Bank.

"It's not much of a jewel anymore." Sunny vividly recalled how people used to line up to rub the paws of the two bronze lions that had once perched at either side of the entrance, guarding the bank. So many Chinese believed in the superstition that promised good fortune from the lions' touch that their metal paws had been buffed to gleaming nubs.

"I used to love coming here with you and your father." Jia-Li motioned to the unmarked intersection. "Remember? He would always buy us those delicious *cí fàn tuán* they sold at that corner stand."

"Nothing tasted better," Sunny agreed with a pang of melancholy, thinking about her father more than those achingly sweet sticky rolls. Her father had taken a dim view of the paw-rubbing ritual, like he did most Chinese superstitions. He was a man of science, a dedicated physician and diabetes specialist. He was also a devoted anglophile, and the British bank was his favourite building in Shanghai. He appreciated the towering structure for its grandeur, but he loved the old bank even more for the empire it represented.

A huge Rising Sun now hung from the bank and, today, it flapped listlessly in the breeze. Sunny had no idea what the Japanese used the building for, but soldiers were guarding the entry to keep away civilians. The lions, like her father, were long gone; rumour had it the Japanese had taken them away to be melted down.

"It's been almost five years, *bǎo bèi,*" Sunny said. "I still miss Father as though he died only last week. Will that ever stop?"

Jia-Li shook her head. "Nor should it, *xiǎo hè.* You keep him alive in your memory."

"I hope so."

"I miss him too," Jia-Li said. "He was far more of a father to me than that weak man who passed for mine."

Sunny had fonder memories of Jia-Li's father. He was a jovial man who always had a silly joke at hand or loose change to spare for the girls. However, he had never been around much, and gambling debts drove him to take his own life when the girls were only thirteen years old. Sunny suspected that Jia-Li's feelings had more to do with her father's suicide than how he'd actually treated her. She viewed his death as a betrayal; it had saddled the family with a large debt. But Sunny had learned from previous experience to keep those thoughts to herself.

"Besides, you have Franz now," Jia-Li pointed out.

"Yes, yes, I do," she murmured as she looked out toward the harbour.

Jia-Li pounced on the wistfulness of her tone. "What's wrong, *xiǎo hè?*"

"Nothing."

Jia-Li stopped. "Tell me."

Sunny slowed to a halt. "You know Franz. He carries the burden of the hospital on his shoulders. The whole refugee community, for that matter."

"You think he cares too much?"

"It is all too much. The hospital, the refugees, Simon, Charlie, Ernst—Franz feels responsible for them all. He works himself to the bone, and when he does go to bed, he is so restless. He doesn't sleep more than a few hours each night." She shook her head. "It's simply too much."

"Have you spoken to him?"

"I've tried."

Jia-Li arched an eyebrow. "Tried?"

"The last few months, *bǎo bèi* ..." Sunny searched for the words. "They have not been the same."

"It sounds as though he is just exhausted."

"That might explain it, yes." Sunny knew there was more to it. Whether it was because of her concealed involvement in the Resistance or her guilt about it, a wedge was growing between her and Franz. The previous night as they lay in bed together, Franz had become suspicious when she pressed for more details about General Nogomi's office. "Sunny, why do you keep asking about Astor House?" He sat up in the bed. "What could possibly interest you so much?"

Sunny's mind raced, searching for something plausible. "I can't stop thinking about him, and the power he lords over us all—it's life and death."

Franz looked hard at her. "And what does the location of his desk or the number of soldiers guarding his office have to do with that?"

"Oh, Franz, none of it matters at all." She wrapped her fingers over the sinewy muscles in his forearm. "It's just ..."

"Just what, Sunny?"

"I want to picture it in my head. That's all." She inwardly cringed as she piled one lie upon the next. Sweat started to bead under her arms. She worried that her face would soon start perspiring, too.

His forehead furrowed. "What possible purpose would it serve, Sunny?"

"To fantasize, I suppose."

He eyed her in disbelief. "I do not understand."

She massaged the inside of his arm, loathing herself for this crude attempt at seducing information out of him. "Remember how we celebrated the night the Allies recaptured Sicily? Or when the Solomon Islands fell? Don't you ever dream of what it would be like if the Allies were to liberate Shanghai?"

Franz shook his head softly. "That will not happen any time soon."

"Still, I love to imagine it. I picture General Nogomi standing behind his desk with his head bowed. A shameful surrender. Maybe even handing a ceremonial sword over to the liberators."

The wrinkles in his forehead smoothed. "It's dangerous to think that way, Sunny."

"Why do you say that?"

"It could lead to foolish actions."

"Or it might inspire us to persevere?"

Franz gently pulled his arm free of her hand. "True, hope can sustain a person," he said. "But too much of it can create unrealistic expectations—and heartbreak."

Sunny wanted to tell Franz that hope was not the issue. She had no idea when, or even if, Shanghai would be liberated. She was just so tired of feeling helpless. Every day she had less to offer at the hospital, which had been depleted of almost everything needed to offer meaningful care. She was desperate to somehow contribute to the alleviation of the suffering and misery that the Japanese occupation was bringing to all of her people: the Chinese, the Shanghailanders and the Jews. Besides, despite her mixed feelings, she still valued the sense of purpose that her first assignment had brought her.

Now, as Sunny stood on the pavement across from her best friend, she had to resist the urge to tell Jia-Li about her connection to the Underground. But she had no right to burden her with such a dangerous secret. Besides, she sensed from Jia-Li's distracted manner and uncharacteristic restlessness that she was wrestling with her own troubles. Sunny hazarded a guess as to their source. "Do you think Charlie will stay much longer?"

Jia-Li shrugged. "He says he will leave by month's end, with or without our help."

Sunny looked back out to the bustling harbour. Naval ships and merchant crafts speckled the river. The Rising Sun flew everywhere. Near the dock, she sighted the *Conte Biancamano*, the Italian luxury liner that had carried the Adlers to Shanghai from Europe. The Japanese had seized the ship in the wake of the Italian surrender and were refitting it as a troop transport ship. "Charlie's departure would be both selfish and foolish," Sunny said.

"Selfish?" Jia-Li placed her hands on her hips. "Charlie is being noble. He sees a cause bigger than himself. And he's willing to die for it."

"And how will his death—which will almost certainly come before he has even escaped the city limits—help anyone?"

"You underestimate him."

Sunny shook her head. "I know what he has accomplished. But, *bǎo bèi*, that was when he had two legs and lungs that still worked. In a few more months, he might be stronger. His breathing might improve. Perhaps then he can make it back to his men."

"He doesn't think he can wait any longer."

Sunny was distracted by an unfamiliar warbling sound overhead. She glanced up but could see nothing aside from pillowy clouds. She turned back to Jia-Li. "Then you have to convince Charlie otherwise."

"The man is a war hero. Why would he listen to a prostitute?"

Sunny grimaced. "What kind of nonsense is that, Ko Jia-Li?"

"It's true."

Sunny softened her tone. "Surely you have noticed the way he looks at you."

Jia-Li reddened. "Charlie looks at me no differently than he does Yang."

The warbling sound grew louder. Sunny glanced upward again. "Really? I'm not convinced Charlie is smitten with Yang."

"*Smitten?* With me?" Jia-Li reached out and touched Sunny's shoulder. "Do you think he is, *xiǎo hè?*"

Sunny had hardly ever seen her world-wise friend so flustered. "And he's clearly not alone, *bǎo bèi,*" Sunny said with a chuckle.

Jia-Li touched her throat in mock outrage. "You think that I have a crush on—"

Her words were cut off by the sound of aircraft engines. A formation of planes suddenly broke through the clouds. They descended so rapidly toward the river that Sunny thought they must be in a nosedive. Their engines whirred with a pitch lower than that of the Japanese fighters, the Zeroes, which normally patrolled the skies.

The sidewalk vibrated as the planes flew low enough for Sunny to make out the markings painted across their noses: a pair of predatory eyes and an open mouth full of jagged teeth. Stars and stripes were tattooed along the sides of the fuselages.

"The Americans!" Jia-Li yelled over the roar.

The planes—Sunny counted eight of them—banked simultaneously over the river, flying parallel to the shoreline before swooping down on the *Conte Biancamano*. Their wings spat fire, and water sprayed out of the river. The *rat-tat-tat* of the machine guns almost drowned out the sound of the engines.

Puffs of smoke rose from the turret of a nearby Japanese gunship as it returned fire. The planes banked again and circled tightly for a second strafing run over the ship. An air-raid siren wailed. Other sirens blared too as military vehicles roared down the Bund in both directions. Pedestrians scurried for shelter under buildings' overhangs. Sunny and Jia-Li stood frozen, both of them stunned by the sight of the aerial assault.

The American planes circled and made a third run past the *Conte Biancamano*. Flames began to lap at the ship's stern. The bitter stench of smoke and cordite filled the air.

More airplanes appeared on the horizon over Putong, on the eastern shore of the river. Even from a distance, Sunny recognized the shape of the Zeroes as they zoomed over to meet the Allied planes.

The American fighters suddenly banked ninety degrees and flew directly over Sunny's head, gaining altitude as they began their westward departure. The Zeroes raced behind them in chase, but in moments the American fighters had reached the outskirts of the city. Sunny knew nothing about aerial warfare, but she doubted the Zeroes could catch the Americans. At least, she hoped not.

"Those were the Flying Tigers," Jia-Li whispered in awe when the rumble of machinery finally faded.

Stories about the elite American air squadron that fought alongside the Free Chinese had been circulating in Shanghai for months, but Sunny had never heard of anyone seeing the planes anywhere near the city.

As she looked out at the burning hull of the *Conte Biancamano*, she was filled with a mix of sadness—this was the ship that had brought Franz to her—and optimism. Still, it was proof that the Japanese were vulnerable even in Shanghai. Perhaps their aggression could be countered after all?

As the minutes passed, the sirens subsided and pedestrians reappeared on the sidewalk.

Jia-Li looked at her watch. "I am running short on time. I promised Chih-Nii I would be in early." She cleared her throat. "There are a . . . a number of ships in port this weekend."

Fighting off the image of drunken sailors pawing at her best friend, Sunny leaned forward and wrapped her in a hug. "I will see you soon, *bǎo bèi.*"

"And I will talk to Charlie." Jia-Li broke into a huge smile. "Perhaps he will reconsider now that the Americans have finally shown up in Shanghai."

*   *   *

After Jia-Li left for Frenchtown, Sunny continued southward along the Bund until she reached the Old Chinese City. During the sixteenth century, the area had been surrounded by thirty-foot-high walls to protect it from raiding Japanese pirates. *But those pirates own the city now,* she thought bitterly.

Despite the Old City's reputation as a tourist trap for Westerners in search of what they believed to be "the authentic Orient," the bustling market had been one of her favourite places to visit with her father. Its stores and stalls were a kaleidoscope of colours and sounds, offering everything from furniture to lanterns. Artisans would sit outside their stores as they worked. Jewellers fastened pieces of jade in delicate silver settings, while tailors embroidered astonishing cheongsams. Sunny used to love watching the toy makers carve gorgeous puppets from sandalwood or pine.

As Sunny stepped through the arch of the north gateway, the reality of war wiped away her nostalgia. Half the stores were boarded up or abandoned. The ones still open offered up a meagre selection of merchandise, their windows near empty. Few people were here to buy, and the once lively merchants seemed as lacklustre as their stock. Even their sales pitches, which Sunny remembered as relentless and confident, sounded unconvincing and hollow.

Sunny hurried through the market until she reached the open square that housed the Woo Sing Ding tea house, which sat on stone pillars in the middle of a man-made lake. Two distinctive zigzag bridges connected the ornate two-hundred-year-old tea house to land on either side. She spotted Wen-Cheng sitting on a bench across from the tea house. As usual, he held a newspaper open in front of his face, but she recognized his clothing and posture. Circling the lake toward him, Sunny felt only gnawing regret.

She sat down on the far end of the bench. "How are you today, Soon Yi?" Wen-Cheng asked from behind his paper.

"Nervous," she replied tersely. "Is it necessary to meet in such public places?"

His shoulders rose and fell. "I do only as I am told."

Although the open square wasn't particularly crowded, Sunny irrationally sensed eyes on her from every direction. "Doesn't this . . . work . . . frighten you, Wen-Cheng?"

"It terrifies me." He calmly turned a page. "But it is far too late to second-guess my decision."

"I wish I could be so philosophical."

His lips creased into a slight smile. "My wife, my parents, my job, the family business—they are all gone. This is much less of a gamble for me."

"Than for me?"

"Yes." Wen-Cheng lowered his newspaper. His eyes darted over to her. "I have already lost everything I once held dear. Including you, Soon Yi."

His meaning was unmistakable. Their romance had amounted to no more than a promise, but she still remembered how desperately she had once pined for him. The recollection only compounded her guilt. "Wen-Cheng, you know that Franz and I . . ."

"I know," he said, unperturbed. "I am merely pointing out that I have less to lose than you do. I wish . . ." He hesitated. "That I had never involved you."

His tone surprised Sunny and, if she was honest, disappointed her a little, too. "It was always my choice, Wen-Cheng. Remember? I insisted."

A minute or two of pained silence passed between them while Wen-Cheng continued to pretend to read. Sunny looked to her right and saw the old man in the Zhongshan suit limping slowly toward them. She wondered again how high the man ranked within the Resistance, or whether the organization even possessed that much structure or hierarchy. Did one cell within the Underground even know what the others were up to? Or did it all amount to a series of uncoordinated acts, no more damaging than fleas pestering a dog?

But Sunny held her tongue as the elderly man lowered himself creakily onto the bench between her and Wen-Cheng. He stared straight ahead at the rounded roofline of the tea house. "What have you learned, Soon Yi?" he asked.

Sunny spoke in short bursts, her voice hushed. She told him everything Franz had shared with her about the offices of General Nogomi and Colonel Tanaka. As she held forth, the man remained still and expressionless.

"And Colonel Kubota?" he finally asked.

Sunny shifted in her seat. "The colonel is no longer at Astor House. His office is inside the ghetto. On Muirhead Road."

"Have you been there?"

"No, but my husband has," she said, anticipating his question. "It's a modest space on the second floor."

"Do you believe you would be allowed inside his office?"

"I would have no reason to go there."

The old man's nostrils whistled as he exhaled. "Surely you can find a reason."

"I . . . I do not see the point." Sunny turned toward the man, but his gaze did not shift. "Colonel Kubota is no longer in his previous job. He has suffered a stroke. He has been demoted. Overseeing the Jewish refugees is a far lesser role."

"Soon Yi speaks the truth," Wen-Cheng said quietly. "The colonel is not the man he once was."

"That is none of your concern," the old man said, unmoved.

Sunny sat up straighter. "Are you aware that the colonel risked his life and his career to save the Jewish refugees—including my husband and stepdaughter—from extermination?"

The man showed no response. His eyelids drooped as though he might nod off in the middle of the conversation. Finally, he said, "Are you aware, Soon Yi, that Colonel Kubota lived in Shanghai among us for ten years, all the while pretending to be our friend and advocate?"

His voice was calm, but Sunny sensed rage behind his words. "No, I was not—"

"Do you know, too, that the colonel won our trust for no other purpose than to infiltrate our government and lay the groundwork for Shanghai's downfall?"

But he saved my family, Sunny thought.

"I ask you again, Soon Yi," the man said, his tone turning to stone. "Can you get inside his office?"

Chapter 25

The soldiers arrived at the hospital unannounced and insisted that Franz accompany them to Colonel Kubota's office. Franz had no idea what had prompted the summons but was nonetheless eager for the opportunity to speak to Kubota again. Refugees were dying daily from cholera, typhoid fever and other diseases that could have been treated with basic supplies such as intravenous fluid. The day before, a young father had died of a ruptured appendix. Franz had been unable to operate; they had waited in vain for anaesthetic that Joey's black market contact had promised but never delivered.

Franz stepped into the colonel's office intending to appeal to Kubota's sense of compassion. But his plans evaporated when he spotted the others in the room.

Kubota sat behind his desk, resignation carved into his weary face. Ghoya paced between the desk and the window. But it was the sight of the man on the far side of the room, who stood with arms folded across chest, that froze Franz's blood.

"Thank you for coming, Dr. Adler," Kubota said with his usual politeness. "You remember Colonel Tanaka?"

If he lived to be a hundred, Franz would never forget the chief of the Kempeitai—the man who had overseen his torture at Bridge House.

Sporting a fresh brush-cut and wire-rimmed glasses as thick as bottle bottoms, Tanaka wore knee-high black boots over his tan uniform and white armbands on his jacket sleeves. Franz had come to fear those markings almost as much as the red-and-black swastikas. He bowed his head. "Colonel Tanaka, Mr. Ghoya."

Tanaka did not acknowledge his presence, but Ghoya shook his head at Franz. "It's no good, Dr. Adler," the little man muttered. "No good at all."

Franz waited, but Ghoya volunteered no explanation. "I am sorry, Mr. Ghoya, what is no good?"

"The Jews. I let them—" Ghoya glanced sheepishly over to his superiors. "*We* let them out of the Designated Area to work in the rest of the city. I give them passes. And how do they thank me?"

Again, Ghoya left Franz hanging. "I am not sure, sir."

"They smuggle. They smuggle!" Ghoya cried. "Jewellery, liquor, cigarettes. It does not matter. All for the money. These Jews, Dr. Adler. These Jews, they take advantage of our kindness."

Tanaka swirled his head in Ghoya's direction and scolded him in Japanese. Ghoya's eyes went wide and his chin dropped in deference.

Franz's throat constricted at the sound of Tanaka's shrill voice. He thought back to the squalid torture chamber in the basement of Bridge House, and lying strapped by his head and limbs to a wooden bench. Franz could practically feel the ligatures cutting into his wrists and the foul water sloshing over his face now. He breathed deeper, fighting off the memories.

Tanaka looked over to Kubota and continued in clipped Japanese. Kubota nodded reluctantly before turning to Ghoya and addressing him quietly. Ghoya sputtered an obsequious reply and bowed deeply at the waist. Kubota's left hand shook on the desktop as he held out his good arm to Franz. "We did not invite you here to discuss smuggling, Dr. Adler."

"*Sabotage!*" Tanaka hissed in English.

Franz's shoulders tightened. Against reason, he assumed that Tanaka must already know that Charlie and Simon were hiding in Yang's home. "Excuse me, Colonel?"

"A bomb." Tanaka stabbed his finger at the window. "Right here."

"Yesterday, saboteurs detonated another bomb in Hongkew," Kubota explained. "The explosion occurred just before noon at the wharf at the foot of Muirhead Road. Two sailors died. A merchant ship was damaged."

"So close," Tanaka snapped, his eyes blazing behind his thick glasses. "Were the Jews responsible?"

"Colonel, the wharf is outside the ghet—" Franz caught himself. "Outside the Designated Area."

Tanaka's angry gaze never left Franz, but he waved dismissively in Ghoya's direction. "This one lets Jews come and go. He fusses over jewellery and cigarettes. I worry over bombs!"

Franz opened his mouth. "Colonel Tanaka, there is no—"

"You Jews hate Germans. Admit it!" Tanaka seemed to believe Franz spoke for all of Shanghai's Jews. "All you want is their defeat. So Imperial Japan must also lose. You will do everything to make it so."

"Colonel, we are peaceful." Franz brought a hand to his chest. "The great emperor has given us shelter. And we are most grateful for the Japanese hospitality."

"So you say," Tanaka scoffed.

"No one in the Designated Area has access to explosives." Even as Franz spoke the words, he wondered if they were true. He knew of a few young hotheads, including the three Klein brothers, who were making noises about aiding the Underground. He had warned them and their parents that their reckless talk could threaten the entire community.

Tanaka smirked at Franz. "We will look ourselves."

Kubota stared down and spoke to his desktop. "I'm afraid Colonel Tanaka is correct. We will have to search the Designated Area."

Franz suddenly pictured the Kempeitai crashing through the doors of Yang's suite, catching Charlie and Simon unaware. Hiding his panic, he edged toward the door.

Tanaka suddenly sprang forward, stopping only inches from Franz's face. The hot sour breath made Franz blink. Tanaka pointed his forefinger into Franz's chest, as though poking him with a stick. "If I find anything, *you* answer to me."

"I . . . I . . ." Franz stammered. "There is nothing to find."

Kubota began to speak in Japanese, but Tanaka stopped him with the same sharp tone that he had levelled at Ghoya. Franz could see that his old ally no longer had much standing with the Kempeitai chief. Tanaka turned to Franz with a malicious grin. "If I find anything . . ." Without another word, he wheeled around and stormed out of the office.

Ghoya shuffled after him, head low. He stopped at the doorway and turned to Franz. "The smuggling will stop. It will stop. You mark my words, doctor."

Desperate to warn the others, Franz hurried for the door himself. "Colonel, if you will please excuse me."

Kubota only smiled weakly. "Circumstances have changed in Shanghai. Yours, mine, everyone's. Would you not agree, Dr. Adler?"

"I would, yes."

"No wonder the Reubens declined my offer."

"To be released from the internment camp?"

"We refer to them as 'civic assembly centres,'" Kubota said with a trace of sarcasm. "Yes, they requested not to be relocated."

That the Shanghailander couple had opted for prison camp over the relative freedom of the ghetto struck Franz as proof of just how dire the refugees' situation had become.

"Colonel Tanaka." Kubota shook his head. "His threats are never empty."

"So I have learned."

"We will not tolerate subversion in the ghetto," Kubota said mechanically.

"I would not expect you to."

Kubota looked up from his desk, his eyes burning. "I had no intention of returning here."

"I realize that."

"We Japanese are guilty of pride. Too much pride. I am afraid I am no exception, Dr. Adler. To come back to the city that I once viewed as home . . . like this." Franz was uncertain whether Kubota meant his diminished physical or administrative capacity, or both. "After my stroke, given the choice, I would have preferred to have never awoken."

*   *   *

As Franz left the bureau, he resisted the urge to run. At the ghetto checkpoint, he saw two Japanese soldiers flanking the refugee guard. A thin woman stood in front of them, twitching nervously, while one of the soldiers rooted through her handbag.

When he was done, the soldier returned the bag to the woman and cleared her to re-enter the ghetto. As she crossed through, Franz recognized her as Liese, the nurse who had fallen into the role of the refugee hospital's anaesthetist.

Liese seemed astonished to see him. "Herr Doktor Adler!" she gasped. "Why . . . why are you here?"

"I had a meeting with the authorities," Franz said. "And you? Why did you leave the ghetto?"

Breaking off eye contact, Liese looked acutely uncomfortable. "I hem clothes for a Japanese tailor in Frenchtown. Twice a week I drop off the finished clothes and collect the new ones."

"Is everything all right, Liese?"

She stared at her feet for a long time before answering. "I am not sure whether it is my place to comment, Dr. Adler."

"Comment on what?"

"I had just received my pay from the tailor. He only gives me a few marks for a week's worth but still . . ." She sighed. "After he paid me, I went to the Old City. There is a market there that sells vegetables for a good price when they have anything to—"

Franz regretted asking. "Liese, I do not mean to be rude, but I am in a frightful hurry."

She nodded to herself. "I wasn't snooping, Dr. Adler. I just happened to see them together. On the bench."

"Who did you see, Liese?"

Her voice dropped to a whisper. "Your wife."

"Sunny was in the Old City?"

"Yes." Liese glanced around her before speaking in a hush. "She wasn't . . . alone."

Chapter 26

"Papa sold them all!" Freddy exclaimed as soon as they were alone beneath the eaves behind the school. Laughing, he grasped Hannah by the shoulders and spun her around. "You're a brave one, Banana, carrying all those cartons through that checkpoint."

"It was nothing." She tried not to remember queuing at the checkpoint in her bulky coat, which was lined front and back with cartons of cigarettes, worrying she might faint with fear. But in the end, the guard waved her past with only a few questions and seemingly no interest in what might be under her coat.

Freddy dug into his trouser pocket and pulled his hand out in a fist. "I wouldn't call this nothing." He made a show of slowly unfurling his fingers to reveal the five-dollar bill in his palm.

Hannah stared dumbfounded at the crumpled note. She assumed that the man with the beard was Abraham Lincoln, but she had never before seen anything other than an American one-dollar bill.

Freddy waved it at her. "For you."

"For me?"

"Your share of the profit."

"But Freddy this . . . this is a fortune."

Still laughing, he leaned forward and pecked her on the lips. "No, Hannah, this is just the beginning."

The kiss left her dazed. Warmth swept across her brow and cheeks. She stared wide-eyed at the boy before her, who was suddenly too handsome to bear. Freddy was saying something, but she couldn't follow his words.

He shook her gently by the shoulders. "Next week again, yes?"

"Yes," she murmured, uncertain of what she was agreeing to and not even caring.

"Papa was wondering if this time you might be able to carry a few more cartons?"

"I think so, yes," she said. Anything that might encourage Freddy to kiss her again.

The sound of footsteps shattered the moment. Freddy dropped his hands from her shoulders as though letting go of a scalding pot. He stepped back just as Hannah saw Otto Geldmann rounding the corner.

Otto was a sweet kid whom she had known since her first week in Shanghai. But just then, she wished the earth would swallow him up and leave her alone with Freddy again.

Freddy straightened to his full height and took a step toward the slight boy. "Hey, Otto, you're not spying on us, are you?" he asked in a friendly voice, but with a threatening undertone.

"No." Otto's cheeks reddened. "I was just—I don't know—kind of bored. I came to see if I could find anyone behind the school."

Freddy reached into his pocket and extracted a crumpled box. Hannah counted four cigarettes inside it. "We were just about to have a smoke. You want in?"

"Yes. Yes, please. I would love one," Otto said. He glanced at Hannah, his eyes wary.

Hannah and Otto choked on their cigarettes while Freddy inhaled as smoothly as if he had been smoking for years, then tossed the stub to the ground and crushed it with the heel of his shoe. Hannah and Otto followed suit.

"Those were less than half done!" Freddy exclaimed. "What a waste!"

"Oh, sorry," Hannah said, and meant it. Otto nodded contritely.

Freddy turned to Hannah with a knowing grin. "No matter. I'll be getting a bunch more very soon."

*   *   *

As Hannah headed home after school, she felt light as air. Her belly grumbled, but she hardly noticed another day without lunch. The kiss had happened so quickly that she couldn't even remember how Freddy's lips felt on hers, but her chest filled with butterflies as she considered the promise inherent in that one moment. She resisted the urge to skip: her left foot never cooperated gracefully enough.

Her thoughts turned to the five-dollar bill tucked into her skirt. She would give it to her father without a second thought, except she knew there would be questions. She could not risk revealing what she and Freddy were doing. She considered leaving the money on the floor or tucking it into Franz's coat pocket, or perhaps even Sunny's, but the outcome would be the same. No one in Shanghai could afford to be so careless with that amount of money.

Esther! She would give the money to her. She could trust her aunt with anything.

With that problem solved, her thoughts drifted back to Freddy. *Had they just become boyfriend and girlfriend? Could it really be?*

Caught up in her daydreams, Hannah had already walked a few blocks before she noticed the unusual number of jeeps and trucks collected along the street. Some were parked on the sidewalk or pointed halfway out into intersections, while others blocked the entrances to the alleyways and the networks of homes they concealed.

As Hannah rounded the corner onto Kung Ping Road, she saw three soldiers gathered behind a truck parked at the end of the block. Infantrymen were a common sight in the ghetto, and these men stood at ease, but Hannah still felt deeply unsettled. She almost doubled back to avoid them but instead lowered her eyes to the pavement and continued on her way, staying on the far side of the street.

Just as Hannah reached the truck, the soldiers sprang into action. For a panicked moment, she thought they were heading for her. Instead, they raced over to the door of a nearby apartment building that had just flown open.

Hannah heard the shrieks first. The words were almost unintelligible, but she made out the phrase "Leave me be, you devils!" howled in Shanghainese.

A soldier stumbled out through the doorway hoisting a tiny Chinese woman in his arms. Her long hair had fallen across her face, and she struggled like a cat in a bathtub. The soldier pinned the woman's arms to her sides, but her legs flailed as though she were trying to run on air.

The other soldiers raced over, taking hold of the woman's arms. One soldier slapped her viciously across the face with his palm, then hit her again with the back of his hand. The woman yowled in response and struggled even more vehemently.

Hannah spun away from the violent scene. She was about to run back down the street when the woman called out to her in Mandarin, "*Girlie!* Listen to me!"

Yang! Hannah froze. She cautiously looked back over her shoulder at the woman who had helped teach her Chinese. Yang tossed her head, clearing the hair from her ashen face. Her frantic eyes were huge. "*Wǒ dúzì yīrén!*" she cried. "They found only me!"

Hannah was confused by Yang's odd statement. Had she misunderstood an idiom?

"I was alone!" Yang cried. "Soon Yi must know that I was alone. Tell her."

The soldiers were looking at Hannah now. She began to back away. The man who had slapped Yang squinted hard at Hannah and shook a finger accusingly. "You know the woman?" he demanded in English.

Hannah shook her head. "I . . . I don't speak Chinese."

The soldier stared at her skeptically for a moment before shooing her away. "Go! Leave us!"

Hannah held Yang's terrified gaze for a fraction of a second before she backed away a few paces, then turned and ran down the street.

"Only me! You tell her, girlie!" Yang cried behind her. Then she shrieked again, "Leave me be, you devils!"

Chapter 27

Something was wrong. Sunny sensed it the moment Franz appeared on the ward and shepherded her off to the staff room. Once they were alone, he grimly told her about his interview with Kubota and Tanaka and their threat to raid the ghetto. "Where are we supposed to move Simon and Charlie this time?" he demanded.

"We have to separate them."

"But how? It will take a miracle to find one new safe house, let alone two."

Sunny locked her fingers together. "We have to get Charlie out of the ghetto altogether."

"And Simon? He can't stay around here either. After last year—what happened at Bridge House—someone in the Kempeitai is bound to recognize him."

Only one solution came to mind. "Jia-Li will take Charlie in," she said.

Franz grimaced. "Into her flat? In Frenchtown?"

"Can you think of anywhere else?"

"No. Even still, then what do we do with Simon?"

"Perhaps he can go back to the Comfort Home?"

"Would Chih-Nii really take him back?"

"I'm not sure."

"I can see how we might be able to pass Charlie off as a crippled beggar or something," Franz said, squeezing the bridge of his nose. "But how would we get Simon out of the ghetto past the guards?"

Before Sunny could reply, the door burst open and Hannah rushed into the room, her hair a tousled mess and tears coursing down her cheeks. Sunny had never seen her stepdaughter looking as distraught.

Hannah launched herself into her father's arms. "They have Yang!" she cried.

Sunny went cold. "Who has her?"

"The soldiers," Hannah gasped into her father's shoulder. "I watched them take her away."

Sunny covered her mouth with both hands. The blood-curdling image of Irma being cut down by gunfire flashed to her mind.

Franz gently pried Hannah from his chest and steadied her with his hands on her shoulders. "Slow down, Hannah. This is very important. Did the soldiers arrest anyone else with Yang?"

Hannah shook her head.

"Are you certain?" Franz demanded. "They could have already taken others away or . . ."

"No, Papa. Yang told me." Hannah shook free of her father's grip and turned urgently to Sunny. "She kept saying to tell you that she was alone."

"Are you certain, *Liebchen?*" Franz asked.

Hannah nodded adamantly. "At first I thought I misunderstood her Chinese, but she repeated it twice: *wǒ dúzì yīrén!*"

"'I was alone,'" Sunny said, thinking of just how alone poor Yang really must have felt at that moment.

Sunny felt nauseous with worry. Yang was the closest to a mother that she had known for the past twenty years. They had lived apart only since the Japanese forced the Adlers to move into the ghetto. Even then, despite her dread of the Japanese, Yang had followed them out of loyalty and love. Yang's greatest fear had now been realized, and only because she had offered to help Sunny. "We must do something, Franz," she murmured. "How can we help her?"

He stared back hopelessly. "If only . . ." His words petered out, and he stepped forward to wrap her in a tight hug.

Sunny squeezed back, desperate for the contact. "We had better find the other two," she sobbed into his neck.

"Which others?" Hannah demanded.

"You need not worry over this," Franz said.

Hannah placed her hands on her hips. "I'm not a child, Papa." But her tone was sympathetic, not petulant. "You don't have to protect me this way anymore."

Sunny eased her body out of Franz's embrace. She wiped her eyes with a sleeve and then turned to Hannah with a small smile. "Simon was staying with Yang. Along with Charlie—the man who was at our home last spring."

"The man you operated on in the bedroom?" Hannah asked, looking more grown up than Sunny had ever seen her. "Do the Japanese want to arrest them?"

"I think so," Sunny said. "Yes."

"Can they not stay with us?"

"No, *Liebchen.*" Franz shook his head. "It would be far too dangerous. For them and for us. Trust me. Ours will be one of the first homes that is searched."

"So what can be done?" Hannah asked.

Franz's eyes clouded with puzzlement. "The first step is to find them."

*   *   *

Sunny insisted on returning home with Franz to break the news to Esther. Leaves rustled at their feet in the mild autumn breeze as they silently hurried along. Despite her preoccupation with Yang, Sunny could not shake the sense that Franz was upset with her. Did he somehow know about her contact with the Underground? He offered nothing, and she was too frightened to broach the subject.

They stepped inside their home to find Esther on the couch, cradling the sleeping Jakob in her arms. The sight of mother and son, both so contented, made something inside Sunny break. She had to swallow back a sob.

The moment Esther looked up at them the smile slid from her lips. "*Was ist los?* Something has happened."

Franz looked down. "The Japanese are raiding the ghetto."

Esther twitched and then caught herself. Jakob stirred without waking. She rose to her feet and lowered him carefully onto the sofa. As soon as he was settled, she rushed over to them. "And Simon?" she breathed.

"They haven't caught him, Essie," Sunny said.

"How could you know?"

Franz described what Hannah had witnessed outside Yang's apartment.

"*Mein Gott,* that poor woman," Esther said. "But where would Simon go?"

Franz closed his eyes and shook his head. "There are many places one could hide in the ghetto, Essie."

Esther nodded. It was clear that she was struggling to fight off the tears. But her lips quivered, and she covered her face with her hands.

"Essie, we will find Simon," Franz reassured her.

A soft choking sob emerged from behind her hands. "What if they find him first?"

They fell into a mournful silence. After a few moments, the phone rang. Telephone service had become so sporadic that Sunny had almost forgotten they still had one.

Franz took a step toward it, but Esther darted out in front of him and grabbed the receiver. "*Hier bei Adler!*" she said sharply. Then her tone softened and she brought a hand to her cheek. "Simon! *Gottze dank!* It really is you. Oh, my Simon. Where are you?" She listened and then said, "You are telling the truth? Please, God. You really are safe?" She paused again. "Of course, of course. When can I see you?" Another pause, then, "Yes, yes.

They are right here. Promise me, Simon. You will be more careful than ever. I could not bear . . ." Her voice faltered.

Sunny and Franz shared an uncomfortable glance.

"I love you, too. More than you can know." Esther pulled the receiver from her ear and held it out toward them.

Sunny stepped forward and took the receiver. "Simon! Where are you? Are you safe?"

"Yeah, I'm fine. Charlie too. Another family took us in."

Simon had helped so many refugee families in the city through his work with the CFA that Sunny imagined they would have lined up to shelter him. "Which family?"

He hesitated. "Best not to say over the phone."

"Of course not," she said.

"Don't worry. We are well taken care of." He chuckled. "I already miss Yang's cooking, though."

A lump formed in her throat. "Simon, they have her."

"Oh no." Simon exhaled so heavily that the receiver whistled in her ear. "She wouldn't leave with us, Sunny. As soon as we heard the trucks, we got out of there. Yang insisted on staying. Maybe they found our clothes or . . . I don't know."

"Or perhaps Yang panicked?" Sunny suggested, desperate for a more benign explanation. "Maybe that was the only reason they took her? You know how the Japanese terrify her."

"That could explain it," Simon said hopefully. "Maybe they just took her in for questioning."

But Simon's words rang hollow. There was no routine questioning when it came to the Japanese. "It doesn't matter, does it?" Sunny sniffed. "Even if they didn't find anything in her apartment, what difference will it make to Yang now that they have her?"

Simon's voice softened. "She's a tougher bird than you give her credit for, Sunny."

Sunny swallowed with difficulty. "You will not be able to stay in the ghetto, Simon. Not for much longer."

"Yeah, the Japs are sweeping the place."

"There was a bomb at the wharf. The Japanese are looking for subversives. Raiding the whole ghetto. We need to move you soon." Sunny glanced over at Franz; he held up one finger. "Within a day."

"Charlie and I will be ready anytime."

"How will we reach you?" she asked.

"I'll call you in an hour or two."

"And if there is no telephone service?"

"I'll send someone to carry a message back to us."

Sunny didn't like the idea of including anyone else in the plan, but there was no other option. "All right."

"Listen, Sunny, if something goes wrong . . . You and Franz will take care of Essie and Jakob for me, won't you?"

Sunny looked over at Esther, who was hanging on her every word. "Of course. All will be fine. Telephone us again in two hours, Simon. We will have details then. Goodbye."

As soon as Sunny hung up, Franz motioned to the couch where Jakob was sleeping. "Perhaps we should move as well. At the very least we need to find somewhere for Essie, Jakob and Hannah to stay."

"Why, Franz?" Sunny asked. "We have nothing to hide."

"True, but . . ." Franz refused to meet her eyes. "Who knows where they might take Yang."

Sunny cringed as she imagined Yang being tortured by some vicious interrogator. *I should have never asked her to shelter Simon and Charlie. It's all my fault.*

"Surely she would not tell them about us?" Esther murmured.

"I wouldn't blame her if she did." Franz continued to stare at the ground. "Last year, after they took me to Bridge House . . . I would have told them anything to make it stop."

The door rattled with three slow knocks. There was a pause, followed by four taps. Esther rushed over to Jakob and swept him up protectively in her arms, but Sunny raced over to answer the door. It was a secret signal, dating back to her childhood when she and Jia-Li had lived three doors apart and would sneak over to each other's houses without their parents' approval.

Jia-Li stood at the threshold in a black suit and matching hat, her eyes smouldering. "Everyone is gone," she gasped as she stepped inside. "And their flat was a disaster."

Sunny hugged her best friend. "Charlie and Simon are safe," she sobbed. "But they took Yang."

"Oh, that poor woman." Jia-Li moaned softly. "I'm so sorry, *xiǎo hè*. Do you know where they took her?"

Sunny wriggled out of her friend's embrace. She did not want to consider Yang's plight another moment, let alone discuss it. "Simon and Charlie will not be able to stay much longer where they are. We wondered if you might take one of them into your—"

"I will take them both!" Jia-Li cried.

Franz shook his head. "It would be better to separate them."

"And Charlie should stay with you," Sunny said.

Jia-Li just nodded, but Sunny could sense her friend's eagerness to help.

"Do you think Simon could go back to the basement of the Comfort Home?" Franz asked.

"Chih-Nii was not pleased with what happened last time. The raid." Jia-Li sucked air in through her teeth. "Not pleased at all. She is trying to get rid of the last two who are still with us. I will talk to her, but . . ."

"What about Ernst?" Franz suggested.

"Never, Franz!" Esther cried. "Ernst lives among Nazis!"

Franz nodded. "Which is precisely why the Japanese would not look there."

"He has a point," Sunny said. "For the short term, Simon might be safest living there."

Esther shook her head wildly. "What if they find him? That would be worse than the Japanese." She paused, then spoke softly: "What they did to my Karl . . ."

Chapter 28

Sunny stared out the window, which was cloudy with grease streaks and grime. A massive swastika flapped from a pole mounted on top of the building across the street. This neighbourhood in the International Settlement had always been a German enclave, but it no longer matched Sunny's childhood recollections. She used to happily anticipate attending the Oktoberfest street celebrations with her father, the air rich with festive accordion music and the smell of grilled sausages, pretzels and beer. Now, she sensed only menace from the uniformed Nazis who roamed the streets. And the neighbourhood's palpable military presence only heightened her concern for Yang.

Ernst sat calmly across the table from her. Without asking, he filled her teacup and then lit another cigarette for himself. "My home is always open to Simon." He waved a hand. "However, as you can see, my work has a habit of spilling out everywhere. Hardly leaves much of the *Lebensraum* that the Nazis so covet."

On the other side of the room, a narrow corridor led, Sunny assumed, to the water closet and possibly a bedroom. She wondered if the rest of the apartment was as cluttered as the room she was in, which was littered with canvases, most of them unfinished. A stained armchair occupied the far corner, while the table and two chairs where she and Ernst now sat filled the rest of the space. The odour of oil paint mingled with that of yeast and flour drifting up from the bakery below.

"Space is the least of Simon's concerns right now," Sunny pointed out.

Ernst jerked a thumb to one of the nearest canvases. It depicted a mountainous landscape foregrounded by a field of colourful wildflowers. "He will also have to cope with me painting the rubbish that I pass off for art these days."

"It's lovely, Ernst."

"It's soulless *Scheisse*." He snorted. "Some talented Hitler Youth could have painted one almost as well. Perhaps even the Führer himself could have pulled it off. No wonder the fools lap it up so."

"What will Simon care, Ernst?" Sunny forced a smile. "He is not an art critic. He will be happy to be here."

"And I will be happy for the company," Ernst said. "Please reassure Simon that I'm no longer in the habit of dragging stray men home with me. I hardly even drink anymore. I have become a disgrace to hedonism. I blame the Communists and their dreary asceticism. Regardless, living with me, the biggest threat poor Simon might face is deadly boredom."

Sunny reached out and patted Ernst's wrist. "You still haven't heard from Shan?"

"Not for six months. How could I?" Ernst sighed. "Besides, even if I could reach him, I doubt Shan would want anything to do with me after the way I abandoned him."

"He would understand," Sunny said reassuringly, although she was again thinking again of her amah. How could Yang ever forgive Sunny for putting her in harm's way?

"Shan has so many admirable qualities, but he can be . . . hard-headed." Ernst shooed his romantic concerns away with a roll of his eyes. "Enough of this bleak gabble. It's decided, then. Simon will live here."

"We have to find a way to get him here," Sunny murmured.

Ernst inhaled again, then stubbed out his cigarette in an empty paint tin. He studied her carefully before he nodded to himself. "Something else is troubling you, Sunny."

"I am so worried for Yang."

Ernst leaned into the table, his gaze disconcerting in its intensity. "Of course you are, but there is more to it, isn't there?"

Sunny hesitated. She hardly knew Ernst well enough to pour her heart out to him—and it was neither the time nor the place—but she was bursting to tell someone. And who would understand a secret identity better than a homosexual artist living not just under an alias but behind enemy lines? "It's Franz," she finally said.

"What about him?"

"He has become so distant lately. He doesn't trust me anymore."

Ernst raised an eyebrow. "Does he have cause for suspicion?"

"No! Not in that sense. Never." She glanced around the room as if someone might have crept in without her noticing, and then lowered her voice to a hush. "Ernst, I . . . I got involved with the Underground."

"The Underground?" He frowned, then his face lit up with sudden understanding. "You haven't told Franz, have you?"

"You know how he views people in the ghetto who participate in subversive activities."

"Tell me."

"He thinks it is terribly selfish. That it risks the security of all the refugees. And I've been doing it behind his back." She shook her head.

"So why did you volunteer?"

Sunny told him weakly about her sense of powerlessness and desire to help, her sense of duty. She didn't touch on her guilt over the execution of Irma and the teenagers, or her wish to avenge her father's murder. Nor did she mention her growing regret over the decision to get involved.

Ernst lit another cigarette before he spoke. "I have known your husband for a very long time. Yes, he can be agonizingly proud and exhaustingly stubborn, but what never fails to astound me is his almost boundless capacity for understanding."

"You think I should tell him?"

"I think *you* think that you should tell him."

Sunny laughed in spite of herself. "You are wiser than you let on, Ernst."

"I'm a complete fool, actually. But sometimes even fools recognize the obvious."

As Sunny finished her tea and Ernst smoked, their conversation turned back to the logistics of relocating Charlie and Simon. "So Charlie and Jia-Li will live together?"

"Yes. If we can get him out of the ghetto and to Jia-Li's."

Ernst chuckled. "Can you imagine it, Sunny? It will take a hatchet to cut through the romantic tension in that apartment. I have no idea who either of them thinks they are fooling. It's like watching two teenagers—"

A rap at the door cut Ernst off. Sunny hopped to her feet, spilling the last of her tea. "Are you expecting someone?" she whispered.

Ernst shook his head. He pointed to the corridor and mouthed the word "bedroom."

Sunny took a shaky step forward as she saw the doorknob turn and the door fly open.

Baron von Puttkamer marched into the room as though he owned it, followed by his Korean bodyguard, who assumed a post by the door. "Ah, so you are home after all, Gustav," the tall European bellowed.

"Of course, I . . ." Ernst sputtered.

The baron assessed the cramped quarters with a sweep of his eyes. "I thought your art was selling better than these accommodations would suggest."

"I am as frugal as your average Jew," Ernst quipped.

Smiling, von Puttkamer turned his attention to Sunny. She feared that he would remember her from the spring day when they had met on the streets of the ghetto, but his eyes didn't register a flicker of recognition. He bowed his head and held out his hand. "A pleasure, Fräulein."

Ernst inclined his head in Sunny's direction without meeting her gaze. "A new friend, Baron. She is posing for a painting I have in mind." He cleared his throat, feigning embarrassment, as though the baron had caught them in flagrante delicto. "She will be leaving shortly."

"That's hardly necessary, Gustav." Von Puttkamer waved his hand. "The lady doesn't speak German, does she?"

Ernst shook his head. "She barely understands English. Our communication is more . . . physical in nature."

Still smirking, von Puttkamer said, "Really, Gustav? You and that miserable half-breed? You're an eligible artist. Surely you could do better." He shook his head. "These mixed bloods are the kind of perversity we are striving to wipe off the map."

Sunny's skin crawled, but she pretended not to follow a word of his German. Instead, mustering a bored expression, she collected the dishes from the table and carried them over to the countertop in the galley kitchen.

Von Puttkamer moved across the room to study a painting that rested against the wall. "Do you like it, Baron?" Ernst asked over his shoulder.

Von Puttkamer shrugged. "The craftsmanship is fine."

"Praise does not come much fainter than that."

"It is hardly original, Gustav. Walk the art district of Cologne and you will find a hundred like it."

"Fortunately for me, Cologne is a good long walk from Shanghai."

"You are touchy, Klimper. So like an artist." Von Puttkamer laughed. "I'm not questioning your talent. After all, two of your paintings hang in my home. I merely wonder whether you are truly inspired by the theme. I sense you can do much more with your gift than this."

"You give me more credit than I am due, Baron."

Von Puttkamer turned his attention away from the canvas. "I did not come to here to discuss art. Or even your penchant for sullied races."

"So why have you come?"

"To invite you to dinner, my dear Gustav. This Friday."

"Oh, thank you," Ernst said. "Is there a special occasion?"

"I would like you to meet my wife. She's somewhat of an art connoisseur. She very much enjoys your work."

"Lovely. I would be delighted. No doubt your wife is an enchanting woman."

"At times," von Puttkamer said. "Of course, there will be a few Party members in attendance as well." His eyelids creased. "We have more to discuss on the Jewish question."

Sunny stiffened, but she held her head still while continuing to stare out the window.

Von Puttkamer scoffed in disgust. "It astounds me how freely—how easily—the refugees live here in Shanghai. With their schools, temples and hospitals. Better than many of the good Germans back at home who have to cope with the hardships of war. The Japanese are supposed to be our allies. Yet they allow the Jews to thumb their noses at us all."

Ernst hesitated before speaking. "I wish there were more that could be done."

Sunny glanced over her shoulder and saw that von Puttkamer was smiling. "Ah, but there is more, my friend. So much more."

"Really, Baron?" Ernst said with a calmness Sunny could tell was feigned. "Didn't you tell me that last year, when those SS officers came from Tokyo, they were unable to persuade the Japanese to act?"

"Ah, but that was last year," von Puttkamer snorted. "This time will be different."

"How so, Baron?"

"This time we will not ask the Japanese for permission."

Chapter 29

Franz took another sip of his coffee, but he had been nursing the cup for half an hour and it had gone cold and tasteless. The café's proprietor, Herr Steinmann, shot him another impatient look. The restaurant wasn't crowded, but Franz had been tying up the most desirable table, in the corner by the window, for too long.

Franz far preferred the richer and more bitter coffee that Frau Schilling brewed at her bakery two blocks over. Besides, he couldn't really afford the beverage, in spite of assistance from Jia-Li and Ernst. It sickened Franz to have to depend on the charity of friends. And even with their help, the Adlers might have gone hungry the week before had Esther not sold the last of her mother's brooches.

Franz glanced over at the table beside his, where a couple sat with three young boys, who appeared to range from about four to eight years old. The father was using an old army knife to cut a piece of apple strudel into slices, while the boys watched him, practically vibrating with anticipation. As soon as the delicate operation was complete, the children snatched their slivers in delight. Franz noticed that neither parent reached for the pastry.

Franz heard the café door open and looked over to see Sunny step inside. Their eyes locked across the room. Heartsick, he thought again of what Liese had told him about seeing Sunny with Wen-Cheng. Hard as he tried, he could not shake the mental image of them lying naked together in a rundown rooming house near the Old City.

Franz had yet to find the right moment to confront Sunny with what Liese had told him. Even if he could have put aside the current crises with Charlie, Simon and Yang, he still wasn't convinced that he wanted to discuss it. Where could he possibly begin? As Sunny hurried over to him, her hips swinging ever so slightly with each step, his pulse quickened. He could not imagine losing her.

Sunny had barely settled into the seat across from him when Herr Steinmann appeared at the table, hands on his waist. "Perhaps the lady would like something to eat or drink?" he asked pointedly.

"A cup of tea," Franz answered for her. "And I will have another coffee."

Steinmann shook his head. "And what food might I interest you in?"

Sunny gave him her most disarming smile. "Only the drinks, thank you."

Steinmann snatched up Franz's cup and saucer and marched off. As soon as he was gone, Sunny leaned over the table until her and Franz's lips almost touched. "Everyone is ready," she whispered.

"The soldiers are still outside?" he asked in a tone as low as hers.

She nodded toward the window. "Everywhere."

"*Scheisse,*" he muttered as he saw a pair of infantrymen troop past the window with rifles slung over their shoulders.

"It can't be helped, Franz." Sunny motioned discreetly out the window to the intersection, where Joey, barely recognizable in the rags of a coolie, stood holding up a rickshaw. "When Jia-Li comes to the doorway, I will check the street and signal when it is clear. Then she will hail Joey."

"Anyone might stop them along the way. If one of the soldiers were to recognize Charlie . . ."

"Why would they stop them? They will be just another Chinese couple riding in a rickshaw."

"Who can afford a rickshaw ride these days?"

Sunny squeezed the back of his hand. "There are still people in Shanghai with means."

Franz's chest ached at her touch, but he didn't withdraw his hand. "Not in the ghetto," he said.

"Charlie and Jia-Li won't be in the ghetto for long."

Herr Steinmann came back and lowered a cup in front of each of them with exaggerated care. Franz didn't touch his coffee, but he found the aroma soothing. At an unaccustomed loss for words with Sunny, he stared out the window at the doorway of the building where Charlie and Simon had apparently spent the night hiding in another refugee family's flat.

Sunny sipped her tea. "Franz, what do you think von Puttkamer is planning?"

Franz shook his head. "What are Nazis always up to? Something terrible for us."

"Do you really believe they would attack the ghetto?"

"Without question."

"Right under the nose of the Japanese?"

"I doubt anything would deter them. Their hatred is not rational. It knows no bounds."

"Yes, but how can they just invade the ghetto when their own allies have already claimed it?"

"Perhaps they will raid after dark?" He lifted his cup and whispered into it. "Or maybe they intend to plant booby traps?"

"If Ernst can find out the details, then surely we will be able to stop them."

"Can anyone stop them?" Weariness descended over Franz, exhaustion as intense as any he had ever known. The continual threats to his community's existence seemed to coalesce into one giant storm cloud. "How long can one continue to bail water from a ship that is already submerged?"

"For as long as it takes, Franz. You are—" She suddenly turned to the window.

Franz followed her gaze to the building's entryway, where Jia-Li stood calmly in a black cheongsam, which was uncharacteristically conservative for her with its low hem and high collar. Sunny rose and slipped over to the door of the café. Moments later, Franz saw her rush past the window. Craning his neck to take in as much of the street as he could, he spotted a pair of soldiers—not the ones who had passed earlier—patrolling the intersection at the far end of the street. Sunny must have given Jia-Li the all-clear signal because she waved her arm to hail the rickshaw.

As planned, Joey trotted up to the door. Moments later, Charlie appeared at the entrance, propped up on his crutches, wearing a suit and fedora.

As Charlie and Jia-Li were climbing into the carriage of the rickshaw, Sunny re-entered the café and slid back into her seat.

Franz studied the soldiers at the far end of the block, but they seemed to take no notice of the departing rickshaw. He held his breath as Joey jogged by the café, pulling Jia-Li and Charlie behind him. All three were staring dead ahead.

Sunny reached for Franz's hand again. "As long as no one stops them at the checkpoint."

"Even if they get so lucky, what about Simon?" he asked. "How will we get him out past the checkpoint? The soldiers will assume he is a refugee. They would definitely stop him."

"Not if he's inside a night soil man's barrel."

His stomach turned, but they had yet to come up with a better plan for getting Simon past the guards. As they finished their drinks, Sunny gently caressed Franz's knuckles. He stared down at the table and kept his hand still.

"Franz?" Her voice cracked.

He looked up to see that her eyes had misted over. "Yes?"

Her hand froze on his. "I have something to tell you."

Franz tensed, bracing himself.

"Not here," she said. "Let's walk."

With the dread of a man on his way to the gallows, Franz rose to his feet. He dropped a few coins on the table and followed Sunny to the door.

They walked two blocks in silence before Sunny stopped on the sidewalk and turned to face him. She glanced in either direction and then lowered her voice to a whisper. "Last spring, I . . . I contacted the Underground."

The street swam around Franz. "*The Underground?* What are you talking about, Sunny?"

"I approached Wen-Cheng. I knew he was working with the Resistance." She swallowed hard but maintained her husband's gaze. "He didn't want to involve me, but I insisted."

Franz was speechless. Suddenly everything made sense.

Her face trembled. "The worst part has been hiding it from you all these months. All the secrecy. I am so sorry, Franz."

"So that was why you were in the Old City with Wen-Cheng?"

Her head jerked up in surprise. "How did you know about that?"

"Liese saw you."

"And you didn't say anything?" she asked incredulously. "Why not, for God's sake?"

Franz only stared back at her.

Her mouth fell open. "Oh, Franz, no! I would never . . ."

"I didn't know what to think."

Sunny stepped forward and wrapped her arms around him. She scattered kisses along his neck and cheeks. When her lips found his, he kissed her back, tasting the salt of her tears.

Despite his overwhelming relief, a different form of uneasiness took hold of Franz as they held each other on the street. He realized it might have been better for everyone had his wife's secret been as simple as a romantic dalliance. He broke free of her embrace. "Sunny, if you were to be caught . . ."

Tears flowed freely down her cheeks. "I was so angry with them for what they did to Irma and those boys. For what happened to Father. And I was ashamed with how little I had done. It seems so foolish and rash now, but I only wanted to contribute—to make some little difference—and instead I may have ruined everything."

Franz grasped her upper arms. "What exactly have you done, Sunny?"

"Not so much." She composed herself and wiped her eyes dry. "All they have asked me to do so far is gather information."

Franz suddenly understood. "General Nogomi's office! That is why you were so interested, isn't it?"

"Yes," she admitted, ashamed.

"This cannot continue, Sunny. You must cut your ties with them."

"I want to, believe me, but Wen-Cheng says . . ." Her voice cracked again. "I am not sure they will let me."

"They have to! I will tell Wen-Cheng."

Sunny looked down at her feet. "It's not only General Nogomi's office they are interested in."

"Who else's?"

"They want me to get inside Colonel Kubota's office."

The hairs on Franz's neck stood up. "Are they planning to harm the colonel as well?"

"I . . . I suspect so, yes."

"This is insanity, Sunny. He is the only ally we Jews have ever had here."

"I tried to talk to him, but he wouldn't listen."

"Who?"

"My contact . . . He is the only one I ever met besides Wen-Cheng." She paused. "He's an old man, infirm—pitiable, really. But there is more to him than meets the eye. There is anger, and something else . . ."

"What else, Sunny?"

"There's something . . ." She shut her eyes. "Very dangerous about him."

Chapter 30

Hannah couldn't control her trembling. She had already started toward the checkpoint twice but had turned back each time. She was sweating underneath her bulky coat. The corners of the cigarette cartons dug through her shirt and into her sides, as though she were buried up to her neck in a trash can.

Hannah couldn't help but think again of Freddy and Leah, whom she had stumbled upon at the noon break behind the schoolhouse. They stood, sharing a cigarette, in the same spot where days before Freddy had kissed Hannah. He was his usual unflappable self, but Leah looked as guilty as a child caught with her hand in the cookie jar.

Your imagination is playing tricks! But it was futile. There was no mistaking the intimacy between them. *Why would Freddy ever choose me over Leah? She is so beautiful, and I am just a cripple.*

Hannah suddenly spun around and vomited against the wall of the nearest building. An old Chinese couple stopped to stare at her. Evading their eyes, she wiped her mouth and hurried down the street. *The money will help my family,* Hannah told herself.

But it had never been about money. Besides, Esther had been so suspicious the last time. Hannah remembered her aunt's expression of disbelief as she stared at the five-dollar bill without reaching for it. "Where did you get so much money, Hannah-*chen?*"

"I told you, Tante. A friend from school felt sorry for me—for us."

"For us?" Esther said evenly. "We are among the fortunate."

Hannah nodded to Jakob, who was happily tugging at the buttons on Esther's sleeve. "With the baby and all."

Esther frowned. "Which friend?"

"She asked me not to say."

Esther nodded knowingly. "She did, did she?"

"Please, Tante Essie," Hannah said. "I knew Papa would ask so many questions. That's why I came to you. Besides, what does it matter where the money came from? We can put it to such good use."

The darkness drained from Esther's eyes, and her lips curved into one of her wise smiles. She reached out and stroked Hannah's cheek. "Oh, Hannah, you must understand. It always matters where the money comes from."

In the end, Esther accepted the money, but Hannah knew she could not go back to her aunt with more unexplained cash. Her father would surely find out, and his disappointment would be the least of her worries if she were caught by the guards. It was such a great gamble. *This is the last time!*

Hannah stood up straight and combed her fingers through her hair. She took a deep breath and headed toward the Muirhead Road checkpoint. As she approached the intersection, she saw the *pao-chia* guard on duty across the street. She recognized his lanky frame and sharp features. It was Herr Einhorn, a senior member of congregation at the Ohel Moishe Synagogue. Hannah had often seen him parading self-importantly around the refugees' temple. With his hawkish face and suspicious eyes, Einhorn was one of her least favourite guards.

She considered backtracking to enter the ghetto at the far end, via the Wayside Road checkpoint. However, the Japanese soldiers who had been at the post when she had exited the ghetto were nowhere in sight now, and it seemed better to take advantage of their absence. Nauseous with anxiety, she lowered her chin and crossed the road to the checkpoint.

Hannah waited at the curb while Einhorn scrutinized the exit pass of the man in line ahead of her. After several questions, which seemed to her more detailed than the usual cursory screen, Einhorn finally waved the man through.

Suddenly racked with doubt, Hannah began to back away from the checkpoint, but Einhorn beckoned her forward. "Come ahead, Fräulein." He chuckled. "I won't bite."

Hannah bundled her coat tighter around her and took two hesitant steps toward him.

"I know you." Einhorn smiled coolly. "The surgeon, Adler. You are his daughter."

"Yes."

His eyes narrowed. "You were here last week as well, were you not?"

Fear welled in the pit of her stomach. "I have a Russian friend who lives in Frenchtown," she explained, trying to stay calm.

Einhorn wrinkled his nose. "Neither the French nor the Russians have been great friends to the Jews."

Hannah looked down. "I lost track of the time, sir. I am late to return. I was supposed to help my stepmother prepare dinner."

"Yes," he said. "Your father married that local Oriental woman, did he not?"

"She is Eurasian, sir. Her mother was American." Hannah was baffled as to why she was explaining Sunny's background to this nosy man.

"War changes things." Einhorn shook his head disapprovingly. "And people, too."

Hannah had no idea how to reply to this, so she stared at the ground, praying that he would lose interest in her.

"Well, Fräulein, you had best hurry home. I am sure your stepmother will not be pleased by your tardiness." He laughed to himself. "Not that the Chinese tend to be punctual themselves."

Hannah could have cried with relief. Forcing herself not to run, she kept her eyes glued to the sidewalk as she hurried forward in a fast walk. As she passed close enough to smell his hair oil, Einhorn remarked, "You are wearing a very heavy coat for this time of year."

Hannah froze.

"Would you mind just opening up the front of it for me?" he asked.

Dread enveloped Hannah. She considered bolting but realized that it would only make matters worse. Not trusting her feet to cooperate, she turned slowly toward him. "I have a slight cold, sir." She repeated the words she had been rehearsing much of the way back from Frenchtown. "My father—the doctor—suggested that I remain bundled up."

"Sound advice, yes." Einhorn nodded. "But I'm afraid Mr. Ghoya has given me very clear instructions."

"I have nothing to hide." Hannah coughed into her hand. "But there are many buttons, sir. It is cumbersome to—"

Einhorn looked at her sternly. "Please open your coat, young lady."

Her belly suddenly tensed and she vomited, splashing the front of her coat.

Einhorn jumped back. "What is wrong, Fräulein?"

Hannah's legs buckled. She felt as though she were watching from outside her body as she swooned, then fell to the ground. She landed hard on her buttocks and then toppled backwards.

The sky spun, then Einhorn's face filled her field of vision. Her nostrils filled with the scent of his pipe tobacco. "Are you all right, girl?" he asked.

Mouth dry, she nodded weakly into her collar, which had bunched up around her neck. Einhorn reached out to clear it from her face. Suddenly, his eyes widened and his hands froze on the garment. "What is under this?" he demanded.

She stared at him. "Cigarettes," she finally croaked.

"Smuggling?" he gasped. "This is not good, Fräulein. Not good at all."

"Please, sir. This is the last time. I swear it."

"I have to report this," Einhorn said. "You have left me no choice."

Hannah reached up and grasped his bony wrist. "If my father . . ."

A sympathetic look crossed Einhorn's face, and he glanced around them. "Do you realize how much trouble I could be in if I do not report this?"

"Please," she moaned.

He hesitated, then, with a heavy sigh, began to arrange her coat collar around her neck. "Get up," he snapped in a low voice. "Do not breathe a word of this to anybody. And never ever attempt such foolishness again. Ever!"

"Never, I swear to God," she said as she struggled up to a sitting position, still feeling woozy. "Thank you, sir. Thank you."

As she climbed unsteadily to her feet, she heard the sound of boots slapping heavily against the pavement nearby.

Chapter 31

Sunny nestled her head into the crook of Franz's neck. Her confession had been a relief to her but had resolved little. If anything, the dangers they were facing had only intensified: they had yet to move Simon from his tenuous sanctuary, the Japanese continued to search the ghetto, Yang's fate was still unknown and the Underground still demanded Sunny's cooperation. She and Franz agreed that Colonel Kubota had to be one of its targets.

Still, as Sunny nuzzled with Franz on the old sofa, she felt somehow lighter. Her gaze drifted to Jakob, who was fast asleep in his crib. Her thoughts turned to her stepdaughter, who wasn't back from school. "Where is Hannah?" she asked Franz.

"At a friend's home, I presume," he said. "I hope that she is studying, like she said she would be."

Esther put down the wooden spoon she had been stirring the rice with and walked over to them. "It is not like Hannah to be so late."

Franz eased Sunny's head off his shoulder and sat up straighter. "Perhaps I should go look for her?"

"But where?" Sunny asked.

"She spends much of her time with that boy Freddy Herzberg," Franz said. "I know where the family lives. I will start there."

Esther wiped her hands on her apron. "Franz . . ."

"Yes?"

"Good, *ja*." Esther looked away evasively. "Go see the boy's family."

Franz squinted at her. "Essie, is there something else?"

"No. No. I can't help but worry. I'm just an overprotective Jewish aunt." She chuckled weakly. "Old habits die hard."

"Essie, what is it? What do you know?"

Before she could answer, three soft knocks sounded at the door.

Franz hurried over to answer it. To his surprise, Freddy stood at the doorstep. He was wearing a new bomber jacket, and his hair was slicked back. "Good evening, Dr. Adler. I am sorry to disturb you, but I was hoping Hannah might be home."

"No, she is not." Franz squared his shoulders. "I was just on my way out to look for her."

"I'm sorry to have missed her." Freddy flashed a confident grin. "When she does come home, Dr. Adler, please let her know that I dropped by."

Sunny joined them at the door. "Why are you looking for her, Freddy?"

"She is holding something of mine," Freddy said. "It's not so important. I can pick it up tomorrow."

Franz leaned closer to the boy. "What exactly is she holding for you?"

Freddy's head twitched again. "She has one of my books. For homework. I can do without it for another day." He backed away from the door. "My parents are expecting me home for dinner."

Esther slipped between Franz and Sunny, only stopping when she was inches away from Freddy. "Where did Hannah get that money, Freddy?" Her voice was frantic.

"Money?" Freddy grimaced. "I don't know what you mean."

Esther grabbed him by the elbow. "This coat, it's brand new."

Freddy tried to shrug his arm free, but she hung onto it. "My parents bought this for me. It was a birthday gift."

"Was your family not living in a heim only last year, Fritsch?" Esther replied angrily. "The five dollars Hannah gave me. What do you know about it?"

Franz turned to Esther with a grimace. "Five dollars? What nonsense are you talking, Essie?"

Esther didn't take her eyes off the boy. "You know where that money came from, don't you?"

Freddy's face reddened and he looked away. "I have nothing to do with it."

"I don't believe you," Esther said. "If something has happened to her and you are somehow responsible . . ."

Franz lunged forward. He grabbed Freddy's lapels and shoved him back against the hallway wall. "Is Hannah in trouble?"

"I . . . I don't know," Freddy grunted. "She never came back."

"Came back from where?"

"Frenchtown."

"*Frenchtown?*" Franz gasped. "Why did Hannah leave the ghetto?"

"You should ask her."

"Tell me!" Franz shouted, tightening his grip on the boy's collar.

"Cigarettes," Freddy croaked.

"What was Hannah doing with cigarettes?"

"Bringing them back. To sell in the ghetto."

Esther took her head in her hands. "*Smuggling?* You forced Hannah to smuggle for you?"

Freddy struggled to shake his head. "We never forced her!"

Franz shoved Freddy aside and headed down the hallway. Sunny raced after him. "Where are you going?" she called.

"To Ghoya's office!" Franz said without slowing. "They must have her!"

*   *   *

They were panting when they reached the Bureau of Stateless Refugee Affairs. Despite the late hour, a line of refugees waiting to apply for exit passes spilled out the front door and onto the street. Franz bolted past the queue, ignoring the cries and complaints of the people in line. Sunny followed him as he elbowed his way down the narrow corridor and burst into Ghoya's office.

An older man who stood cowering in front of the desk spun around in surprise. A soldier rushed inside after Sunny and Franz. Ghoya leaned back in his chair, watching the commotion with an amused grin. He waved the soldier out of the office before he turned to the old man. "No pass for you today. Go. Go. Leave me now!"

As the old man scuttled out of the room, Ghoya turned his attention to Franz. "I believe I know why you have come here, Dr. Adler. Yes, yes. I believe I do."

"Mr. Ghoya, please, sir," Franz said as he approached the desk. "Where is my daughter, Hannah?"

Ghoya motioned to the ceiling. "Right here, Dr. Adler. We have her. Right here."

Franz clasped his hands together. "May I see her, Mr. Ghoya? Please."

Ghoya leaned back and patted his belly contentedly. "Such a big lunch today. Do you know the Café Aaronsohn?"

Franz gaped at him, bewildered. "On Tong Shan Road?"

"Yes, yes! Mr. Aaronsohn and me, we have an understanding." Ghoya nodded knowingly. "I eat lunch there. Every day at twelve thirty. They feed me; I sign his wife's pass. She buys their supplies on Nanking Road." He laughed again. "A good deal for everyone. The wife, she needs a pass. And me? I need lunch."

"Mr. Ghoya, I have to—"

"Today I had such a big plate of *gebratenes*." Ghoya butchered the Yiddish word. "Too much, too much! But the chicken was so good. The Aaronsohns, they cook good chicken."

Franz held out a hand imploringly. "Mr. Ghoya, about Hannah . . ."

Ghoya shook his head repeatedly. "Do you know what your daughter has been up to? Do you?"

"I have heard only just now."

Ghoya put his hands on the desk and launched himself to his feet. "I warned you," he cried as he raced around the desk toward them. "Did I not tell you? The smuggling must stop!"

Sunny stepped forward. "She is just a girl, Mr. Ghoya. She didn't know what she was doing."

"Who are you, woman?" Ghoya demanded.

Sunny reached for Franz's hand and squeezed his damp palm. "I am Mrs. Adler."

Ghoya turned to Franz, his face scrunched up. "This? This is your *wife?* You are not married to a Jewess? But the girl—she has no Chinese in her."

"Hannah's mother is dead. Mrs. Adler is my second wife. Mr. Ghoya, please, Hannah is only a child—"

Ghoya raised a finger and let it sail up over his head. "Child or not. This must stop! Examples must be set."

Franz thrust out his hands in surrender. "Then take me instead. Let me be the example."

"No, no, no!" Ghoya shook his head wildly. "The girl is the smuggler. We must punish her."

"Mr. Ghoya, I put Hannah up to this!" Franz cried. "She didn't want to do it, but I insisted. The cigarettes were for me to sell. You see, Hannah doesn't need a pass to leave the ghetto, so I—"

Ghoya's eyes widened in fury. "I will stand you in front of a firing squad right this instant!"

"It's not true!" Sunny exclaimed. "My husband didn't know. I swear to you. We both only found out minutes ago. The children planned this themselves."

Ghoya's face calmed and he nodded to himself. "The girl told me the same."

"For God's sake, she is only a child," Franz murmured. "You can't put her in front of a firing squad."

Ghoya raised his arm and slapped Franz across the cheek so hard that Sunny winced. "Who do you think I am? I do not shoot little girls!" he screamed. "Still, examples must be set. Yes, they must be set!"

Franz recovered and stared at Ghoya. His face bore an angry welt and a long scratch left by Ghoya's ring. Sunny resisted the urge to reach out and stroke his cheek.

"What kind of example, Mr. Ghoya?" Franz asked.

"Tomorrow at noon." Ghoya's tone turned conversational. "Your daughter will face her punishment in the street."

"What kind of punishment?"

"She will be flogged."

Franz wiped the blood from his cheek. "No . . . please. Lash me instead."

Ghoya raised his hand, ready to strike again. But a moment later he dropped it back to his side. A smile crossed his lips. "Yes, of course. Why not both of you? That would be a better example still."

Chapter 32

The windowless cell reeked of sweat and urine. Franz crouched in the corner, as far from the filthy pail that served as a toilet as he could get. At least an hour had passed since the soldiers had tossed him into the concrete box. He assumed that they planned to hold him until the flogging.

Ghoya had let Sunny go—that was some consolation—but Franz's concern for his daughter consumed him. He kept picturing Hannah terrified and alone, cowering in a cell of her own.

Franz didn't fear the whipping, not after the torture he had lived through at Bridge House. But the idea of having to watch as they flogged his daughter in front of him broke his heart. No father should have to endure that.

"*Damn that Herzberg boy,*" Franz said under his breath. But he was just as upset with himself for not having kept a closer eye on his daughter. Esther had always predicted that Hannah's spirit and curiosity might lead her into trouble. He'd already caught Hannah sneaking out of the ghetto once; Franz cursed himself for not paying more attention since.

A key turned in the lock. Franz rose to his feet as the heavy door creaked open.

Colonel Kubota stepped into the room and heaved the door close behind him. Leaning heavily on his cane, he made his way toward Franz.

"Thank you for coming, Colonel." Franz bowed deeply.

But the resigned look on Kubota's face dimmed Franz's hope before it could even take shape. When Kubota finally spoke, his tone was subdued. "Dr. Adler, I am afraid that Mr. Ghoya is perfectly correct in this instance."

Franz said nothing.

Kubota tapped his cane on the floor. "We can no more turn a blind eye to unlawfulness in the Designated Area than we can tolerate subversion."

"I understand, Colonel, I do."

Kubota's expression softened. "You are looked upon as one of the leaders in your community, Dr. Adler. It reflects poorly on you for your daughter to be caught smuggling. On us as well."

"Of course, but Hannah is only thirteen. She doesn't know better. I only ask that you punish me instead."

Kubota closed his eyes and exhaled slowly. "I would not interfere with your punishment even if I could, Dr. Adler."

Franz nodded vehemently. "But surely Hannah . . ."

Kubota turned clumsily and hobbled back to the door. He pulled it open. "You may come in, young lady."

Hannah took a tentative step into the cell, stopping just inside the doorway. She hung her head.

Franz rushed over to her with arms extended. "Hannah, darling!" he said as he enveloped her in a hug.

She trembled wordlessly against him like a puppy in a cold rainstorm. "I'm so sorry, Papa," she murmured into his chest. "So very, very sorry."

Franz inhaled her hair's familiar scent. "Everything will be all right, *Liebchen.*"

"You are in such trouble," she said. "It's all because of me. I had no—"

Franz held her face between his hands. "We are together again, Hannah-*chen*. Nothing else matters. You understand?"

"If only it were so simple, Papa. What have I done?"

Franz stared into his daughter's eyes. Something had changed in her.

He could sense the difference but could not quite put it into words. It was as though she had lost something.

She reached up and eased his hands away. It was then that Franz spotted the welts on her cheeks. Rage ripped through him at the thought of Ghoya hitting his daughter. He caressed her wounds delicately while he imagined tearing Ghoya's limbs out.

Hannah removed his hands from her cheek again. "They don't hurt, Papa."

Franz kissed the welts. "You are brave."

Kubota coughed. "You and your daughter may return home now."

Franz turned to him with a grateful smile. "Thank you, Colonel."

Kubota shook his head. "Tomorrow, Dr. Adler, you will be required to report to Mr. Ghoya shortly before noon." His gaze shifted uncomfortably to Hannah. "You as well, young lady."

"But . . ." Franz began.

"The girl will not be lashed. I have seen to that." Kubota's eyes found Hannah's again. "However, you will have to witness your father's flogging. I'm afraid it is . . . only fitting."

Her lips twitched as she fought off the tears. "I understand, Colonel."

Franz stroked her hair. "It will be all right, Hannah-*chen*."

Kubota turned for the door. "I will leave you two now."

Franz called after him. "Colonel, may I have another word?"

"There is nothing left to discuss, Dr. Adler."

"It has nothing to do with this . . . incident."

Back still turned, Kubota nodded.

Franz glanced looked over to Hannah. "Wait outside, *Liebchen*. Please. We will just be a minute or two."

She shot him a reluctant look before slowly walking to the door and closing it behind her.

Kubota turned to face Franz. "What is it, Dr. Adler?"

Franz moved a step closer and lowered his voice. "Colonel, I have heard a rumour." He paused. "Concerning you."

Kubota chuckled humourlessly. "If rumours were raindrops, Shanghai would be underwater by now."

"It's more than just a rumour."

Kubota cocked his head. "How so, Dr. Adler?"

Franz closed his eyes. Once he said the words, there would be no backtracking. But regardless of the risk, he could not remain silent. He owed this man too much. "I have reason to believe that certain people are plotting against you."

Kubota's face told him little. "Plotting to assassinate me?"

Franz nodded.

"Which people?"

"I don't know who they are," Franz said. "I have never met them. I only know that they are involved with the Underground."

"And how do you know this?"

Franz held out his hands. "I . . . I cannot say. I am not involved. Nor is the person who told me. That I promise you."

"Then why are you telling me?"

Franz motioned to the door. "You just spared my daughter from a public flogging. And last year you helped save us from the Nazis. I can never repay that debt."

Kubota frowned. "Nor can you tell me who is behind the plot to kill me."

"I do not know. I swear to you! You can hand me over to Colonel Tanaka. Even if I spent another week in Bridge House, it would not help you find the people responsible."

"Are you aware of any specifics?" Kubota asked. "When or where? Or what they are planning?"

"No, nothing," Franz said helplessly. "I only know that they are very interested in the layout of your office, here in this building. A bomb, maybe?"

Kubota bowed his head slightly. "Thank you, Dr. Adler," he said without a trace of alarm. "I appreciate you sharing this information."

"It's not my place to say, Colonel, but I hope you will take precautions. Perhaps you could post more guards?"

Kubota tilted his head in genuine surprise. "Why would I do that?"

"Surely if your life is in danger—"

"There must be thousands of people in Shanghai who would want me dead. I cannot blame them. In their shoes, I would feel the same." Kubota sighed resignedly. "Besides, good men—men whose lives are ahead of them, not behind—are dying every day. What right do I have to ask for special protection?"

"You are their leader."

Kubota laughed to himself. "I was not sent back to Shanghai to lead."

"Why were you sent back, then, Colonel?"

"To remind me of my dishonour."

"Dishonour? How is that possible? You risked your life to stand up for the refugees."

"Disobedience is dishonourable, regardless of the circumstance," Kubota said. "Our culture is sometimes difficult for an outsider to understand, Dr. Adler."

"In this case, yes."

"There is an old Japanese proverb: *Karo tōsen.* It literally means 'summer heater, winter fan.'"

"I do not understand, Colonel."

Kubota spoke softly. "Sometimes one has to recognize when one has outlasted his usefulness."

*   *   *

Two soldiers escorted Hannah and Franz from the building and released them without a word. Threats would have been superfluous, though. There was no question that Franz would be back as ordered; he had nowhere to hide.

With her head hung low, Hannah held Franz's hand weakly as they walked home. Her shame was so evident that, despite his curiosity, Franz held his tongue.

A block from their home, Hannah slowed down and freed her hand from his. "Papa, I thought . . ."

Franz turned slowly to face her. "What did you think, Hannah?"

"That I could . . . help somehow."

"*Help?* By smuggling cigarettes?"

"No—well, yes—by raising money. For the family. To contribute somehow."

The good intention behind her reckless actions only fuelled his anger. "Was this *contribution* worth risking your life—all of our lives—over?"

"Freddy's father, he said—"

Franz pulled his daughter toward him. "What did Herr Herzberg tell you?"

"That there would be no risk," she said miserably. "That they would never search a girl my age."

Franz felt as though every muscle in his body had tightened at once. "Go straight home, Hannah," he choked through clenched teeth.

"Papa, you are not going to—"

"Go home!" he barked.

Hannah eyed him, frightened, then turned and hurried away.

Franz headed down Ward Road, passing the hospital without even glancing at it. He continued until he reached the corner of Thorburn Road, where he had once collected Hannah after a visit to Freddy's home.

Franz had no idea which of the drab buildings the Herzberg family lived in. He stopped to ask an elderly refugee who was slumped on a frayed bamboo chair that appeared as fragile as the man it held. The man responded to Franz's German in Yiddish and pointed a knobby finger toward a flat on the ground floor of a nearby apartment building. Franz headed straight for it.

Freddy answered the door. At the sight of Franz, he instinctively edged back from the threshold.

"Where is your father?" Franz demanded.

"It is suppertime, Herr Doktor Adler. Perhaps he can call—"

Franz brushed past Freddy into a well-appointed sitting room. Herr Herzberg stood up. The wingback chair he'd been sitting in looked to Franz like it belonged in the Comfort Home's drawing room. The aroma of boiled meat reached Franz's nostrils just as Herzberg crossed the floor.

Herzberg was Franz's height but thicker across his chest and waist. He gave Franz the same easy smile Franz had seen from his son. "Ah, Herr Doktor Adler, we met once before." He extended a hand. "Last year, at the Ward Road heim. You were looking after a friend of mine who had stomach pains. Alfred Glockstein. Perhaps you do not remember me, but—"

"I remember you," Franz said but failed to meet the man's handshake.

Unperturbed, Herzberg dropped his arm to his side. "To this day, Glockstein tells anyone and everyone who will listen that you saved his life that night. Ah, doctors, how would we ever get by without you?"

Franz motioned to Freddy with his eyes. "We need to speak, Herr Herzberg. Outside."

Herzberg swept the suggestion away. "The boy's practically grown. Almost as tall as me. Whatever this concerns, he can hear it, too."

"Outside!" Franz turned for the door without waiting to see if Herzberg was following.

Franz stood at the curb with his arms folded. Herzberg kept him waiting but eventually joined him on the sidewalk, wearing a new-looking hat and coat. The salesman-like smile was still glued to his face.

"My daughter, Hannah," Franz began.

"Such a sweet girl, that one. And so clever. I've had the pleasure of watching her speak Chinese to a local—"

"They caught her!"

Herzberg's face crumpled with concern. "The Japanese?" He gasped. "Where? How?"

"At the Muirhead checkpoint. Smuggling cigarettes into the ghetto." Franz scowled. "*Your* cigarettes."

Herzberg brought a hand to his forehead. "That poor girl. Where is she? What will they do to her?"

"You could have gotten her killed, Herzberg!" Franz snapped. "Do you understand?"

"Could have?" Herzberg's expression softened and understanding lit up his eyes. "Have they released her, then?"

"How could you have done such a thing to Hannah? To any child? Risking her life to smuggle your booty."

Herzberg shrugged good-naturedly. "Honestly, I never expected them to search a girl as innocent looking as your daughter. Had I thought that she was in any danger of being searched . . ."

Franz held his hands tightly at his sides, suspecting he might otherwise grab the man's throat. "You turned my daughter into a scapegoat, Herzberg. The victim of your crime." Franz left out that he himself would be the one to face the consequences.

Herzberg seemed unconcerned. "No one forced Hannah," he said calmly. "She volunteered to go. And we gave her a share of the profits."

"She is thirteen years old!" Franz's jaw fell open. "How do you sleep at night?"

"Not bad," Herzberg said. "Certainly, much better than when I used to live in that overcrowded heim off two cups of watery soup a day. We are doing better, true, but look around you, Dr. Adler. Who among us can afford the luxury of high moral standards?"

"High moral standards? Are you a lunatic? You risked a child's life! You used my daughter to do your dirty work!"

Herzberg shrugged. "Why don't you place the blame where it truly belongs?"

"And where is that?"

"With the Nazis. With Hitler! He forced us into this wretched place." Herzberg watched a Chinese man in a traditional straw hat struggling to balance a bamboo pole across his shoulders. "To live like these peasants. Like animals."

"Hitler? He made you take advantage of children?"

Herzberg exhaled. "He has forced me do whatever is necessary to protect my family."

Franz grabbed Herzberg by the collar of his coat. "You will stay away from Hannah. Far away! Do you understand me?"

Herzberg stared back at him but made no attempt to resist. "Yes, Herr Doktor. You are most easy to understand."

"And you and your son will never involve another child in your schemes. The smuggling stops now, Herzberg. Am I clear?"

"What we do with our business is not your—"

Franz pulled harder, hoisting Herzberg up on his toes. "No more smuggling!" he cried.

Herzberg clamped his hands over Franz's wrists and began to pry them free. "And what can you do about it?"

"If I hear of you selling so much as a single cigarette in the ghetto, I will tell Mr. Ghoya precisely what you have done."

Herzberg froze, and his eyes filled with terror and conciliation. "No, of course. No more smuggling. Never again," he sputtered.

Chapter 33

Refugees and Chinese citizens alike gathered at the intersection of Muirhead and Wayside Roads to watch the soldiers erecting the wooden post in the middle of the street. Hannah had heard that floggings in the ghetto always drew a substantial crowd. She assumed that people came out of morbid curiosity, and it disgusted her to see such a gathering for the sole purpose of witnessing her father's whipping. She would have given anything to not have to watch.

Freddy had promised to be there, too, but he was nowhere in sight. Hannah was glad not to see him. She had only told him out of spite. She wanted Freddy to feel guilty, like she did. But it hadn't worked; she saw through his feigned concern. All he cared about was that she had not turned him in and that his own family had been spared the whip.

What a fool I was! She had fallen so hard for Freddy's American-style charm. Only now she could see how he had manipulated her. Even the kiss that had shaken her world had just been an act. She had been his pawn from the first day. Undoubtedly, Freddy would find a replacement; perhaps even Leah Wasselmann.

Hannah's stomach churned. She worried about vomiting again, especially when her father reappeared.

They had walked together from the hospital to the Bureau of Stateless

Refugee Affairs, but Ghoya had whisked Franz into the building as soon as they arrived. She had not seen him since. Hannah had never felt so alone. She wished Sunny was with her. She longed to hold her hand.

On the way over, Hannah had asked her father why he insisted that they keep the flogging from his wife.

"What good would it do to tell her?" Franz asked.

"She would want to be here for you."

"For what, Hannah?" he snapped. "So she could suffer, too?"

"I . . . I . . ." she stuttered. "This is all my fault."

"What's done is done, Hannah-*chen*." He exhaled. "I wish to God you didn't have to see this, but they have given us no choice."

"It should be me, Papa."

Franz placed an arm around her shoulder and brought his daughter to a halt. His eyes locked onto hers. "Do you not understand how much worse that would have been for me?"

She shook her head. "I am responsible."

"The Herzbergs had no right to involve you."

"But—"

"Just as I have no right to involve Sunny," he said. "You know she would insist on being here, too."

"She would want to be here," Hannah repeated.

"Sunny has so many worries right now. Yang's arrest has been so hard on her. She does not need to see this. Neither do you." He squeezed her shoulder. "Hannah, promise me that you will look away or cover your eyes."

"I . . . I have to watch, Papa. That colonel said so."

"Promise me, Hannah."

"I will try."

She was snapped from the memory by the sight of Ghoya leading her father out of the building. Two soldiers were with Franz, but they didn't need to detain him. He walked calmly, with his head held high.

Hannah burned with guilt to see her father, who always dressed so fastidiously, clad only in an undershirt and trousers. As he passed her, he nodded once, as though to remind her of her promise, and then gave her a tight reassuring smile.

As soon as the contingent reached the post in the middle of the intersection, Franz stepped forward and leaned against it, holding up his hands so one of the soldiers could bind them with rope to the rusty metal ring that hung above him. Once Franz's wrists were secure, the soldier grabbed her father's undershirt and ripped it apart, exposing his bare back. The other soldier stood back from the post, a thick black whip in his hands. Its tail was so long that it gathered at his feet like a coiled snake.

Hannah smelled aftershave and turned to see Ghoya sidling up to her. "Do you see, girlie?" he demanded. "Do you? This is what happens to smugglers."

"I have learned my lesson, Mr. Ghoya," she blurted. "I swear to God! Please do not punish my father."

Ghoya grinned widely. Then, without warning, he slapped her across her bruised cheek. The pain stung worse than the first blows the day before, but she bit her lip and stifled her tears, desperate to stay strong for her father.

"Examples must be set," Ghoya hissed into her ear. "You should be on that pole, too. If not for Taisa Kubota . . ."

Realizing that it was futile to plead anymore, she looked down at her feet.

Ghoya reached out and pinched her jaw, then forcibly rotated her face in the direction of the post. "You must watch this, girlie! Every lash, every single lash. They are for you, too."

The soldier nearest her father hollered in Japanese. Hannah only recognized the last word—"*ichi*"—which she knew meant "one." The soldier holding the whip cocked back his arm.

Franz squared his shoulders and raised his head higher.

Ghoya maintained his grip on Hannah's face, but Hannah averted her eyes upward. Even so, she saw the whip uncoiling overhead. It cracked through the air. The next thing she heard was a revolting snap.

A gasp escaped Franz's lips.

Hannah couldn't help but look over. She was horrified to see a raw wound coursing the length of her father's exposed back. His knees buckled slightly and he stooped forward against the post, bleeding.

"You see, girlie?" Ghoya asked. "Do you?"

"I do," Hannah breathed.

"Yes, yes. Everyone must see." Ghoya turned to the watching crowd and bellowed, "This is what happens to smugglers! Tell the others: next time it will be a firing squad. Yes, yes! Tell them that, too!"

The first soldier called out, "*Ni*"—"Two."

Franz straightened his legs and arched his spine.

Hannah glanced skyward again. She tasted bile as the lash sizzled overhead.

Chapter 34

October 11, 1943

Sunny hurried along Thibet Road on her way to Frenchtown. Despite the warmth of the autumn day, she kept her hands tucked in her coat pockets and her chin buried in her collar as she passed one Japanese soldier after another. She imagined each of them snapping a whip, and her rage simmered.

Half an hour after she'd applied salve and bandages to Franz's back, Sunny could still feel the rough edges of his wounds against her fingertips. She was amazed that infection had not set in over the past week. She had to fight back tears every time she changed the dressing.

For his part, Franz hid his suffering behind smiles and occasional jokes. He had even returned to work to assist Sunny on an urgent amputation and a perforated colon repair. Still, she knew he was in agony.

Sunny's anger wasn't limited to the Japanese. She was furious with Hannah, too, and had yet to forgive Franz for keeping the flogging a secret. Sunny had only learned of it when a Jewish woman burst into the hospital hysterical with the news. Upon sprinting to the site, Sunny found Franz half-naked and curled up at the foot of the whipping post. There was so much blood caked over his back that it appeared painted on. The sight of Hannah was almost as distressing. The girl rocked silently on her knees beside her father, tears streaming down her cheeks. Franz was unable to rise to his feet, and Sunny had to ask a pair of young men to carry him home over their shoulders.

Forcing that day from her mind, Sunny focused on the more hopeful news that Joey had delivered the day before. He was shouting as he burst onto the ward. "I found her, Soon Yi! I found her!"

Sunny raced over to him. "*Yang?* You found Yang?"

"Yes!"

"Where?" She threw her arms around Joey and danced him around in a circle. "Is she here with you? Outside?"

He shook his head, beaming. "No. She's in Lunghua. Can you believe it?"

Her arms fell away. "The prison camp?"

Joey knit his brow, puzzled at her tone. "With the Americans and the British, too. Lunghua is not so bad, Sunny. There are even children inside."

It was true. Sunny had heard that the conditions at Lunghua were more bearable than at many of the other sites that the Japanese still referred to as "civic assembly centres." "How do you know Yang is there?"

"Guo-Zhi." A silent labourer, Guo-Zhi had worked at the refugee hospital longer than Sunny had. "His wife went out to Lunghua Camp to take food to her former employer—you know, that widowed Englishman. She saw Yang being unloaded off a truck out front."

"Did Yang look well?"

"Her face was bruised and she had a limp, Guo-Zhi told me." Then he hurried to add, "But at least Yang was on her feet. This is so much better than what the news could have been."

Joey was right. Sunny found solace in the knowledge that Yang was at a relatively safe camp, rather than in some torture chamber like Bridge House or buried in one of the mass graves, as she had come to fear. Still, she couldn't help but wish for more. She wanted Yang home with her.

The thought faded as Sunny saw the gentle curve of the Cathay Building ahead of her. Despite Shanghai's general dilapidation, the grand building—a fusion of Gothic and art deco design styles—gleamed as brightly as ever, sunlight reflecting today off its gilded motifs.

Sunny slipped in through the ornamental copper doors and hurried across the lobby to the elevator. As the car rose higher, so did her trepidation. She rarely visited Jia-Li at her home; her best friend often hosted clients there. Sunny had never before arrived unannounced, but today she had no choice. The whole neighbourhood had lost telephone service again. Besides, word had swirled through the ghetto that the Japanese were closely monitoring the phone lines. Few were willing to risk discussing anything on the line, especially any matters that could be construed as remotely sensitive.

Sunny stepped off at the ninth floor and approached Jia-Li's flat at the end of the hallway. She rapped three times on the door, then paused and tapped four times. Their signal.

A few seconds passed, long enough for Sunny to wonder whether Jia-Li was out or indisposed. Then the door opened a crack. "Are you alone?" Jia-Li whispered.

"Yes."

The door opened wider and Sunny stepped inside.

Wearing only a black silk robe, Jia-Li greeted Sunny with a hug. Beneath her jasmine perfume, Sunny detected a trace of sweat and something else. Assuming that she had interrupted a client's visit, Sunny wriggled free of her friend's embrace and back-pedalled toward the door. "I am sorry to surprise you, *bǎo bèi*. I will come back later."

Jia-Li reached for Sunny's forearm, pulling her back. "What is this foolishness, *xiǎo hè?*"

"Honestly, it is no inconvenience," Sunny said. "I'll return later. When you are more available."

Jia-Li glanced down at her short robe and then looked up, suddenly understanding. She cleared her throat. "Oh, Charlie is home with me. We, um, slept in late this morning."

The two friends stared at each other for a moment before breaking into simultaneous laughter, which soon evolved into a fit of giggles. "Perhaps Charlie would have been safer staying with that refugee family after all," Sunny choked out between laughs.

"He might have gotten more sleep," Jia-Li joked.

A clopping noise drew Sunny's attention. She turned to see Charlie, shirt untucked, making his way toward her. The sound of his crutches against the wooden floor reminded her of hoof beats. "Nice to see you, Soon Yi." He smiled without a trace of self-consciousness.

Jia-Li wiped a happy tear from her eye and then locked elbows with Sunny. "Come, sit with us. I'll make tea."

As they settled themselves, Sunny shared the news about Yang. It led to another hug and more giggles of relief. The women sat down side by side on the couch, while Charlie eased into the room's sole wingback chair. Sunny noticed how empty the apartment was. On her last visit, it had been filled with decorative objects: paintings, sculptures, rugs and ornaments, including a massive gilded candelabrum and an ornately painted Ming vase. Sunny wondered if Jia-Li had hocked her possessions to help support the Adlers with "loans" that they would never be able to repay.

"As you can see, *xiǎo hè*, I have uncluttered somewhat."

Sunny squeezed her hand. "All your beautiful decorations, *bǎo bèi* . . ."

"Were out of style anyway. I think it looks better this way. Better feng shui." Jia-Li looked over to Charlie with a loving grin. "Besides, none of my vases stood a chance with my one-legged rhinoceros stampeding about."

He laughed. "I am still light as a feather. Even on only one foot."

Despite his gauntness, Charlie looked more robust than he had on Sunny's last visit. "You are feeling stronger, Charlie?" she asked.

He flexed his elbow. "I could lift you both with one arm."

"You have done enough lifting for one day." Jia-Li laughed and this time Charlie reddened slightly.

Jia-Li's joy was contagious. Sunny was also relieved that, unlike on her previous visits, Charlie had yet to mention his impatience to return to his troops. As though reading her mind, he leaned forward in his chair and said, "I still intend to get back to my men, but priorities have shifted."

Sunny looked from Charlie to Jia-Li. "So I see."

"No, no," he said. "I mean the Flying Tigers."

Jia-Li eyed Charlie warily, but he didn't seem to notice.

"The American planes?" Sunny asked.

"Exactly!" He almost jumped out of his chair with excitement. "They crossed overhead on their way to the river again this morning. I counted them as they flew home. They did not lose a single fighter."

"So American planes will keep him in the city," Jia-Li said to herself as she lit a cigarette. "At least something will."

"You know how important this is, precious," Charlie said. "It means the war is coming to Shanghai."

Suddenly uneasy again, Sunny asked, "Hasn't the war been here since the first bomb fell on Hongkew?"

"That battle was lost years ago. Our incompetent generalissimo wasted half his army trying to defend the city without adequate air support." Charlie motioned to the ceiling. "Now, with the help of the Americans, we can finally turn the tide against the *Rìběn guǐzi*."

Jia-Li turned to him dubiously, a cigarette dangling from her lips. "You don't mean us, Chun? Surely not." It was the first time Sunny had heard her use his Chinese name.

"I do." He nodded enthusiastically. "From inside the city, too. No longer out in the countryside."

"But how can you help the American planes, Charlie?" Sunny asked.

"The *Rìběn guǐzi* can only move troops and supplies in and out of the city via the river or the railway," he said.

Jia-Li sat up straighter. "Then why can't the Americans bomb those?"

"So far, they have sent only fighters. No bombers. I suspect the Allies have not yet gathered the air power for such a mission." Charlie shrugged. "Regardless, we can reach the railway terminal just as easily as any bomber. And the Japanese transmitter is in Hongkew. Right outside the ghetto."

"Reach them how?" Jia-Li nodded in the direction of his crutches. "Besides, what would you use to blow up the terminal or the transmitter?"

Charlie's grin only widened. "Fireworks, if need be."

"Charlie, you are in no condition for that," Sunny said. "You are still recovering from—"

Jia-Li leapt to her feet. "This is nothing but fantasy!" she cried, waving her cigarette wildly. "You see yourself liberating Shanghai. A hero. The same way I imagine myself as a wife, and even a mother someday. A woman of virtue. Not what I really am: a glorified wild pheasant."

Charlie stared at her, his smile tempered but not gone.

Jia-Li dropped to her knees in front of him, grabbing his hand in hers. When she spoke again, her voice trembled. "The truth is we are both damaged beyond repair. You and I . . . we are only dreaming, Chun."

*   *   *

As Sunny walked through the International Settlement, she reflected on Jia-Li's outburst. Her best friend was smitten to a degree Sunny had never seen before. Pleased as she was for Jia-Li, Sunny worried over the risks of this new romance. Not only could Charlie be gone or lost in an instant but Jia-Li would remain in grave danger every moment that she spent with him.

As Sunny crossed the Bund and entered the Public Garden, her mind turned to the real purpose of her trip out of the ghetto.

Wen-Cheng was sitting on the same park bench as always, holding a newspaper in front of his face. A quick look around her confirmed that no one else was in the gardens. Sunny dropped down onto the far end of the bench.

"How is Franz?" Wen-Cheng asked without lowering the paper.

"Better."

"I am pleased to hear it." He paused. "And Charlie?"

"What about him?"

"Have you found him alternative accommodations?"

"Yes."

"Where?"

"With Jia-Li."

Wen-Cheng nodded. "And you, Soon Yi? How are you?"

"I am no longer . . . comfortable."

Wen-Cheng turned a page but said nothing.

"Our contact—the old man," Sunny continued. "Do you know much about him?"

"He was a friend of my father's. Before the invasion, he was involved with the municipal council."

"That must be how he knew Kubota. The colonel used to work in the mayor's office." Sunny nodded to herself. "I knew they must have had some kind of previous relationship. You can tell by the way he speaks about him."

Wen-Cheng eyed her momentarily before turning back to the newspaper. His voice took on a sudden urgency. "I warned you: once you commit, there is no way out."

Sunny felt a heavy weight descend on her shoulders, but she could only nod.

"You feel a debt of loyalty toward the colonel. I understand that." Wen-Cheng exhaled. "But it is not up to you or me to decide such things. We are like . . . soldiers. We must do as we are told. Otherwise it will become very dangerous for us."

"How can I simply—" Sunny detected movement out of the corner of her eye. Her pulse raced as she watched the old man in the grey Zhongshan suit limping down the pathway toward them. He moved at a leisurely pace, stopping every few yards to stare at the weed-riddled lawn.

Sunny knew that the old man and his network were not the enemy. The members of the Resistance were risking so much—their lives and those of their loved ones, too—to liberate her city. She admired their bravery and selflessness, but at that moment, all she wanted was to see the old man turn and walk away forever. By the time he finally reached the bench, Sunny's mouth had gone dry.

He stood with his back turned to them, holding his arthritic fingers interlocked behind his back. "Soon Yi, we need you to set up an appointment with Colonel Kubota."

"An appointment?" Sunny shook her head. "I cannot do that."

The old man stood absolutely still. "Cannot or will not?"

"I cannot get in to see the colonel," Sunny said, remembering what she had practised saying earlier that day with Franz. "I already tried, last week."

"Oh?" The old man turned slightly in her direction. "And why were you trying to see the colonel?"

"To stop my husband from being flogged," Sunny lied. "I went to his office and begged the guards to allow me in. I waited outside for hours, and when the colonel finally came out, he just breezed past me and got into his car. He did not even acknowledge me."

The man shrugged slightly. "Perhaps if you are calmer when you return."

"It won't make a difference." Sunny willed indifference into her tone. "My stepdaughter was caught smuggling cigarettes into the ghetto. My husband is *persona non grata* with the Japanese. I doubt the colonel would see me under any circumstances."

"Sunny is right," Wen-Cheng said from behind his newspaper. "Perhaps it would be better to revise the plan."

The old man just turned his head and gazed out at the river. The breeze blew a few blades of brown grass across Sunny's feet. Her heart thumped as she waited for his next words.

"I had assumed you would be more resourceful, Soon Yi," the old man said with a small sigh. "Considering how the Japanese mistreated your illustrious father, I thought you would at least be dedicated to our cause."

"I am dedicated," she insisted. "Those savages killed my father. They whipped my husband. I would do anything to be rid of the *Rìběn guǐzi*."

"Then you will find a way to meet with the colonel," he said sharply. "This week."

Sunny went cold. "And if I cannot?"

The old man looked skyward. "The battle lines have long been drawn, Soon Yi. All that is left is for you to decide exactly where you stand."

Chapter 35

Franz leaned back in his chair and immediately regretted it. His back stung as though someone were digging their nails into the open wounds, but he bit his lip and fought off the pain. Hannah was watching.

"Can I get you anything, Papa?" she asked as she hopped to her feet and headed toward the kitchen.

"I am not an invalid, Hannah."

How quickly the roles are reversed, he thought. A year and a half earlier, he had hovered day and night over his daughter's bed as she fought a cholera infection that had nearly proven fatal. At the time, he had been cognizant of her every movement; even the smallest suggestion of discomfort launched him into action. Now, it was Hannah treating him as the patient.

His daughter had changed; there was no denying it. Even through her moodiness earlier in the spring, she was still his little girl and, though she didn't seem to realize it at the time, needed him as much if not more than ever. But this was different. Franz was proud of her sudden maturity, but there was more to it—a burgeoning independence. And he didn't yet feel ready to let go of the child in her.

"There are still a few leaves left, Papa." Hannah lifted a small teapot. "I can steep more tea for you."

"One more cup and I will sweat green." Smiling, he leaned forward to take the pressure off his searing back. "How is school, Hannah?"

"Same as ever"

"And with Freddy . . ."

She crossed her arms over her chest. "I do not speak to him."

"Perhaps he is not as much to blame as you think." When she didn't reply, Franz added, "His father should never have involved either of you with those cigarettes."

"Freddy knew what he was doing."

Franz would never trust the boy again either, but he was willing to defend him if it helped protect Hannah's feelings. "People do desperate things in desperate times, Hannah-*chen*. Especially if they believe they are doing it for their family."

"I have seen Freddy for what he really is." Her expression was stoic and her eyes clear.

The door opened and Sunny stepped inside.

One glimpse told Franz how upset she was. He turned to Hannah. "Your aunt will be home soon with rice. We will need hot water for dinner."

Without a word, Hannah grabbed the rusty pot off the counter and headed out the door.

As soon as she had left, Sunny plunked down beside him and took his hand in hers. "I met the old man from the Underground."

Although her tone was emotionless, Franz sensed her anxiety. He sat up straighter and leaned back into the chair, hardly noticing the pain. "Was it an ultimatum?"

"Perhaps. I am not sure."

"And what does that mean for you? For us?"

She held up her free hand, then let it drop to her side.

He nodded to himself. "I will speak to Wen-Cheng."

"No, Franz. He is as helpless as we are."

"He got you into this."

"*I* did that myself."

"I blame him!" Franz suddenly found an outlet for all his indignation—toward the Herzbergs, the Underground, the Japanese and even Sunny. "Why did Wen-Cheng ever come to the refugee hospital?"

"To help."

Franz squeezed her hand so hard that she had to tug it free. "For no other reason than you, Sunny. He came for you."

"You are not thinking clearly."

"Nonsense. I have known it for months. Perhaps you are the one whose perspective is clouded."

Sunny cocked her head. "Franz, are you accusing me of something?" she asked softly.

He could not let go of his anger. "Wen-Cheng could have volunteered anywhere. To help with his own people. He is from Shanghai, after all. Instead, he chose a German Jewish refugee hospital. Why?"

"He knew that we worked there."

"*We?*" Franz grunted.

"All right, me, then."

"Exactly."

Sunny stood up and straightened her skirt. "Whatever Wen-Cheng's motives for coming to the hospital, they did not affect my actions. For the longest time, he would not even admit to being involved, let alone introduce me to anyone involved in the Underground. I insisted. I wanted to participate." She hesitated. "I needed to."

He frowned. "You *needed* to?"

"Yes, darling," she said evenly. "If I were not born here, I would not understand it myself. I felt that I needed to do something. Anything. If only to honour the memory of my father."

"You are correct. I do not understand."

They sat in silence for a few moments. Franz's anger dissipated, but worry only filled the void. "I warned Colonel Kubota," he finally said. "What else can we do?"

His wife shook her head, her light brown eyes glistening.

"What if they come for you, Sunny?" he asked.

"Oh, Franz. Those people from the Underground—they are decent people."

"Maybe so, but if they believe you defied them or, worse, think for one moment that you might collaborate . . ."

She leaned forward and placed her fingers lightly on the back of his neck, careful to avoid his wounds. "We will be all right."

"How can you be sure?"

"Simon." She laughed. "You know how he likes to compares us to cats. For always landing on our feet."

"It's not even true of cats. Let alone us."

"We will get through this." She kissed him on the lips and then pulled away. "I must go freshen up."

As Sunny headed to the bedroom, Franz's thoughts drifted to his American friend. He had last seen Simon two days earlier, at the refugee hospital, as they waited together for Joey to show up with a vehicle to move him.

Dressed in the straw hat and ragged pants of a coolie, Joey arrived rolling a honey wagon ahead of him like a wheelbarrow. Even the normally unflappable Simon was distressed by the stench that seeped out from the oversized barrel.

"I washed it myself, Mr. Simon," Joey explained apologetically. "And look." He reached into the barrel and pulled out a worryingly full bucket of waste.

Franz and Simon peered inside the barrel and saw that the space beneath the bucket, where Simon was to hide, appeared relatively clean. Simon looked a little green, but he forced a chuckle. "Wonder if my family back home still thinks I'm living in the lap of luxury."

Joey brought a hand to his chest. "Boss, with me driving, it will be a short ride."

Simon motioned to the sloshing bucket. "Slow and steady, Joey, while I'm riding under that thing." He closed his eyes. "Slow and steady."

Franz patted Simon's shoulder. "It will not be too long."

Simon breathed through his mouth. "I can survive an hour or two. I think."

"I meant that we will soon find somewhere more suitable for you to live."

"I'm kind of looking forward to rooming with Ernst," Simon said. "I get a kick out of him. He's so cynical—he would make a good Jew. A good New Yorker, too, for that matter."

"Except he lives in the heart of Germantown."

"So what?" Simon rolled his eyes. "I'm not marching in any parades."

"The last time Sunny visited, Baron von Puttkamer came over unannounced."

"I'll keep a low profile," Simon promised. "As long as I am near Essie and my boy, I don't care if I have to hide under the sofa while Göring and Goebbels have tea."

Joey helped Simon into the barrel. As he crouched down inside, he looked back up at Franz with uncharacteristic hesitation. "This . . . this can't last forever, can it?"

"The tide is turning against the Japanese and the Germans," Franz said, hoping he didn't sound as half-hearted as he felt.

"Ready, boss?" Joey asked.

Simon gave him a wry grin. "Remember, Joey: slow and steady."

The young man slid the waste-filled bucket into the slot above his head and carefully wedged it into place.

Franz was still thinking about Simon as the door to the flat opened and Esther entered, holding Jakob over her shoulder. As soon as she lowered the baby to the floor, he stirred, reaching for his favourite wooden rattle, giving it a drowsy shake.

Franz noticed Esther's pallor. "What is the matter, Essie?"

"Oh, that man . . ." Her voice was shaky.

"What man?"

"Mr. Ghoya."

"What has he done now?"

Esther's eyes swept down to Jakob before focusing on Franz. "I went to see him to ask for a pass to visit Simon."

"And?"

"He asked me all sorts of strange questions. Still, he seemed to be in a good mood. Everyone in line had said so. He even signed my pass."

"So what went wrong?"

"Well, he asked me where I lived." She squeezed her forehead. "When I told him, Ghoya asked if I knew you."

As Franz rose to his feet, the wounds on his back throbbed. "You didn't tell him that you lived with Hannah and me, did you?"

"I didn't know what to say. That little man, he became so agitated. He started screaming." Her face crumpled. "He jumped onto his desk, Franz! Can you imagine? Such a scene."

"You told him?"

"Only that you used to be my brother-in-law. Not that we lived together."

"What did he say?"

Esther slumped down into the chair that Franz had just vacated. "Ghoya said that no one in our family would ever leave the ghetto again. No, he didn't say it. He shrieked it."

"Oh, Essie."

"What am I to do?" Esther murmured. "I will never be allowed out, and Simon cannot get back inside. He will never see his son again."

"Yes, he will," Sunny said from the doorway. "I will take Jakob to him."

Chapter 36

October 18, 1943

Jakob hadn't made a sound during their journey through the International Settlement, but despite the baby's cooperation, they made slow progress. Sunny stopped to feed him a bottle of milk and then again a block later to change his diaper in the backroom of a teashop that was run by a friendly old Shanghainese woman. Sunny couldn't resist taking other breaks along the way, too, to rub noses with him, tickle his belly or swoosh him through the air—anything to elicit another one of his giggles.

Sunny was happy for the distraction. She'd spent much of the past few days, and sleepless nights, thinking about her last conversation with Wen-Cheng. Two days earlier, he had whispered a request to meet her in private. As soon as they were alone in the staff room, Wen-Cheng asked, "Have you found a way into Kubota's office yet?"

She held out a hand, palm up. "I cannot do it."

"Cannot or will not?"

"You, too, Wen-Cheng?" She hung her head. "Does it really matter which?"

"No." He sighed. "It's better this way. Whatever the Underground intends for you to do will only have terrible consequences."

"What will they do now?"

"The old man and the others, they have grown impatient."

"So they will make other plans?"

"I believe they already have."

She hesitated. "What does that mean for me?"

He broke off eye contact. "I . . . I am not certain."

"These men. They are fighting for China. For us."

"It's true." He paused and then added, "And they will do whatever they deem necessary to protect their cause."

There was no mistaking his tone. Sunny shivered. "I see."

"I never should have let it come to this."

"Stop it, Wen-Cheng. We have been through this too many times."

Wen-Cheng's expression was suddenly melancholic. "If only I had had the courage five years ago to leave my wife. It could have been so different for us."

Sunny reached a hand out but stopped short of touching him. "Everything has happened for a reason. You cannot blame yourself."

"I feel no blame, Sunny. Only regret."

She didn't know what to say, so she bit her lip and nodded.

His expression hardened. "You will be all right, Sunny. That I promise you."

She smiled. "Wen-Cheng, what can you possibly do?"

"Whatever I have to," he murmured and then repeated in a firmer tone, "Whatever I have to."

Sunny shook off the unsettling memory of the determined look in Wen-Cheng's pale eyes. She pulled Jakob against her chest. It felt so natural to cradle him that way. She wondered again when she and Franz might have a baby of their own, though she recognized the absurdity of the thought, particularly in light of what Wen-Cheng had implied about the Underground's intentions.

As Sunny reached the edge of Germantown, she saw swastikas fluttering overhead like laundry on a clothesline. Before she had met Franz—before war had decimated Shanghai—she used to giggle through the newsreels that played before the matinees, the goose-stepping Nazis with their ubiquitous flags. She thought of the nightclub comedian she had once seen: his Hitler impersonation had evoked convulsions of laughter from the audience.

No one was laughing anymore.

Sunny made eye contact with a tall European man in a homburg who stood on the other side of the street. He returned her gaze, but his expression was hostile. She turned and hurried up the steps to Ernst's apartment. Without thinking, she rapped on the door using the secret knock she shared with Jia-Li.

"*Ja?*" Ernst asked through the door. "Who's there?"

"Sunny."

The door flew open and Ernst stepped out in a tattered, paint-speckled shirt. A cigarette burned between his fingers. "Well, if it isn't my mixed-blooded courtesan herself," he joked, kissing her on both cheeks and pulling her by the elbow inside the flat. He nodded at Jakob. "And look. You've come bearing gifts."

Even more canvases now cluttered the small room. Some lay on the floor while others were stacked against the walls. Most of them appeared unfinished, with whole sections that were sketched and uncoloured, or completely blank. She even spotted a portrait of herself—presumably sketched to cover Ernst's lies about their relationship—propped against the wall.

Simon's head popped out from the corridor. As soon as he spotted Jakob, he dashed across the room with arms outstretched. "My boy!"

Simon eased Jakob out of Sunny's arms and covered his head in kisses. He brought his face up to his son's and cooed. Jakob responded with a happy squeal. Simon laughed. "Name one thing in this world that smells as good as my boy—just one thing!"

"Have you ever cracked open a fresh bottle of Hennessy?" Ernst asked. "Its bouquet is not of this world. Beyond compare."

"Do you hear that, Jake?" Simon said. "Uncle Ernst thinks you don't smell as good as hooch."

"Please, never 'hooch,'" Ernst protested. "Only the world's most delicious cognac."

Simon glanced at Sunny. "Where's Essie?"

"She couldn't come, Simon."

His back stiffened slightly. "She's okay, though?"

"She couldn't secure a pass."

"Next time," Simon assured his son. "Mommy will visit Daddy next time, isn't that right, fella?"

Sunny laid a hand lightly on his shoulder. "Esther can't leave the ghetto, Simon."

His face fell. "Ever?"

Sunny told him about Esther's run-in with Ghoya. Simon gritted his teeth. "That miniature tyrant. He can't stop us."

"Of course he can, Simon. Dwarf or not. In this new world, all that matters is the size of the gun," Ernst muttered. "Those with the biggest, they make the rules now."

Simon bounced Jakob in his arms. "I'm sick of their stupid rules," he exclaimed.

"What choice is there?" Sunny asked.

Simon looked up at her with a sad, almost apologetic, smile. "Look, Sunny, I know what a burden I've become for you all. I hate it. But I have no choice. It's my family. I got out of the internment camp to be close to them. Same for the Comfort Home. And I will leave here, too—in a heartbeat—to see Essie again."

"Simon, what happened with Ghoya . . . it's all still very raw," Sunny said sympathetically. "See what the next few weeks bring before you do anything rash." She stopped herself from offering any hollow reassurances about Ghoya reconsidering.

"She's right." Ernst extracted a crumpled pack of cigarettes from his shirt pocket and offered one to Simon, who, to Sunny's surprise, accepted.

With the baby in his arms, Simon waved off Ernst's lighter. Instead, he tucked the cigarette behind his ear. "I can wait a week, maybe two. But no longer, I swear. I will go right out of my head."

"A week or two," Ernst echoed through a cloud of smoke. "In that time, I will transform you into a painter." He gestured toward one of the smaller canvases propped up against the wall. "Look, Sunny. The work of our American hero. What do you think?"

Sunny overcame her surprise and stepped closer to examine the painting: a greenish-blue vase bursting with yellow daffodils. Although it looked amateurish beside Ernst's work, it wasn't bad. "I had no idea you could paint, Simon."

"You gotta be kidding, Sunny," he grunted. "Poor old Van Gogh must be spinning in his grave."

"I doubt that tortured soul ever stops spinning," Ernst said. "Still, Sunny is correct. You have ability. That one is rubbish, of course." He waved his hand at the paintings scattered around the room. "But really not so different from the tripe I paint these days."

Simon pointed at a stack of canvases in the far corner. "Show her the real one, Ernst."

"*Ach*, why would she be interested?"

Sunny nodded encouragingly. "Please, Ernst. Show me."

"It's hardly more than a doodle." He exhaled a puff of smoke. "I had to do something of . . . of substance before I went out of my mind with this flea market work."

Sunny stepped over to the corner of the room.

"The one closest to the wall," Simon instructed.

Sunny moved two large canvases aside, picked up a smaller one buried behind them and turned it outward. At first glance, she mistook the subject of the portrait for Jia-Li. On closer inspection, she saw that the model had a fuller figure and a wider face than Jia-Li's, with crow's feet that had yet to visit the corners of her friend's eyes. Still, the woman's expression hinted at the boredom she so often saw in Jia-Li's. Ernst had painted the woman in the same stark style of his pre-war portraits: naked on her back, with legs crossed and arms held above her head, hands folded behind her neck. Sunny could not tell whether the woman was lying on a mattress or the ground, since the background was unpainted. Her skin was nearly as pale the canvas but for her pink nipples and the wisps of dark hair between her legs. But Sunny was most struck by the ragged horizontal lines that ran up the woman's arms like rungs of a ladder.

The scars reminded her of a teenager she used to see at the Country Hospital. The girl had witnessed the rape and murder of her own mother during a Japanese raid, from inside the wicker box where the woman had hidden her. In the ensuing months, her father brought the girl to the hospital on several occasions for care of self-inflicted slash wounds to her wrists. One day, the man returned to the hospital alone to tell Sunny that his daughter had cut the artery too deeply for anyone to help.

Sunny angled her head to study the painting. "What does it represent, Ernst?"

"Represent?" Ernst snorted. "Nothing. It's just a painting."

"I see beauty and vulnerability," Simon said. "And pain, of course. Agonizing pain. All those scars on her arms that will never heal."

"Such nonsense," Ernst scoffed. "You sound exactly like Franz, finding meaning where there is none. All this symbolizes is my revulsion over having to paint yet another Brandenburg Gate or Alpine meadow for those Nazi philistines."

At the mention of the Germans, Sunny peeled her eyes from the canvas. "Ernst, that dinner at von Puttkamer's? Did you go?"

"I did, yes."

"What was it like?"

"The food was divine. There was a scrumptious sauerbraten. The meat was done to perfection, and it was served with delicious claret. The company, on the other hand . . ." He exhaled heavily.

"Who was there?" Sunny asked.

"Oh, I don't know. Obersturmführer this, and Sturmhauptführer that. All those self-important fools and their pompous titles and uniforms. Like a bunch of children playing dress-up."

"What about the ghetto?" Sunny asked. "Did they talk about their plans for the refugees?"

"Only in the vaguest terms," Ernst admitted. "I tried to bring it up with von Puttkamer, but he said he didn't want to discuss anything so unpleasant at such a happy occasion."

"So unpleasant?" Sunny balled her hands into fists. "What did he mean by that?"

"Who knows? The baron probably spouts anti-Semitic rhetoric in his sleep. After dinner, when von Puttkamer was really quite sauced, I asked him again. He just carried on about showing 'those Jews' what's what and suchlike. No specifics at all."

"Perhaps they have given up?"

"You heard what von Puttkamer said—right here in this very room." Ernst shook his head. "No. They have a plan."

Simon hoisted Jakob above his head. The baby squealed again in delight. "Maybe we need a plan of our own."

"A plan for what?" Sunny asked.

"Dealing with the baron."

"Here we go again." Ernst turned to Sunny. "Our American friend here spends half his time scheming. He believes we can cripple the Third Reich with a decisive attack on Germantown. Apparently Shanghai, not the Eastern Front, is Hitler's Achilles heel."

"Why not?" Simon demanded.

Sunny's nerves felt raw. "Why not what?"

"Deal with von Puttkamer. A pre-emptive strike."

"You are not serious, Simon?" she gasped.

As Simon rocked Jakob his face turned to stone. "Would it be better to just sit back and wait for those animals to attack the ghetto? To just hope they don't kill too many women and children?"

*   *   *

Sunny left Ernst's flat feeling more disheartened than ever. Even Jakob, nestling in her chest and snoring softly, could not lift her spirits. Sunny could see that Simon was serious. She understood his point, too. Perhaps an attack on von Puttkamer was their best hope for protecting the ghetto.

"It would never work," she murmured to herself. The Nazis reminded her of some kind of multi-headed Hydra. Lopping off one head would only engender angrier replacements.

Her sense of suffocation intensified as she crossed back over the Garden Bridge and re-entered Hongkew. Threats seemed to lurk in every nook and cranny these days: the Japanese, the Nazis and even the Underground—her own people. She glanced down at Jakob in her arms. *I must be out of my mind to even fantasize about bringing a baby into such a dangerous world.*

As she reached the intersection, Sunny saw the ghetto checkpoint a few blocks ahead. She was about to cross the street but paused when she saw an approaching motorcade. Two motorcycles rushed toward her, followed by a military car with a Rising Sun flapping from its antenna.

The vehicles slowed to round the corner, and Sunny spotted two uniformed officers sitting together in the back seat. The one closest to the window was Colonel Kubota. Their eyes met momentarily, and she saw a hint of a smile cross his lips before the car drove away.

Sunny was still thinking about the colonel when, a block further along, the ground beneath her shifted and shook. A thundering boom rattled the nearby shop windows. Her ears rang from the blast. She dropped to her knees and hunched forward to protect Jakob in her arms.

Then it was chaos. Gunfire crackled: single shots, followed by the spitting clatter of machine guns. Men shouted and screamed in Japanese. Jakob howled. Sirens blared. Military vehicles raced up and down the street from every direction.

Jumping to her feet, Sunny kept Jakob pinned tightly against her body. He squirmed, but she held him close as she ran toward the ghetto.

Only one thought ran through her head: *I must get him home to his mother.*

Chapter 37

Franz and Max Feinstein glanced at each other across the patient's bed. Below them, Herr Hirsch picked up on their exchange. His eyes darted from one doctor to the other, while his narrow face paled in fright. *"Was ist los?"*

"We call it diverticulitis, Herr Hirsch," Max explained. "From little pouches on the wall of your colon. We all develop diverticula after a certain age."

"I'm only forty-two," Hirsch protested.

"Old enough for diverticula," Max said. "And now some have become infected."

Hirsch winced as though the words alone caused him physical pain. "What can be done?"

"We have to operate," Franz said.

"So you cut out these pouches?"

Franz folded his arms across his chest. "No. We have to remove a section of your colon."

"Mein Gott!" Hirsch croaked. "You will cut out my bowels?"

"Only part of it, Mr. Hirsch."

Hirsch brought a hand to his mouth. "Afterward, will I be able to eat? And . . . to still move my bowels?"

Franz nodded. "In a week or so, I believe so. Yes."

Hirsch's face relaxed, but his eyes remained wary. "When will you do this surgery?"

"Today, before your fever gets higher or the infection spreads." Franz considered his next words carefully, concerned about their effect on the nervous patient. He knew Hirsch, an accountant who now did bookkeeping for several local businesses, through the synagogue. He liked him. "Without it, your life may be in danger."

Hirsch sighed. "So go ahead then. Operate."

"We are . . . lacking supplies," Franz said. "We do have a little morphine left, but we have been without ether for most of the month."

"What are you saying, Herr Doktor?"

Max clasped his hands together. "Dr. Adler will have to perform surgery without anaesthetic."

Hirsch's jaw dropped. "Oy," he groaned. "You intend to slice me open when I am still wide awake?"

"There are other options," Franz said.

"Such as?"

"Ethanol."

"Spirits," Max clarified. "Wine, or if you prefer brandy or even gin."

Hirsch looked horrified. "To make me *shikker?* I don't ever touch a drop—"

Franz heard rapid footsteps behind him. He turned to see Joey rushing toward them. "The Japanese!" Joey cried. "They are here!"

Franz spun away from the bed. "Where, Joey?"

"Outside. On the street." He motioned wildly toward the door. "Three or four trucks. More coming."

"Is it a raid?" Max demanded.

Joey shook his head. "They are unloading stretchers. Wounded men. One is covered in blood."

The three nurses on the ward gathered around to listen. The patients who had enough strength sat up in their beds. No one spoke. Everyone's eyes were trained on Franz, waiting to see what he would do.

"Berta, Miriam, go prepare supplies and dressings," Franz instructed. "And, Liese, get the operating room ready."

Franz, Max and Joey shoved four empty beds to the front of the ward. They were lining them up, side by side, when two Japanese soldiers burst into the room bearing a stretcher that held an older man in a naval uniform.

Franz recognized him immediately: it was Vice-Admiral Iwanaka, the senior naval commander in Shanghai. His white jacket was splashed with red. Blood seeped from a bullet hole that had ripped through the fabric covering his abdomen. The blood was pooling sluggishly at the wound, and Franz knew that if Iwanaka wasn't already dead, he would be at any moment.

Four more soldiers flew into the room carrying two loaded stretchers between them. They hoisted a second wounded man onto the nearest bed. The man's shrill voice, which Franz could hear barking orders in Japanese, sent a shiver down Franz's spine. He turned to find himself staring into the eyes of the man who had nearly killed him at Bridge House the year before. Clutching the right side of his chest, Colonel Tanaka struggled to sit up. Bright blood oozed out between his fingers. Tanaka shook a finger at Franz. "*You!* You fix me now!"

Shocked and fearful, Franz stepped closer to the Kempeitai colonel. "May I examine your injury?"

Tanaka tentatively pulled his fingers away from his chest. Franz could see a gash that tore through the uniform just beneath the armpit. The blood began to flow more briskly, obscuring the wound. As Tanaka thrust his hand back to his chest, Franz heard a faint hissing sound: air leaking out from his lung. "A hemopneumothorax," Franz muttered to himself.

"What is this?" Tanaka demanded.

"Your right lung has collapsed, and the space around it is filling with blood and air," Franz said. "Was it a knife?"

Tanaka nodded. "The saboteurs! You fix me now!"

"Colonel, I still must examine the others—"

"Me first," Tanaka hissed. "Or the hospital is finished. All you Jews, finished!"

A younger man in a Kempeitai officer's uniform bustled over to the bedside, his face contorting into a sneer. "You heard Taisa Tanaka," he said in accentless English. "You will fix his wound immediately."

"We don't have any ether in the hospital." Franz held out his palms. "No anaesthetic. No gas. You understand?"

"We will get you the gas." The young officer turned to a soldier and barked at him in Japanese. The second soldier then spun and raced for the door.

"No gas!" Tanaka cried. "You fix me."

"To fix you, Colonel, I will have to cut your chest wide open. Perhaps remove part of your lung."

"No gas. You do it!"

"While you are still awake?"

"Now!"

Franz turned to the nearest nurse. "Miriam, take Colonel Tanaka to the operating room." He glanced from side to side. "Where is Mrs. Adler? And Dr. Huang, is he here? We could use the help."

As Franz scanned the room, his gaze fell on the third wounded man who had been carried in. He lay quietly on the furthest bed. From his vantage point, Franz could only see the man from the chest down, but he noticed that his green uniform was blood-stained in patches over his lower abdomen and left thigh.

As Franz took a step toward the man, Berta called out, "Dr. Adler. Herr Doktor!"

Berta was holding the admiral's wrist, two fingers locked over the spot where the radial pulse was supposed to be. She shook her head very slightly, then released the man's arm and reached for the sheet at his feet.

"The admiral," Franz heard someone ask weakly. "Is he dead?"

Franz's heart sank as he recognized the voice of Colonel Kubota. He rushed over to the injured man's bedside. "Yes."

"I see." The colonel's tone was flat. "They were waiting for us."

"Saboteurs?"

Kubota nodded. "It was an ambush. There was some kind of explosion. They blocked the street and shot our motorcycle escorts. They attacked our car from both sides. One shot the admiral and me, and the other stabbed Colonel Tanaka."

Franz reached for Kubota's belly. "May I examine you?"

Franz took the man's slight shrug for permission. He untucked Kubota's shirt and pulled it up. The bullet wound to his abdomen had stopped bleeding. Franz gently touched the moist skin at its edges. The abdominal muscles contracted involuntarily, but Kubota did not even wince in response.

"At least I was forewarned," Kubota said quietly.

Distracted, Franz shook his head and mumbled, "I'm sorry, Colonel."

"You warned me that the attack would come."

"But my warning did you no good."

"In life, it always helps to be prepared."

Franz turned his attention to the wound on Kubota's thigh. "You must be in pain."

Kubota tilted his head slightly. "It is bearable."

Franz called over his shoulder, "Berta, please prepare morphine."

Kubota reached out with his steady hand and grabbed Franz's wrist. "Give me a substantial dose, Dr. Adler. Please."

"We will make sure you are comfortable. I promise."

Kubota squeezed tighter. "That is not what I am requesting."

Franz pulled back to study Kubota's face. "Surely you do not mean ..."

The colonel swallowed. "My time has come. Let me go. Please."

Franz's neck tightened as he considered how quickly the colonel, in his vulnerable state, would stop breathing following a liberal dose of morphine.

Just then, Miriam called out to him, "Herr Doktor, they are ready for you in the operating room."

Franz's gaze lingered on Kubota before he turned away. "Berta, please give the colonel as much painkiller as he requests. Double the dose, if he asks for it."

Franz hurried down the hallway to the operating room. Outside, he donned a surgical gown and mask and then scrubbed his hands at the sink. He was nearly finished when Sunny appeared, breathless, at his side. "I was there, Franz," she panted. "Jakob and me. The bomb exploded so near us! And then the shooting began."

He motioned to the operating room. "Tanaka is inside. Knife wound to the chest."

"Colonel Kubota, he smiled at me from the back seat of the car." Her face reddened and she dropped her gaze to the floor. "They got to him, Franz."

"Without your help."

"I want to believe that, too."

Franz waited as Sunny slipped into her surgical gown and hurriedly scrubbed at the sink. They entered the operating room together. Tanaka was already on the gurney covered in sheets, except for the exposed patch of skin surrounding his stab wound. Liese held a blood-soaked gauze to his chest. On the other side of the bed, a surgical tray lay at the ready.

Tanaka's breathing was laboured, but he was wide awake. He eyed Franz hostilely. "Why the wait? Fix me!"

"Should we not wait for the ether—the gas—to arrive?"

"I told you. No gas. Begin!"

Franz nodded to Sunny, who stepped up to the gurney. Liese slid out of the way, and Franz moved into the spot across from his wife. Sunny passed Franz an antiseptic-soaked towel, and his nose filled with the acrid smell of iodine. He swabbed the wound in slow circles.

Tanaka gritted his teeth in obvious pain. "So close to the Designated Area," he grumbled.

"Pardon me, Colonel?" Franz asked, wondering if the colonel was delirious or in shock.

"The attack. So close to the Designated Area."

"I suppose so, yes."

"The Jews," Tanaka said. "They are the saboteurs."

"I'm sure it is not so."

Tanaka gave him a look of sheer loathing. "The Germans are right. You Jews only make trouble."

Franz's throat tightened. "We were not involved."

"I will put an end to it," Tanaka grunted.

Franz tried to fight off a sudden sense of doom. "An end to what, Colonel?" he breathed.

"All of it," Tanaka muttered to himself. "We should have listened to the Germans last year. No more. Next, we deal with you Jews!"

The younger Kempeitai officer barged into the operating room, bearing a black bottle of ether in his hand. He raised it up to show it to Franz. "Is this what you need?"

Stunned by the threat Tanaka had just uttered, Franz could not even respond.

"Yes," Sunny said as Liese hurried over to take the bottle from the officer.

Tanaka craned his neck to address the young Kempeitai man in clipped Japanese. The officer nodded and turned to Franz. "The colonel has ordered me to stay and observe." He glared at him. "To make sure everything is proper."

Robotically, Franz turned back to Liese. "Please begin."

Liese's hand shook slightly as she applied the ether mask to Tanaka's face. She tilted the bottle, allowed four or five drops to fall and waited. In a matter of seconds, Tanaka's eyes began to flutter. Liese added two more drops. She brushed a finger over his eyelashes and watched for a response. None came. She looked up at Franz. "He is asleep, Herr Doktor."

Sunny passed Franz a scalpel. He placed it against the skin underneath Tanaka's armpit and sliced, following the curve of the fifth rib all the way to the level of the breastbone. Air whooshed out of the wound. Sunny dabbed at the freshly oozing blood as she exchanged the scalpel for a pair of scissors.

Franz pressed the scissors to the cartilage adjoining Tanaka's breastbone. He had to squeeze down with all his might to cut through it. As soon as it was free, Sunny inserted a retractor into the incision and pulled the ribs wide apart, exposing pink lung. More blood dripped from the wound.

Franz put his hand into the warm chest cavity, exploring the spongy surface of the deflated lung. He could feel the rapid vibrations of Tanaka's heart. His own pulse quickened as he considered what devastating form of retribution Tanaka might have in store for the refugees.

Franz moved tissue out of the way with one hand while mopping up blood with the other. "More light, please."

Liese adjusted the overhead lamp, allowing Franz to spot a large vessel that was leaking blood. He motioned to it with a pair of forceps. "Do you see it, Sunny?"

She nodded. "A lacerated pulmonary vein?"

"Yes," Franz muttered. "Needle and thread, please."

Sunny passed him the catgut-threaded instrument. Franz's hand moved to repair the vessel, then froze. The thought hit him so suddenly and so powerfully that it left him numb. He turned slowly to the junior Kempeitai officer. "A large blood vessel in the colonel's chest has been cut. I am not certain I can stop the bleeding."

Sunny eyed Franz quizzically but said nothing.

"You repaired General Nogomi before," the officer snapped. "You will do the same for the *taisa*."

To Franz's astonishment, his hand was steady as he inserted the instrument inside the colonel's chest. He pressed the needle through tissue just a fraction of an inch from the leaking blood vessel. He tied off the suture and then repeated the procedure, missing the injured vein by the same distance. He held up the long end of the thread. "Cut, please," he instructed Sunny.

She looked down into the wound and then up at him, aware that he had deliberately sutured the wrong site. Without a word, she reached inside the wound and cut the ends of the suture.

"That is the best I can do to repair the vessel," he announced for the benefit of the other Kempeitai officer. "Forceps, please."

Sunny passed him the long clamp-like instrument. Hand still steady, he dug the forceps' teeth into the wall of the leaking vein and tugged slightly. The trickle of blood quickly became a gush, and Franz watched the vessel disappear in a pool of fresh blood.

Chapter 38

Exhausted from a sleepless night, Franz looked out at the muted rays of daylight that filtered through the small window. Sunny's hand skimmed across his bare back, lightly fingering the ridges of his scabs. Her need to console him was as strong as ever.

The evening before, Sunny's efforts to comfort him had been more forcefully intimate. He had resisted, initially, his mood dark after what had happened in the operating room. But Sunny was persistent, and coaxed him to arousal with her touches and persuasive kisses. Still, the relief was only temporary. Afterward, as he lay next to her, their legs and arms intertwined, the guilt crept back like a hand to his throat.

"What choice did you have, Franz?" Sunny murmured into his neck.

"I took an oath."

"Could any oath apply to our circumstances?"

"'To never cause harm.' It always applies."

"And what about the harm Colonel Tanaka might have caused? You heard him—he blamed the Jews for the attack. Based on nothing."

"I was his doctor, not his judge or jury."

Sunny rested a finger on his waist. "You did what you had to do to protect us."

"What I did was wrong," he said flatly.

"And what about Hermann Schwartzmann?" Sunny asked, her voice rising in frustration.

"What about him?"

"You risked everything to operate on his wife—to give her a chance—even though her husband worked for the Nazis."

Three years before, Schwartzmann, a Nazi diplomat, had come to Franz desperate for help for his wife, who had bile duct cancer. Franz was the only surgeon in Shanghai capable of the operation. Eventually, he took pity on the suffering woman and risked his job and his family's standing by operating on her at the Jewish hospital. Schwartzmann had more than repaid Franz: he'd provided not only money to keep the hospital running but also crucial information about a secret SS plan to exterminate the city's Jews. Ultimately, Schwartzmann had taken his own life after the Nazis found him out.

"Precisely," Franz said. "Remember how much Hermann helped us? He sacrificed his life for us. What would have happened to all of us had I ignored my oath when he first approached me?"

"It's completely different," Sunny snapped. "Hermann was a victim of circumstance. Tanaka was evil. He took pleasure in your suffering. If he had survived, he might have wiped out the entire community."

Franz rolled over to face her. "I understand what you are saying. I love you even more for trying. But nothing will change the fact that I deliberately killed a patient. For a doctor, it is unconscionable."

"You don't have to view it that way, Franz."

He kissed her, letting his lips linger on hers before he sat up, his legs swung over the edge of the bed.

"If there is one silver lining to all of this, darling," Franz pointed out as he slipped on his trousers, "at least the Underground achieved its objective without involving you."

"Have they?" she said distantly. "We saved Colonel Kubota's life. They are not going to be pleased."

"No, I suppose not." Franz felt torn: Kubota had not even wanted to survive the assassination attempt.

"What if they come for the colonel?" Sunny asked.

"At the hospital?"

She nodded.

"The Japanese have posted guards." Franz finished buttoning his shirt. "I am far more concerned about your safety."

"Wen-Cheng said he will not let anything happen to me."

"It's not his role to protect you."

She laughed emptily. "Oh, Franz, you are not still jealous?"

"I only wish I could do more for you."

Sunny stared at him for a moment and then, eyes reddening with tears, she rolled away.

He studied the supple curve of her spine and resisted the urge to touch it, to run kisses down its length. Instead, he turned for the door.

*　　*　　*

Franz spotted few other refugees on the street, but soldiers were everywhere, patrolling the roads in armoured vehicles and occupying intersections with machine guns. In the wake of the assassinations, fear of retribution had swept the community, and with good reason. Ghoya had closed the checkpoints and revoked all exit passes. Overnight, people had been dragged away; raids were still happening. A firing squad had gunned down a pair of innocent spinsters who had panicked and tried to flee their home during a random raid. The Jewish community's mood was painfully reminiscent of Vienna in the days following Kristallnacht.

Keeping his head low and eyes to the ground, Franz hurried the three blocks over to Seymour Road, but he hesitated out front of the Ohel Moishe Synagogue.

Franz had always admired the red and brown brick temple. It had been built by Russian Jews in the early 1920s, before they abandoned Hongkew for Frenchtown. As always, its distinctive row of columned arches caught his eye. He had long wished to photograph it, but film was scarce and the risk of drawing Japanese suspicion with a camera was too great.

Franz had often accompanied Hannah and Esther to the temple on Saturdays and High Holidays. He enjoyed the ritual, but he had never been religious. As he stood staring at the carved wooden door, Franz realized that, for the first time in his adult life, he had come to a house of worship in search of guidance.

Franz dug inside his coat and extracted a yarmulke. Adjusting the skullcap on his head, he pulled open the doors and stepped inside a cavernous room that was filled with rows of benches and ringed by an upper balcony. At the front of the room stood the ornately gilded doors of the ark of the Torah. The faint fragrance of melted wax drifted to Franz. He scanned the room but saw no one. He wandered toward the bimah, the decorative table on which the sacred scrolls of the Torah would be unrolled for readings. As Franz reached the first row of benches, he heard footsteps behind him and turned to see Rabbi Hiltmann walking toward him in a black suit and yarmulke.

"Good morning, Dr. Adler." The rabbi chuckled. "You do realize that today is not Saturday?"

Franz smiled uncomfortably. "I do, yes, Rabbi. I was hoping to speak to you."

The rabbi eyed him for a moment and then motioned toward the benches beside them. "Come, sit with me."

Franz took a seat beside the rabbi, feeling out of place and suddenly regretting his decision to come. Embarrassed, he studied the Torah's ark before them.

"So? What can I do for you, Dr. Adler?"

"I need . . ." Franz coughed into his hand. "I was hoping for your opinion, I suppose."

"Not medical, I hope," the rabbi joked.

"I did something, Rabbi." Franz could feel the flush crossing his cheeks. "Something I am ashamed of. A sin."

"I am not a priest." Hiltmann smiled good-naturedly. "You understand we rabbis are not paid to take confessions."

Franz's face heated further. "I need your advice."

"Ah, advice. Of that I have loads to give." The rabbi laughed again. "After all, I am a Jew, am I not? So tell me."

"I broke one of the commandments," Franz said.

"Oh? Which one?"

"Thou shall not commit murder."

The rabbi turned slowly toward him. "You . . . you killed someone, Dr. Adler?"

"I did."

Hiltmann did not move, waiting for an explanation.

"He was a patient, Rabbi," Franz continued. "A Japanese colonel, the head of the military police . . ."

The rabbi folded his arms across his chest and listened as Franz described what had happened in the operating room. Even after he had finished, the rabbi said nothing. Franz finally broke the silence. "Well, Rabbi?"

Hiltmann shrugged. "I am not a policeman. I am not a judge. You alone have to live with what you did. What else can I tell you?"

"You are a spiritual man, a rabbi," Franz said, taken aback. "It's a sin what I have done, surely. How would this appear in the eyes of God?"

"I try not to speak for God." The rabbi sighed. "I am, however, fond of reading his teachings and the Talmud's interpretation of them."

"So you must have at least a theological opinion, no?"

"This Japanese colonel." The rabbi looked at him gravely. "He is the one who would have handed us over to the Nazis last year?"

"Yes."

Hiltmann nodded slowly. "Before the operation, you said he threatened to harm the Jews again?"

"I believe so, yes. But he was not specific. He only said that he would 'put an end to it.'"

"Or, perhaps, an end to all of *us?*"

Franz shook his head. "Perhaps, but he was critically ill at the time. Who knows what he might have done had he survived."

The rabbi tilted his head. "Let me ask you, Dr. Adler, did you act out of spite or vengeance?"

Franz considered the question carefully. He thought back to the week of torture he had endured in Bridge House at Tanaka's hands. More than the humiliation and agonizing pain, Franz remembered how deeply he had hated Tanaka when he had threatened Sunny. Given the opportunity, at that moment, he would have strangled Tanaka with his bare hands. But that incident never crossed his mind inside the operating room.

"It is a difficult question for you to answer, Dr. Adler?" Hiltmann prompted.

"No," Franz said firmly. "I was not thinking about revenge. I was only thinking about my family."

"Hmm." The rabbi stroked his silvery beard. "In Leviticus, the Torah commands: *tëlëkh räkhiyl B'ameykhä—*"

"I do not speak Hebrew, Rabbi."

"As a Jew, you really should," Hiltmann said, sounding exactly like Rabbi Finkler, the perpetually disappointed cleric of Franz's youth. "It means 'Nor shall you stand idly by while your neighbour's life is at stake.'"

"But how can I know that my neighbour's life was truly at stake?"

"The Talmud is also clear on this issue," the rabbi said. "In the six hundred and thirteen mitzvoth, or commandments, a faithful Jew is required to save a person who is being pursued. Even if it means killing the pursuer. The Torah further commands that one should not take pity on the aggressor. He is to be killed before he has a chance to kill the one he pursues." He pulled his hand away from his beard. "You understand? The Torah is endorsing a preventive strike under such circumstances."

"I see," Franz mumbled.

The rabbi shrugged again. "That is only what I know from my reading, Dr. Adler. I am not your judge."

Franz nodded. "God is."

"Always, I suppose." The rabbi's eyes lit up with amusement. "But, Dr. Adler, in this particular instance I was thinking of you, not God."

*   *   *

As Franz headed back to the hospital, he felt only a small degree of consolation. Regardless of what the Torah commanded, his bible was still the surgical textbook. And nowhere inside it could he find justification for his actions.

A Japanese soldier was guarding the entrance to the ward with a rifle across his chest. Inside, people walked on eggshells. No one was speaking. Nurses and patients exchanged nervous looks. Franz headed toward the bed in the far corner, which was shielded from the rest of the ward by curtains.

At Franz's approach, the young soldier guarding the bed stood at attention and raised his rifle. Franz touched his lab coat. "I am the colonel's doctor."

The soldier eyed him with indifference until Kubota's voice croaked out from behind the curtains. The young man relaxed his shoulders and lowered his weapon.

Franz stepped through a gap in the curtains. The colonel was covered up to his neck by a blanket, his face pale and eyes sunken.

"How are you . . . feeling . . . today, Colonel?" Franz stammered.

"I am alive." Kubota's voice was weak and his tone inscrutable.

Embarrassed, Franz lowered his gaze. "Are you in much pain?"

Kubota shook his head slightly. "The injections help."

"Colonel, the bullet damaged your colon. We had no choice but to fashion a colostomy. To bring a loop of bowel out to the wall of your abdomen."

"So I will evacuate into this bag from now on."

"Only temporarily," Franz said. "Once the swelling recedes and the wound heals—in a few months—I will be able to reattach the two ends of the bowel again."

"A few months," Kubota echoed hollowly.

"Colonel, I couldn't just let you . . ." Franz looked up and met the military man's despondent gaze. "I am sorry, Colonel. I truly am."

"You saved my life, Dr. Adler." Kubota stated it as though reporting the weather outside. "You have a duty as a doctor. I am a soldier. I understand duty. I had no right to ask you to do otherwise."

Franz nodded. "I was hoping that, in time, you might feel differently."

As Kubota gazed into the distance, he seemed to be fighting pain. "I never was so fortunate to find a wife, Dr. Adler. My parents are long dead, and my brother was a captain. He went down with his ship at Guadalcanal."

"You have friends," Franz said. "And so many admirers among my community."

"Shanghai," Kubota said dreamily. "I was always so contented here. When I arrived on my first posting, I felt as though I had found a home. The city was so full of wanderers and adventurers from around the world. I belonged, Dr. Adler. You understand?"

"I have no doubt you did."

"I was saddened when war came to Shanghai, but I understood the need for it. But once we went to war with the Allies, everything changed. It was difficult to watch my Shanghailander friends suffer so." Kubota paused. "Then the Germans came to me with their barbarous plans for your people."

"What you did for us, Colonel, was heroic."

Kubota shook his head. "To have not intervened would have been dishonourable."

"Still, it took great courage."

"My choice was never the sacrifice you make it out to be, Dr. Adler. By that point, my fate had already been sealed. My superiors had lost patience with my divided loyalties." Visibly tiring, Kubota stopped for a few breaths. "Truth be told, I wanted to go."

"To leave Shanghai?"

"The Shanghai I knew—the place I still think of as home—that city is long dead." He looked at Franz wistfully. "And yet, somehow, I live on."

Chapter 39

Sunny pressed the towel to the surgical wound on the man's abdomen. "Will it ever heal, Frau Adler?" Herr Hirsch asked, his tone plaintive.

"A little time and patience do wonders for healing, Herr Hirsch." She sounded to herself like the old matron she had worked for at the Country Hospital. The woman had a gift for silencing even the most demanding of patients.

"If only God will grant me enough time to be patient."

"You are over the worst of—"

A sudden commotion cut her off mid-sentence. Sunny heard something crash to the floor and someone shouting in Japanese. She dropped the towel and raced over to Kubota's bed.

The young Japanese soldier who always stood at the foot of the bed was motioning wildly with the barrel of his rifle toward the bed. The colonel was propped up on a pillow, eyes open but absolutely still, his lips dark blue.

Sunny thrust her hand up to Kubota's mouth but didn't feel so much as a flutter of air against her palm. She placed her fingers on his neck. A pulse still beat weakly beneath them. Sunny saw that his pupils were the size of pinholes. She doubted he could still be conscious, but she sensed awareness behind his glassy eyes. His expression verged on serene.

As she stood there, helpless, Sunny felt his pulse drain away beneath her hand.

Even the guard could see what was happening. He shrieked at her in Japanese, demanding action. Sunny only shook her head. A lump formed in her throat as she pulled her hand from Kubota's neck and lifted the sheet over his head. The guard let his rifle fall to his side, its muzzle dangling toward the ground, as he gaped in disbelief.

Sunny turned to see Berta standing at the door to the ward. The other nurse absorbed the scene immediately. "How did this happen?" she asked. "I checked on him just a few minutes ago. He was stable."

Sunny hurried over to her. "Did you give him painkillers?"

Berta shook her head. "No, but Dr. Huang did. When he changed the dressings."

"Wen-Cheng?" Sunny gasped and then covered her shock with a small cough. "Dr. Huang changed the colonel's dressing?"

"And administered morphine, yes." Berta lowered her voice to a whisper. "There is something else."

"Yes, Berta?"

She cleared her throat. "The morphine."

"What about it?"

"You must understand. I am not accusing Dr. Huang."

"Tell me, Berta."

"After Dr. Huang prepared the colonel's injection, the other morphine pills—our last ones . . . they went missing."

Sunny managed to maintain a neutral expression. "You think Wen-Cheng took them?"

Berta held up her hands helplessly. "Who else could have?"

"Perhaps Dr. Huang needed them for patients outside the hospital?" But Sunny already knew what he had done with them. "I will speak with him."

*   *   *

Sunny assumed that Wen-Cheng would have left the hospital long before, so she was surprised to find him sitting alone at the table in the staff room, smoking a cigarette and staring at the wall.

She sat down across from him. "The colonel is dead."

Wen-Cheng showed no response. His gaze was fixed somewhere beyond her.

"He didn't die from his injury," she continued.

"What then?" Wen-Cheng asked mechanically.

"Morphine toxicity."

"How can you be certain?"

"I was with him, Wen-Cheng. He stopped breathing. His pupils were constricted. I have seen more than enough opium and morphine poisonings to recognize the signs."

Wen-Cheng avoided her eyes. "Accidental narcotic poisoning is a common occurrence on surgical wards."

"This was no accident."

"You do not believe so?"

Sunny shook a finger at him. "You poisoned the colonel!"

Wen-Cheng smoked in silence for several tense seconds. Finally, he met her eyes. "And it's fortunate for you that I did."

Sunny leapt to her feet. "How can you say that?" She struggled to keep her voice low. "He was a good man. The one decent Japanese officer I have ever known."

"Maybe so, but they wanted him dead."

"You mean that bitter old man did."

"More than just him," Wen-Cheng said. "Besides, he is a very important man, Soon Yi. A person not to be crossed."

"I haven't crossed him!"

"Nor did you do as he requested."

She hung her head. "No."

"I meant what I told you, Soon Yi," he said quietly. "I will do whatever is necessary to protect you."

"What does that have to do with Colonel Kubota?"

"The others. They don't know that the targets were brought to our hospital for treatment." He paused. "*Their* targets."

Sunny nodded, suddenly understanding. "If the Underground learned that we operated on Kubota. That we saved his life . . ."

"They would come for him." Wen-Cheng shook his head. "For you too, I'm afraid."

"I see."

"Decent man or not, I do not regret what I did, Soon Yi."

Sunny realized that Wen-Cheng had poisoned the colonel to protect her. Guilt pressed down on her shoulders as acutely as it had after she had witnessed the deaths of those teenaged boys and Irma, which felt like so long ago now. "Is it over now?" she asked.

Wen-Cheng looked away again. "They see only black and white. Either you support them . . ."

"Or what?"

"You are a collaborator."

"That is what they think I am? *A collaborator?*"

"The old man, he never believed that you could not get to Kubota. He thought you were protecting the colonel."

She slumped back into her chair. "I have heard how the Underground deals with collaborators."

He sat up straighter and folded his arms. "I will not let them harm you. No matter what, Soon Yi. I will protect you."

IV

Chapter 40

December 18, 1943

Sunny bundled her coat tighter around her, bracing against the biting wind. Her foot slid on a patch of black ice and she barely kept her balance. Her elbow still ached from a fall the day before on the slick pavement.

Winter had descended early on Shanghai. The week before, there had been snow flurries. But Sunny knew that something more dangerous than the bitter chill or the black ice was keeping the sidewalks in Frenchtown as deserted as those inside the ghetto.

She had expected things to deteriorate after Tanaka's murder, but even still, the Japanese reprisal was shocking in its vitriol. In the weeks since the assassinations, the authorities had launched a ruthless crackdown on all so-called "hostile" citizens, from Chinese locals to the stateless Jews. No one in the ghetto seemed to know who had replaced Colonel Tanaka, but the Kempeitai's collective paranoia was at an all-time high. The men in the white armbands were ubiquitous, and treacherous. Impromptu arrests, whippings and executions were commonplace.

The refugee community was still reeling from the death of one of its most respected members, Albert Neufeld. The week before, Neufeld had returned from a meeting with a group of Russian Jewish leaders fifteen minutes past curfew. Rather than revoking his pass for a month—the standard punishment for missing curfew to that point—the soldiers at the checkpoint had gunned Neufeld down in the street.

Sunny felt more vulnerable than ever. She had had no contact with anyone from the Underground, not even Wen-Cheng, in the past seven weeks. He had disappeared after their tense discussion in the staff room. Sunny had not told anyone about his role in poisoning Kubota, but she suspected Wen-Cheng found it too risky to stay on at the hospital. She hoped that he had vanished of his own accord.

Sunny stepped through the doorway of the Cathay Building, hurried across the marble-floored lobby and took the elevator to the ninth floor. Reaching Jia-Li's door, she knocked with the secret signal.

Jia-Li pulled her into the living room with an exuberant embrace. Sunny did a double take at the sight of her best friend. Her face free of makeup, she wore casual trousers and a sweater, and her hair was pulled into a tight bun. She reminded Sunny of the woman in the famous Marxist poster they'd seen throughout their childhood, glorifying the female prole-tariat. Jia-Li didn't even smell like her old self. Sunny couldn't detect a trace of either her usual jasmine fragrance or her favourite Russian cigarettes.

Charlie was kneeling on the floor of the living room with his crutches at his side. He looked over his shoulder and gave Sunny a quick smile before turning his attention back to the pliers he was using to tighten a screw onto a thin metal cylinder. "A pencil detonator," Charlie explained before Sunny could ask. "It works as a time-delay fuse."

Sunny frowned. "For a bomb?"

His back still turned to her, Charlie shrugged. "Not much purpose in a fuse without an explosive."

Sunny lowered her voice. "A few months ago, you mentioned the rail-way station. Is that what it's for?"

"Perhaps." Charlie's tone was flat as he focused on the equipment in his hand. "The targets have not been decided yet."

"Where did you get the supplies?" Sunny asked.

"Some of his men smuggled them into the city for us," Jia-Li said.

"*Us?*" The last time they had discussed sabotage, Jia-Li was outraged that Charlie would even consider it. Now she seemed to be part of it. Sunny found the change in her best friend dizzying; it was as though she were staring at a stranger.

"Someone has to do it, *xiǎo hè*," Jia-Li explained happily.

"But why you two?" Sunny asked. "Charlie is a wanted fugitive, hobbled by his . . . injury. And you, *bǎo bèi*, what do you know of sabotage?"

"What did you know before you got involved with the Underground?"

"Nothing!" Sunny cried. "And look how much I regret it. You are no more a saboteur than I am. It's not our purpose."

Jia-Li met her gaze. "I am obliged to support my husband."

"Your husband?" Sunny grimaced.

"He will be soon." Jia-Li broke into a huge smile. She dropped to her knees and threw her arms around Charlie's neck, kissing him. "Chun proposed, *xiǎo hè*. Only yesterday. I couldn't wait to tell you!"

"Congratulation. That is . . . wonderful news," Sunny sputtered.

Jia-Li sprang to her feet, dashed over to Sunny and flung her arms around her, wrapping her in another hug. "Oh, *xiǎo hè!* I have never been so happy."

"I am happy for you. Both of you." It was surreal to be discussing an engagement while Charlie assembled a bomb on the living-room floor, but Jia-Li's happiness was infectious. "Have you chosen a date?" she asked, wriggling free of her friend's grip.

Charlie lowered what he was holding to the floor and reached for his crutches. "As soon as we find someone to marry us." He stood up. "Today would not be too soon."

"How about your old reverend?" Jia-Li asked. "Is he still alive?"

Sunny shook her head. "He has been interned with all the other Americans."

"And that rabbi, *xiǎo hè?* The one at your wedding."

Sunny grimaced. "Rabbi Hiltmann? Seriously?"

Charlie made his way over to Jia-Li, put an arm around her waist and drew her close to him. "A rabbi, a judge, a sea captain . . . Anyone short of a Japanese officer would do. Can doctors perform weddings?"

Sunny shook her head. "At this point, I don't know who in Shanghai has the legal authority to officiate."

"It does not have to be legal. Only official." Charlie stroked Jia-Li's cheek and stared at her adoringly. "So one day we will be able to tell our children."

Sunny detected a note of fatalism in Charlie's tone, but Jia-Li didn't seem to notice. She planted a lingering kiss on Charlie's lips before turning back to Sunny. "I have found a real gem, haven't I?"

"I agree." Sunny looked up and down, indicating Jia-Li's plain outfit. "But this change in you—it's so dramatic."

"I am done with the old me, *xiǎo hè*. The outfits, the Comfort Home, Chih-Nii . . . all of it! Oh, how I have wasted my life." She put her hands on her hips. "No more. For the first time, I have found a purpose. A role that I can take pride in."

"That's wonderful," Sunny said. "I am happy for you. Franz will be too. Really. But sabotage, *bǎo bèi?*"

"Whatever it takes to free Shanghai. To rid our country of this Japanese scourge. It is the first step." She stole a quick glance at Charlie. "And then maybe we can consider a family."

Sunny realized that there was no arguing with her friend. She knew Jia-Li never did anything halfway, and never before had she seen her friend's eyes burn with such fervour.

*   *   *

On her way home, Sunny crossed over the Garden Bridge and headed along Broadway. Although far quieter than usual, the city's busiest thoroughfare still buzzed. The cries of the merchants were as shrill as ever. Coolies hauled crates or carried loads on bamboo poles across their shoulders. Despite the early hour, several wild pheasants—most of whom looked to Sunny like teenagers at most—loitered at the dockside, approaching soldiers and other passersby. The smell of burned oil from the street kitchens wafted through the air. Her stomach rumbled, but hunger pains were something she hardly paid attention to anymore.

Sunny noticed a crowd of Chinese gathered a block or two ahead of her. Not until she reached the edge of the gathering did she see the wooden beam that had been rigged up between two lampposts like a scaffold. Then she spotted the bodies. Tethered to the beam with thick ropes were eleven corpses hanging no more than a foot or two apart, their shoes clearing the ground by roughly the same distance.

They had been badly beaten around the face, a few beyond recognition. All were men, Sunny could tell, but they ranged in age from young to old: one looked to Sunny as if he might have been a teenager. Blood, dirt and what Sunny assumed was vomit stained their shirtfronts.

Sunny's gaze landed on the hands of the body hanging nearest to her. His fingernails had been ripped out, and his fingers appeared to have been dislocated or fractured. They pointed every direction but straight. The other victims' hands had been similarly mutilated.

Sunny fought off the urge to gag. Desperate to flee the grisly scene, she started to turn away when her eye was caught by something about one of the bodies. The man's nose had been bashed in and his lips were swollen, but his hooded eyelids gave him away. "Oh, God," she whispered under her breath, recognizing the old man as her Underground contact.

Sunny elbowed her way through the crowd until she could make out the faces of the dead men. Afraid to breathe, she prayed that she would not see Wen-Cheng among them. Her eyes reached the end of the beam without spotting him.

Her relief was short-lived when she considered what the men might have confessed under torture. Her eyes moved back to the old man's crumpled face. *Did you tell them about me?*

Chapter 41

"I should leave straight away," Sunny murmured to Franz as they sat side by side on the sofa, fingers interlocked. "It's too dangerous for me to stay. It's not fair to any of you, especially Hannah and the baby."

Franz squeezed her hand reassuringly. "If the Japanese knew anything, they would have already come for you."

"How can you be so sure?"

"We know by now how the Japanese behave. They would never wait. If they suspected you, they would pounce."

She nestled her head into the crook of his neck. "To have to leave you, Franz, that would kill me."

He stroked her hair. Even though she had not been able to bathe in days, somehow her hair was still soft and smelled like soap. "This might actually work to our advantage."

She jerked her head from his shoulder. "*Our advantage?* How is that possible?"

"What they did to those men from the Underground—that was beyond barbaric." He squinted in disgust. "But surely it no longer matters whether or not the old man thought you were a collaborator. No one will be coming for you now."

"No, I suppose not," she said. "The old man, maybe he didn't tell the Kempeitai about me after all."

Franz looked at his wife. Sunny's eyes danced with both affection and desire. He couldn't remember her ever looking more beautiful. Slowly, almost teasingly, she lowered her lips to his. They shared a long kiss, and she gently ran her fingernails across his neck and shoulders. He resisted the urge to slide her dress up over her hips and instead, reluctantly, pulled his face away from hers. "Esther and Hannah could return at any moment," he said.

"We live in dangerous times, Dr. Adler," she said throatily.

The others had gone to the shop for rice and hot water. Hannah loved carrying Jakob through the streets. It reminded Franz of how she used to insist on lugging her beloved rag doll, Schweizer Fräulein, with her everywhere when she was younger. For his part, while Jakob adored his cousin, he had begun to resist being held. He had started crawling a few weeks before and was far more interested in exploring the ground for himself.

Just as Sunny leaned in for another kiss, the door shook with three heavy knocks. She went rigid in his arms. Another softer series of raps followed. "Franz, it's me," Ernst's voice could be heard through the door.

Sunny's body relaxed. Franz rose to his feet and hurried over to the door.

After a quick handshake, the artist marched over to Sunny and kissed her on both cheeks. "You just grow more gorgeous by the day."

Sunny waved away his mock flirtation. "Is everything all right, Ernst?"

A cigarette and a lighter materialized in his hands. "Well, I am still trapped in that twisted little neighbourhood—Wiesbaden on the Whangpoo, I call it—but I have few complaints otherwise."

"And Simon?"

"Ah, that reminds me." Ernst dug in his back pocket and fished out a crumpled envelope. "For Essie, of course."

"How is he managing?" Sunny asked.

Ernst heaved a sigh. "I am not certain how much longer I will be able to retain my house guest. Hard to blame him, though. He's desperate to be with his family."

Franz folded his arms. "Even if that means endangering us all?"

Ernst lit his cigarette. "In my experience, seldom do common sense and emotion correlate."

"Yes, I have noticed the same," Franz conceded.

"Simon simply has to wait," Sunny declared. "Never has the time been worse for reckless behaviour. I will speak to him."

"Best of luck with it." Ernst whistled out a stream of smoke. "You are right about the atmosphere, though. On my way over here, on Broadway, I saw something . . . ghastly."

Sunny looked down at her feet. "Those men hanging from the beam?"

"You saw them, too?"

"They were from the Underground," she murmured. "I knew one of them."

"It's a hazardous business, this subversion." Ernst's eyes narrowed as he looked quickly from Sunny to Franz. "Unfortunately, the Japanese are not the only ones in Shanghai in a vengeful mood."

"What are the Nazis up to now?" Franz asked.

Ernst whistled. "Von Puttkamer's plans are heating up."

"He told you so?"

"No, he wouldn't include me in those kinds of discussions. But there has been more activity. More meetings."

"How do you know it concerns the Jews?" Sunny asked.

"You remember Gerhard?" Ernst said, lowering his voice. "That young man in the baron's entourage?"

Franz had only a vague recollection of the young man who had accompanied von Puttkamer on his tour of the ghetto. What he remembered most clearly was the boy's unflinching scowl. "What about him?"

"Gerhard has taken a bit of a shine to me." Ernst rolled his eyes. "Not in *that* way, of course. Apparently, I remind the lad of his uncle or some other ungodly relative who is under the impression that he can paint. Regardless, Gerhard has taken to confiding in me of late."

Franz took a step closer. "What has he told you?"

"Believe it or not," Ernst said with a chuckle, "Gerhard is suffering a crisis of conscience."

"Why?"

"Gerhard doesn't care what happens to the adult Jews—'it's a better world without them,' as he so charmingly puts it—but he is troubled by the idea of harming children."

"*Scheisse!*" Franz groaned. "What are they planning?"

"A bomb."

Franz felt as though his innards had turned to stone. "They're planning to bomb the ghetto?"

"Where? How?" Sunny's voice cracked.

"Even Gerhard doesn't know. Von Puttkamer has not shared the target with anyone, it seems like." Ernst viewed them with a helpless shrug. "All I know is that the baron has promised something . . . *spectacular.*"

"'Spectacular.'" The word lodged in Franz's throat.

Sunny rubbed her temples. "Do you have any idea when they will do this . . . this terrible thing, Ernst?"

"Soon," Ernst said. "Gerhard doesn't know the precise date, but von Puttkamer is intent on carrying out the attack before the New Year."

"But that's less than two weeks," Franz said.

Sunny reached out and clutched his elbow, squeezing tight. "We cannot just wait. We must do something."

"Do what?" Franz cried. "Tell Ghoya? The Kempeitai? No. Colonel Kubota is the only one who would have listened to us."

Sunny turned back to Ernst. "You must get more details from Gerhard."

"And if he doesn't know any more?"

Sunny looked over to Franz, her expression businesslike. "We have to mobilize the ghetto. Post our own watches outside public buildings."

"Organize the young men. A good idea, yes," Franz mumbled, snapping out of his shock. "What about after curfew? How can we watch at nighttime?"

"The Germans will not be allowed on the streets after curfew either," Sunny pointed out.

"Let's hope not," Ernst said.

*　　　*　　　*

Halfway up the pathway to the hospital, Franz stopped to study the old structure. Five years earlier, before it had been converted into a hospital, the building had barely withstood the Japanese aerial bombing. As his gaze ran over its patched roof, taped windows and pockmarked walls, he realized it wouldn't take much for it to collapse now.

As Franz made his way onto the ward, he wondered what the point was in continuing to offer patchwork medical care to the wretched Shanghai Jews. Even if the Nazis didn't target the hospital, how could he be of any help if the saboteurs attacked the ghetto? What did he have left to offer anyone? It all seemed so futile.

Still, Franz suspected that he would go out of his mind if he deviated from his routine. There were post-operative patients to tend to and, other than Sunny and him, no other surgeons were left at the hospital.

Franz had not been sorry to see Wen-Cheng go. His suspicions about Wen-Cheng's involvement in Colonel Kubota's death aside, Franz had never fully curbed his jealousy. Although he trusted Sunny completely, he couldn't jettison his doubts, irrational as they were, that Wen-Cheng might somehow find a way to win her back.

Franz spotted Max down the hallway and caught up with the internist as he stepped into his makeshift laboratory. Max pointed to the slides beside his desktop microscope. "Two more confirmed cases of cholera," he sighed. "Even the parasites are not taking a winter break from tormenting us Jews."

"We have bigger problems."

"Than cholera?" Max raised an eyebrow. "You remember our last outbreak? That daughter of yours turned out be one of the luckier ones. We were burying people for days and days. I doubt we have ever seen—"

"The Germans are planning to bomb us, Max."

The older man's face fell. "What? Here in the hospital?"

"Somewhere in the ghetto."

Max slumped into his chair and listened in silence as Franz shared what he knew. "We have to convene an emergency meeting of the community leaders," Franz concluded. "We must organize a watch."

"To monitor the ghetto?"

"It's not so large," Franz said. "There can only be so many possible targets. Besides, it wouldn't be easy for the Nazis to sneak in unnoticed, *if* we were watching for them."

"So let's say one of our young men is fortunate enough to catch the Nazis planting a bomb," Max said. "Then what? How would we stop them?"

"We haven't worked out those details. At the very least, they would be able to warn people."

Max cupped his chin in his hand. "Why bother, Franz?"

"To save lives."

"Yes, but for how long?" Max asked. "Next month—next week, perhaps—it will be something else. Starvation? Another disease? A bigger bomb? Or some other Nazi scheme that is even worse than the last?"

"You can't think that way," Franz said, though he couldn't help share in his friend's pessimism.

"Don't you see, Franz? The Nazis ... Hitler ... they will never let us be. And for whatever reason, God refuses to intervene. 'The chosen people?'" Max scoffed. "Couldn't be further from the truth! It would be far more accurate to call us the 'cursed people.'"

Franz thought of Max's daughter and her family. The man had every right to his views, but Franz would still need his help in mobilizing the community. "Listen, Max, this is a crisis. Now is not the time for—"

The sound of heavy footsteps cut him off. He heard shouting from somewhere down the hallway and hurried out of the lab to investigate, Max on his heels.

Two soldiers stormed toward them. Franz froze at the sight of their white armbands. *Not now! Don't take me now, of all times.*

A gaunt Kempeitai officer stopped in front of them. He swung a finger from Max to Franz and back. "Feinstein, Maxwell!" he barked.

Max's face paled and he shot Franz a terrified glance. "Don't tell my Sarah, Franz," he whispered. "Her weak heart. She cannot know that—"

"Feinstein!" the Kempeitai screamed.

Max stepped forward. "I . . . I am Dr. Feinstein," he stammered.

"You come!"

"Why?" Max held up his hands. "I have done nothing wrong."

"Come now!"

Max turned to Franz. "Think of an excuse, Franz. Anything! Sarah can never know what—"

The Kempeitai officer slammed his fist into Max's stomach. As Max doubled over in pain, the soldier caught him by the hair. He jerked Max's head forward and swung his knee into it, breaking his nose with a crunch.

Franz moved toward Max, but the other Kempeitai man clamped a hand across his shoulder and spun him backwards.

Gasping for breath, Max struggled to straighten up. Blood poured from his nose and down his face. His lips parted into a grotesque smile. "The chosen people, *ach!*" he grunted. "Protect my Sarah, Franz."

Chapter 42

Franz's fingers had gone numb despite the gloves' wool lining. He had been standing in the cold outside the Bureau of Stateless Refugee Affairs for hours. Even though he had reached Ghoya's headquarters minutes after the curfew lifted at seven o'clock, at least twenty refugees were already lined up ahead of him. The queue now snaked behind him as far as he could see, and the doors still had not even opened.

As Franz waited in line, his imagination ran wild with possible scenarios involving von Puttkamer and his "spectacular" bomb plot. He had no interest in conversing with the others in line, but the talkative man one spot ahead of him had insisted on drawing him into conversation, even though Franz had turned away and feigned difficulty hearing.

"You remember me from the hospital, Dr. Adler? *Ja*, surely. I am Samuel Eisler. My sister, Gisela Silverstein, Frau Silverstein, yes? You removed her gall bladder in the spring of '40."

"Ah, of course, yes," Franz said, but he had only a faint memory of the operation and none whatsoever of Eisler. "How is your sister?"

"She is fine, but she is a real kvetcher, you know? Always troubled by something or other."

Eisler wanted to talk. He had apparently been a successful tailor in Munich and had married the most beautiful girl at his local synagogue before his *Goldgräber* of a wife ended up leaving him for a rich lawyer. Franz learned this and much more as they waited for Ghoya's office to open.

"Did you hear that American broadcast last week?" Eisler said next, heedless of the risk of being overheard. Listening to Allied stations was forbidden—people had been shot for less—and there were at least a few Japanese soldiers within earshot.

Franz turned away. "I have no access to a wireless of any kind," he said, loud enough for the nearest guard to hear.

Fortunately for Eisler, the soldier didn't seem to understand German. "Edward Murrow on CBS," the foolish man continued. "I am fortunate to have a good grasp of English, you understand. That man Murrow went with RAF bombers on a raid over Berlin. Oh, you should have heard his description. So marvellous! It sounded as if those brave pilots pummelled the Führer's city. Murrow called it 'orchestrated hell.' It's so wonderful, is it not, Herr Doktor?"

Franz looked back at Eisler. "How can 'orchestrated hell' be wonderful?"

"Berlin, man!" Eisler exclaimed. "The Allies are pounding the Nazi empire at its core."

"And yet the Nazis still dominate Europe," Franz pointed out. "I am told they refer to it as *Festung Europa*."

"You watch, Dr. Adler. Watch how quickly Fortress Europe collapses as the Allies advance."

"I have heard the same for almost two years," Franz snapped. "How the Nazis will capitulate the moment the Americans and British invade the continent. But where is this invasion? Hitler still has the run of Europe." He motioned to the checkpoint and lowered his voice. "Meantime, we line up in the freezing cold to grovel to a Japanese Napoleon for permission to cross the street."

"Any day now, Herr Doktor." Eisler laughed. "You will see."

Movement in front of them drew their attention. Franz looked up to see that the door had opened and people had begun to file inside the building. He shuffled ahead with the rest of the queue as it relocated inside the narrow hallway that led to Ghoya's office. Franz was relieved to see Eisler turn to the person ahead of him. "Do you listen to the wireless?" Eisler exclaimed. "That Edward Murrow is my favourite . . ."

The door to Ghoya's office was wide open, and the little man's voice, even at its quietest, carried the length of the hallway. Franz could tell that his behaviour was as predictably unpredictable as usual. He joked and laughed with some of the refugees and berated, accused or struck others. Anything could launch him into a tirade.

Some people in the line appeared resigned, even bored. Franz assumed that they faced Ghoya regularly and had grown oblivious to his volatility. Others were ashen with terror or fidgeted nervously. Franz even caught himself shifting from foot to foot and cracking his knuckles.

Over an hour passed before he made it to the head of the queue. Franz had rehearsed arguments in his head, but as his turn neared, he still had no idea what he would say to Ghoya when he finally faced him.

An expressionless soldier at the door nodded for Franz to enter. At the sight of him, Ghoya hopped up from his seat and rushed around his desk. "No, no, no!" He waved both hands wildly. "No passes for anyone in your family. I was clear." He turned his head from side to side as though conferring with imaginary colleagues. "Was I not clear? I believe I was clear."

"You were, Mr. Ghoya." Franz lowered his gaze and bowed before the little man. "I have not come regarding a pass."

Ghoya's irritability vanished as abruptly as a hailstorm ending. He sauntered around his desk and sunk back into his chair. A thoughtful look crossed his face as he touched his fingertips together in a diamond shape. "Not for a pass? So why have you come?"

"I am . . . concerned for a friend."

"Which friend?" Ghoya asked.

"Max Feinstein. A doctor. He works at my hospital and—"

A knowing look came to Ghoya's eyes as he raised a hand to cut Franz off. "Maxwell Feinstein from Hamburg, Germany. Yes, yes. I know him!"

"Dr. Feinstein was arrested by the Kempeitai."

Ghoya laughed. "Of course he was! You think I do not know this? I know everything that happens in the Designated Area." He patted his chest. "After all, I am King of the Jews!"

"But, sir, why was Max arrested?"

Ghoya shook his head gravely. "Maybe I should give you a pass for one day. Yes, maybe. To go see the exhibit on Broadway Street."

Dread overcame Franz, but he pretended to be unaware of the mass public executions. "Why is that, Mr. Ghoya?"

"Traitors," Ghoya grunted. "They hang there for everyone to see. Those cowards who killed our brave officers."

"But I do not understand." Franz raised a hand. "What do they have to do with Dr. Feinstein?"

"He spies for the Resistance, too."

Franz felt his pulse pounding in his ears. "That is not possible, sir. He is a doctor. He has no interest in war or politics."

"Your doctor friend is a spy!"

"But Max speaks only German. How could he possibly communicate with anyone in the Underground?"

"A spy, I tell you. *A spy!*" Ghoya clenched his fists as he screamed. "We know it to be so!"

Franz saw it was futile to argue. His heart sank. Was Max even still alive? It almost didn't matter. If the Japanese believed him to be a spy, his fate was sealed.

Ghoya's tone suddenly became calm, almost pleasant. "You do understand that your friend is gone?" For a moment, Franz thought Ghoya still meant Max. "Now that Colonel Kubota is no longer with us, no one is left to protect you. You have only me to answer to. Only me." He laughed again. "No reason to concern yourself, Dr. Adler. I am a very fair king."

Franz said nothing.

"Mrs. Aaronsohn tells me every day at lunch how thankful the Jews are for my benevolence," Ghoya said, clearly proud of his choice of words. Then his eyes narrowed and he tut-tutted. "The smuggling

. . . the spying . . . it all comes back to that Jewish hospital of yours. The hospital where both colonels and the admiral died. Where that spy Feinstein was working."

"Mr. Ghoya, the hospital is not associated—"

"Why should the Jews have their own hospital? What is so special about you people? Tell me!"

"Nothing is special about us," Franz blurted. "We are a miserable people. A cursed people. And it is hardly a hospital at all anymore."

"It is true! Your hospital was of no use to our wounded officers. No help at all! Perhaps the building could be put to other uses."

Franz had run out of arguments, so he simply dropped his chin and nodded in defeat.

But Ghoya seemed to have lost interest in the hospital. He leaned back in his seat. "Colonel Tanaka, he never trusted you Jews."

At the mention of Tanaka, Franz experienced a familiar twinge of guilt.

Ghoya jutted out his lower lip. "Without the king, who knows what the colonel would have done to you Jews."

"We are grateful for your help, of course."

Ghoya held out his hands. "What is a king without his people?"

Franz decided to seize the opening. "You know, sir, Colonel Tanaka is not the only one who wishes ill toward us Jews."

"Yes, yes, I know," Ghoya cried gleefully. "The other Germans! They hate you Jews."

"The Nazis, yes. You are absolutely correct." Franz nodded. "They will probably attack us at any moment."

"Attack you?" Ghoya frowned.

"Yes in the ghet—the Designated Area, sir. We have heard a rumour that they are planning to launch an assault any day. Of course, you must already have heard this, too."

Ghoya cocked his head but said nothing.

"Surely, Mr. Ghoya, they would need your permission before they could plant any bombs in—"

"*Bombs?*" Ghoya launched himself to his feet. He stared at Franz and when he spoke, his voice was hardly more than a whisper. "What is this talk of bombs?"

Chapter 43

Jakob tugged at Hannah's hands while she covered her face and peeped.
"Kuckuck!"

She opened her hands like shutters. As usual, her left hand moved
less smoothly than her right, but her nephew was oblivious. He giggled
uproariously. The ten-month-old couldn't get enough of his favourite
peekaboo game. Hannah was happy for the distraction, too. Jakob's presence counterbalanced the rising tension at home.

School wasn't much better. Hannah and Freddy hardly spoke. What
hurt far more than seeing him with Leah was his cheerful indifference. It
confirmed what Hannah had feared: for Freddy, she had only ever been
a means to an end. Lately, she had been spending more time with Otto
Geldmann than any of her other classmates. While there was a degree of
consolation in his sweet attentiveness, Otto never gave her butterflies the
way Freddy always had.

Jakob swung a hand at her face, demanding more peekaboo. "You are
such a determined little one," she laughed as she swept him off the floor
and swung him through the air.

Jakob struggled against her until she brought her lips to his belly and
blew, which elicited another fit of giggles. "Time to change your diaper,
Schatzi," she said.

As Hannah lowered Jakob to the floor, she looked over to the couch, where Esther had been reading Simon's letter. Tears now ran down her cheeks and the letter dangled from her fingers. Hannah had not seen her aunt cry in years, not since those dark months after Kristallnacht when the storm troopers had killed Onkel Karl. "What's wrong, Tante Essie?"

Esther wiped her eyes with the back of her hand. "*Ach!* It's nothing really. I am only being foolish."

Hannah passed Jakob his favourite rattle, which he took to shaking energetically. She got to her feet and hurried over to the couch. Reaching for her aunt's hand, she sat down beside her. "Tell me, Tante, please . . ."

"Simon—he worries about us."

"He always worries when he is not with you," Hannah pointed out. "It's only natural."

Esther smiled through her tears. "This time is different, Hannah-*chen*."

"How so?"

"Simon says he cannot wait any longer. That he will not. He insists on coming to join us."

"Here? In the ghetto?"

Esther nodded. "There couldn't be a worse time for him to sneak across the checkpoint. You have seen how vigilant the Japanese are being ever since the Underground—" She caught herself.

"Killed those Japanese officers," Hannah finished her sentence.

"Of course, you too would have heard about that."

"Everyone has. And I know they died at Papa's hospital." Hannah stifled a sigh. Her aunt was as overprotective as her father, both of them believing they could somehow shelter her from the bad news that was as predictable in Shanghai as the winter rain. "Last month there was a rumour going around at school that a group of former students was behind the killing."

"That's nonsense, Hannah. It was the Resistance."

"I never believed the gossip."

Esther went quiet. When she finally spoke, her voice was hoarse. "If

Simon were to be caught, they would not simply take him back to a camp. No, they would . . ." She shuddered. "I cannot even bear to think of it."

Hannah thought of the women who were shot for trying to escape their home during a raid. She squeezed her aunt's hand tighter. "We have to convince him to stay put."

"He will not listen to us."

"Why not?"

"In light of the, er . . ." Esther hesitated. "Recent events. He feels he has to be here to protect us."

"You mean the bomb the Nazis are planning?"

Esther grimaced. "You know about that, too?"

Hannah nodded. "Last week, I overheard Sunny and Papa talking about it."

"Yes, but—"

"I am not a child," Hannah huffed, aware that she sounded like the epitome of a petulant teenager but too angry to care. "In a few months, I will be fourteen. You do not need to protect me from this anymore."

"I'm sorry, Hannah. You are right. You're practically grown up. God knows you are wise beyond your years." Esther mustered another smile. "I cannot help myself. Sometimes when I look at you, I just see my precious little niece, not the young woman you are becoming." She pointed to Jakob, who was trying to eat his rattle while hauling himself to his feet against the side of the couch. "I want to protect all of you from the misery in this world."

Hannah leaned closer to her aunt. "I want to help you, Essie. Let me."

"I know, Hannah-*chen*," Esther murmured. "I love you for it, too. But I don't think anyone can stop Simon. Once he sets his mind to something . . ."

Hannah pulled her hand free of Esther's and snapped her finger. "Tell him you will leave."

"Leave?" Esther frowned. "I do not understand."

"Warn Simon that if he tries to come for you, you will take Jakob and go somewhere where he will never find you."

"I can't make a threat like that," Esther said, more in surprise than anything else.

"Even if it stops him from doing something so rash?"

Esther stared at Hannah for a moment. "I suppose it might be worth it. Yes, it just might."

The door opened, and Hannah looked over to see her stepmother enter.

Sunny picked up on Esther's distress from across the room. She looked quickly over to Jakob and, seeing that he was fine, hurried over to the couch. "What's wrong, Essie? Is it Simon?"

Esther waved the letter in her hand. "He is planning something . . . something suicidal."

Sunny took the letter from her hand and read it silently, then folded it and passed it back to Esther. "I will speak to him."

"You will?" Esther said.

"I will make him listen."

"Oh, thank you, Sunny. And will you take him something from me?"

"Certainly. Another letter?"

Esther glanced at Hannah and then turned back to Sunny with a shake of her head. "An ultimatum."

Chapter 44

Sunny couldn't draw her eyes away from the painting. Though it was Post-Impressionist in style, and only half finished, its macabre theme was unmistakable. Many of the figures on the canvas were just ghostly outlines, their features still undefined. Nonetheless, she was mentally catapulted back to Broadway and the morning she had stumbled across the execution site. Ernst had captured the electric mood of the crowd that morning. Sunny experienced another pang of pity for the victims. They must have suffered horribly before their undignified deaths. And clearly time had proven Franz right: the old man from the Underground must have kept her identity from the Kempeitai.

"Not my best work, I realize." Ernst stood beside her, smelling of oil paint and tobacco. "Let me see if I can salvage it yet."

"It's gripping." Sunny finally peeled her eyes away. "But Ernst, after the last time, with those paintings you did of the Nanking Massacre."

"What about them?"

"They just about got you drawn and quartered." Simon spoke up from the window ledge where he was sitting. "You think it's wise to go over that waterfall again?"

Ernst addressed Sunny. "This, from a man who single-handedly wants to storm the ghetto?"

Simon rose and strolled over to them. "No storming. I only want to make sure my wife and son are safe. Is that too much to ask?"

"Don't you see, Simon?" Sunny said. "By trying to reach Essie and Jakob, you would only be putting them in more danger."

"What choice do I have, Sunny? Better that I stay cooped up here and just hope they keep out of harm's way?"

"Sunny has a point," Ernst said. "Your return will not go unnoticed. The Japanese are everywhere."

"It's not the Japanese who concern me," Simon said.

"They should, my friend." Ernst wiggled a finger at his painting. "They really should."

"Even the yellow peril—" Simon flashed Sunny an apologetic look. "The Japs, I mean. What they can do doesn't compare to what the Nazis have in mind."

Sunny turned back to Ernst. "Have you heard more from the baron?"

"Nothing specific." Ernst pulled a pack of cigarettes from his shirt pocket and tapped one out. "I tried to visit him yesterday but couldn't get in."

"The son of a bitch doesn't trust you anymore," Simon snorted.

"I doubt that," Ernst said through a cupped hand as he lit the cigarette. "I imagine von Puttkamer is being extra cautious, now that his plans are in the final stages."

"Final stages?" Sunny stiffened. "What have you heard, Ernst?"

"Gerhard believes the attack is imminent."

"What does that mean? Today? Tomorrow? Next week?"

"Von Puttkamer told him to be prepared at a moment's notice," Ernst said. "Gerhard thinks the attack will come in the next few days. A week at most."

A chill ran down Sunny's spine. "Days . . ."

"Right in the middle of Hanukkah," Simon said to himself.

"Christmas is only a few days away," Ernst added.

"Yeah, but Hanukkah will bring all the Jews together in one spot," Simon said.

Sunny stifled a gasp. "At the synagogue! Of course!"

Simon nodded. "On Saturday. It's Shabbat."

"That has to be where the Nazis will attack!" Sunny exclaimed. "When everyone is gathered for the service."

"Saturday is also Christmas Day," Ernst pointed out.

Simon grimaced. "You don't honestly think that would stop them?"

"No, I suppose not. Probably their idea of a Christmas present."

"Even if we know the day and location, how do we prevent it?" Simon wondered aloud.

"Will they not cancel the service?" Sunny asked.

"I doubt they would." Simon's hands fell to his sides. "Besides, those snakes would just find another time and another place. Remember when von Puttkamer came to the ghetto? He sniffed around the hospital and the school, too."

"Still," Sunny said. "If we think this is when they intend to strike, we must do something to stop it."

"I wish we had gone after von Puttkamer months ago." Simon shook his head bitterly. "When we still had time."

"How would you have accomplished that?" Ernst asked. "Jews are hardly allowed out of the ghetto."

"I could do it myself."

"I never really pictured you as the assassin type. Besides, what would you use for a weapon?"

"A knife? A brick? My bare hands if need be. The son of a bitch wants to blow up my family!"

Ernst exhaled a plume of smoke. "You think von Puttkamer is the only Nazi who has it out for the Jews?"

"He's the one with the bombs right now," Simon said.

Sunny thought again of the multi-headed Hydra. "Killing von Puttkamer would only antagonize them."

"Maybe it would, maybe it wouldn't," Simon said. "Either way, I am not going to sit here while my wife and son are stuck in the ghetto. Not with Nazis waltzing around with enough dynamite to flatten Brooklyn."

Sunny clutched Simon's arm. "Esther doesn't want you there, Simon."

"It's not her decision."

Sunny knew Simon too well to believe that any of her arguments would sway him. Instead, she reluctantly reached into her coat pocket and withdrew the letter from Esther.

* * *

As Sunny walked away from Germantown, she shook off the image of Simon's crestfallen face. Still, she had no regrets. She was confident that he had been persuaded by Esther's note to abandon his foolhardy plan to return to the ghetto.

On her way home, Sunny veered off toward Frenchtown. Walking at fast as she could without drawing attention to herself, she reached the Cathay Building in just a few minutes. When she reached her friend's apartment, Jia-Li greeted her as though she had been expecting the visit. Interlocking their arms, she led Sunny into the living room.

Charlie sat on the floor, just where Sunny had last seen him. He smiled as he fiddled with what she assumed was an explosive device, though she did not recognize the grey metallic box that he was working on.

Across the room, Sunny spotted an old baby pram pushed against the far wall. All of a sudden, she felt joy, concern and envy all at once. Before she could even ask, Jia-Li held up her hands and shook them vigorously. "No, no, *xiǎo hè*. Not what are you thinking. No."

"Then who is the pram for?"

Jia-Li shook her head. "It's not for a baby at all."

Bewildered, Sunny stared at her best friend before the truth washed over her like ice water. "For a bomb?" she gasped. "You are going to plant a bomb inside a pram?"

"Do you have a better idea for sneaking one into a train station?" Jia-Li asked.

"Charlie cannot wheel a pram," Sunny sputtered. "Not on crutches."

Jia-Li dismissed the idea with a wave. "Obviously not. A man wheeling a pram would draw far too much attention."

"No, *băo bèi!*" Sunny turned angrily to Charlie. "You cannot let her do this, Chun. It's not right."

"It was not my idea." Despite his impassive tone, Sunny saw reluctance in Charlie's eyes.

Jia-Li kneeled down beside Charlie and slung an arm over his shoulders. "I am the only one who can do this." She kissed his cheek and then turned back to Sunny, her expression more determined than ever. "You will never talk me out of it, *xiăo hè.* Never."

Sunny crouched down in front of them. She grabbed Jia-Li's free hand and squeezed it urgently. "Listen to me, *băo bèi.* I know a better way for you both to help."

Chapter 45

The light snowfall continued to colour the streets white. Despite the evening's chill, Franz paused outside the entrance to Ohel Moishe Synagogue. Rather than framing it mentally for a photograph, as he had done several times before, he scanned the brick building for points of structural weakness. It looked sturdy enough, but his eyes kept drifting back to the ground-floor arches. He imagined the rumble of the supporting walls giving, and the upper floor and roof crashing down on the congregation.

He willed the nightmarish vision out of his mind. *What do I know about sabotage or demolition?*

He put on his yarmulke and entered the synagogue. Rabbi Hiltmann stood at the front of the room hunched over the bimah, polishing the tabletop with a yellow rag. The rabbi did not turn around right away at the sound of Franz's footsteps on the tiled floor, finishing his inspection of the tabletop first. "Ah, Dr. Adler." His grey beard bobbed and his lips curved into a smile. "Visiting *shul* outside Shabbat yet again? Is this some kind of new habit?"

"I need to speak to you." Franz lowered his voice. "It's urgent, Rabbi."

Hiltmann carefully folded his rag into a square. "This is not related to your previous visit, then?" Franz shook his head. "So have you made your peace with your actions?"

"In a way, yes," Franz said, though it was far from the truth. Not a night had passed without him thinking about Colonel Tanaka on the operating table. No amount of rationalization could overcome his sense that he had betrayed both a patient and his profession. But this was not the time for introspection. "Rabbi, I have concerns about the security of the synagogue."

Hiltmann frowned. "Security? Of the *shul?* What do the *misrachdik* have in mind for us this time?"

"No, not the Japanese, Rabbi. The Nazis."

The rag dropped to his side. "The Nazis?" Hiltmann repeated slowly.

"We have reason to believe they intend to bomb the synagogue."

The rabbi's head jerked up as if he had been slapped. "How could you possibly know this?"

"I have a friend. He is Austrian. A gentile." Without mentioning Ernst by name, Franz shared what he knew of von Puttkamer's plans. "Rabbi, you must cancel the Shabbat service tomorrow morning."

Hiltmann stared up at the ark of the Torah for a long moment before answering. "You are certain that the temple is their target?"

"We can assume it, Rabbi. The school is closed for Hanukkah. And attacking the hospital would not have the same ... impact as targeting the synagogue. Especially not tomorrow."

"So you are also assuming the attack will come tomorrow."

"When else?" Franz groaned. "Much of the refugee community will be gathered here for the Hanukkah service. And for the goyim, it's Christmas Day."

The rabbi sighed so heavily that his lips whistled. "But to cancel prayers on a Sabbath?"

"Surely it's acceptable if lives are at risk."

Hiltmann stroked his beard. "*Pikuakh nefesh,*" he muttered.

"I am not familiar with that term."

"*Pikuakh nefesh.* A principle in Jewish law whereby the preservation of life overrides almost all other religious considerations."

"Yes, exactly. There couldn't be a more fitting application."

The rabbi considered this. "They have taken everything from us, have they not?" he finally said. "Our homes and all our possessions. They divided our families and drove us across two oceans. Yet it seems that is still not enough for them."

"Nothing will be, Rabbi."

"On Kristallnacht, I watched from the apartment across the street as they burned my synagogue to the ground." Hiltmann's eyes drifted over to the ark again. "Out front, they made a bonfire from the scrolls of our beautiful Torah. Our cantor, Yitzhak Hirschberg. Yitzhak was young and so naive." He shook his head gravely. "Yitzhak ran out and begged them to stop. You know what happened?"

"I can only imagine."

"They clubbed Yitzhak until he was unconscious and then . . . they . . ." Hiltmann swallowed. "They threw him on the fire."

Franz thought again of his little brother, Karl, lynched by storm troopers that same night. "I remember Vienna, the morning after. Seeing our family's synagogue—where my parents and my brother were married—reduced to a pile of rubble."

The rabbi nodded to himself. "So now they want to repeat their marvellous feat here in Shanghai. To destroy our only place of worship. To kill as many of us as possible."

"We can rebuild the synagogue," Franz said. "But what can you do if the roof collapses on the congregation?"

Hiltmann was quiet again. "You do understand the significance of Hanukkah, do you not, Herr Doktor?"

"The oil that burned for eight days when it was only supposed to last one?" Franz said, vague on the other details. If Hannah were here, she could have filled in the gaps.

"Ah, that is the miracle we remember, but it's not the essence of Hanukkah." The rabbi's expression hardened. "Hanukkah commemorates a great moment of Jewish defiance. The time when the brave Maccabees, outnumbered though they were, drove the Assyrian oppressors out of

Jerusalem." He held up both hands. "And why did they fight? To reclaim the Holy Temple in the name of God."

"Yes, but were the Assyrians armed with explosives, Rabbi?"

"How can we abandon our synagogue on this day of all days?"

"What about *Pikuakh nefesh?*"

The rabbi shook his hands in front of him. "Where is your proof that the Nazis will attack tomorrow?"

"Proof?" Franz groaned. "I am not privy to the specifics. We were fortunate that my friend caught wind of this at all."

Hiltmann eyed him defiantly. "Without proof, I will not cancel the service."

Franz brought his hands to his chest in appeal. "Rabbi, you would risk so many lives?"

"We can post young men outside to watch for signs of trouble. They will warn us."

"And if the warning comes too late?"

"This is a house of God, Dr. Adler." The rabbi's voice trembled. "How can we allow the Nazis to chase the faithful from it, just because of innuendo and rumour? Where will it end?"

*   *   *

Outside, the snow was thickening on the ground. Franz half walked and half skated on the slick sidewalks as he hurried from the synagogue to the hospital.

He found Sunny there and led her into the staff room, then filled her in on his conversation with the rabbi. "I did not expect the man to be so obstinate," Franz sighed.

Sunny kissed Franz on the cheek and then offered him a small smile. "Stubbornness?" she said in mock surprise. "From a Jew?"

Franz laughed in spite of himself. "I don't know how you put up with us."

"I love you," she said. "Besides, I consider myself very fortunate to be part of your wonderful community, bewildering though it sometimes is."

"I love you, too." He kissed her on the lips. "Despite your peculiar view on what constitutes good fortune."

The smile slid from her lips. "So it is up to us to ensure the safety of the synagogue."

"With Charlie's help?" he asked.

Sunny nodded.

Franz exhaled heavily. "Charlie will be taking a huge risk even showing his face in the ghetto, with all those soldiers about."

"He is determined to help us. To repay our kindness, as he puts it. Besides, who else knows anything about explosives?"

"What if Charlie doesn't find the bombs?"

"If they are there, he will find them."

"Can you be so sure? Would you risk the lives of Hannah, Esther and the baby on it?"

Sunny's eyes widened. "They are not planning to attend the service? Surely not."

"They want to."

Sunny reached out and cupped his face. "You cannot let them, Franz. They must stay home. Promise me."

Before Franz could answer, the door to the staff room burst open and Ernst rushed in, his coat dusted with snow. "There you are, thank Christ!"

"What is it, Ernst?" Franz demanded.

Ernst brushed snowflakes from his coat and head, even out of his beard. "This evening," he said. "Von Puttkamer and his men are coming tonight."

"To the ghetto?"

"Yes. To see Ghoya."

Franz grimaced. "He is asking Ghoya for permission to attack us?"

Ernst waved off the idea. "No. He is coming with food and presents. To show Ghoya and the others a traditional German Christmas."

"It must be a ruse."

"Of course it is." Ernst patted his pocket in search of cigarettes but came up empty. "But one that will get them inside the ghetto after dark."

"After curfew," Sunny murmured.

Ernst nodded. "Precisely."

Franz interlaced his fingers and squeezed them until they hurt. "So his men will have free rein to plant their bombs, at the synagogue and wherever else they want to, without us being able to watch."

"That is the general idea, no doubt."

Franz once again pictured the walls of the synagogue buckling. "As soon as the curfew is lifted in the morning, we will have to scour every inch of the synagogue's grounds."

Sunny turned to Franz, her eyes frantic with worry. "What if we're wrong, Franz?" she murmured. "What if the synagogue is not their target? Perhaps they plan to explode bombs tonight. In the heime or the other buildings where the refugees live."

But Franz felt certain in a way that he rarely did outside the operating room. "Going to all this trouble to bomb a few apartments would not satisfy the Nazis. No. Von Puttkamer promised something spectacular."

"I know, darling, but what if . . ."

"We need to spread word among all the refugees. Everyone must guard their homes and look out for signs of unusual activity."

Ernst jutted out his lower lip. "*Ja*. It's a good idea."

"Our telephone exchange is still not working," Franz said. "Someone needs to go tell Charlie. We will need him in the morning, first thing."

"I will go," Sunny offered.

Ernst held up a hand. "No, Sunny, let me. Frenchtown is practically on my way home."

Sunny shook her head. "Ernst, you have already risked more than enough for us."

Ernst stroked her cheek. "Do you remember last year? When the Japanese were hunting for Shan and me? You risked everything to hide us here in the hospital. In plain sight among the cholera patients." He chuckled. "In retrospect, it was not really much of a plan."

"We did shave your head," Sunny pointed out.

"My beautiful locks." Ernst ran a hand through the wild tangles of hair that were part of his current disguise. "After what you risked, this—this is nothing. Besides, I fear that the real danger is yet to come."

Chapter 46

"I suppose it would not be appropriate to wish you Merry Christmas or Happy Hanukkah," Charlie said as he approached Franz where he stood in the lane behind the synagogue.

"No, not today," Franz whispered, adjusting his old camera around his neck. The Kodak Brownie box camera had originally belonged to Sunny's father. Franz had been out of film for months but, the day before, had sent Joey to trade a pair of Sunny's earrings for a fresh roll on the black market.

Franz might not have recognized Charlie were it not for the crutches. Under his snow-covered straw hat and mismatched, tattered clothes, Charlie could have passed for one of Shanghai's beggars.

"I do not remember Shanghai ever being this cold." Charlie's cloudy breath obscured his face.

Franz was almost oblivious to the temperature. Sunny had found him an old pair of her father's woolen long johns. And adrenaline had coursed through his veins since Ernst's visit, helping to keep him warm and alert despite his lack of sleep.

He had stayed awake through the night, vigilantly watching out the window for any sign of Nazi saboteurs. Each moan from the pipes or creak of the floorboards sent his heart up his throat, but the hours had passed without incident. He had heard no reports of unusual activity in the ghetto, which cemented his belief that the Hanukkah service at the synagogue had to be where and when von Puttkamer planned to strike.

Charlie turned back to the temple and slowly scanned it. "The snow provides the perfect camouflage for planting bombs." Unlike Franz, he seemed calm.

"I used to love the cold winters in Austria," Franz said. "But today I hate the snow."

"Well, it also presents certain challenges to the bombers."

Franz frowned. "What do you mean?"

Charlie let a few snowflakes fall onto his tongue. "Igniter cord will not burn reliably through snow. They would have to use an alternate fuse. A pencil detonator, probably."

"What is that?"

"A narrow cylinder packed at one end with a detonator. You crush the copper tip with pliers." Charlie held up his forefinger and squeezed its tip between the fingers of his other hand. "Acid is released inside and eats through the wire holding the striker away from the detonator. The small explosion detonates the bigger charge."

"How long does the fuse take to ignite?"

"Depends on the detonator. Anywhere from a few minutes to several hours."

"Several hours?" Franz coughed. "So they might have triggered the detonators already and left?"

Charlie pointed to the thin layer of snow around the building. "Do you see any footprints?"

"Surely they could have triggered them last night when the bombs were planted? The fresh snow would cover tracks."

"No. Long-delay detonators are unreliable in such cold weather." Charlie's eyes narrowed. "How much time do we have before the service begins?"

Franz glanced at his watch, dismayed to see that it was already past seven thirty. "An hour at the most. How can we search the whole area with all this damned snow?"

"We do not need to search the whole building."

"Why not?"

"They would only place explosives at load-bearing points. Where the most damage would be done to the target."

The target. Franz winced at Charlie's choice of words, but it must have been exactly how the Nazis viewed the temple and the Jews inside it. "Shall I go around to the front and collect the volunteers?"

"Let's first see what we are facing."

Franz followed Charlie around to the rear of the building. As he slipped and slid on the snow, Franz was impressed by the other man's stability on crutches. Charlie stopped to stare up at the upper levels of the synagogue. He shifted right and left, then settled on a spot. "Here. This is where I would plant it." He laid his crutches against the wall and lowered himself to the ground.

Franz hurried to the synagogue's back door, where the shovel Rabbi Hiltmann had promised was waiting. By the time he brought it back, Charlie had already cleared away a patch of snow at the base of the building that was at least ten feet wide.

"Should I shovel more snow?" Franz offered.

Charlie shook his head. "Safer to do this by hand." He carefully patted the patches of ground that he had exposed.

Taking care with his camera, Franz kneeled down beside him. The knees of his pants were soaked on contact with the ground. Not knowing how else to help, he began to extend the cleared area by patting away armfuls of snow.

"Here," Charlie said in a hush. "Right here."

Franz turned to Charlie, who was gently pawing at the ground. After a few moments, Franz made out the edges of a green object about the size and shape of a loaf of his favourite *Schwarzbrot*—black bread. Charlie cleared dirt from the top of the object. Franz spied two metal cylinders stuck into it like stubby antennas. "Pencil fuses. They placed two for good measure." Charlie ran his fingers up and down the cylinders and then said, "Not activated yet."

Franz's throat constricted. "So someone will return during the service to ignite them."

"Yes. They must have a short delay." Charlie skimmed his fingers along the edges of the green block and let out a low whistle. "Plastic explosive. British issue. Highly effective. The Americans dropped us some for our work in the field."

"Let me take a photograph," Franz said, rising unsteadily to his feet.

Franz angled the camera to capture the bomb, along with as much of the wall as he could. It was awkward: he was accustomed to photographing architecture, not weapons of mass murder. He shot the scene from three different angles to ensure that he had documented it sufficiently.

Franz dropped back to his knees and joined Charlie. Together they gingerly excavated the explosive. Franz reached out to touch its surface, but just as he made contact with the smooth block, Charlie's hand shot out and clamped onto his wrist. "Leave it," he snapped.

As soon as Charlie's grip loosened, Franz jerked his hand away as if he was pulling back from a flame. Charlie eased his fingertips under the edge of the explosive and gently pried upward. He raised it an inch or two. He snaked his other hand around and swept along its undersurface, then stopped suddenly. "Booby-trapped," he murmured.

Franz's heart leapt into his throat and he resisted an overwhelming urge to run away. Instead, barely breathing, he watched as Charlie slowly eased one side of the block up off the ground until he exposed a string dangling beneath it.

Franz spotted a round green object attached to the far end of the string. Half-buried in dirt, it resembled a dark pear. "Is that a . . . a grenade?"

Charlie didn't reply, just extracted a knife from under his coat and sliced through the string with a flick of the blade. He lifted the brick up off the ground in one smooth motion. "The trip wire is attached to the grenade's pull cord. A favourite booby trap of the Germans."

Charlie wrestled with the detonators to tug them free of the bomb. He stuffed them in his pocket, then placed the explosive beside his crutches. "How much time do we have?" he asked.

Franz checked his watch again. "Forty-five minutes, if that."

"We must find the rest of them."

Franz stared down at the brick they had found. He could not imagine the force that it was capable of unleashing. Even though he had expected to find bombs, seeing the object itself was jarring, almost surreal. "How many do you think they would have planted, Charlie?"

"At least four, possibly as many as six."

"So much ground to uncover," Franz said.

"Only the load-bearing points," Charlie reminded him. "And if someone was coming to set off the detonators in broad daylight, they must have planted them in other spots behind the building. And no deeper than this one."

"Should I go get the others now?"

"Yes." Charlie nodded to the hand grenade, which stuck out of the hole they had made as a deadly reminder. "But no shovels."

Chapter 47

Rabbi Hiltmann was waiting inside the synagogue's main entrance along with nine or ten male volunteers. The stale air smelled of sweat and fear, and the young men crowded around Franz, hanging on his words. When he got to the booby trap and the bombs, the men exploded into a frenzy of chatter and wild gesticulations.

Hiltmann clapped his hands above his head. When the room went quiet, he spoke only two words: "*Pikuakh nefesh.*"

Franz exhaled in relief. "You will cancel the service, Rabbi?"

"Even I can distinguish between defiance and martyrdom." Hiltmann's gaze ran across the collection of volunteers, several of whom Franz knew. None looked to be older than twenty-five, and they all wore similar wool coats over the dark suits they had dressed in for the service.

The rabbi gestured toward a curly-haired volunteer and the young man standing beside him. "Sol and David, go tell everyone. The service is cancelled." He looked around the room. "The rest of you, go outside and assist Dr. Adler."

In tense silence, the volunteers followed Franz outside to where Charlie had already discovered another bomb and was in the process of defusing the grenade underneath it. The others watched in awe. After Charlie cut the trip wire with his switchblade, he held up the plastic explosive—its two detonators still wedged into the surface—to show them what to look for. Franz translated his English into German. Charlie then divided the men into teams of two and directed them to spots around the synagogue's perimeter.

Soon, the building was surrounded by men in suits crouched on their hands and knees as though they were praying to the Western Wall. They nervously swept away snow and examined the surrounding dirt with their fingers. Within fifteen minutes, they had located two more booby-trapped bombs. Within half an hour, Charlie declared the temple free of explosives, and the group pushed the snow back against the building, making it look as natural as possible. They finished two or three minutes before eight thirty, just when the day's service had been scheduled to commence.

From a distance, Franz thought, the temple's snowy perimeter looked undisturbed, similar to how they had found it, but he realized that it would be unlikely to fool anyone who got much closer. Fortunately, snow was continuing to fall, covering their tracks.

The volunteers wanted to stay outside to guard the synagogue but Charlie insisted otherwise. "Go inside and make noise. Chant and sing," he instructed. "Be loud. Convince anyone who nears the building that a service is underway."

As the men reluctantly shuffled back inside the synagogue, Charlie motioned to the columned archways. "We will wait there. Behind the pillars."

"What if they come around from the front?" Franz asked.

"No. They cannot afford to be seen. They will come from behind."

"And if they are armed?"

Charlie pulled open his coat to reveal a pistol tucked into his waistband. Franz had no idea what Charlie planned to do with the bombers if and when he caught them, but the sight of the gun helped to calm his nerves.

Following Charlie's lead, Franz squatted down behind one of the pillars. Neither spoke a word as they peered out from behind the brick columns.

Half an hour passed. The cold wind nipped at Franz's ears and snaked under his coat until he began to shiver. Just as he was about to lift his arm to check his watch again, he heard Charlie cough quietly, as if clearing his throat.

Franz directed his gaze over the field of snow and saw something in the lane that ran along the property's border. Two young men strode purposefully down it. They were dressed in wool caps and parkas, with packs slung over their shoulders as if they were headed for a hike in the woods. As the men approached the synagogue, they shared a glance and then separated, slinking off in opposite directions.

Franz watched in trepidation as the first man approached the temple, but he did not seem to notice that the snow had been moved. He stopped about ten feet back from one corner of the building and then carefully paced off three steps. He then made a quarter turn and headed straight for the spot where one of the bombs had been uncovered.

The man lowered himself to his knees, no more than ten yards from where Franz and Charlie were hiding. Franz's shallow breathing sounded like cymbals in his ears. But the man kept his head down and cleared snow away with gloved hands before he reached inside his pack for a small spade.

Out of the corner of his eye, Franz saw Charlie manoeuvering his crutches before vaulting silently to standing. Franz quickly got to his feet.

Charlie brought a finger to his lips. They studied the trespasser, who was hunched over on his knees, digging at the dirt with the spade. Charlie mouthed the word "now" and then bolted, moving as fast on crutches as Franz could on his own two feet.

Charlie was only a yard or two away when the young man's head swivelled around. Just as he dropped his spade and pushed himself up to his feet, Charlie flung his crutches away and lunged. Landing on the man's back, he slammed him headfirst into the snowy ground.

Charlie's arms were a blur. By the time Franz reached them, Charlie had locked one arm across the man's chest and was holding a switchblade against his throat. "Not a sound," he hissed.

The young attacker's acne-studded face was pale. His eyes darted wildly from Charlie to Franz. "*Ich verstehe nicht,*" he croaked.

"He doesn't speak English," Franz whispered to Charlie.

"Tell him."

Franz translated, and their captive blinked his agreement.

"How many bombs did you plant?" Franz asked.

"Why would I tell you, you filthy Jew?" the young man snarled, though his eyes belied the defiance in his words.

Without waiting for a translation, Charlie slid the knife along the captive's neck until blood trickled along the blade.

"Four!" the man gasped, holding up four fingers. "Four bombs in all."

"Are there others here beside you and the other one?" Charlie demanded.

"*Nein,*" the man replied. "We were the only ones sent to the synagogue."

Franz began to relay the answer to Charlie but stopped mid-sentence. He spun back to the captive. "What do you mean the only ones sent here? Where were the others sent?"

"I . . . I . . . No, we were the only ones."

"Tell me," Franz growled.

Suddenly another voice cried out from somewhere behind Franz: "*Eine Falle!* It's a trap!"

Franz spun around to see the second bomber appear from behind the corner of the synagogue, a gun swinging in his hand as he ran.

The young German struggled violently in Charlie's grip. Franz heard a whooshing sound and felt something warm spray his cheek. He glanced over to see the man go limp in Charlie's arms, blood gushing down the front of his parka. Charlie lowered the bloody knife from his throat.

Franz heard the crack of a gunshot overhead as particles of brick showered down on them. Instinctively, he dropped to his chest.

Charlie tossed the saboteur's body aside and yanked the gun from his waistband. He aimed at the second man, who was sprinting across the snow, making for the lane. But Charlie lowered his weapon without firing a shot.

Franz stared at him questioningly.

"The soldiers out front." Charlie motioned to street. "If they hear more gunshots . . ."

Franz watched the man disappear behind one of the apartment buildings in the lane. They could never catch up to him.

Charlie struggled to balance himself upright. Dazed, Franz rose and retrieved Charlie's crutches from where they had landed in the snow.

"Go get your camera," Charlie instructed.

"There's no time now."

Charlie gestured to the body of the young German, the snow around his head and shoulder stained red. "You must photograph this."

Franz knew that they would eventually need the evidence, but at that moment it was the least of his concerns. "He was lying, Charlie. I saw it in his eyes. There are other Nazis in the ghetto. Other targets, too."

Charlie's eyes locked onto his. "The hospital?"

"Sunny!"

Chapter 48

Franz's heart pounded in his throat with every step as he sprinted for the refugee hospital. Rounding the corner onto Ward Road, he slipped on the snow and fell, landing heavily on his right shoulder with a crunch. The pain was sharp, but he picked himself up and set off in a run, holding his arm like a damaged wing.

A soldier patrolling the street shouted and angrily gestured for Franz to slow down; he eased up for a few yards, resuming his sprint the moment the soldier's back was turned. All he could think of were the explosives he had seen at the synagogue and how Sunny had insisted on overseeing the hospital that morning. "Please, God," he muttered repeatedly under his breath.

With every step, his dread rose. He expected to hear the crackle of an explosion at any moment, or to smell smoke. As he slid around the final corner, relief washed over him: the hospital was still standing. He raced up the pathway and burst through the doorway. "Sunny? Where are you?" he cried, running down the corridor.

Even before he reached the ward, he heard a flurry of activity: the frantic voices of nurses barking instructions and patients calling out for help.

Inside, Berta and Miriam were lining up gowned patients at the doorway. Franz had to scan the room twice before he spotted Sunny in the far corner, struggling to transfer an old woman from her bed to a wheelchair.

He raced over and helped her lift the heavy woman, igniting a searing pain in his shoulder. "Sunny, we found bombs," he said breathlessly. "Outside the synagogue—"

"There were gunshots, Franz," she interrupted. "Not more than five minutes ago. They came from behind the building."

He grabbed her by the shoulders. "Where is Joey?"

"I haven't seen him for maybe half an hour." Her eyes were frantic. "Joey was outside, Franz."

"I was just outside. Everything is quiet now."

"Still, we must clear the building."

The old woman looked up at them in horror. "What is going on?"

Sunny ignored her and waved toward the beds, several of which were still occupied. "None of those patients can walk. And we have just the one wheelchair."

Franz shook his head gravely. "We can only do what we can do."

"We can't just leave them behind."

"Lower them onto blankets. We'll drag them if need be. Can they crawl? We have to get out now!"

Calmer now, Sunny held his gaze and then nodded. She shoved the wheelchair toward the exit.

"Miriam, Berta!" Franz called. "Take the patients out front!"

Just then, Charlie came rushing into the room on his crutches, his face pale and rigid.

"There was gunfire behind the hospital," Franz exclaimed. "We're clearing the building."

"Come with me!" Charlie wheeled around. "There are footprints outside and . . ."

Franz squeezed past the patients and raced out the door after Charlie. He followed him around the side of the hospital. Charlie came to a halt just as Franz noticed the body lying on the ground ahead of them. The man lay slumped on his side, his head turned into the snow. Franz couldn't see his face, but he immediately recognized the old navy suit. "Oh no. Joey!" He lunged toward his fallen friend.

Charlie grabbed Franz's shoulder, launching another wave of pain. "Leave him," he snapped. "It's too late. He is dead. Shot through the heart. We have to find the bombs."

Rage, sorrow and fear cascaded through Franz, jolting him into action. He followed Charlie past Joey's body and behind the building.

Charlie waved at the many footprints they could see cutting through the snow and leading to spots against the wall. "There. The explosives will be there."

Reaching the heavily marked area, Charlie dropped to his one knee and swept frantically at the snow in front of him, then leaned further forward and began to brush more gently.

Leaning over Charlie's shoulder, Franz caught a glimpse of the same green plastic they had seen at the temple. Charlie swept away snow until he exposed the protruding pencil detonators. He ran a finger up one cylinder. "The tip. It's been crushed. The fuse is live."

Franz leaned back instinctively. "How much time do we have?" he asked.

Charlie wrestled the first detonator out of the block and threw it over his shoulder. He had to struggle harder to free the other, but it finally slid free. He tossed it away. "No way to know," he panted. "Could be any time now."

"But there were four bombs outside the synagogue."

Charlie reached for his crutches and pushed himself upright. "Follow the footprints!" He hurried along the wall, following the tracks in the snow.

Franz rushed past him to the next accumulation of footprints. He fell to his knees and swept his arms back and forth through the powdery snow, trying to ignore his throbbing shoulder. Suddenly his hand came in contact with something hard. His breath caught in his throat. Following Charlie's example, he delicately wiped the snow away from another half-buried explosive.

Franz examined the detonators and saw the pliers' teeth marks. *The bomb is live!* He fought the urge to scramble away.

Willing his hand steady, he reached out for the icy-smooth detonator with his right hand while stabilizing the explosive block with his left. He tugged on the cylinder but it hardly budged; his shoulder burned. He switched hands and braced his left elbow against the ground, then jerked even harder. The detonator gave way. He tossed it aside and reached for the second one, but this one resisted fiercely. The cylinder wouldn't budge.

His heart hammered against his rib cage. Melted snow dripped into his eyes, obscuring his vision. Behind him, he heard Charlie moving past, searching for the next charge.

Franz almost called to him for help, but there was no time. He considered grabbing the bomb and hurling it as far from the hospital as he could, but the thought of the grenades attached to the explosives at the synagogue stopped him.

He wiped his eyes clear and jumped to his feet. Planting his right foot firmly against the bomb, he again took the slippery detonator in his left hand, yanking back as hard as he could. It came loose and he toppled backward as it flew free of the explosive.

On his back, he arched his arm and threw the detonator with all his might away from the hospital. Just before it hit the ground, Franz saw it spark red, then explode.

Chapter 49

Light snow fell on the gathering in the clearing behind the hospital. The crowd was so big that people were forced to stand shoulder to shoulder to make enough room around the graveside.

Sunny could not stop her tears as she watched three coolies lower Joey's casket into the shallow grave that they had chipped out of the frozen soil. He was being buried on what would have been his twenty-second birthday—though there was an arbitrary element to that date. Joey had known only that he was born sometime in early winter, and when Sir Victor Sassoon had insisted on throwing him a lavish nineteenth birthday party a few years earlier, they had settled on December 27, primarily because it worked best for the tycoon's busy social schedule.

Joey was an orphan without any known family, so his funeral arrangements had fallen to Sunny. He had been neither religious nor, unlike so many rural Chinese, even remotely superstitious. Sunny had opted for a traditional but non-denominational Chinese burial. The casket was covered with the white and yellow paper that, according to folklore, warded off evil spirits.

Sunny was moved by the large turnout. The hospital staff stood in groups of two and three, a few patients were huddled under blankets, and a handful of coolies shivered in the cold. Others from the refugee community clustered around the gravesite, some sobbing openly. Only Simon was absent. It had taken every ounce of Sunny's persuasiveness to convince him not to attend. Only after she had suggested that he write a sermon Esther could read, rather than risk his life to sneak into the ghetto to pay his respects, did he finally agree to stay away.

Sunny crouched down, scooped up a handful of cold dirt and tossed it onto the coffin. Franz stepped up beside her and did the same. The other mourners formed a line to repeat the Chinese ritual. It reminded Sunny of the Jewish custom of mourners placing dirt back into a grave during the funeral ceremony. Again she was struck by the parallels between her native and adopted cultures.

Sunny took a last look at Joey's coffin, then stepped back. Franz's hand tightened over hers. She squeezed back, incredibly grateful that her husband had survived the recent events with no more than a broken collarbone. But her relief dissolved into melancholy as she thought of the last time she had seen Joey alive, a huge grin on his face as he had headed out the hospital's door promising to "sweep the Nazis away like fallen leaves."

"Thank you, darling," Franz murmured.

"For what?"

He motioned to the mourners. "You gave Joey a hero's funeral. No less than what he deserves."

"He deserved to live."

He held her hand tighter. "So true. But think of the lives he helped to save."

"Charlie and you did too. You are all heroes." Sunny wiped her eyes. "It's just that . . . Yang, Max, Wen-Cheng and now Joey. They are all gone."

Franz caressed her cheek with his free hand. "I know."

She caught his hand and gently pulled it away from her face. "Franz, how can we be sure that von Puttkamer will not simply try again?"

"We can't be sure. Not really."

"So where does that leave us?"

Franz exhaled heavily and his clouded breath obscured his features. "I must speak with him."

"Von Puttkamer? You can't be serious, Franz."

"I don't see another way."

Sunny tensed. "How would you even get a pass to leave the ghetto?"

"I will have to get von Puttkamer to come to me."

"Why would he agree to that?"

"I'll offer him certain . . . incentives."

"What kind of incentives?"

"Photographs," he said. "Listen, Sunny. You must take a message to Ernst. Something he can relay to von Puttkamer."

She shook her head. "We cannot involve Ernst. If von Puttkamer even suspects that he was the one who told you . . ."

Franz's forehead creased. "*Ja,* this is true."

"Let me do it," Sunny said.

"Walk into Nazi territory with a message from me, a Jew? You must be joking."

"Now that Joey is gone, who else can leave the ghetto?"

"We will find someone," Franz said. "One of the other refugees. Someone with one of Ghoya's precious passes."

She reached for his right elbow, and he winced in pain. "Sorry, darling." She released his arm. "Let me, Franz. I can do this."

He shook his head. "It is too risky."

"I will only be the messenger." She feigned a thick Chinese accent and continued in pidgin English: "I bring chit to master. He pay my cumshaw."

Franz's smile was fleeting. "No. It is too dangerous. I cannot allow it."

"And I will not allow Joey's death to have been in vain." Sunny put her hands on her hips. "I must do this, Franz."

*   *   *

Sunny had never worn this much makeup before. Her face was caked in powder, lipstick and rouge, and her hair tied in a constricting bun. She could feel her skin tighten every time she moved her lips. She felt as if she could have almost passed for one of the wild pheasants on the dock. Even though she barely recognized herself in the mirror, she still felt vulnerable. *What if he recognizes me from Ernst's flat?*

As she walked through Germantown, she imagined running into Ernst or Simon in this getup. She could picture Ernst's look of horror, and almost hear Simon's laughter. It calmed her to think of her friends.

The further she ventured into Germantown, the more uniformed men she encountered. She forced herself to sashay theatrically down the street, drawing both scowls and leers from the men she passed.

Von Puttkamer's building was the grandest on his block. A sign out front of the ground-floor office advertised itself as the German Information Bureau. A bell tinkled as Sunny opened the door and entered the office.

The baron's Korean bodyguard stepped out from behind a desk to meet her. "*Haben Sie sich verlaufen?*" he grumbled.

She pretended not to understand German.

"Are you lost?" he asked sharply in English.

Sunny dug into her coat and produced the envelope Franz had given her. "My come to see Baron. I bring chit."

The man extended his hand. "Leave it with me."

"I supposed to give baron."

"The baron is not here," the man snapped.

"Jewish doctor say give only baron."

"Give it to me now!"

A door behind the desk opened and von Puttkamer entered the room, impeccable in a grey three-piece suit. He smiled disarmingly at Sunny without so much as a glimmer of recognition. "Good afternoon, young lady," he said in smooth English. "Do I understand that you are carrying a letter for me?"

Sunny squinted and shook her head in mock confusion.

"The envelope, Fräulein." He touched his chest. "I am Baron von Puttkamer. Is that for me?"

Sunny thrust her hand out. "Yes, good Mr. Baron, yes."

"Thank you." Von Puttkamer bowed his head. When Sunny showed no sign of leaving, he shooed her away. "Go now. You can tell your master I have received his letter."

"Jewish doctor, he say wait for answer."

"Answer?" Von Puttkamer grimaced. He tore open the envelope and pulled out what was inside. A photograph fell out from the folded page and fluttered to the ground, landing face up.

Even in black and white, it was still ghoulish. The dead Nazi lay with his throat slashed against snow that was stained with his own blood. The bomb was visible above his head, eerily resembling a tombstone.

Von Puttkamer read Franz's note. After a long tense moment, he reached for the photograph. When he looked again at Sunny, his face was tight and his cheeks flushed. "Tell that *Jewish* doctor of yours that I will be there."

Chapter 50

Esther and Hannah exchanged worried looks but remained grimly silent as Sunny stepped inside the flat. Only after Sunny had scrubbed off her makeup and changed into regular clothes did Hannah speak up. "What did he say, Sunny?"

There was no point in trying to shelter Hannah. She was already aware of the bomb plot and her father's role in averting that disaster—it was the talk of the ghetto. "He will meet your father," Sunny said quietly.

"*Got hilf im.*" Esther reverted to Yiddish and laid a protective hand on Jakob, who slept on the couch beside her. "Who knows what the madman will try."

"Von Puttkamer will not try anything," Sunny said. "At least not in such a public setting."

"But he won't just forget, will he?" Hannah said.

"No," Sunny conceded. "That is why your father has to speak to him."

"To talk some sense into him?" Hannah scoffed. "To make him see the errors of his Nazi ways?"

"Hannah!" Esther cautioned.

Sunny understood that behind her angry words, Hannah was terrified for her father's safety. "Your papa knows what he is doing, Hannah. What he *must* do, to discourage the Nazis from striking again."

Hannah's confident expression gave way to one of sheer anxiety. "How can he possibly know that?"

Sunny was weighing how to answer when someone knocked lightly at the door. She glanced over at Esther, who just shook her head.

Sunny crept over and cracked open the door. It took her a moment to recognize Wen-Cheng. Typically fastidious about his appearance, Wen-Cheng was a mess: his hair was dishevelled and a patchy beard spotted his cheeks. She could smell unwashed hair and clothes, rather than his usual cologne.

She yanked the door open and moved to hug him, but he shrank from her. "Where have you been all this time?" she demanded.

"We must speak," he said in a hush.

Sensing his urgency, Sunny didn't bother to invite him in. Instead, she grabbed her coat and followed him outside.

They walked a few blocks in silence. Looking anything but calm, Wen-Cheng reminded Sunny of how jittery Jia-Li used to become during her episodes of opium withdrawal, but she doubted drugs were to blame. Wen-Cheng suddenly ducked down a narrow lane and Sunny followed. He halted after about ten paces and surveyed the homes on either side of them. "I have very little time," he muttered.

"We were so worried, Wen-Cheng. Where have you been these past months?"

"Everywhere. Nowhere."

"The old man from the Underground and the others—you heard that the Japanese caught them?"

He nodded, his eyes refused to meet hers.

"Did they come for you, too?"

"I am safe," he said, but his jumpiness told her otherwise. "I have come to warn you."

"Warn me about what?"

"You must stay away from your friend," he said.

"Which friend?"

"Jia-Li."

"Jia-Li? No, never. She has nothing to do with this." But even as she spoke, Sunny thought of the pram that her friend intended to take to the railway station—and what it would contain.

"They know, Soon Yi," Wen-Cheng said. "The Kempeitai know about Jia-Li and Charlie. They know he is living with her."

Sunny's hand flew to her mouth. "How could they possibly know?" she gasped.

Wen-Cheng continued to scan the lane as if he was anticipating an ambush. "Does it matter?"

Desperate with worry, Sunny could think of nothing else. "I must warn her."

"No!" Wen-Cheng cried.

"I have to."

"Can you not see, Sunny? It is too late."

"Too late? How could it be too late?" She paused. "What is happening, Wen-Cheng? How could you possibly know what the Japanese are planning?"

"Stay away from Jia-Li. I beg you, Sunny."

The truth struck her like flying shrapnel. "Oh my God!" she exclaimed. *"You told them."*

Wen-Cheng's face reddened and he dropped his head. "I did what I had to do."

"To save your own skin!"

"My fate is sealed," he said softly. "No. I did what I did to save you."

"How dare you!" She slapped him across the cheek, so hard that her palm stung.

Wen-Cheng stared at her and then emitted a humourless laugh. "They were going to kill you, Sunny."

Her head swam. "Who were? The Japanese?"

"No, the Underground. It was only a matter of time. They had labelled you as a collaborator. A traitor."

"For not helping them murder Colonel Kubota?"

"That, and treating the Japanese officers at the hospital after the assassination attempt," he said grimly. "They knew all of it."

"So you . . ."

"Betrayed my own people. Yes. I became a collaborator. For the *Rìběn guǐzi*, no less. I turned in my own cell. How do you think they knew where to find the old man and the others?"

"Oh God." She suddenly thought of Max's arrest. "And Dr. Feinstein?"

"The Japanese, they were so suspicious of my work at the hospital. They insisted there must be others."

"Why Max?"

"He had helped treat one of the local Underground leaders when he had gout."

Sunny's legs felt unsteady. Her knees began to buckle. "So you told them Max was your contact at the hospital to draw suspicion away from me?"

Wen-Cheng held out his hands. "I had to give them a name or they would have gone after you and Franz." He dropped his arms to his sides. "I vowed to protect you."

"But at what cost?"

He looked her straight in the eye. "At any cost."

"And Jia-Li? Why her?"

"They are such relentless masters, Sunny. Always demanding more. More names, more spies. I thought if I gave them someone as important as Charlie . . ."

Tears welled in her eyes again. "Oh, Wen-Cheng, what have you done?"

*   *   *

Sunny raced over to the Cathay Building in a haze of terror and confusion. Expecting the worst, she was surprised to find the street quiet and still covered in unblemished snow. The serenity of the scene did little to quell her mushrooming sense of foreboding, however. As Sunny entered the lobby, she wondered if the Kempeitai were already watching the building.

A middle-aged Chinese couple stood waiting for the elevator. Sunny didn't know who she could trust anymore, so she opted for the stairs. She was breathless by the time she had climbed all nine floors, but she still sprinted down the hallway.

Sunny rapped the secret signal on Jia-Li's door. When a few moments passed, Sunny feared that she might already be too late, but then the door flew open. Before Sunny could say a word, Jia-Li pulled her inside.

"I have news," Sunny blurted.

"Oh, I do as well, *xiǎo hè!*" Jia-Li practically sang. "Such wonderful news. The best news!"

"There is no time, *bǎo bèi*. You must listen—"

But Jia-Li wouldn't. Still gripping Sunny's arm, she guided her into the living room. On the far side of the room, Charlie knelt in front of the pram, adjusting one of its legs with a screwdriver. Beside him stood a stack of green blocks: the explosives he had seized from the Germans.

"Listen to me, both of you," Sunny pleaded.

Jia-Li held up her left hand in the air and waved it until Sunny noticed the narrow silver band encircling her ring finger.

"You and Charlie . . ."

"Are married!" Jia-Li cried joyfully. "Just this very morning."

The news stunned Sunny. "*Married?* How could that be?"

"I went out for rice this morning. On the way home, I ran into a neighbour. He was escorting an old monk back to his flat. It turns out the monk was his great uncle." She giggled gleefully. "A cleric in our very building! We couldn't pass up the opportunity. We would have waited for you but . . . Oh, how I wish you could have been there." Her voice cracked. "Married, *xiǎo hè*. Me! To that beautiful man. Can you believe it?"

"I am so happy for you. I am." Sunny's heart cracked. "But there is no time for celebrating. They are coming for you."

Jia-Li angled her head. "Why do you say this?"

"The Kempeitai. They know. Wen-Cheng is an informant. He told them that Charlie is here, *bǎo bèi*."

The screwdriver in Charlie's hand dropped to the floor. Jia-Li's face fell. "Why?" she asked. "Why would he do this?"

In a few rushed sentences, Sunny shared what Wen-Cheng had told her. Before she had even finished, Charlie leapt up, grabbed his crutches and darted to the window. As he peered out, he said, "You must leave now."

Trembling, Jia-Li nodded. "Chun is right, *xiǎo hè*. You had better go."

"Both of you," Charlie commanded.

"Leave you?" Jia-Li extended a hand to Charlie, but his back was still turned. "On the day we are married? I won't. Never!"

"I will meet you in the Old City," Charlie said without taking his eyes off the street. "We must make separate escapes. If they see us leaving together, we are doomed."

"No, Chun," Jia-Li pleaded. "If we leave right this moment, then surely—"

Charlie shot up a hand to cut her off. The room went silent. The faint sound in the quiet street carried all the way to the ninth floor.

Charlie released the curtain and let it fall into place. He wheeled back to them. "They are here!"

Jia-Li ran over to Charlie. He held her against his chest and kissed the top of her head. "You are everything to me," he murmured.

"I could not love anyone more," Jia-Li whimpered.

He wriggled free of her and pushed her toward the door. "Our only hope is for you to leave. Now!"

Jia-Li hesitated. "Promise you will meet me, Chun." Sunny could see the emotion in her misting eyes. "Promise me."

Charlie closed his eyes and nodded.

"In the Old City?"

"The Old City," Charlie said. "Now go. Take the stairs. Do not look back!"

Jia-Li's gaze lingered on him for one more moment and then she turned for the door.

Sunny followed, but Charlie's voice stopped her. "Wait, Sunny. You need to leave separately. It's the only way."

Sunny's mouth went dry as she stopped and watched Jia-Li dash out the door.

"Take the elevator down, Sunny," Charlie instructed. "Leave the building as though you were heading out for a stroll. As though it were any other day."

"You go first," Sunny croaked. "They are not looking for me."

"No. I will go soon. But first I need to create a diversion." Charlie moved over to the stack of green bricks, lowered himself to the ground and reached for a narrow metal cylinder. "Sunny, if . . ."

"Yes?"

"Tell her, Sunny . . . tell Jia-Li how happy I am I found her. Tell her that I did not waste my life hunting the ghost of my father."

She swallowed. "I will tell her, Charlie." She then turned and rushed out the door to the elevator. As she waited for the car to arrive, she shrunk back against the corridor wall, afraid that Kempeitai men might burst out of the elevator at any moment. But the car was empty when the doors opened. Inside, she felt lightheaded and her hands trembled. Her nervousness grew as she watched the indicator light above the doors steadily shift from "9" down to "L." She could hear shouts and stomping boots even before the car reached the lobby.

The doors opened and Sunny was greeted by the sight of a rifle barrel. She thrust her hands up and stumbled back against the elevator wall.

A Kempeitai man who stood beside the soldier holding the rifle pointed at her accusingly. "You come now!" he shouted in English.

Sunny took a few tentative steps into the lobby. Numerous soldiers filled the space, and more were piling in through the front door.

The Kempeitai man clamped a hand on her upper arm. "Who are you?" he demanded.

"I . . . I am only a visitor. My friend, Ling Mei"—she said the first name that came to mind—"she lives on the seventh floor."

The man stared at her, then snapped his fingers at the soldier beside him, barking out orders in Japanese. The soldier lowered his rifle, stepped forward and grabbed Sunny by the other arm. As the Kempeitai man released her arm, the other soldier jerked her toward the front door.

"I am only a visitor," Sunny pleaded again.

The soldier took no notice of her words as he dragged her to the door. There were only a handful of soldiers left outside, but the street was lined with trucks and troop transports.

"*Xiǎo hè!*" Jia-Li cried from somewhere.

Sunny craned her head to see her best friend struggling against two soldiers who were hauling her toward a military vehicle.

Before Sunny could say anything, flames lit up the sky above her and an ear-shattering boom rocked the ground beneath her feet. She felt something sharp hit her head as glass and debris rained down on them.

Finally free of the soldier's grip, Sunny dropped to the snow and covered her head with her hands. The soldiers on the street, including her escort, scrambled back toward the building for cover.

Sunny swivelled her head and saw Jia-Li sitting in the snow, her guards gone. Sunny pushed herself up to her feet and raced over to her friend, scooping her up by the shoulder.

Jia-Li looked at her with a pitiful stare. "The explosion, *xiǎo hè*. Charlie. My Charlie!"

Chapter 51

Sunny could not clear the smell of smoke and cordite from her nostrils, and she was still picking slivers of glass from her hair and clothes.

After the explosion, the Cathay Building's panicked residents had poured out onto the street. Soldiers and Kempeitai men had raced around in confusion, detaining some civilians while ignoring others. Capitalizing on the mayhem, Sunny had just quietly guided her dazed friend away from the building, whispering repeatedly, "Keep walking *bǎo bèi*. Just keep walking."

No one stopped them as they hurried arm in arm toward the Old City. After entering through its north gate, they walked up and down every twisting street and lane within its walls. They passed certain shops and temples three or more times, but Jia-Li did not want to stop. Her eyes were clear and her expression rigid as she scanned the streets. She must have already realized that her husband of only one day would never appear to meet them, but Sunny did not have the heart to share his final words with Jia-Li yet. So instead, Sunny silently remained at her friend's side while she searched in vain for Charlie.

When they reached the main square for a second time, Jia-Li veered off toward the Woo Sing Ding tea house and slumped down onto a bench. As Sunny joined her, she realized this was the place she had last met with

Wen-Cheng and the old man. The uncomfortable memory of their terse exchange darkened her thoughts further.

It's all my fault! Had Sunny found a way inside Colonel Kubota's office, Wen-Cheng would never have felt the need to betray the old man, Max and, ultimately, Charlie. Her face flushed with guilt and she avoided eye contact with her friend. *I am the link to all their deaths.*

Jia-Li stared at the tea house for a few minutes. Finally, in a low, angry tone, she said, "He promised."

"Oh, *băo bèi,* Charlie would move heaven and earth to be here." Sunny's voice cracked. "Perhaps he is still trying."

"He will never keep his promise."

Sunny reached out and gripped Jia-Li's limp hand. "He would have said anything, *băo bèi.* Anything to make you leave. He loves you that much."

"He is my husband," she said, unmoved. "I should never have left. And he should never have sent me away."

Sunny squeezed Jia-Li's hand even tighter. "For love, *băo bèi.* Charlie only did it out of love."

Jia-Li slipped her hand free. Her eyes were red and her cheeks flushed now. "I would have wheeled that pram full of dynamite into the train station, *xiăo hè.* Even if it meant I would never come back out."

"I have no doubt, *băo bèi.*"

"Not for Free China. Or the Underground. Or the stupid Communists." Jia-Li's voice trembled. "Only for Chun. Always for him."

"I know."

Jia-Li buried her face in her hands. Soon her shoulders shook. "My home is gone," she choked out between sobs. "So is my husband."

Sunny struggled to find reassuring words but could think of none. She couldn't look her friend in the eye. She felt responsible for incinerating Jia-Li's happiness.

"Where do I go now, *xiăo hè?*" Jia-Li murmured.

Sunny's eyes misted over. "Come home with me, *băo bèi.*"

"And get you all killed?" Jia-Li scoffed. "Even the children?"

"You cannot go back to the Cathay Building."

"What is there to return to?"

"The Japanese know who you are, *băo bèi*," Sunny said. "They will be looking."

"Perhaps it's best if they find me."

"Stop it," Sunny snapped. "You can't think like that. Imagine what Charlie would say."

Jia-Li only shrugged. "What else would you have me do?"

Sunny sat up straighter. "The Comfort Home."

"Is the first place the Japanese will look."

"They have searched there before—many times, right?—and never found the hideaway."

"Why would Chih-Nii take me in as a fugitive? After how I walked out on her."

"You are like family. She has always had a soft spot for you."

Jia-Li gave a bitter laugh. "She had a soft spot for the money I brought in."

Sunny rose from the bench and reached for Jia-Li's arm again. "Come. We will go talk to her."

Jia-Li remained seated. She looked up at Sunny with pained eyes. "Can we give him a few more minutes?"

The minutes turned into more than an hour as they sat together and quietly reminisced about Charlie and his brief presence in their lives. At last, Jia-Li wiped her eyes and rose to her feet. "Let's go," she declared.

As they left the Old City, Jia-Li kept her head still and her eyes straight ahead, her search abandoned.

Arriving at the Comfort Home, they circled the block to ensure no Japanese vehicles were in the area before they approached the walkway that led to the elegant old villa. There was something tranquil yet surreal about the snow-covered trees that lined the path.

As they neared the mansion, an enormous man stepped out to greet them. "Ushi!" Sunny rushed up and hugged him, barely able to get her arms all the way around his waist. "It is good to see you."

"Hello, Sunny." He patted her on the back.

Ushi and Jia-Li just stared at one another. Eventually, his eyes fell to her left hand and he motioned to the ring. "Is it true? Are you . . . married now?"

Jia-Li nodded.

Ushi gave her an awkward smile. "I am happy for you."

"Oh, Ushi." Jia-Li hurled herself into his arms.

Ushi held her tightly. Somehow he seemed to understand everything. "I am so sorry, *bǎo bèi*," he whispered.

Jia-Li broke free of the hug. "I have nowhere left to go now, Ushi."

Ushi turned for the door. "Come. We will speak to her."

They found Chih-Nii in her small office, sitting behind her Qing dynasty desk. She was counting the previous night's take, having neatly separated it into various currencies, from American greenbacks to Japanese yen. She looked up only after she had finished with a wad of bills.

Chih-Nii wore her usual glamorous cheongsam, but there was something drawn about her overly made-up face. She eyed Jia-Li blankly. "As a rule, I do not send presents to couples who exclude me from the wedding."

"No one else—not even Sunny—was there," Jia-Li said softly.

"And so where is the proud groom?"

"He . . . he could not make it."

Chih-Nii's eyelids creased and her tone turned sharp. "And you have come back here for what, precisely? To gloat?"

Jia-Li folded her arms across her chest and said nothing.

Ushi looked over at Sunny, urging her with his eyes to speak.

"She has nowhere else to go, Chih-Nii," Sunny said.

Chih-Nii's gaze drifted from Sunny to Jia-Li. "Is this true?"

Jia-Li looked down at her feet. "My Charlie . . . he's gone," she murmured.

The bills fluttered to the table as Chih-Nii propelled herself to her feet. She rushed over and wrapped a thick arm around Jia-Li's shoulder. "Tell auntie, little flower. Tell her everything."

Chapter 52

The rain pelted down, turning the streets into a mush of puddles and slush. The city's usual strong smells, trapped under ice and snow for so long, returned with a vengeance. Franz's eyes watered as he passed a drainpipe that reeked so strongly he guessed something larger than a rat had to be decomposing inside it.

Across the street, Franz saw the sign for the Café Aaronsohn. Even if he could have afforded to eat there, he wasn't partial to its food and wouldn't have chosen it as a lunch destination. Besides, with his stomach flip-flopping and the taste of bile on his tongue, food was the last thing on his mind. Still, the popular café met his needs from a strategic perspective.

As Franz stepped through the door, he patted his coat pocket, reassured by the bulky outline of the envelope. The clock above the counter read two minutes to twelve; he was early. He was relieved to see that, despite the foul weather, the restaurant was more than half full. Claiming a table in a far corner, he ordered an espresso and tried to look casual.

The wait only intensified his anxiousness. He never doubted that von Puttkamer would show, but he hoped the man would be as punctual as a typical Prussian.

Just then, the door chimed and the baron entered with his bodyguard. Von Puttkamer sniffed the air and made a face, as though the mere scent of kosher cooking was objectionable. Without even removing his jacket, he approached Franz's table.

Heads turned and the chatter dropped to a hush: many of the patrons recognized von Puttkamer. But the baron appeared oblivious. He eased into the chair across from Franz while his bodyguard slipped into the corner, his back to the wall as he eyed the other customers blankly.

Von Puttkamer laid his damp homburg on the table and folded his leather gloves inside it. "Not the easiest of journeys in this weather, Dr. Adler. My car got stuck twice. I do hope we are not wasting one another's time."

Nervous as Franz felt, he was in no hurry to get to his point. "In my five winters in Shanghai, I cannot remember seeing so much snow or slush."

"Fascinating," von Puttkamer said. "Is this what you summoned me across the city to discuss? The turn in the weather?"

Forcing lightness into his tone, Franz asked, "Would you like a coffee, Baron?"

"Here?" Von Puttkamer chuckled. "No. No, thank you."

Franz lifted his cup. "As good as back home."

Von Puttkamer tilted his head in surprise. "I am curious, Herr Doktor. Do you really consider Germany your home?"

"Austria."

"Is part of the greater Reich now." Von Puttkamer shrugged. "Still . . ."

"Only in the sense of it being the country where I was born and raised," Franz admitted. "I would certainly never view it as my home now."

"That is convenient, considering that we would never view you as a true German." Von Puttkamer nodded. "Now that we have settled that . . ."

Franz glanced at the clock above the counter. He needed to draw the conversation out for another ten minutes or so. "Have you spent much time in Vienna?"

"As little as possible." Von Puttkamer made a show of checking his pocket watch. "Frankly, I never enjoyed the city much."

"Why not, Baron?"

"Too overwrought," he sighed. "The architecture. The music. The painting. It was all too precious for my taste. And so, so many of *your* kind." He shook his head. "Berlin. Now there is a wondrous city."

"I have only been there once, but I would have to agree," Franz said. "So many architectural marvels."

"*Ja,* in comparison, it makes Shanghai look like the colonial outpost it is and always will be."

"Will you be returning again soon?" Franz asked.

"That is hardly any of your business, Herr Doktor." Von Puttkamer pushed his seat back from the table and began to rise. "Clearly, coming here was pointless."

Franz's neck tensed with worry, but he managed to keep his expression neutral and his tone conversational. "We have not yet decided what to do with all your plastic explosives, Baron."

Von Puttkamer dropped back into his chair. He shot Franz a murderous glare but said nothing.

Franz shrugged. "We even wondered if perhaps there might be some demolition work required in Germantown."

"You wouldn't dare," von Puttkamer snarled.

"Probably not, no." Franz shook his head. "Unlike you, we are too civilized to slaughter innocent men, women and children."

Von Puttkamer leaned into the table. "You had no difficulty murdering Hans," he hissed.

"You view him as innocent?" Franz asked in disbelief. "The man who was about to bomb our temple? You and I must have slightly different understandings of the word."

"The world is at war, Adler," von Puttkamer scoffed. "Honour, bravery, duty—those qualities are more important than questions of guilt or innocence under these circumstances."

"Really, Baron? Is there honour in blowing up a synagogue full of worshippers? Or bravery in collapsing a hospital on top of its patients?"

"If they are filled with enemies of the Reich, then why not?"

Franz wrestled back his emotions. "Because we will not let you," he said softly.

"Next time, no one will inform you beforehand."

Ernst! Franz wondered if his friend was already under suspicion. "No one informed us," he insisted.

Von Puttkamer raised an eyebrow.

"We spotted your men arriving after curfew," Franz bluffed. "Our people are always watching. Day and night."

Unperturbed, von Puttkamer laughed. "Well, you should sleep well then."

"It will never happen again!" Franz exclaimed.

Von Puttkamer's frigid smile held firm. "How can you be so sure?"

Franz reached into his pocket, pulled out the yellowing envelope and slid it across the table. Von Puttkamer eyed Franz warily before picking it up and extracting the photographs. Franz mentally flipped through the photos as von Puttkamer examined them. Together, they provided a clear picture of the booby-trapped bombs outside the synagogue and the dead German bomber lying next to the temple wall.

Von Puttkamer stuffed the photographs back into the envelope and shoved it, spinning, back to Franz. "So what? You have photographs. They prove nothing!"

"I believe they establish your intent quite clearly."

"And even if they did?"

"Did you get permission to do this? From the Japanese?"

"Permission?" Von Puttkamer glanced incredulously over to his bodyguard. "To rid ourselves of a blight on the good name of the fatherland?" He turned back to Franz. "We do not need anyone's permission."

"And yet you crept into the ghetto on Christmas Eve under the false pretense of delivering gifts," Franz pointed out. "What do you imagine the Japanese would think of such duplicity?"

"Who gives a damn?"

"Do you not remember last year? When Josef Meisinger from the Gestapo came to the Japanese about attacking the Jews?"

Von Puttkamer reached for his gloves. "What about him?"

"The Japanese banished Meisinger from Shanghai," Franz said, though he knew it was not the whole truth. Jia-Li and Sunny had actually blackmailed Meisinger into leaving the city with photos of the colonel with a teenaged male prostitute, snapped with a hidden camera at the Comfort Home. Franz saw the irony in the fact that, just a year later, they were again trying to deter the Nazis with incriminating photographs.

"So fortune has smiled on you twice in one year." Von Puttkamer smirked. "Can you not see, Adler? You are merely delaying the inevitable."

"I do not see it at all, Baron," Franz said evenly. "Especially now that Germany is losing the war."

"We are losing nothing," von Puttkamer snarled. "In every long war, there are swings in momentum. It will swing back in the Reich's favour soon enough. Regardless, you Jews have already lost. Long ago."

"And yet, we are still here."

"For the time being." Von Puttkamer shook a glove at him. "If you think for one moment that you can blackmail me . . ."

Franz was relieved to hear the door chime again. He looked up and saw that the clock read 12:34. Ghoya strutted into the café, escorted by two soldiers. The small man looked around, appraising his seating options. As soon as Ghoya's gaze found them, he rushed over to their table.

"What have we here?" Ghoya's attention swung from Franz to von Puttkamer and back. "A Nazi and a Jew having coffee?" He laughed. "A Nazi and a Jew! What will come next? The sun out at night and the moon in the day?"

Von Puttkamer stood up and bowed his head. "Good afternoon, Mr. Ghoya."

"Baron von Puttkamer." Ghoya bowed in turn, still laughing. "Tonight I will look for the sun at midnight. I will. Yes, yes, I will!"

"Enjoy this while you can, Mr. Ghoya," von Puttkamer said. "I promise you, you will not witness this sight again."

Ghoya squinted at Franz. "What about all your talk of the Nazis attacking the Designated Area? Now you meet them for coffee?" He turned back to von Puttkamer. "The doctor told me you intended to bomb their church and their hospital."

"Bomb them, indeed?" Von Puttkamer chortled uneasily. "Such nonsense."

"Yes, yes! That is just what I said." Ghoya laughed again. "Nonsense! My exact word was 'nonsense.'"

Heart pounding in anticipation, Franz caught von Puttkamer's eye and slid the envelope very slightly toward Ghoya. The baron's brow creased, but Ghoya was oblivious, his gaze never leaving the other two men.

"These Jews. With their small worries and crazy ideas." Ghoya flung up his hands in exasperation. "Everyone is always after them! Yes?"

Continuing to inch the envelope forward, Franz held steady eye contact with von Puttkamer.

The baron hesitated and then nodded once crisply: a concession. "Most paranoid, I agree, Mr. Ghoya." Sighing heavily, von Puttkamer brought a hand to his chest. "Regardless, I have just given the doctor my word that we will not bomb the Jews or harass them in any other way they might imagine. We have far more important concerns than their wretched little community."

Chapter 53

January 1, 1944

Sunny was bleeding when she woke up. Her period had arrived four days late, which was unusual: normally, she could have set a calendar by her cycle. The timing for a pregnancy couldn't have been much more disastrous, and she realized that she should have been overcome with relief. Still, as she washed herself, she felt tears threatening and she had to fight back sobs.

Sunny cried for more than just the end of a baby that might have been. The past year had been one of such terrible loss. Irma, Joey and Charlie were dead. Max and Wen-Cheng could be, too, for all she knew. Even Yang's status inside the internment camp was uncertain. As Sunny scrubbed the last traces of blood from her hands, she felt another twinge of guilt over the role she had played—inadvertent as it was—in their downfalls.

Brushing her hair from her face, she dried her eyes and headed out of the bathroom to join the celebration.

Esther had promised them a traditional New Year's Day brunch. "Just as my mother used to serve in Linz—only without all the delicacies, good cheer or optimism." Esther's disclaimer notwithstanding, the scrumptious aromas of coffee, cinnamon and fried meat wafted through the flat. Usually, breakfast consisted of rice latkes or a pudding assembled from the previous night's scraps. Sunny's stomach rumbled in anticipation as she headed into the main room.

Esther was a flurry of activity in the kitchen and kept insisting there was not enough space for anyone to assist her. Hannah bounced Jakob on her lap and sang him a traditional nursery rhyme: "*Hoppe, hoppe, Reiter.*" The boy cried in delight every time Hannah reached the end of the verse and dropped him between her knees, catching him by his wrists.

Franz reclined on the couch, fighting a smile as he watched them. Sunny dropped into the seat beside him. She couldn't remember when she had seen her husband so relaxed or contented. She wouldn't hide the truth from him again, but deciding her news could wait, she reached for his hand and slipped her fingers between his.

Hannah was swinging Jakob between her legs when the door flew open. Ernst bustled into the flat with a bottle tucked underneath his arm. "*Prosit Neujahr!*" he cried. "Happy New Year!"

Hannah lowered Jakob to the floor and hopped up to greet him. "What have you brought us, Onkel Ernst?"

Ernst pulled the magnum from under his arm and shrugged with false humility. "This? It's nothing. Surely everyone should celebrate the New Year with a sip or two of bubbly?"

Franz shook his head. "Where on earth did you find it?"

"While I might reside in Hitler-*dorf*—squarely in the heart of the Dark Ages—mercifully, Frenchtown is not too far away. At the Café Palais. I traded a sketch of the proprietor's charming wife for this equally charming champagne. A good year, too—'38."

Franz glanced over at Sunny with a tender smile. "The year we met."

"Your timing is impeccable, Ernst," Esther called from over her shoulder. "You will join us for brunch." It was not a question.

He heaved a mock sigh. "Oh, if you insist, Essie."

Sunny shuffled closer to Franz to make room on the couch for Ernst. Enjoying the pressure of her husband's thigh against hers, she squeezed his hand tighter.

Ernst eyed them with a sly grin, but said only, "You spoke with the baron after all, then, Franz?"

"How did you hear?"

"Gerhard." Ernst shook his head gravely. "The boy is petrified that he will be found out. And he just might be, if he doesn't stop acting so jittery."

"Reassure him, Ernst. Von Puttkamer believes our watchers spotted his men in the ghetto."

Ernst nodded. "I take it that the baron was not amused by what you had to show him?"

"I would say not, no."

"I caught his last radio broadcast," Ernst said. "Von Puttkamer was even more venomous than usual. This time he was complaining about Jewish doctors: 'Blood sucking snakes, the lot of them.' Though I imagine he had one in particular in mind."

Franz shrugged. "As long as he leaves us alone."

"Do you think he will?"

"He promised as much. In front of Ghoya, for what that is worth. I hope the photographs will be enough of a deterrent."

Ernst wagged his head from side to side, unconvinced, before turning to Sunny. He draped an arm lightly over her shoulders. "Tell me, how is your poor friend coping?"

"Jia-Li is heartsick. Ruined." Sunny held up a hand. "But at least she is somewhere safe."

"That would have meant everything to Charlie." Ernst exhaled sadly.

They lapsed into silence. Finally, Franz admitted, "I'm sure Charlie's men will be crushed to hear of his death."

"But how will they find out? No one can get word to them." Ernst pinched the bridge of his nose. "I am beginning to doubt that I will ever see Shan again."

"One day, Ernst," Sunny said. "You will find him."

"You think so?"

She patted his knee and smiled warmly. "I am sure of it."

Embarrassed, Ernst cleared his throat. "Such melancholic nonsense. I almost forgot why I've come." He dug into his pocket. Sunny expected to see a pack of cigarettes emerge, but instead he extracted an envelope. "I am here on official business. As Simon's mailman."

Esther rushed over, wiping her hands on her apron, and plucked the letter from Ernst's hand. "Excuse my manners, please. It's my first letter in a week." She sliced it open and turned away from them. As she read, her shoulders began to tremble. At first, Sunny thought she was crying, but then she heard an unexpected sound.

Hannah stood and hurried over to her aunt. "What is it, Tante Essie?"

Esther turned back to the table, laughing as tears rolled down her cheeks. "Simon is being Simon."

"What does he say?" Hannah demanded. "Tell us."

"He has agreed to remain at Ernst's provided that . . ." Esther stopped to consult the letter. "Someone sends him a decent pair of earplugs."

Ernst rolled his eyes. "So he needs quiet from me? *Ach!* I put up with all his talk about that ridiculous baseball. And then the big band music . . ." He made a face. "All day long with the same nonsense."

Esther's grin grew. "And with the Allies advancing in Italy and Russia, Simon is convinced that the war will be over by the end of this year." She returned her attention to the letter again. "He writes, 'Forget Jerusalem, next year in the Bronx!'"

Franz and Hannah shared a chuckle, but Ernst shook his head in bewilderment. "It's an old expression," Esther explained. "At the end of Jewish holy days, we say 'Next year in Jerusalem' to signify optimism for the coming year."

"Only one more year, can you imagine?" Sunny asked of no one in particular.

Franz laid his other hand on top of hers. "Simon is a dreamer, darling."

She kissed his cheek, letting her nose linger on the soft stubble. "Every so often even dreamers get it right."

"Look!" Hannah cried as she pointed across the table.

Sunny turned to see Jakob wobbling upright. He took a tentative step, then another, and two more in rapid succession before toppling down onto the floor. He appeared stunned by his accomplishment, then broke into a giggle that sent a wave of laughter through the room.

"Your first steps!" Esther cried, rushing over to scoop Jakob up in her arms and smother his face with kisses. "Oh, *Schatzi,* wait till Papa hears."

Sunny ached with joy and longing. She nestled her head into Franz's neck. "I don't care where I am next year as long as I am with my family. And perhaps ..."

A smile lit up her husband's face as he brushed his lips over hers. "Perhaps a playmate for Jakob?"

Acknowledgments

As usual, I have more people to thank than space available to name them all, but I'm compelled to single out a few.

As rewarding as I find the process of writing a novel, the challenges—particularly with a book in which I feel such an obligation to be historically accurate—can be mightily intimidating. I wouldn't even have attempted the feat without the uncomplaining support of my friends and family, in particular my wife, Cheryl; my mother, Judy; and my daughters, Chelsea and Ashley.

Of course, I need more than just moral support. As with all my previous novels, I relied heavily on the insights and input of Kit Schindell, a wonderfully skilled freelance editor. I am also grateful to my agent, Henry Morrison, for his ever wise and even-keeled guidance.

I am pleased to continue my relationship with the team at Tor/Forge. It's a pleasure to collaborate with consummate professionals such as Tom Doherty, Linda Quinton, and Paul Stevens. And I can't express gratitude enough to my friend and editor, Natalia Aponte. She worked with me through the entire process, from the glimmer of an idea to the final polished draft, bettering the product each step of the way.

Finally, I have to acknowledge the people who lived and died in Shanghai during the Second World War. Nineteen forty-three was a year of hardship and sorrow for most of the city's residents, particularly the Chinese, the Shanghailanders, and the Jewish refugees. Yet, the resilience, bravery, and selflessness so many of them demonstrated is inspiring. I hope this novel conveys a sense of my deep admiration for them.